every
bone
a
prayer

ASHLEY BLOOMS

Published by Sourcebooks Landmark, an imprint of Sourcebooks
P.O. Box 4410, Naperville, Illinois 60567-4410
(630) 961-3900
sourcebooks.com

Library of Congress Cataloging-in-Publication Data

Names: Blooms, Ashley, author.
Title: Every bone a prayer / Ashley Blooms.
Description: Naperville, Illinois : Sourcebooks Landmark, [2020]
Identifiers: LCCN 2019042346 | (trade paperback)
Subjects: LCSH: Psychic trauma--Fiction. | Healing--Fiction. |
    Self-actualization (Psychology)--Fiction. | Speculative fiction.
Classification: LCC PS3602.L667 E94 2020 | DDC 813/.6--dc23
LC record available at https://lccn.loc.gov/2019042346

Printed and bound in the United States of America.
VP 10 9 8 7 6 5

A Word from the Author

Dear Reader,

I wrote this book because I wanted (and needed) to explore the ways that trauma impacts individual, familial, and community identity. How trauma takes shelter in our bodies, passing from one generation to the next. And, most of all, I wanted to write a story about what comes after the hurt—how we find a way back to each other and to ourselves.

It seems impossible to write a book about trauma, vulnerability, and healing without considering the reader's own history. I don't know what you're carrying in your hearts or bodies, but I want all of you to be able to engage with this book on your own terms. As a survivor and as someone with PTSD, trigger or content warnings have helped me live more comfortably and experience the media that I love safely. These warnings are, essentially, about transparency and choice. If you know what you can expect from this book, then you will be better equipped to know if you can engage with it.

So, before you read *Every Bone a Prayer*, I'd like you to know that it contains depictions of sexual abuse between children, domestic violence, emotional abuse, portrayals of Evangelical faith, and body horror/grotesque imagery. If you're interested in further details about the appearance of these things, you can visit my website for more information: ashleyblooms.com/triggerwarnings.

And please know that if you need to set this book aside, there's nothing wrong with that. It's okay to protect yourself. Misty would want you to be safe, so would the crawdads, and so do I.

With love,
Ashley

Shift

*Before a crawdad can grow, it must
shed the hard shell of its body.
First, a new skin forms beneath the shell.
This skin is soft, but grows stronger.
It is a process of separation, of
letting go of the old shape.
A slow goodbye to the body that existed before.*

One

Everything that Misty needed was behind her bedroom door, but she couldn't open it. She planted her toes into the carpet and leaned her full weight against the wood, twisting the knob back and forth. For a moment, the door slipped open, revealing a sliver of darkness about an inch wide. Somewhere inside that darkness was her bed piled high with pillows, her favorite T-shirt, and her box of treasures. Misty stretched her fingers, hoping to slide them through to grab the door, but it slammed shut before she could.

"Penny, let me in," Misty said.

A muffled "no" came from the other side.

Misty tried again, but her sister was too strong, no doubt digging her heels into the same carpet, her sister two years older and three inches taller, her sister a weight Misty could not move. It would be so much easier if Misty could talk to Penny the way she talked to everything else, so much better without words.

"You can't keep me out of my own room," Misty said.

She pushed again, and again the door jerked forward an inch, a space just big enough for Penny's voice to slip through: "Then go tell Mom on me."

Misty let go of the door and it slammed back into place. "I can't."

On the other side of the trailer, her parents' voices rose and fell in argument. Misty could only make out every tenth word from behind their closed bedroom door, and those words didn't make sense alone—*won't, should, really, right, leave.* They needed everything in the middle to be complete, all the parts that Misty was missing. Her mother's voice stood out the most, a sharp spike against the dull rumble of her father's voice, and together they made a slow, slack creature whose fists pounded against the trailer as it dragged itself closer and closer to Misty.

She slid to the floor and pressed her knees to her chest. Muffled sounds came from behind her, too—Penny crying alone in their room. It would normally hurt Misty to know that her sister was sad, but it only made her angry this time. She pounded her fist against the door, trying to jar Penny's head. Trying to punish her for shutting Misty out.

But Penny just balled her fist together and punched back, and the wood reverberated between them, their spines pressed to the same spot on the door, and together they made their own strange creature with its own strange heart pounding and pounding.

Misty didn't stop punching until her father walked out of the bedroom with one hand held in the air and the other empty by his side.

"I'm done talking about this," he yelled.

Misty's mother followed him. Her ponytail slumped against her shoulders, little baby hairs catching the light around her face, making her glow. "You don't get to decide everything on your own, you know that? You're *married.* You're a *father.*"

"I don't need you telling me who I am."

"Apparently you do. You sure seem to have forgot awful quick."

He snatched his keys from the coffee table and turned toward the door. "Like you'd ever let me forget a damn thing."

Panic rose in Misty's chest at the sight of her father leaving. She looked for something to distract her parents with. She'd done it before, stepping between them when they started to argue, holding up her art project or reciting the Bible verses she'd memorized from Sunday school, and the sight of her was often enough to startle them out of their fight. Misty became a blush rising to her mother's cheek, the spasm of her father's hand clenching tight and then releasing—a freckled truce with her father's wide nose and her mother's brown eyes.

But then her father opened the front door and light flooded the room so quickly that Misty and her mother winced against it. Misty's father turned to say something else until he spotted Misty sitting on the floor at the end of the narrow hallway. He stopped.

Her parents stared at her and Misty stared back at them.

This was usually the part where they would stop fighting. Her mother's voice would lift to a false high, her father hugging Misty even though he rarely showed affection. Even their attempts at happiness felt wrong.

But this time Misty's father looked away from her without smiling. He looked at her mother and said, "This is what *you* wanted, Beth. You're the one who has to tell them," then slammed the door hard enough to rattle the glass in the windows.

Misty's mother stood with her arms crossed over her chest. She stared not at Misty but through her to some far and foggy place that Misty had never seen. She went there often enough that Misty knew how to handle it, how to be patient, to wait for her mother to come back to herself. Back to Misty. But this time, her mother touched her fingers to her mouth, walked back across the trailer, and disappeared into her bedroom.

The trailer was quiet without her parents' noise. There were so many small and empty spaces in need of filling.

Misty dug her heels into the carpet one last time. She pressed her full weight against her bedroom door so fast that her sister didn't have time to prepare. Something thudded behind her and the door jerked back a few inches, the dark space of their room yawning by Misty's side until her sister growled and pushed back even harder. Misty's feet burned as she lurched across the carpet, and she fell to the floor on the outside of everything she wanted.

anything, but you can ask for things, too. You open up and wait for God to speak to you. Close your eyes now. Close your eyes." So Misty listened to her mother and she listened for God—her chest a door flung wide open; her heart the golden light spilling onto the floor, eating the darkness whole. She invited everything inside.

But instead of God, Misty heard the mouse living in the walls of their trailer.

The mouse showed Misty the tangled nest she'd made for her children from the torn scraps of the science folder Penny had lost the week before. The mouse filled Misty's nose with the scent of mothballs and her bones with the hum of the pipes in the walls. The mouse showed Misty what it felt like to be a mouse, furred and quick and small.

Eventually, with practice, Misty got better at reaching out to the world. She learned that everything had a name. Not the name that most people knew them by, but something different, an underneath name made of sounds and memories and feelings, a name that shifted and grew and evolved. Some things had many names, and some had only one. Some things had names that she couldn't speak inside herself, they were so long with age, so heavy with time.

Misty had a name, too, that lived beneath and beside her other name all the time, and this name was long and twisting, filled with memory and sound. She could choose parts of her name, selecting the memories or moments she held closest, but other parts were beyond her control. The crawdads had tried to explain it to her once—how names were made from things remembered and lost, things passed down from generations before, and things that the body knew that the mind forgot. Sometimes she understood how names worked, but sometimes she still wasn't sure.

But she knew that in order to speak to the world, she had to offer her name, like holding out her hand, one half of a bridge built between her and everything else. The crawdads could respond with their name and join Misty, sharing thoughts and memories and feelings. Misty knew what it felt like to be small and clawed and slick. She knew the safest places to hide during squalls when the creek swelled with water and the current threatened to tear the crawdads away. She had seen the pictures the crawdads etched into the sand with their tails in the deepest parts of the creek, messages like prayers that the minnows carried downstream. She could smell an oil spill in an eddy and she had felt the weight of eggs gathered on her belly and she had molted with the crawdads a hundred, hundred times. And she knew all of this because the crawdads knew and they shared it with her. They shared themselves.

Misty conjured her name as she stood in the creek with her nose hovering inches above the cool water. The name bubbled inside of her, dozens of images and feelings connected by the thinnest of strands—her hand reaching out for her grandmother's when Misty was barely old enough to walk, the paper-thin feeling of the older woman's skin inside Misty's palm; the rattle of her mother's breathing when she and Misty were both sick and her mother carried Misty from room to room, rocking her, shushing her, begging her to sleep; the first time Misty had ever tasted snow, bright and shivering cold; her father's voice from a different room, muffled and rumbling; a doe in the woods, blood on its hip and pain in Misty's leg, pain in her chest; Penny standing beside her in church and singing along to a song she didn't know, making up the words until Misty's sides ached from trying not to laugh; the feeling of a crawdad skittering over her shoulder, tangling in her hair; her mother sitting on the couch with her head in her hands; her father's truck peeling out of the driveway, gravel pinging against the metal sides of the trailer; her mother's arms crossed over her chest that morning, the faraway look in her eyes, a feeling of sadness like many small stones stacked inside her stomach, weighing Misty down, down, down.

Misty's chest ached with the memories and she almost pulled away, almost ended her name before it ended itself, but she held on. Names were honest things. They didn't hide. They didn't lie. They couldn't, as far as Misty knew, and the only way to speak to the world was to be true.

But it was getting harder to be honest with the world as her name gathered sadness and heartache and weight. Her name growing heavier by the day.

Then the crawdads answered with their name—a stirring in the dark, a rustling, deep-blue something. The crawdads were silt running between her fingers, the hushed crinkle of a morning glory closing its petals for the day, the pop of a bone from its socket, and they were there, in Misty's head, in her chest, in her legs. They shared her body with her and they helped her carry the weight of her thoughts, her memories.

"Come see me," she said.

And though she only meant to speak to the crawdads, the light Misty shone into the world attracted all sorts of things and they called out to her with their own voices.

A black snake shared the crunch of a field mouse's neck, a bright bubble of blood bursting in the center of Misty's chest.

The minnows shone silver flashes against the backs of her eyes, and the force of the water against their scales as they swam against the current, the dim green taste of the deepest water filled her mouth until her tongue was mossy and thick.

Her fingers spasmed with the flutter of a bluegill's tail a few feet away.

But it wasn't just Misty that got a sense of the other creatures' bodies; they got a sense of hers, too. They were always shocked at first. She knew them as a little weight that perched along her spine, looking up at her like someone walking into a cavern and finding that it was a cathedral. They marveled at the space of her, the strange proportions of her body. They rocked with the rhythm of her lungs and curled against the hollow of her clavicle, but all of them eventually settled in her legs. They begged her to walk, to carry them a while. They asked her to wiggle her toes, to jump, to kneel. They crowded in her joints, their minds like a hive of bees, their excitement pumping Misty's heart faster, faster. They'd never felt anything like her before, never known a body so small but so great at the same time, and they filled Misty, however briefly, with a love of herself as a strange thing, marvelous and new.

And though she couldn't see it with her eyes closed, all around her, a circle formed. All manner of things that lived in the creek swam closer. The air itself rippled with a faint heat as Misty called the crawdads near. Even the birds felt a certain pull, a shift in the wind that drew them to the trees that lined the creek, and they looked down with small, black eyes at the little girl standing below.

The crawdads hurried through the water and grabbed hold of the bend in Misty's knees, pulled themselves up in pinches and stutters. They clung to the hem of her shorts and crawled over one another's backs, grasping for purchase.

Misty opened her eyes and ended her call. She swayed to the side, part of her still convinced she was the water. She took a deep breath and wiggled her fingers. She pressed her tongue against the roof of her mouth and swallowed just to feel the muscles in her throat contract. The door inside her chest was heavier now, harder to close, and a little piece of her remained open as she straightened her back and waited for the dizziness to pass.

It was hard to share her body with something like the creek that believed absolutely the truth of its existence when she didn't believe the same of herself. It was hard to convince her body to return to her when it longed to be clawed and slick or hard and slithering or winged and feathered and gone, gone, gone.

But it was a girl body instead.

It was small and pale-skinned and freckled with squat calves that were bruised from falling. It was a here-and-now body with a sore spot on her tongue from eating corn bread straight out of the oven last night and an ache behind her eyes from crying that morning. It was still a short body, a good-at-hiding body that fit into the dark corner by her parents' bedroom door and listened to the things they said to each other when they thought no one was listening. Dark-haired and dark-eyed and at least three inches shorter than she wanted it to be, it was her body and it was impossible to ignore.

Misty stood up slowly and walked even more slowly in the direction she had come. The crawdads clung to the sleeves of her T-shirt. They tangled themselves inside her hair and swayed with her as she walked through the water. Her body felt wrung out, emptied of everything she had brought—every need, every worry, every fear. When she reached the creek bank, she dropped to her knees on the soft sand. She rested her forehead against the ground and closed her eyes. She heard, in the distance, the familiar grind of her mother's car engine. Misty was supposed to go grocery shopping with her this time since it was Misty's turn to pick out the ice cream, but the tires crunched over the driveway and were gone without her. A pang of sadness rippled through Misty and the crawdads felt it, too, as they fell from Misty's clothes one at a time. They gathered around her, worried. They searched for wounds on her body, murmuring back and forth, and the sound of their shared conversation was like leaves crunching inside her head.

"I'm okay," Misty said as the crawdads worked at the hem of her T-shirt, trying to find a way beneath.

They didn't believe her. They shared images of small things— acorns and newly laid eggs and the round blue pebbles buried beneath the creek bed. This was how the crawdads, how everything, spoke to her. Not with language that she understood, but with a mix of images and sensations that Misty translated. Sometimes it was hard to interpret what the crawdads meant, and even harder to make herself clear to them. But Misty knew what they meant when they shared these images with her. They were telling her that Misty was like the acorn, the egg, the pebbles. She felt small that day, and the crawdads wanted to know why.

Misty turned her head so she could see a half dozen of the crawdads keeping watch over her. "I'm just tired. I don't want to go back home."

And at once the sensation of fifteen small hands holding her in place, asking her to stay.

"I can't." Misty held out a finger and the crawdads crowded around it, touching the tips of their claws to her skin. "I have to go back. My bed is there. And my mom. She'd be sad without me."

The crawdads sent her a fuzzy feeling in her lips and the image of a night sky, which had always been their way of asking why or telling her that they didn't understand.

Misty sighed. "I don't know. I don't think my family is happy." She shared a rush of images. Her mother standing by the front door with her head in her hands. A window in an empty house that they passed every Sunday on the way to church that made Misty feel lonely. Penny slamming a door in her face. The little lines of light that etched across her favorite quilt when she hid beneath it, the light tracing the seams, the light pointing out all the places that were worn and frayed and falling apart.

The crawdads gathered nearer.

"I wish I could talk to them like I talk to you," Misty said. "They don't listen to me much when I do talk, but if I was in their heads, then they couldn't ignore me."

Misty laid her cheek against the sand. She'd thought of telling her family about how she could speak to the world but she wasn't sure how they'd react. They might not believe her at all. She had no way to explain what she did, no proof besides a few crawdads crawling over her skin. Or worse, if they believed her, they might also believe she was bad. Her aunt Jem told stories sometimes about strange people and strange things that had happened in their family, and Misty's mother hated the stories. She never wanted to listen. If she found out that Misty was a strange thing, too, then she might hate her or turn her away, might never trust her again.

After a while, some of the crawdads returned to the creek. Some started to burrow beneath the ground, digging narrow tunnels where they could hide, until only one crawdad remained before her. It was almost impossible to tell them apart, and even if she could, it was impossible to give the crawdads names of their own. She had tried before, but the crawdads rejected them. They knew themselves as crawdad and nothing else. They were a collective, a group. When she called, they answered together, and when they left, they left together. They didn't want to be known apart.

A crawdad returned from the creek with a shed crawdad skin in its claws. The crawdads had shared their memories of molting with Misty, the way they shed their old bodies so they could keep growing. She'd felt the itch of a too-tight skin, the fevered panic of shedding, the need to be released. She knew what it was like to expand, to grow, and she loved to look at the shed skins, to touch them, gently, and feel the way they gave beneath her, like she was holding light inside her hands. The crawdads shared them with her, and Misty collected them in a box under her bed. Looking at them made her feel steady, like there was nothing in the world that couldn't be undone or redone.

Misty stroked her finger along the back of the molted skin. It was only partially intact—the tail and one claw had been torn away, leaving a fragment of the crawdad who had shed its body. A bell chimed nearby and Misty jumped. She kicked her feet out of the water and scrambled to her knees. She'd hung a string of bells in the bushes weeks before to warn her when someone came too close. The only person who came looking for her these days was her neighbor, William. She hadn't known him before they moved into Earl's trailer, but now he was the closest thing to a best friend that Misty had ever had. He was the same age as her, but a grade behind because he'd missed too much school last year. William could tie knots and spit, and he cursed when no one was around to hear. He listened to her when she complained about Penny and he was nice enough, but she didn't trust him with her crawdads. His BB gun had been taken away for shooting at robins from his back porch. Without the gun, she worried he might turn his attention on the crawdads. They were so easy to corner, to catch.

So Misty pounded her fist against the ground three times. With every blow, a jolt shot through the air, something like a shout, like thunder. The crawdads skittered back to the creek or crawled into their burrows. As William crashed through the underbrush on the hill above the creek, the last crawdad's tail swished into the water and disappeared.

"Hey!" he called. "What're you doing?"

"Playing," Misty said.

"Is them your bells back there?"

She nodded. "That's my alarm."

"That's pretty smart," he said. "Have you thought about adding something? Like some spikes. Or maybe digging a pit or something for people to fall into. The bells is good but they won't stop nobody from coming down here."

"It ain't supposed to stop nobody. It's just got to tell me they're coming."

William shrugged. "Let me know if you change your mind. I could draw something up for you and show you how it'd work. If you're interested."

"Yeah," Misty said. "What're you doing anyway?"

William smiled. "Going to the barn. All of us are."

"Who's us?" Misty asked.

"Me and Penny and you."

"Why?"

He grinned. "I got a game for us to play."

"What kind?"

"You have to come and see. I bet you ain't never played it before though."

"What is it?"

William turned and ran through the high weeds without answering. He sent the bells ringing again, louder this time than before, and

Misty felt the pluck of his fingers against the string inside her chest, her own ribs fluttering with the sound.

She dipped her hand into the creek before she left, searching for any crawdads that might have lingered. The slow current altered the image of her hand, making it appear as though her finger crooked away at the knuckle, like somewhere beneath the surface of the water her hand was broken and she just hadn't felt the pain yet.

Three

The barn was old and creaking and filled with things that Misty shouldn't touch—things sharp and jagged and flowered with rust, things sagging with stale water, bloated until it was impossible to tell what the thing was in its life before. The wooden planks that made up the barn's walls and roof might have been golden once, but they had since faded to a cloudy gray and grown soft in places where they shouldn't be soft. Even the breeze stopped at the barn's door, so the air grew stagnant inside, too warm. It seemed that nothing stirred except for the dust, which lifted from the ground, from the tools, even from the walls, like the barn was shedding itself by inches. One day Misty might wake up and the barn would be gone, carried off by a strong breeze a few miles down the road, rearranged slightly so no one might notice it had been a barn once instead of a bird or a church or whatever barns became when they forgot their making.

The barn belonged to their landlord, Earl, and he had forbidden Misty and Penny and William from going inside. He called them a liability, saw them like a wound waiting to open. He lived in the trailer across the driveway from the barn. Earl owned the bottom where Misty stood and everything on it—three trailers, the barn, the crumbling fence, and the tilted mailboxes. His front yard was a garden where nothing ever grew, no matter how hard he worked. The garden soil was dark and dry and peppered with small stones that Earl tossed across the road when he dug them up. All summer long the stones plinked and skittered across the blacktop and Earl grunted and cursed and sighed, needing the earth so much to be something that it wasn't.

The garden was one of the few things that Misty didn't speak to. Earl had begged the ground for so long to be something that it wasn't—called it *growing*, called it *now*, and *green*, and *hurry*, that the garden had become something else. Misty felt it like a loose tooth, an aching, unsettled feeling that buzzed in the palms of her hands every time she looked at it. There was something different about the garden, something sad and strange.

Misty had thought of reaching out to it before, of offering her name, but speaking to something that was injured could be dangerous. Misty had learned that the hard way the summer before. She'd been trying to befriend the deer that sometimes grazed in the woods behind her trailer, but they were cautious things. Wide-eyed and slender-legged, they moved through the trees like shadows, and no matter how hard she tried, Misty could never seem to get close to them. She'd offered them pieces of her name, waiting for them to offer their own in return, but they never would. Prey animals were often more guarded. They made Misty work harder to get to know them and took longer to share themselves with her. She still didn't understand why they saw her as a threat, but she tried to respect them.

She'd gone to the woods every day for weeks and was on the verge of giving up when she found the wounded fawn.

It was the first time she'd seen one alone. They were usually close to their mother's side, their wide, dark eyes peeking out at Misty from a distance. But this fawn was alone, and bleeding. Its back hip was covered with dark-red blood, the fur matted and thick. Its back legs had slumped to the ground, but the front legs were still stand-ing. They trembled so hard that the whole doe was shaking, its ears twitching back and forth like a light bulb blinking on and off, like any minute the fawn might disappear altogether.

Bloody as it was, the fawn still tried to run when it saw Misty, but it was too weak to do more than shuffle a few steps before tipping into the underbrush. Misty thought about turning back. She could get her mother, or her father, or even Earl. Anyone might know better than her what to do with something this hurt. She'd never seen that much blood before, and the smell of it was enough to make her stomach twist.

But she stayed. And she did the only thing she could think to help the deer.

Misty offered her name, which was shorter back then, and not quite so sad. Her name spilled out of her all in a rush, and the moment it ended, Misty was racked with pain. She dropped to one knee and cried out, but there was no one there to hear her but the fawn, who struggled toward her. Pain swelled in her hip, spreading to her knees and ankles, all her joints on fire. Her fingers spasmed, and her mouth tasted like dirt and blood. Shards of the fawn's memories lodged in Misty's mind, temporarily blocking out the fawn in front of her. Misty saw the woods and trees as the fawn did, and she saw her mother, a doe, and the smell of their den, and then there was a shot.

A crack like thunder, but there was no rain, no clouds in the sky.

Her mother bolted through the trees and the fawn tried to follow, but her leg wouldn't move. Then the pain came. Bright. Strange. She'd never felt anything like it before.

She stumbled through the trees. She cried out for her mother, but her mother was gone.

And the fawn cried out still, filling Misty with its pain, with the scent of its mother. Misty tried to pull back, to shut the door in her chest long enough to breathe—all she wanted was a breath of air—but there was no way to do it. The fawn was so panicked, so afraid. It was in so much pain that it couldn't stop itself. It just wanted not to hurt anymore, and it clung to Misty as long as it could.

And without the fawn's name, it was harder to break the connection, harder to see beyond anything but its hurt, harder to know herself as something separate from the pain. Without something to anchor the fawn, all its feelings bled over into Misty, became Misty. She struggled to breathe, to speak.

Then the fawn's mother came.

Misty wasn't sure where she'd come from, but she was there and the world dimmed like the sun was setting in the middle of the afternoon. Misty had never passed out before, but she felt a kind of looseness behind her eyes, a sense of falling. A cold muzzle pressed to her throat once, briefly, and when Misty looked up again, she was alone. The grass rustled in the distance. The wind dried the sweat on her forehead and she shivered.

It took nearly half an hour for Misty to walk the quarter mile back to her trailer, and by the time she stumbled into the yard, her mother was looking for her. Misty had collapsed into her mother's arms and smelled nothing but warm fur and milk.

Her mother took her to the local clinic, who said it must be a cold, and then to the hospital, who said it must be heatstroke. They both ordered bed rest, and Misty spent the next week on the living room couch with the fan sputtering cool air onto her calves. Her mother hovered nearby and even Penny let Misty choose what they would watch on television every night for a week. They were always so kind when she was hurting. It almost made her wish she was hurt more often.

Misty didn't speak to anything for almost a month after that. Every time she tried, the pain of the fawn seared through her and she let go, retreating to the silence in her head. Eventually, the pain of the memory faded, and Misty went to the creek, to the crawdads. The fawn was still part of her name, its bloody hip ingrained on Misty like a scar.

"Are you coming or not?" Penny leaned through Earl's barn doors and squinted against the sunlight.

Misty shivered. She tore her eyes away from the garden and hurried past Earl's trailer. No matter how much she'd like to help the garden, she couldn't risk that kind of pain. Not again.

Four

Inside the barn, William climbed onto a rusted camper shell and squinted at the hayloft overhead as Penny squatted in the nearest corner, all of them looking for the same thing.

"What do we need a bottle for anyway?" Misty asked.

"For the game," William said.

"But everything in here is broke," Penny said.

"Including you," William said.

"You know, I got plenty of other things I could be doing other than digging around some flea-bitten barn on a Saturday with the likes of you." Penny rose from the corner and planted her hands on her hips again.

"There's got to be one bottle in this whole damn place," William said. "Mom says that Earl drinks like a fish."

"That's another thing," Penny said. "I don't like being in here when Earl could come creeping back to his trailer any minute. He might chop us up into little pieces like he did his wife."

"Quit, Penny," Misty whispered, but Penny just rolled her eyes.

"That's just a story," William said.

"A true story," Penny said. "Aunt Jem says that he never got convicted because he's a Dixon. His uncle's a preacher at our church, and he vouched for Earl when it happened and made everything go away with all that money his family's got."

"They wouldn't vouch for him if he really did it," William said. "Besides, people said his wife was right quare. She was all the time talking to animals."

"So?" Penny said. "Misty's all the time playing with crawdads. It don't mean anybody has a right to hurt her."

"What's wrong with liking crawdads?" Misty asked.

"Well," Penny said, "Aunt Jem said that after Earl's wife went missing, her sister lost it. She wanders through the woods now with a lantern in her hand looking for her. She don't even eat anymore."

William pointed a finger at Penny. "It's fire, not a lantern. She conjures it in her hand like this." He held out his palm and wiggled his fingers so they might have been writhing and orange instead of short and pale.

"What was her name?" Misty asked.

"What?" William said.

"The lady," Misty said. "Earl's wife."

"I don't know," William said.

"It was something with a *C*. Carol. No, Caroline, I think."

"Oh," Misty said. "That's a pretty name. Caroline."

There was something in saying her name that made the barn feel heavier. Something about her name that charged the air between them. That she was a real woman with a real name made it harder to share the stories because it made the stories easier to believe. The conversation fractured, and the three went back to their separate corners searching for a bottle.

Misty found one first, nestled in a pile of broken glass. Her bottle was a deep, true green with a white smudge on the front where the label used to be and a crack that snaked from base to mouth. The crack rose up a little, just enough to tear her skin if she wasn't careful.

The bottle's name was hiding there, trembling along the thin crack that Misty felt all through her chest like a spine bent and creaking. If the bottle broke, its old name would still be there, changed only a little by the breaking.

Names were shaped through addition. The bottle's name grew when it went from something small and dark in an endless sky to something spinning and joined, to something solid and deep in the earth, to something outside of it, to something heated and shaped, to something green and slick, to something labeled and sold, to something here in the palm of her hand. It was all of those things, always. It carried its own shadow in its sounds, little imprints of the life it had lived, and the bottle's life had been long. Misty ran her fingers gently along the length of the bottle before she stood.

"Here," she said.

William let go of the board he was hanging from and dropped to the floor. He took the bottle and twisted it between his hands, searching for defects. The bottle cast a faint green shadow over William's nose and mouth, turning him momentarily into something far away and sinking, a drowned boy with his face pointed toward the sun.

"This here's the one," he said.

"We have to hurry though," Misty said. "Mom'll be home soon."

Penny crossed her arms over her chest. "She's right. Mom'll skin us alive if she finds us in here. Or Earl will. We must be a bunch of idiots."

"That's what makes it fun," William said.

Penny took the bottle from William and held it upside down, letting a few drops of brown water drip out. "Yeah, but your mom won't take a switch to your bare legs if she catches you. She'd have to be home first to even notice you was gone. She's probably out with that new feller of hers. The one that drives that blue truck."

Something dark flashed across William's face as he jerked the bottle from Penny's hand. "That ain't her feller. And if you'd quit talking for half a second, we could get started and then nobody has to get in trouble, how about that?"

They sat so their bodies formed a triangle, there in the corner of the barn among puddles of rainwater grown scummy in the June heat, where the air smelled of stale hay and staler beer. That way, William said, no one could see them from the road if they drove by.

"Ain't we supposed to have more people?" Penny asked.

"What, you want me to go find Earl?" William said.

Penny frowned. "I'm just saying. There ain't that many of us playing, so what happens if my bottle lands on Misty, huh? What then?"

"You ain't never kissed your sister on the cheek before? We'll figure it out, all right. The game ain't even started and you're picking it apart. Here." William held the neck of the bottle between two fingers. "You just spin it like this. Not no little spin, neither. It's got to go all the way around at least twice."

"What if it don't?" Penny said.

"Then you lose your spin."

"You're making this up," Penny said. "Spin the bottle ain't got that many rules."

"Have you ever played this game before?" William asked.

Penny lifted her chin. "I've seen—"

"Seeing ain't the same," William said. "My cousin taught me how to play with her and her friend, and they're both sixteen. And I reckon they know a lot more than you do about kissing games. They showed me—well, they showed me how to do this, for one. So until you know more than me, I reckon I'm the one to listen to."

William took the first spin without hesitating, and they kissed what the bottle gave them. Wooden beams. Metal pipes. Once, for William, a grasshopper. The bottle seemed to find only the gaps between them, the space that separated their knees from other knees. It didn't land on a body, not even after William moved them three times, convinced that it was the ground or the moisture from the puddles that was warping the bottle's path. Nothing changed when they moved, except for the light falling through the spaces between the barn's wooden sides. The light soured, turned to a kind of dirty yellow that no flower had ever grown.

Misty's lips grew chapped from kissing so little skin and so much else. Her tongue tasted first of dirt and then of iron and then of nothing at all, but they kept spinning, because even one kiss would change something between them. Misty could feel it in the way that they all leaned forward as the bottle spun, that something was about to happen. She opened her chest for the bottle, let it fill her with its memories, with the feeling of its glass against the cold earth, the tremor of every spin jarring through her spine, like they were spinning together, and she could have asked the bottle to land on William if she wanted. She could kiss him there, in the dank barn while her sister watched, but she didn't want to. Her nerves coiled around the bottle's name until they both pulsed together under her skin and she hoped it might never land, that it would spin and spin until someone's mother came home and called them from the barn.

It was Misty's turn, and she told the bottle to land where it would, to choose for itself where it wanted to be, and the words coursed through her like a lightning strike, all spark and light, all warmth. She pressed her fingertips along the crack in the bottle's glass and felt the bottle call back, a distant, glimmering sound, but then William grabbed the bottle's neck and twisted. The bottle seesawed back and forth against the damp ground, the glass clinking louder every time it touched the earth. Misty leaned back in case the glass shattered. She pulled away from the bottle until she heard nothing but her own thoughts, felt nothing but her own skin, solid and sheened with sweat.

A car drove past the barn, a cloud of dust yawning in its wake. A door slammed and Misty's mother called their names. Penny jumped to her feet and ran outside before their mother could notice what direction she was coming from. Misty leaned back, about to follow, but William darted forward at the last second. His lips were warm and dry against Misty's cheek as he kissed her. He didn't look at her as she stood to leave, but his own cheeks were stained a deep, deep pink. Misty's skin tingled in the breeze as she walked out of the barn, leaving William behind with the green bottle, still spinning.

Five

That night, Misty and Penny and their mother watched their mother's favorite show, the one about the missing people, who almost always turned out to be missing women. Missing women usually turned out to be dead women, murdered by their husbands or boyfriends or coworkers. Dead women whose bodies were often found in parts, scattered along empty highways, shoved into boxes or freezers, or left in shallow pits in unfamiliar woods. The lives of women seemed to be thin strings held taut in someone else's hands, and at any moment someone, some man, might come along and cut that string in half.

Misty sat beside their mother on the couch while Penny lay on her belly on the living room floor. Penny scribbled furiously in her notebook, though she refused to share what she was writing. Their mother had a plastic tray of cookies in her lap. Misty had eaten the entire middle row that week, the one where the cookies were half vanilla and half chocolate, leaving only the vanilla and chocolate cookies on either side. So their mother took one of each kind, wiggled them apart and then stuck the odd pieces back together. She handed one of these cookies to Misty and kept one for herself. Every now and then Penny looked up at the television to mutter "What an idiot" or "What a jerk," and their mother just shook her head.

It was Misty's favorite night of the week. Her mother had just gone grocery shopping so there was plenty of food in the cabinets—more, it seemed, than their family might ever eat. Misty had already showered, and her long, damp hair dripped cool water onto her neck, which made her shiver and scoot closer to her mother, and her mother smelled just the same as always, like dried flowers and sweat.

Misty had tried to talk to her mother the way she talked to the rest of the world, but it had never worked. When she tried, her chest felt tight with a mixture of loneliness and tenderness that she associated with her mother, but she heard no other sound, no grumblings or roarings or quickenings, no memories, no stories. It was that way for everyone she knew. She had never learned her family's other names and she wasn't sure where to find them, or if she could. She wasn't sure why it was that way, either, though she wondered if maybe it was because people lied so much and so often. Names were honest. They had to be in order to work, and sometimes it felt like there wasn't a day that passed that her family didn't hold something back. But if she could find her own name, then maybe she could help her mother find her name. And things would be different between them. They could talk to each other all the time and share everything that they had to share, and Misty would never have to wonder if her mother was lonely or sad or scared, because she would know. And she could help. She might even be able to help her mom and dad stop fighting so much. She could become the bridge between them.

Everything would be better if she could just talk to them the way she talked to the crawdads. All she had to do was figure out how.

Headlights arced across the living room window as a car pulled into the bottom. The light skittered across their mother's eyes, and she walked to the window to peek outside.

"Is it Dad?" Misty asked. The night would be better if he were home, too, sitting in his recliner with his face stained dark by coal dust.

Penny snorted. "Not likely."

Their mother glared at Penny, but she said to Misty, softer, "No, Little Bit. Your dad will be home tomorrow. That's just Miss Shannon coming home from work."

"Is that blue truck behind her again?" Penny asked.

"How'd you know?"

"That same truck was here last weekend," Penny said. "I *told* William that she had a new boyfriend. You'd think he'd be happy that she's finally seeing just one feller instead of three or—"

"Penny Lee. It ain't your place to comment on who Miss Shannon spends her time with." Their mother closed the blinds and sat back down beside Misty.

William's mother, Shannon, worked at a gas station a few miles away. She was a cook in the kitchen that served hamburgers and pizza and fries. She always came back smelling of grease and charred meat, and sometimes she brought Misty free onion rings. But her hours were long and always changing, and William was never sure when she'd be back. Misty had seen William waiting for his mother a thousand times, and every time it was the same. First he lingered in the driveway with the cordless phone in his hand. Every now and then he'd put it to his ear, wait for a moment, and then drop the phone back down. Then he waited on the porch steps. His knees drawn up under his chin, a bag of potato chips or cookies sitting by his side, or sometimes clutching a pillow he'd brought from his bed. Eventually, when the sun started to set and the gnats worried at his skin, he went inside the trailer and closed the door. The only light that flickered in his living room window came from the television show he watched alone. Misty always wondered if he watched the same show that she did with her mother and sister, if he saw the same women die, if he called his mother again, and if, that time, she answered.

Misty checked the locks on the doors twice. It was part of her bedtime routine. She checked the back door, tapping it once with her finger when her father was home and twice when he was gone. The doorknob spoke to her with a gentle voice, its name a string of hands twisted together at the wrist, a rope that stretched through decades—the warmth of Misty's small palm and the rough calluses of her father's hand and the quick, tight twist of Penny's hand as she flung the door open and stomped outside, and Misty's mother's touch, tentative, soft. There were other people, too, who Misty had never met. People who had lived in the trailer before with cold hands and hands dripping hot water and hands stained with grease, hands bleeding and frightened and grasping, hands tired and glad to be home. All of those hands reached back to her through the doorknob's memory as Misty tapped the lock twice, asking it to keep her family safe, and the doorknob promised it would try.

Misty and Penny's room was on one side of the single-wide trailer and their parents' room was all the way on the other end. If Misty stood in her doorway, she could see her mother's doorway, which was never closed but always cracked a little. She checked for the crack—a little beam of golden light, her mother's shadow sweeping across the floor as she changed clothes.

Misty's room was small, and felt even smaller because of the dark wood paneling on the walls. There was a single window above

Penny's bed that looked out onto William's trailer and Earl's garden. Their mother had tacked a blanket around the window frame at the beginning of summer to keep the sunlight from heating the room. A box fan leaned against the door, blowing cool air against Misty's bare calf. They had inherited their beds from their cousins Jerry and Jamie, two sturdy metal frames nicked from years of use. Misty's bed had belonged to Jamie and had a curse word carved into the bottom of the headboard where no one could see. Penny's had belonged to Jerry and had vines etched along the bottom post, their leaves the color of static. The beds were meant to be bunked, but the ceilings in the trailer were too low so their father had pushed each mattress to opposite walls instead, leaving a wide-open space in the middle, which was usually strewn with cast-off toys and clothes.

Misty's bed was on the left side of the room, the one without a window. The side of her bed next to the wall was lined with stuffed animals. She checked on each of them before bed, kissing their foreheads or booping her nose against theirs or shaking their tiny stuffed paws. Penny groaned Misty's name from the other side of the room. She hated Misty's bedtime routine, but Misty just ignored her.

Her stuffed animal lineup rotated every night so that each animal got a chance to be at the head of the bed, which meant they were closest to Misty. She rearranged them as she said good night, moving Carol the Octopus from the head of her bed to the foot and shifting the line along until Culver Penguin was just beside her cheek. She scratched at a stain on his belly until something pale yellow flaked away.

"You know them animals don't care who sleeps beside you, right?" Penny said. "They got fuzz for brains."

"So do you," Misty said and smiled when Penny scoffed.

"Isn't it time to give those animals away?" Penny asked. "I gave all my stuffed animals to the church when I was ten. Mom and Dad got me a bike for giving them all up. Don't you want a bike?"

Misty rolled her eyes. Ever since Penny turned twelve, she liked to pretend that she was grown. "I have what I want."

"Well, if some of them animals start disappearing, don't blame me. It was probably a wolf that ate them."

Misty walked to the center of the room and drew a line down the middle with her finger. "The force field is up."

"Oh no," Penny mumbled.

Misty climbed into bed, and a pillow flew across the room. Penny giggled. "That's some force field you got there. Can't even keep a pillow out."

Misty closed her eyes.

"Hey, will you get my pillow for me?" Penny asked.

"Get it yourself."

"Please?"

Misty held out as long as she could, but the minute she refused her sister, she had begun to feel guilty about it. If she didn't pick up the pillow, Penny might never speak to her again. She would pretend that she couldn't hear Misty talking like she sometimes did, until Misty panicked, convinced that she'd slipped through the cracks in their home at last, become a ghost at last, and she got so afraid that she would yell at Penny until Penny yelled back at her. Sometimes the only way that Misty knew she was real was if someone else told her it was true. Misty kicked the covers away, picked up Penny's pillow, and tossed it at her head.

Penny smiled with her eyes closed and adjusted the pillow beneath her. "I won't bother your dumb animals, okay?"

"Okay."

Penny turned off the lamp beside her bed.

"Hey, Penny?" Misty said.

Penny sighed.

"Do you think Dad'll come home tonight?"

"No."

"Why not?"

Penny didn't answer for so long that Misty thought her sister had fallen asleep, so she said a little louder, "Hey, can I ask you something else?"

Penny sighed.

"It's important this time. Dad said something before he left. About how Mom had done something and she was supposed to tell us. What do you think he meant?"

"I don't know," Penny said. "I didn't hear him."

"But if you had to guess."

"Then I'd guess it was something bad," Penny said. "Or sad, probably."

"Yeah," Misty said. "I thought so, too."

Penny's mattress creaked as she turned over on her side, and the sheets rustled as she tucked them under her feet.

"Hey, Penny," Misty said.

"*What?*"

"Can you do the thing?"

Penny's hand was a silhouette in the darkness as she reached up and loosened the tack holding the quilt in place over their window. She wrenched it loose and tucked the quilt onto the frame so a thin sliver of light shone through from outside. The light came from the sodium lamp beside Earl's barn. It was the pale orange of a dying fire, and it wasn't much, but after a while it was enough to see the whole room by.

Misty leaned over and slid a shoebox from under her bed. Inside, the crawdad skins in her collection were thin and papery white. They rustled like dry leaves when Misty lifted them into her palm, and it was the sound she imagined ghosts made. Like someone's pale lips pressed to a keyhole and whispering every secret they'd ever kept, fierce and quiet and gone. She counted the skins three times—seven in all—before Penny finally began to snore.

Misty counted to one hundred, listening to the rattle of Penny's snore like there was a leaf caught in her chest that kept catching her breath and shaking and shaking. Only when she was sure that Penny was totally asleep did Misty stow her collection under her bed and slip from under the covers. She and Penny were never allowed to go outside after dark, never alone, and never, never anywhere near Earl's trailer unless their mother was with them, but sometimes Misty liked to do all three. She'd taken to sneaking outside after everyone else had fallen asleep. She'd never gone much farther than the barn, once going so far as to stand on the one-lane blacktopped road that twisted along her holler, just to feel the heat of the day rising up from the pavement and into the soles of her feet. She liked being alone, and she liked doing something that even Penny wasn't brave enough to do.

And no matter what their mother said, or their preacher, or the show about the missing women, or their teachers at school who told them never to trust strangers, it was hard to believe that anything bad could happen to her so close to home. Still, Misty held her breath as she crept through the living room, unlocked the back door, and slipped outside into the night.

Six

The bottom felt strange at night, like the darkness had swallowed the world Misty knew and left something else behind—a place filled with different animals, different sounds, different light. The withered maple tree at the end of the yard called out its name to Misty. Its trunk was full of beetles, and the beetles called out, too, roaming restless through the tree's graying bark. They made Misty feel many-limbed and deeply rooted, her body stretched across a dozen smaller bodies and through more branches than she could count. The earthworms beneath her feet filled her arms with slick, wet earth, and an owl showed her what she looked like from above.

They were still hesitant with her, these night things, but they were growing more and more accustomed to her presence. Misty treated that trust like a piece of glass—something fragile, to be protected. Some people might look outside and never even wonder about the way that bats played games with one another or how owls sometimes told stories going forward and then in reverse and Misty could never really tell which way was the right way. They might seem dull, these animals. Just responding, never thinking, never dreaming, but it wasn't true. Some people just didn't look hard enough or didn't understand that there were a lot of ways to pray, to hope, to feel. A lot of ways of being alive.

Misty stopped as she rounded the corner of the trailer. Miss

Shannon walked onto her front porch with a man following close behind. Misty crouched in the grass, her knees sinking into the soft dirt.

The man was taller and broader than Misty's father, and when the moonlight struck his face, it revealed a full, dark beard and small, dark eyes above it. As Shannon walked down the steps, he reached under the long T-shirt that she wore and lifted the hem, revealing her underwear. Shannon laughed as the man pressed her against the hood of his truck, his hands buried deep in her hair. Shannon's back arched against the metal. Misty's cheeks burned so she stared at the shadows on the grass instead, inspecting the quick, skittered movements of the bugs crawling through the yard.

When Misty looked back at the truck, the man had picked Shannon up, hoisted her onto his waist. Her legs were long and pale as they wrapped around his back, one foot swaying back and forth in its own little rhythm. It was easy to forget that William's life was very different from Misty's despite the many things they had in common. William talked about his mother often and the men that she brought home—her boyfriends, her flings, her test subjects, she called them, jokingly. Sometimes, William said, he listened to the noises that his mother and the men made together at night. Sometimes, she sounded like she was drowning.

Finally, the man set Shannon on the ground again and they parted ways. She watched his truck from the bottom step until even the dim red of its taillights had disappeared around the road, then walked back inside alone.

Misty slunk along the wall of her trailer, one hand gliding over the thin metal of the underpinning. Their front porch was squat and wooden. It had been painted white long ago, but the paint had chipped and faded until it was nearly gone. The bottom was covered on three sides by white latticework that someone had nailed into the boards but never secured to the ground, so over time the lattice got tossed by the wind until one side broke away completely and the other three sides were damaged, bloated with rain and age. A wasp's nest hung from beneath the far corner of the porch, but its edges were dried and brittle, long abandoned. Spiderwebs stretched from one rail to the next, connecting the porch with thin, glistening threads, and a roach skittered out of her way as she crawled beneath the porch. A crawdad chimney that Misty had never seen before hid among the shadows. She knelt before it and strummed her fingers gently against the dirt until a crawdad broke through the chimney. Its claws were cool and slick and a little damp against her finger. The crawdad shared its name and Misty shared hers, building a bridge between them.

"What're you doing here?" Misty asked.

The crawdad shared an image from earlier that day—Misty lying on the bank of the creek—and then other images—acorns scattered across the ground, flies buzzing above something long dead, the heaving thrum of their wings like drums inside her head. The crawdads still believed that Misty was sick or that something was wrong with her.

"So you came to check on me?"

An image of a crawdad with eggs attached to the underside of its long tail. The water pulsed past them, warm and steady, but it never separated them. The feeling of something so close that it was almost herself, a second self, twinned. The crawdads hatched into babies with shells so thin that they were nearly transparent. The hatchlings stayed near their mother's side.

When something was small, it needed to be protected.

Misty was small, so she needed them.

Tears welled in her eyes. She ran her finger gently along the length of the crawdad's back. "Won't you get all dried out under there?"

The crawdad showed Misty the water inside its burrow. Deep down beneath the earth, cold water, pure and sweet smelling. Water buried in pockets if one knew where to look. Water coursing beneath them and around them all the time. The crawdad would make a home there for a while so it could be near Misty. So she wouldn't be alone.

A door creaked and Misty jolted, thinking it must be her mother looking for her, but the porch remained empty. Across the yard, William walked through the high grass and stood in front of Earl's garden. He wore a white T-shirt that glowed under the moonlight and a pair of ratty shorts. His feet were bare and his hair was flattened in the back from the time he'd spent in bed trying to sleep. His shoulders bowed slightly like he might have been searching for something on the dark ground or he might have been praying.

He looked different at night. Different alone when no one else was looking. Smaller, somehow. More like her. Misty hesitated. It felt wrong to speak to William without anyone else around in the middle of the night. Like something that her mother wouldn't approve of.

But he looked so small. So familiar.

Misty crawled from beneath the porch, sharing one last thing with the crawdad—the feeling of her aunt Dolly's hugs, the warm, tight embrace of someone who loved you through and through, the kind of feeling that made it okay to be smaller than something else, to fit inside something else.

Then Misty crept across the yard toward William. She paused

before she reached him and said, "Are you okay?" in her smallest voice.

William whipped around, startled. He dropped the bottle that was in his hand, and it clanked against the ground.

"Shit," he said, and then grinned. "What're you doing out here?"

"I come out here sometimes," Misty said. "Is that the spin-the-bottle?"

William picked the green bottle off the ground and twisted it slowly between his fingers, letting the moonlight glint off its dark surface. "Yeah. I was gonna take it back to the barn. I didn't think Mom'd like it if she found it in my room. I think she's afraid I'm going to grow up and be a drunk just like Earl."

"I saw her outside a few minutes ago…" Misty bit back the words, but William already knew what she meant. He sat down on the grass beside the garden and twisted the bottle in his hands.

"She was saying good night to her boyfriend." He said the last word like it tasted bitter in his mouth.

"With the big beard?"

"That's him. Harold. He's training to be a boss in the mines."

Misty sat down in the grass, careful not to let her bare feet touch the garden. She didn't think anything bad would happen if she did, but it still felt wrong somehow. Sadness crept into her throat just looking at it.

"He's hung around longer than most of the men has," William said. "But they all leave eventually. And then it's just me and Mom again. She says I'm the only one who'll never leave her, and she's right. I just wish he'd get to the leaving already. Mom works all the time, but now she spends half her time with Harold. I don't see her near as much as I used to."

Misty nodded. "My dad ain't home much, neither. And when he is…"

"What?"

Misty shrugged. "I don't know. Him and my mom fight sometimes."

"About what?"

"I don't know. They just seem mad all the time. About everything."

"He don't hit her, does he?"

"No."

"That's something, at least," William said.

"I guess."

William turned the bottle upside down and tried to balance it on the dirt, but the ground was uneven and the bottle kept tipping to the side. They each tapped the bottle with their fingers, bouncing it between them, trying to help it catch someplace in the middle, someplace it wouldn't fall. The bottle finally fell onto the garden and rolled across the torn-up ground. Earl had tilled it that very morning, so the dirt was still loose and dark. William stretched across it, careful not to touch the ground, and he dragged the bottle back into the yard.

"I don't know why Earl keeps trying to make this into a garden," he said.

"I wish he'd leave it alone. It feels mean to keep trying to make it grow when it don't never grow. Maybe it don't want to be a garden."

"Yeah. He's done everything he can to it already." William twisted the bottle in his hands. "You know what I was thinking before you came over?"

"What?"

"That it kinda looks like me. The garden."

Misty looked at the side of William's face. There was a scratch on his cheek, its edges ragged and red even in the dark, and his nose was freckled from all the time he spent in the sun. His hair had grown out more over the summer, and it curled behind his ears and fell into his eyes no matter how many times he brushed it away. She looked between him and the garden, and she could almost see the sameness in them. The sadness.

"That's stupid, ain't it?" he said.

"No, it ain't stupid."

William lifted his chin and smiled at Misty. She smiled back at him.

She said, "What if we left it something?"

"What do you mean?"

"The garden," Misty said. "What if we gave it something. Like the bottle."

Misty pressed her finger against the long, green neck of the bottle, spinning it around until it faced her.

William frowned. "What good would that do?"

"I don't know. It's better than leaving it alone again."

"Yeah," he said. "Yeah, I guess it is."

William knelt over the garden and began to dig into the soft dirt with his bare hands. Misty watched, but didn't offer to help. The thought of touching the garden still made her stomach feel queasy. She took the bottle in her hands instead and called out to it with her name. The bottle answered her the same as it had that morning, except not. Now its name included the game Misty had played and the weight of all three of their hands around its neck. She asked the bottle if it could hold a message from her to whatever was inside the garden.

"Tell it we're sorry," Misty said, "and we hope that it feels better soon."

William stared at Misty when she opened her eyes. "What were you doing?"

"Oh," she said. "I was giving it a message. You know, to give the garden."

"Oh." William took the bottle from her hand. "I don't think that'll work."

Misty shrugged. "It's worth a shot."

He closed his eyes for just a moment before he set the bottle into the hole that he'd dug. Then William covered the bottle with dirt, careful to make it look just like the rest of the garden in case Earl noticed something different in the morning.

"There," he said when he was finished. "What if it don't help anything at all?"

"At least we tried," Misty said.

William trailed his fingers through the dirt slowly, his eyes almost shut, and Misty wondered what he might be saying to the garden, to himself. Something rattled nearby and they both jumped. The sound of muffled footsteps from inside Earl's trailer.

"Hurry," William said. "Go!"

They both scrambled to their feet and took off in opposite directions. Misty paused at the corner of her trailer to look back at William. He waved frantically at her from inside his front door as a light flicked on in Earl's kitchen, spilling golden light onto the dark ground where they had sat moments before. Heart in her throat, Misty crept back into her trailer as quiet as she could and slipped back into bed.

Seven

Misty woke to the sound of shouting.

It sounded like her mother's voice, her mother scolding, her mother hurting, and Misty struggled out of bed, her legs tangled in the sheets. She didn't know what was wrong, but she knew that she needed to see her mother, that she could help, somehow, if only she was there. She slammed her shoulder into the doorframe on her way out of her room; the bruise would last almost a week before it yellowed and faded. The porch burned the soles of her bare feet as she stumbled outside.

Her mother wasn't there.

Neither was Penny.

For a moment Misty stared at the bottom as though it was hiding from her and at any minute the real world would shutter into place and her mother would appear, shouting and crying in the middle of the yard. Misty rubbed her fingers against her eyes as her heartbeat slowed.

Her father stood by Earl's garden. She hadn't seen him since the morning before. He'd left after he fought with their mother and didn't call, didn't come home. He worked on the powder crew at a surface mine nearly an hour's drive from their home, and all that Misty knew about his job was that he was one of the men who blew the mountain apart so other men could reach the coal inside. He'd always worked long hours, but lately he spent more time gone than he did at home.

Another man stood in front of her father, but Misty didn't recognize him. She walked a little closer, lifting her hand above her eyes to block the sun. She stopped.

The man in front of her father wasn't a man at all.

Misty wasn't sure what it was, except that it was made of green glass. It had a head shape sitting on its shoulder shape and a long, narrow body. It was taller than Misty's father and broader, too, but it didn't have a face like him or a face at all that she could see. There were no features—no nose, no ears, no hands—but there were little dips in the glass where those things might have grown once, or might grow still. Its body was the exact same shade of green as the bottle Misty had found in the barn, except the green glass man had no crack running through it. Its body was perfect and whole, and the glass shone in the morning sun with bright pricks of light on its shoulders. The light left thin trails in Misty's vision when she turned away—little worms of yellow and purple that wriggled across the yard until they disappeared into the sky.

She looked for William, wanting to ask him about the green glass man and the bottle they'd planted in the garden, but he was nowhere to be seen. Shannon's truck was still parked in the driveway, but the door to their trailer was shut.

Earl walked across the yard and handed Misty's father a beer. They stood together, staring at the green glass man staring back at them.

Speaking to her father without her mother or sister nearby always felt strange, like maybe Misty should reach out and shake his hand, introduce herself to him. *Hello, it's Misty, your daughter. Hello, do you remember?* But she walked up to him all the same and stood in the place where all their shadows converged. Her father looked down at her and smiled. He ran his fingers through her bangs, raking them down onto her forehead like he always did, and like always, Misty waited until he turned his head to brush them away again.

He said, "About time you got up, Little Bit. It's almost eleven o'clock. You get some breakfast yet?"

Misty shook her head.

"Not even a biscuit? I swear you eat like a robin. You need at least three biscuits and a side of ham."

Misty wrinkled her nose. "I don't like ham."

"Don't like ham? You sure you're my youngin' then?"

Misty knew that it was a joke, but the thought of not belonging to her father still sent panic scrambling through her chest, little sharp-toed beasts squeezing at her heart. She squinted at the green glass man and said, "I thought I heard Mom."

Her father glanced at Earl and away again. "You just missed her. She ain't too big a fan of this, ah, this new addition."

"This miracle," Earl said.

Misty's father laughed, but Earl didn't.

"I don't know what else you would call it," Earl said. "Last night I went to bed and this ground was empty as it's ever been, and this morning there's this."

"Uh-huh," Misty's father said.

"Have you ever seen something like it?" Earl said. "Touch it. It's cold as ice. Even in the middle of this heat. You can touch it, Misty. Something like this, something that God Hisself made, it belongs to everybody. Not just me. All these years I been telling myself that if I kept trying I could find—"

Misty's father squeezed her shoulder. "Why don't you go around back, baby? See if you can find your mama and Penny."

"All right," Misty said.

Earl was still talking as she turned away. He didn't even notice her leaving, his eyes were so fixed on the green glass man.

Around back, the yard was smaller than out front, but it was made of the same dry, yellow grass. The woods behind the yard extended left to the creek and right toward the barn. The trees were thick and green with a heavy layer of leaves beneath them from last year's fall. The leaves exhaled cool puffs of air when Misty stepped on them, as though she was walking on the edge of something's soft teeth while that something was asleep and dreaming about little girls with soft-bottomed shoes.

A clothesline ran the length of the yard, attached on one end to the trailer and on the other end to a maple tree. The rug that usually covered the living room carpet hung over the line, and the line sagged beneath its weight. Penny stood by the woods with her arms folded over her chest, watching as their mother lifted an old broom handle over her shoulder. She did this often. Sometimes after being shut up in the bedroom with their father. Sometimes after a long day alone with Misty and Penny. Sometimes after church.

Their mother brought the handle down, and a plume of yellowed dust swallowed her whole. She held her breath while the dust settled, then exhaled loudly, pulled back the broom handle and swung again. The rug shed grayness for redness, becoming, by degrees, more of its original self, though there were some stains that couldn't be beaten out—a dark smudge in the corner that might have been coffee and a smattering of faint bleach stars.

Misty stood beside her sister and crossed her arms, too.

"You sure picked a day to sleep in," Penny whispered. "Mom yelled."

"At who?"

"Earl. She kept going on about how that thing wasn't from God. False idols and all that. I was happy about it up until Earl balled up his fist and stepped toward her like—" Penny shook her head. "Sometimes I wish Mom would break bad on all of them."

"Just not us," Misty said, and Penny nodded.

"What is it though? That green thing?"

Penny shrugged. "I don't know. Nobody does."

They watched their mother beat the rug until all three of them were covered with sweat for different reasons. Eventually, their mother's arms gave out and she dropped the broom handle. She rinsed her hands with cool water from the garden hose.

"I thought I told you to go inside," she said, looking at Penny, then to Misty. "When did you get up?"

Misty and Penny shrugged in tandem.

Their mother dried her glistening palms on the knees of her long denim skirt, then held them out to the girls. Misty and Penny each took one of their mother's hands, then took each other's. Their mother asked them to bind together in prayer every time something went wrong or someone was hurt so Misty fell into the ritual without question. She bowed her head and closed her eyes as their mother said, "Dear Heavenly Father, you said where two or three or more were gathered in your name that there you were in the midst of them and that whatever they asked believing they would receive. Today we're asking for discernment, Lord. That you help us understand what's happening in the garden. That you let us know how to respond and that you keep us close to you until we know the best thing to do. Watch over us, Lord, and protect us. In Jesus's name we pray. Amen."

Their mother squeezed Misty's hand before she pulled away. She looked at each of their faces. "I want you to promise me you won't touch that thing in Earl's garden."

"Is it bad?" Misty asked.

"I don't know. I don't know what Earl's done. I don't know what he's capable of, and I don't know what that thing is. Until I get some kind of answers, I need you all to listen to me. All right?"

"All right," they said.

"Good girls," she said, and walked into the trailer alone.

"It just showed up," Penny said. "That's the worst part of it. If it had been growing for a while, then it wouldn't be so bad, you know?"

Misty nodded and curled her knees to her chest. William sat beside her in the tall grass by his front steps and Penny sat on a step higher up, her long legs splayed by Misty's side. William's mother had left for work not long after Misty had woken up, and William was having Grippo's for dinner. He shared the open bag between the three of them and they snuck handfuls, chewing slowly, watching for Misty's mother. From this angle, they could see the green glass man only from the side. His chest was flat but deep enough that Misty's father or Earl might have fit inside him with room to spare on every side.

"Maybe it's been growing for a while, though," Penny said. "Just growing where we couldn't see it. It could go all the way down for all we know."

"Down where?" Misty asked.

Penny shrugged. "Hell."

"It don't come from Hell." William jerked the chips toward him. "You sound just as bad as your mama, you know that?"

"Oh, hush," Penny said. "I do wish they wouldn't act so stupid, though. One little statue pops up, and every adult in five miles is acting like the Rapture's come."

"Is that what it is?" Misty asked. "A statue?"

"That's what it looks like to me. Like in a museum or something. Maybe we could call somebody and have them take it away. I bet somebody would pay to have it in their yard instead."

William frowned. "You can't move it. Earl tried earlier. Wrapped a rope around its middle and pulled and everything, said he was afraid somebody might hurt it, but it won't budge."

"See," Penny said. "Who knows how deep down it goes."

"It's cold, you know." William scooted a little closer to the garden, a little further from Misty and Penny. "Like ice. I bet if you stuck your tongue to it, it would freeze in place like that. Have you touched it yet?"

"I don't *want* to touch it," Penny said. "It looks like an alien."

"I think it kinda looks like me," William said.

"It don't look like nobody I've ever seen," Penny said.

William frowned. "Well, it's still the prettiest thing in the county. That's what I think."

Penny snorted. "Well, you sure are the only one."

"Earl likes it. And my mom'll like it, too, after she gets used to it."

"Not if she's got any sense," Penny said.

"She will," William said. "She's got to." His mouth was parted slightly, and he leaned toward the garden. There was a hungry look on his face, the skin beneath his eyes dark with need.

"I bet Earl did it," Penny said.

"Why did it have to be Earl?" William growled.

"Who else could it be?"

"There's lots of people," William said. "Just because it's Earl's land don't mean he had anything to do with it. Whoever did it must be special, though."

Penny stood up. "I'm tired of talking about this. And my mouth is on fire from them chips. You coming, Misty?"

"I'll be there in a minute." Misty waited for the screen door to slam behind her sister before she shifted from the step to the ground beside William. She watched his face from the side. His nose, short and blunt, his eyelashes long and blond. "It looks like the bottle, don't it? From the barn?"

William nodded. "I don't know what else it could be."

"Does that mean the garden did it?"

"How?" William shook his head. "I think Earl must be right. It had to be God."

"Why does it got to be God?"

"Because if it wouldn't him, then it had to be the Devil. They're the only two things that could do something like this."

Misty bit her lip. "I guess so."

"And it has to be from God because it's a good thing and He only does good things. We asked the bottle to help the garden, and now it's growing something. That's what Earl wanted, ain't it? That means he might leave it alone, like you said. And—and my mom almost stayed home with me today because of it."

"Why?"

"She was scared or something, but she'll come around. She said she ain't never seen anything like this before. And maybe your dad will stay next time, too."

Misty looked toward the driveway where her father's truck had been. He'd stayed less than an hour after she woke up before he was gone again. She'd seen the bag he packed, stuffed with clothes, but when Penny asked him where he was going, he just kissed the top of her head and promised he'd see them soon.

"Yeah," Misty said. "Maybe."

They sat together that way, without speaking, until near dusk when William scrambled inside his trailer to answer the phone on its second ring. Dark came an hour after that and still Misty sat alone by his porch. She had watched the green statue in all the light that the day had to offer—bright and golden, harsh and white, waxing, and fading, and gone light—and still the green man glowed around his edges—still he shone. There was something familiar in the statue's shape, as if Misty had seen him once a long time ago. As if he might be there at church next Sunday, sitting three rows up, his shoulders gleaming under the overhead lights. He could be in the bleachers at her next school assembly, standing between all the parents, and no one might notice anything was different. He had slipped into their world so quick, so quiet. He might not stop at the field.

And there was something about the statue's presence that felt almost like a threat. Like the more they wondered about it, the more the statue would unravel everything they understood about the way the world worked. The way God worked.

But the statue had to mean something.

She and William had planted it together. She had sent the garden a message in the bottle, and then the green glass man had grown. Maybe it was from Misty's memories—the bottle turning into her father because he was gone or William because he had kissed her. Or maybe it was shaped after something William asked for as he'd dug the hole where the bottle was buried.

Misty closed her eyes and reached out to the bottom. She didn't offer her name but waited as the crow nestled on the roof of the barn offered its name and the crawdads under her porch and the June bugs with their mouths full of leaves and all the other familiar things that Misty had come to know.

But there was something else, too.

A faint knocking at the back of her mind. A new presence. Something she'd never spoken to before.

Misty waited for it to offer a name, but the presence faded like a hand slowly lifting from her shoulder. Misty tried to follow it, but it was smoke-thin and shifting, then gone.

Misty opened her eyes and stared at the garden and the green glass man. She had tried to do something kind by offering the bottle to the garden, by sending it a message, but now she wasn't sure what she and William had done.

Maybe the garden had woken up now. Maybe it was ready to speak, finally.

Maybe that was a good thing. But maybe it wasn't.

Eight

Their mother didn't tell Misty and Penny that they weren't allowed to go outside the next day, but she stopped them every time they walked toward the front door. Every time she had some new task for them, a bed to make or clothes to fold. So the girls spent the morning cleaning the kitchen from ceiling to floor. The cabinets were dark wood, and a tan countertop separated the kitchen from the living room, its surface nicked with a thousand tiny cuts. The linoleum was a flowered pattern colored dirty orange and green and yellow, and if Misty stared at it too long, the colors seemed to wobble and trade places. A small window trimmed with pale lace curtains overlooked the backyard where the girls often played, the soft wear of their feet still visible in the grass, like they'd only been there a moment ago, or might be there still, some ghost of them standing out there while they were working in here.

They washed every dish and every pot and rearranged the cabinets. They pulled the refrigerator from its nook with their mother's help and swept beneath it. They found Penny's missing bracelet, a handful of Cheerios, eighty-seven cents in loose change, and a thin line of dark mold growing on the wall. The mold crooked like a finger at the tip, inviting Misty to join it there, in the damp, in the warmth, and she couldn't push the fridge back into place quick enough.

Their mother supervised them from the living room. She worked quietly, too, taking all of the porcelain figures from the television stand and setting them on the carpet beside her before wiping a damp cloth across the stand's surface. When their mother finished, she placed each of the figures gently back in the exact place it had been before. There was something peaceful in watching her clean. Something in her movements, so precise, so sure, that felt as though she was putting the whole world to right. That somewhere a crumble of brick and stone became a house again all because Misty's mother had swept the dust from the television stand.

When she could, Misty stole glances out the living room window, but only when her mother wasn't watching. No matter how many times Misty looked outside, William and Earl were always there, their position just slightly changed—sometimes standing beside the garden, sometimes sketching on a battered notebook, sometimes crouched directly in front of the green glass man, bathing in its shimmering light.

And every time Misty looked, she felt a gentle nudge at the back of her mind, a faint knocking like the night before. She waited, still, for it to offer a name, but it never did. It just waited at the edges of her thoughts like a cat stalking through high grass.

"Come away from there, Little Bit," Misty's mother said. Her hand was warm and clammy as it cupped Misty's elbow and pulled her away from the window. Their mother frowned as she glanced outside, then closed the blinds with a snap.

Penny had been scraping a small black stain in the corner of the kitchen, but she stopped and lifted her head. "You know it's just a piece of glass, right? It ain't like it's done nothing to hurt anybody. And even if it did, you can't hold us hostage for the rest of our lives."

Penny looked right at their mother as she said it, and Misty
wanted to pinch the back of her arm. Sometimes it seemed like Misty
caught all of the sadness, the grief, and the guilty that Penny refused
to take as her own. Penny shrugged it off and Misty was there to pick
it up because somebody had to feel it. Somebody had to be sorry.
Somebody had to be quiet, or else the whole world would be filled
with noise and nobody would stay together and there'd be nothing
left for Misty to call home.

"Hostage?" their mother said. The knuckles on both her hands
were scalded bright red by the steaming dishwater.

"I just meant…" Penny dropped her head. "I'm bored. I want to
go out and do something else for a little while."

A muscle in their mother's jaw clenched and unclenched. "You
can go sweep the porch for a little while. But I better not hear your
feet hit the grass, all right?"

Penny waited until their mother turned her back to roll her eyes,
then crept onto the front porch without looking back. Their mother's shoulders slumped when Penny shut the door. Whatever held her
up when she was angry must have cost her a great deal, because she
was always wrung out afterward, all her joints suddenly loose and
yielding as a sheet hung out to dry.

She said, "Sometimes I just want to throttle her."

Misty smiled. "Me too."

Their mother leaned against the kitchen counter for support. "I
told Aunt Jem and Aunt Dolly about that thing of Earl's."

"What'd they say?" Misty asked.

"Dolly's going to pray. Jem wants to see it, of course. She's always
been that way. Casting about looking for something new while Dolly
tells her she can't have it and I run along behind trying to keep them

both from getting hurt or hurting each other." She smiled and looked about to say something more, but paused. It was a familiar gesture. Misty's mother had probably eaten more words than she had spoken, bitten them off mid-syllable and swallowed them somewhere deep inside, someplace even beyond the reach of echoes.

She walked over to the front door and, without looking outside, shouted, "Both feet on the porch, Penny Lee, or it'll be my switch on your hind end."

Their mother had turned to the vacuum when she noticed a faint crescent of lime-green light against the wall. The light had been there all morning—Misty had seen it trembling over her mother's shoulder once and mistaken it for a moth. The light was the exact shade of green as the statue that had grown in the garden. Their mother walked over and placed her hand against the light like it was a stain that she could rub out of the paneling. The light shone on her hand instead, and she yanked her hand away as though she'd been burned.

Misty watched from the kitchen floor as their mother rearranged the curtains on the living room window. She cinched the blinds open and closed. The outside world stuttered to life for one too-bright moment before the living room fell back to dimness.

But still, the light persisted.

It landed on a different place each time—first in the very center of the wall, then it retreated to the corner of a worn throw pillow for almost half an hour before Misty spotted it. Their mother descended on the window again, and this time the light glinted off the thin glass frame of a family photo. It hovered at Misty's throat, small and bright and green. Their mother pulled the photo from the wall and laid it on the kitchen counter, facedown.

Penny walked back inside and said, "The sheriff is out there,

Mama. Earl's building a fence around his garden and talking about intruders and how he wants a patrol or something. And Miss Janet from church and her sister are there, too. And my old history teacher Mr. Morris is out there with his uppity daughter Heather, and they're all talking about—" She stopped and looked between Misty and their mother. "What's going on?"

"There's a green light," Misty said. "We're trying to find it."

Penny leaned her broom against the wall, and Misty left her dishrag on the floor of the kitchen. The air was heavy with the scent of lemon and burnt grease as they chased the light all across the room, from crease to corner to ceiling. They followed it over the sagging couch with its creaking springs, over the recliner where Misty's father sat in the evenings, a ring of coal dust staining the place where his neck rubbed against the fabric. The porcelain figures shook as Misty and Penny stomped back and forth, taking turns in front of the window, blocking the light's path, but it always found some way through, some slight slip that they couldn't catch, never for long. Their mother's face was pulled into a tight expression as she searched, all the little muscles in her face knitting themselves together like they were scared to be alone.

Hours passed this way, and if Misty grew hungry, she didn't notice. None of them stopped to eat or drink. None of them even mentioned stopping.

"How's it keep getting inside?" their mother asked. "I know it's coming from that thing in the garden. The light's the same color." She clutched her hands in front of her chest, and the air grew heavy with something that Misty couldn't name. She'd felt it before on the nights when her parents fought the loudest or in church before the Holy Ghost fell. It was moments like this that Misty felt most desperate to speak to her mother, to close her eyes and call her mother's true name and hear her mother's voice inside her head. It would be her only chance of reaching her mother in moments like this when she seemed so far away, so separate and alone.

There was no way to know exactly where the light was coming from, but it made Misty even more wary of the garden and the strange things happening around it. She still felt the nameless presence hovering near her like a ghost staring over her shoulder. It put her on edge, like any moment she might scream at the garden or the statue or her sister—anything at all to let the feeling loose. Maybe that was how her mother felt, too.

Finally, the sun dipped behind the trees and the green light darkened to the color of a holly leaf. One moment it was there, on the middle of a couch cushion, and the next moment, they had lost it. Misty sank down the wall nearest the kitchen, her shirt crackling like static behind her. Penny squatted near the door, and their mother stood with one long-fingered hand on her throat.

Even when it was gone, the light still didn't feel gone. It felt hiding, waiting. It felt almost. Their eyes darted over the ceiling, the furniture, each other, but the light still didn't come back. Half an hour passed in silence before their mother's hoarse voice croaked, "Get ready. We're going to church."

―――――――――

The church smelled like fresh lumber, wooden but not woody, not like the trees behind Misty's house, even though the two had been nearly the same once. The church had been rebuilt a year before, but still seemed unused, like the doors had been unlocked only that morning. The newness made it hard to feel comfortable. There was always a sense of something being undone by the presence of people—flattening the fresh carpet as they walked, smudging the gleaming pews with their fingerprints, cracking the hymnals' spines with their searching.

The church resisted this intrusion, resisted its new self. There was a shock to being remade. A time of forgetting, of mourning as the church accepted that it was home to different kinds of things now. The blue jays and gray squirrels of the woods had been replaced by instruments and leather shoes and prayer requests. A few years from now, the church would start to remember who it had been before, the memories surfacing like dreams, all muddy and blue. It would join its selves together, the then and the now, and it would be easier for it to speak to Misty. Until then, the church was quiet as it searched for itself, roaming through its own walls, scouring its foundation, and the hum of it trembled in the back of Misty's mind.

Misty's aunts were already waiting in their pew—two round-faced women with soft hands that smelled always of baby powder. Dolly sat with her husband and her daughter, Charlene. Dolly's older child, Sam, had refused to come to church, claiming that God was a story people told to make themselves feel better. Charlene was only eight, which made her the baby of the family, and she had no choice but to come. So she sat in the floor of the pew with a book propped on her seat, mouthing the words under her breath as she read.

Aunt Jem was at the other end of the pew with her two sons, Jerry and Jamie. Jerry's head was bent toward a sketchbook on his lap. He drew something that Misty couldn't make out from this angle—a curve that might have been a face or a wheel or a sun. His older brother, Jamie, wore a bandanna around his long hair. As Misty sat down, Jem plucked the bandanna from Jamie's head and tucked it into her purse, mumbling about blasphemy under her breath all the while. As she did, Jamie took another bandanna from his pocket and tied it over his hair, which had grown out almost to his shoulders. Jem's eyes widened when she looked back at him. This time she ripped the bandanna away and stuffed it into her bag as Jamie pulled yet another bandanna from his pocket—this one bright yellow—and tied it back into place.

After the fourth round, Jem finally relented and asked Jamie what he wanted from her. The two of them fell into whispered negotiations of which Misty heard only a few words—paintball gun, kitchen floor, backyard. When it was over, Jamie sat up straight with his hands folded in his lap, a perfect gentleman with a slight smile tugging at the corners of his mouth.

Misty's family sat in the middle of her aunts so that Misty was wedged between her cousin Jerry and her mother.

Jem sighed. "Beth, you look like how I feel right now. You ain't getting sick, are you? I'll get the preacher over here with his holy water if you are."

Misty's mother swatted at her sister. "I'm not sick. I'm just tired."

"Well, you came to the right place then," Dolly said. "Is that Claudette over there? Sitting with Phillip's family?"

"They got back together," Misty's mother said. "I saw them down at the gas station the other day."

"After she ripped her way up and down the county?" Dolly whispered.

"This is the house of the Lord," Jem said. "At least say 'fornicated.'"

The women went on talking about their week at home, about the coal mines and whether or not Earl was still drinking, the price of double-wides and laundry detergent, and how the beans were withering in the garden. It was Jem who finally asked about the green glass man.

Misty's mother shook her head. "I'd rather not talk about it."

"Oh, come on now. You know what I keep thinking? Earl's been tending that land for years now and finally something grew. It'd be a real inspiration if he wasn't such a creep."

"I don't see why he cleared the land in the first place," Dolly said. "It used to be covered in the prettiest dogwood grove you ever seen. And that old swinging bridge, you remember? I used to walk out there when Wayne and I was first married and we'd have a fight. That place always calmed me right down. Made everything feel all right."

"I never understood how he could afford it," Jem said.

"He got all the money from that settlement. Don't you remember? Something happened to him in the mines. Broke his neck or something."

Jem huffed. "Nothing seems broke to me, except his head. You know, there always was something off about that place. You remember when Earl first set them trailers there? He couldn't keep nobody in them for more than a month or two."

"People said they was haunted," Dolly said. "Wayne's cousin lived in one for a while, and he said that birds nested in the walls."

"Did they say anything about a light?" Misty's mother asked, but Jem just shrugged.

"Whatever it was, I reckon it was God's way of punishing Earl for what he did to that wife of his. Lord knows he's never gonna see any justice in this life."

"She always was a quare thing," Dolly said, "but she never deserved him."

Misty felt her cousin Jerry stiffen at the word *quare*. She'd heard the word often, sometimes aimed at herself, sometimes at Jerry, sometimes at strangers. It was supposed to mean strange or different, but it meant something else, too, something that Misty hadn't quite figured out yet. Jerry had, though, and it hurt him every time he heard it, so Misty laid her head against his shoulder and whispered, "I like that girl you're drawing."

He huffed out a breath and his body loosened a little. "It's supposed to be a bird."

"It will be," Misty said.

He pressed his forehead to hers for a brief moment—his skin cool and soft, the smell of cologne clinging to his shirt—then turned back to his drawing.

"Can we talk about something else?" Misty's mother asked.

Jem picked up a tithing envelope and fanned her face with it. "I know you don't like what's happening, but not talking about it ain't going to make that thing in the garden go away. You do know that?"

Penny leaned forward and whispered, "That's what I said," but Misty's mother didn't answer. Jem took the silence as permission to keep talking.

"It's just like great-aunt Susie when the mountain behind her house started slipping. She didn't pay it any mind, said the mountain had held for a thousand years, it could hold for a thousand more. Then she woke up one morning with her lap full of mud. Nearly buried her alive. Of course that's how she made the Mud Man. He wasn't much of a looker, but he sure helped out around the farm."

"Oh, will you hush with those stories," Misty's mother said. "Half the things you say never happened to anybody, let alone our family."

"Oh, ye of little faith," Jem said. "If we don't remember them, then it won't matter what they went through and I for one think that—"

"Jem," Dolly said, loud enough to make a handful of people look over their shoulders. Misty's mother and aunts smiled and adjusted their skirts until the people turned back around.

Misty's mother spoke quietly between her teeth. "I don't know no more about that thing in Earl's garden than the two of you do, except what it looks like, and I wished I didn't know that. I'm praying. That's all I know to do. Pray and ask God to take it away before…"

Penny rolled her eyes, and Misty wrapped her finger in the hem of their mother's shirt. "It's okay, Mom."

"It's not," she said. "But Jem never could leave anything alone."

Dolly shot Jem a look until she took a deep breath and said, "I'm sorry, Beth. I didn't know it was getting to you like that, or I wouldn't have said a thing to begin with."

"It's probably just some crackpot scheme of Earl's," Dolly said. "That man never was right. Who knows what he's cooked up living alone in that trailer all these years. I bet it'll all blow over in a week and we'll be back to talking about Maxine's low-cut blouses and school supplies. I have to buy Charlene new cleats for softball this year, and I reckon I'll have to take a second mortgage out on the house just to swing it."

"Jamie has some that he grew out of a few years ago. I used to mow the yard in them but they're still in good shape. Have Char walk down and see us tomorrow, and we'll dig them out. You hear me, Char?" Jem said.

Charlene didn't look up.

"That's good," Jem said. "She's probably over there reading how to dispose of bodies, plotting my murder. She's got that look in her eye, you know? The one Delroy Baker's boy had before he—"

"See," Dolly said. "Everything's going to be just fine, Beth. Charlene will bury Jem out back with the Mud Man and we'll all mourn her, of course, but we'll move on. And the pastor's going to speak on that—what did you call it—that statue in Earl's garden. People have been asking him about it, too. He'll tell us what do."

Misty's mother stared straight ahead. The piano began to play and all conversation died as the preacher took the pulpit. He reminded the congregation that Revival was just a month away and he knew their church would receive a touch from the Lord. He saw them like so many hands outreached for a blessing. His words dimmed in Misty's ears as her mother took out her Bible and turned to a verse, the pages bright with highlighter and littered with her fine, neat writing in the margins, the corners of the pages worn smooth by her fingers. Misty didn't hear much else the preacher said, but she studied the wooden beams that crisscrossed the ceiling of the church instead. She imagined herself walking across them with her arms outspread, her toes clenched tight against the veneer, her panty hose slick and smooth beneath her, waiting for someone to look up and notice her, but no one ever did, not even in her fantasies.

Sometimes she imagined that Penny was with her on the beams, but she knew deep down that Penny wouldn't play with her like that, and the fantasy crumbled. So she imagined William instead. If anyone would stand barefoot above the cross and their preacher and half the county on a warm Sunday evening, it would be William. She smiled to herself as she imagined him doing a handstand as she cartwheeled back and forth over the beams. She wasn't sure that either of them could really do those tricks, but in her mind they could do anything. The lights would shake with Misty's footfalls as she tipped end over end, stirring dust that fell like soft snow on the heads of all the people who refused to look up and see them.

The nameless presence had faded from Misty's mind once they left for church. Everything Misty spoke to had a certain reach—a distance they could speak across—including herself. For most things, it was fairly small. A hundred feet, maybe more, and the more Misty spoke to something, the greater their reach grew. She closed her eyes and concentrated as hard as she could on the crawdads in her creek, weaving their name over and over like a long strand of steady rope growing between her fingers. She cast it toward them until she felt them calling back to her from all that distance. Their connection wasn't as strong as it would have been had Misty been standing in the creek, but the crawdads were still there in her mind. And they shared the creek with her. They shared cool water and deep shadows, the current rippling over their shells, the flutter of their tails as they propelled themselves backward into the dark.

For the first time that day, Misty felt relaxed, almost happy. All the tension in her body eased away and she could have slept under the bright lights of the church, surrounded by her family with the low drone of the preacher's voice like a fan blowing in her ears.

Misty's mother tapped her on the knee and Misty startled. Her connection with the crawdads snapped like a twig, separating them. Without thinking, Misty sat up higher and crossed the leg that her mother had touched. Her thighs had slipped apart as she spoke to the crawdads, her body sinking into the pew until her dress pulled up, exposing her bare knees and an inch of pale thigh. And even though no one could see her skin except her mother and aunts, Misty still had to be careful. Of what, she wasn't sure, but she knew that it was wrong for her dress to slide up, for her shirt to be cut too low, for her body to be shown to anyone, even her family. She had to be careful of herself.

At the pulpit, the preacher's message drew to a close. He shut the Bible on his podium and placed one hand gently atop it as he looked out across the congregation. This was the preacher Penny talked about in the barn. He was Earl's uncle, but it was hard to see any resemblance in him as he stood at the pulpit in his white dress shirt and dark slacks, the tips of his shoes gleaming beneath the lights.

"Before I send y'all home tonight, I'd like to speak a little more on community. I've heard some rumors are being spread about something happening on Preacher's Fork. I'd remind you all what the Book of the Lord says about idle gossip. It's our job to spread the word of God, not the word of man. Now, I will be praying on this and seeking His counsel. But for tonight, all we should be worried about is getting our hearts ready for Revival next month."

A smattering of applause rippled through the church, but Aunt Jem snapped her hymnal closed so hard that dust flew from the pages. "Gossip, my rump. He just don't want us talking about what his nephew is up to."

"The church protects its own," Dolly muttered, "but so do we." She nodded at Misty as the pastor bowed his head and led the congregation in a final prayer.

Nine

Penny was quiet on the ride home from church. The kind of quiet that felt like waiting, like plotting, like Misty would soon have something to worry about, so she wasn't surprised when she woke from a bad dream to find Penny's bed empty.

She knew it was empty before she rolled over and saw the quilt kicked to the bottom of Penny's bed, her pillow slumped to the floor, the same way that Misty could tell when the television was on in the living room even if the sound was muted. There was a kind of hum, a warping of the air that life made. All someone had to do was walk into a room to change it, to bend everything around themselves like water rushing past a stone.

The room spun a little when Misty got out of bed. She touched the walls to keep her balance as she walked down the narrow hallway. All the furniture had turned to hard-edged darkness, making it impossible to tell one shape from the next. The green light was there where it had first appeared. It swung slowly back and forth in a way that made Misty think of a smile.

The front door was open just a crack, which meant Penny must be outside. Misty almost shut the door, almost locked it, too, leaving Penny to get into trouble on her own this time. She would deserve it. But the bad dream was still wedged in the corners of Misty's eyes. Something about the green glass man, the sound of glass breaking, and trees all around her. Penny had been there in her dream, and the dream made Misty just afraid enough to open the door and check on her sister.

The air tickled the back of Misty's neck as she stepped barefoot onto the porch. A single light burned in William's trailer, in the room Misty knew was his own, though she'd never been inside. His mother's truck was parked in its usual spot, the muffler tied up with a loose string. When the wind blew, the muffler bounced up and down, tapping out a little message against the gravel. Lights flickered in Earl's windows, and the front door was propped open so television noises drifted across the yard. The lawn chair he kept by the garden glistened under the moonlight, and Penny was there, too, standing in front of the green glass man.

Penny looked smaller than Misty had ever seen her look, or maybe it was the statue that looked bigger in the sight of Penny. It loomed above her. Its shoulders sparkled with white moonlight and orange lamplight.

Misty crept down the steps and crawled beneath the porch where the moonlight fell in pale-blue diamonds. Her bare knees were cold against the hard ground. There were more crawdad chimneys now—three where there had only been one before. Misty drummed her fingers across the ground to draw the crawdads out, but she kept her eyes locked on Penny.

Earl had started building a fence around the garden. He'd used old wood that had fallen off the barn, soft wood that had gone gray in the center, started to rot. The boards lay on the ground, hammered together in the shape they would soon keep, but were too weak to stand on their own just yet. Penny walked over the boards, dragging Earl's plastic lawn chair behind her. The moonlight poured through the green glass man and cast a deep-green shadow on the ground and on Penny, too. She swam through the green light, her skin bubbled and shivered like she was changing into something else as she climbed onto the chair. Penny held her arms straight out for balance, and when she straightened her legs, she stood almost even with the statue.

Misty jumped when a crawdad skittered over the back of her hand. She cupped its small body in her palm and drew it to her chest. The crawdad shared murky images—snakes' holes buried into the bank of the creek, a mouth stretched wide open, two sharp fangs glistening. Misty's chest contracted and her arms pinched to her sides like she was being swallowed whole.

They were scared of the green glass man.

"I don't like it, either," Misty said.

They filled her body with the feeling of water rushing back from the shore, drawing something away. Pull her back, they urged, because even though the crawdads weren't that fond of Penny, they knew that Misty loved her.

"I can't," Misty said. She felt rooted to the spot. She was sure that stopping Penny would be worse than watching her. She wouldn't even give Misty a chance to explain why she was there, but would stop speaking to Misty and refuse to play with her. She would use loneliness like a punishment and Misty didn't want to be more alone than she was already.

So she waited beneath the porch with the crawdads gathered close.

Penny's body was solid and pale next to the statue, which was clear and bright and green. His body of light and shade, hers of cotton and skin. No two things ever looked more and less alike than they did.

The breeze picked up and whipped Penny's sleep shirt to the side, revealing the backs of her pale thighs. The grass rattled and shook, the sound of it like whispers in church, like everything in the bottom was watching as Penny placed her hands on the green man's shoulders. The moonlight stained the tips of her fingers bright green, and for a moment, it seemed like Penny might be sinking into the glass, like he was taking her, inch by inch. Soon, she'd be submerged to the wrist. Soon, her arms wouldn't be arms at all, but clear, bright glass. She'd be nothing but a bubble in his chest, another shade of green for the sun to pass straight through.

Penny leaned forward and pressed her lips to the green glass man.

Misty's stomach twisted with shock and embarrassment and fear as Penny kissed the place where the statue's mouth would have been, had he been a real man instead of glass. Her fingers clutched at his shoulders. Her legs stiffened. She held herself there until she shivered violently. The plastic chair tipped to the side, and Penny stumbled to the ground.

She looked up at the green glass man and touched her fingertips to her chin like she was making sure she was still there, that she hadn't left something behind when she fell. And even though the night was warm and balmy, Penny's breath formed a little cloud of mist when she exhaled. It was like winter had come while she was kissing the green man, like the deep, dark cold of the earth was deep inside of him and Penny had let a little of it out. She had let it inside herself.

Misty slunk further beneath the porch as her sister backed away from the garden. Penny didn't even glance in Misty's direction as she ran up the porch steps, her bare feet pounding against the wooden boards, Penny a flash of pale skin and the twirl of an oversize T-shirt before the front door clicked shut.

The crawdads inched closer, crawling across Misty's thighs, bunching together at her belly. She stroked their hard shells and stared at the place where her sister had been. She didn't know exactly where the statue had come from. She didn't know if it could hurt anything or anyone. If it could hurt Penny somehow.

But it might.

There was only one way that Misty knew to find out. Only one way that she could know for sure what the garden or the statue or the nameless presence wanted.

She had to share her name with it.

She had to speak to the garden.

Ten

"I have to go," Misty said. She placed the crawdads gently on the ground.

The feeling of a thousand reeds cast across her bones, pulling her down, keeping her in place. The crawdads shuffled forward, their claws damp and cool against her skin.

"I have to," Misty said. "I won't get hurt."

The ropes tightened, then loosened. The crawdads eased back to their burrows.

"I'll be careful. I promise."

Misty crawled from under the porch and stood barefoot in her front yard. The light in William's room was gone now. Earl's front door was propped open with a chip of concrete. Faint television noises seeped through the open space, and pale-blue light flickered on his porch. Misty hurried to the garden and knelt behind the plastic lawn chair so it might camouflage her if Earl came outside.

The green glass man's light pooled on Misty's thighs and her outstretched palms. She turned her hands over and the green light swam over her skin, bubbling and twisting as though it were made of water instead of light. She balled her hands into fists and closed her eyes. She wasn't sure which she should speak to—the garden or the statue—so Misty aimed her voice outward, to the bottom. She didn't ask any one thing in particular to answer, but invited any answer. Any voice.

Misty's name stirred inside her chest—her hand reaching out for her grandmother's when Misty was barely old enough to walk, the paper-thin feeling of the older woman's skin inside Misty's palm; the rattle of her mother's breathing, rocking her, shushing her, begging her to sleep; the first time Misty had ever tasted snow, bright and shivering cold; her father's voice from a different room, muffled and rumbling; a fawn in the woods, blood on its hip and pain in Misty's leg, pain in her chest, swelling until it blotted out every other feeling and she almost let go. She almost halted her name right there, afraid of feeling that kind of pain again, but she held on and watched Penny standing beside her in church and singing along to a song she didn't know, making up the words until Misty's sides ached from trying not to laugh; the feeling of a crawdad skittering over her thighs, resting against her belly; her mother sitting on the couch with her head in her hands; her father's truck peeling out of the driveway, gravel pinging against the metal sides of the trailer; the faraway look in her mother's eyes, a feeling of sadness like many small stones stacked inside her stomach; green light swimming on her face, on Penny's face, the press of lips on skin; the press of William's lips against her cheek, warm and soft; a small cloud of cold breath hanging in the air.

Misty braced herself. She expected pain, hurt, despair. She waited for a swell of the garden's feelings, and she hoped she wouldn't be washed away by them.

Dozens of other voices answered instead.

The barn called back to her and so did Shannon's truck, the tailpipe tapping out a little message as the wind picked up. A few birds stirred in their nests and cooed their names, an owl circled overhead, watchful, and a dozen rats scurried out of their hidden homes to get a closer look at Misty kneeling by the garden. All of them spoke to her, but she pushed them all back, held them at an arm's length and listened, listened.

Until a voice she'd never heard before answered back.

"Hello," the voice said.

Misty whipped around, expecting to find someone standing behind her, but the bottom was empty of everything but moonlight and cricket song. The voice wasn't like that of the crawdads or the snakes or the owls. It didn't speak in images, but in words, like hers. It spoke like Misty spoke, and she'd never heard a voice like that inside her head.

And there was no pain, not yet, though her hip ached like there was shrapnel lodged inside, slowly working its way to her surface. Misty looked up at the green glass man's face. "Are you the statue?"

"No," the voice said. "Not statue. Not glass."

There was an oily quality to the voice. Slick and sliding. Misty imagined it like something long and sleek, something hidden under the surface of dark water, and she could only make out its shape by the waves it stirred inside her mind. And because she thought it, the image swam between them, murky and gray.

"Are you the garden then?" Misty asked.

"That's what he called me." An image of Earl flashed between them, his back bent over the garden with a hoe in his hands, the feeling of a dull blade digging into Misty's shoulder, pulling her apart. "That's what you can call me, if you need to call me something."

"Don't you have a name?"

The garden hesitated. "I used to. Once."

"What do you mean?"

Misty felt something like fog collecting in her skin, sweeping up from her elbows and into her chest. It was a cold feeling, damp and lonely. But it wasn't unbearable, not like speaking to the injured fawn.

"I don't remember it now," the garden said. "I lost it. Gone, gone when the bad thing happened. I don't know it anymore."

"What bad thing?"

Branches. A woman's pale face looking back over her shoulder, searching for something in the dark. Her fingers pressed to the trunk of a dogwood tree. Misty heard birdsong inside her head, dozens of different voices, panicked, overlapping.

"Who's that woman?" Misty asked.

"It doesn't matter now. She's gone, gone, too. She took my name with her."

"I don't know if I can keep talking like this," Misty said. "I've never talked to something without a name before."

"I won't hurt you." Weight curled inside the palm of Misty's hand like fingers touching her palm, tentative, cold. "You're the only thing I've spoken to in a hundred dark nights. I was sleeping 'til you woke me."

Misty shook her head. "How did I wake you?"

"The bottle," the garden said. "You and the little boy, the little bruise."

"William?"

"Yes," the garden said. "Him. I heard your voice in the bottle's name. You were calling to me. And I was asleep for so long, down deep in the under, dreaming, down where the nameless things go. I never thought I'd come back again, but you were so...sweet. Are you always that way? Little gentle girl."

"I don't know," Misty said. "I try, I guess."

"And you're so good at speaking for such a little tadpole girl. You must be very brave."

Misty blushed and dropped her face to hide the color creeping into her cheeks. "Penny is the brave one, not me."

"Is she the one who kissed the statue?"

Misty nodded. The statue's green light twisted across her skin, and for a moment she almost felt its touch like cold, like frost. She shivered and scooted a little further away from the garden. "Did you make the statue grow?"

Silence.

Misty tried to feel for the garden in the darkness, in her own body, but it was hard to pin down. Since Misty had shared her name, the garden could see all of her thoughts, could tell if she was lying or holding something back, but without the garden's name, Misty couldn't do the same in return. She was a vessel that could be filled with whatever the garden offered, good or bad, true or not, and there would be no way for Misty to tell the difference.

And just because she'd never heard of a nameless thing didn't mean they couldn't exist. There was still so much about names that she didn't understand, and she'd never had anyone to talk to about it, no one to teach her.

"Did you make the statue?" Misty asked, more frantic.

"No," the garden said. "No. I'm not the statue."

"Then where did it come from?" Misty asked.

"I don't know," the garden said. "What are people saying about it?"

"Mostly that it's a bad thing. Except Earl and William. They like it."

"Earl likes it?"

Something swirling and dark flickered between them before it disappeared, but Misty could taste rage in her mouth, bitter as coffee grounds.

"I don't like it, though," Misty said. "It scares me sometimes. I keep thinking—"

"What?"

"It's stupid."

"No," the garden said. "Your thoughts are important."

Misty smiled. "Well, it's stupid because it won't happen. But sometimes I still think that the statue might move. Just start walking or talking. I don't want to know what it might say." Misty shivered.

The garden filled her with warm sunshine on bare earth, the way the heat crept down into the shadowy parts, the places that hadn't known warmth for a long, long time. It said, "No more scary thoughts. Night is a bad time for those."

"I like it out here at night, though. It's so quiet."

"I'm scared of night," the garden said. "Sometimes I can't tell the difference between dark and gone."

Misty conjured the feeling of her favorite sweater, the one her mother had bought brand new for her from a store, not secondhand. It was so soft inside and out that Misty had almost worn a hole in the sleeve just from rubbing it between her fingers.

"I like that," the garden said. "Soft and warm. You're a sweet girl."

Misty smiled. "I should get back inside now."

"Will you come back sometime? And talk to me?"

Misty curled her knees to her chest. The garden seemed nice. It hadn't filled her full of sadness and hurt the way she thought it might. It did seem lonely and it did seem hurt, but not so much that it scared her. And its voice was the first of its kind she'd ever heard inside her head, the first voice she didn't have to struggle to translate or worry so much about sending the wrong message. It was what she imagined it would be like if she could talk to her mother or to Penny. So easy and quick. So comfortable.

"I could come back," Misty said, "if we figured out your name."

The garden was quiet for so long that Misty thought she might have lost touch with it. Then the voice returned, softly. "You could do that?"

"I don't know," Misty said. "I've never done it before, but I could try."

"And I could help. Somehow. I know all kinds of things about names and speaking."

"Sure."

"And you'll come back? Like a friend?"

"Yeah," Misty said. "Like a friend."

The sunlight feeling returned, heating Misty's shoulders and cheeks as though she was sitting outside in the middle of the day, not the middle of the night.

"You should hurry," the garden said. "He's stirring."

A board creaked nearby. Misty whipped her head toward Earl's trailer. A shadow moved on the wall, followed by a deep, wet cough.

"Go," the garden said. "Quick, quick."

Misty had barely ducked around the corner of the trailer before Earl stepped into his doorway. He wore a dark shirt and a pair of weathered work pants. He braced his arms on either side of the door as he slid down until he was sitting with his legs splayed on the porch. He drifted a little to the side like he was still half-asleep.

Hatred boiled inside Misty's chest at the sight of him. It heated her limbs until she clenched her hands into fists. The feeling surprised her. It came on so sudden and so strong, and it faded almost as quickly. Like the feeling had never been hers at all.

Misty looked at the garden. She couldn't blame it for hating Earl after the way he'd worked the earth, all those years of emptying and tilling and breaking. It would be hard to forget something like that, and even harder to forgive.

But maybe Misty could help the garden, and it could help her. Maybe it knew a way for Misty to speak to her family. Maybe everything would be okay.

Eleven

Back in her room, Misty sat on the edge of her bed listening to the sound of Penny's snores. Any fear or worry from kissing the green glass man must have worn off because Penny was splayed on her back with her limbs sprawled across the bed like she had fallen there from a great height. Misty wanted to shake her awake and tell her about the garden. Penny was always the person Misty told when she had a strange dream or lost a tooth, Penny the most likely to tell Misty to go away but the least likely to follow through on it. Penny who listened even when she seemed like she wasn't.

But Misty couldn't tell her sister anything.

She had no way to prove that it was true. Penny couldn't talk to the garden like Misty could. And even if Misty tried to tell her about names and about talking to the world, Penny would say she was making it up and that it was ugly to lie.

Speaking to the world felt special, but it wouldn't look very special to anyone else. It would look like sitting, like waiting. It would look quiet and there was nothing special about quiet, not to people like Penny who were always saying something, always moving, always seeking. If Misty was ever going to share her gift with her family, she'd have to show them firsthand. She had to learn how to talk to them.

Misty curled onto her side and reached out to the trailer. She could speak to the doors and the windows and even the linoleum in the kitchen if she wanted, but she could speak to the trailer, too, the whole that all the little parts made. The trailer's voice was warm and familiar, if a little nervous. Its name a blurred tally of all the things inside it, including everyone who had ever lived there, scented with honey and woodsmoke and bathed in the golden light of one Easter morning many years before Misty was born. The trailer was a thunder of footsteps across its floors and a thousand nails piercing its sides to hang pictures of different faces; the slam of a door closing behind someone who had called the trailer home for the last time.

And when Misty asked the trailer to show her something nice, the trailer obliged, and countless images flooded behind her eyes. Her toes grew cold when the trailer remembered winter, and her cheeks were warmed by the light of a sunrise she'd never seen as the trailer strung together a whole whirl of memories.

Once the trailer had sat on a high hill with a sycamore tree growing just outside the kitchen window. The morning light that fell through was dappled and dancing. It shivered and shook over the floor, and it looked like glitter falling through the air. Misty saw families that she had never met. A little girl taking her first steps in the same spot where Penny had lain watching television. A mother that wasn't Misty's making breakfast in their kitchen, humming a song under her breath that Misty had never heard. Earl was there, too, though much younger. He was pointing through the open front door with a hammer in his hand, and a woman was behind him. She was thin and small with long brown hair and a bruise on her arm in the shape of someone else's hand. It was the same woman that the garden had shown her earlier, the woman who was gone, gone, too. Earl laughed at something, but the woman just stared at the hammer. The trailer kept going, linking memories of everyone that had ever lived inside it, and because the trailer missed all of these people, the memories were tinged with longing, and Misty felt it all, and, filled to the brim, she fell asleep watching other people's memories.

Twelve

Someone knocked on the front door with a heavy fist, a loud, banging knock that shook the glass in the windowpane.

Misty paused midstep in the hallway. Penny looked up from the television show she was watching, and their mother came from her bedroom with a needle in her hand, a long strand of white thread trailing beneath it like a comet's tail.

They didn't get many visitors and the people who visited—like the aunts or cousins—never knocked, so they all stared at the door as though it might open itself. The knock came again, gentler this time, as though apologizing for the noise it made before. Finally, their mother dropped the needle on the kitchen counter and dusted her hands across her thighs, even though they weren't damp or dirty. She opened the door an inch and frowned.

"Hello, Earl," she said.

"Miz Combs," Earl said. "I hope I ain't interrupting nothing."

"No, no. Just a regular day." She eased the door open another few inches, and a beam of light landed on Penny's upturned face. She scooted away from it, back into the shadows where she could watch without being watched. "Is there something I can help you with?"

"There may be," Earl said. "I don't want to frighten you or nothing. It could turn out to be nothing at all, but I told myself this morning that it was worth telling a mother and her children about just in case it turns out to be something. I know it's what I would want somebody to do if I had little ones of my own."

"Oh?"

"Have you seen or heard anything suspicious lately?" he asked.

Their mother glanced at the statue gleaming in the garden. "Like what?"

Misty took a few steps closer until she could see a sliver of Earl in the crack between the front door and its frame. His shadow landed on the carpet by her mother's feet, and the shadow seemed too long, too thin to be his. Rage flared in Misty's chest, sudden and warm. She curled her hand into a fist and felt the anger like an extra row of teeth inside her mouth just begging to clamp down. The feeling passed quickly, just like it had the night before, but it still left Misty a little unsettled.

"Well, for one," Earl said, "I walked out on the porch last night and found a car idling on the road. I went up to ask them just who exactly they was, but they drove off before I could get to them. Same thing happened early this morning, except this one wasn't coward enough to leave without saying hello. Claimed they was a friend just dropping by to see you."

Misty's mother shook her head. "No, we haven't had any company."

"I didn't think so. I reckon people's heard about what's happened in the garden, and they're coming to steal a look. But this is private property, and we don't want them looking where they ain't welcome."

"The girls play by the road sometimes. If someone isn't looking—"

"That's right. It's a danger. Don't you worry, though. I'll figure out a way to take care of them. I got a friend in the Sheriff's Department who can help."

Misty's mother crossed her arms over her chest. "Is there anything else?"

"Well…" Earl paused. His shadow head turned to look behind him and his long shadow feet shifted. "There've been other things. Maybe you've heard it, too. A, uh, a buzzing. Like a phone ringing over and over, but it's muffled. Like it's hidden somewhere in the walls and you can't ever pin it down no matter how close you get."

Their mother shook her head. She looked at each of the girls in turn, and they each shook their heads, too. "No," she said. "I don't think we heard anything like that."

"Nothing?" he said.

"I'm sorry."

"It's not your fault," Earl said, and Misty could hear the smile in his voice. "Not your doing. There's just one more thing."

"Yes?"

"The birds."

"What birds?"

"Crows, mostly. But starlings, too. Blackbirds of all kinds. They've been gathering on my roof for the last two nights. Peeping in the windows. They keep tapping. Just tapping their beaks against the glass. And every time I go to chase them off, they've already gone. They must hear me coming. That's the only way they'd make it out in time."

"No birds here," their mother said. "At least none like that."

"No," Earl said, "I thought not." He was quiet for a moment and Misty's mother stepped back to shut the door, but then his shadow turned toward her again. "Do you remember Ephesians 6:12?"

The muscles in their mother's throat contracted as she swallowed. She glanced up at the space between the door and ceiling. The green light hovered there, bobbing up and down slowly. "'For we wrestle not against flesh and blood…'"

"'But against principalities,'" Earl said. "Against darkness. Would you remember me in your prayers tonight, Miz Combs?"

"I will," she said.

"Thank you."

Their mother waited until Earl made it all the way back to his trailer before she shut the door and locked it. For a moment, none of them moved. Then Penny turned off the television, sighed, and said, "I swear that man's corn bread ain't done in the middle."

Misty laughed. Even their mother exhaled something that might have been laughter before she turned and walked back toward her room.

"I'm going to get some blankets," she said, "and tack up these windows. Come help me, Penny. And you girls…" She paused and looked them both in the eye. "Don't go wandering around the barn or Earl's trailer when I ain't around, you hear me? Corn bread or not, I don't want you anywhere near that man." Her eyes darted back to the space above the door, but the green light had moved again. It hovered on the ceiling above Misty's head, shaking and trembling.

It was midday before Misty got a chance to go outside. Her mother left the front door open so she could hear Misty if she called, but Misty headed for the backyard instead. Earl nodded at her once as she rounded the corner of the trailer. He knelt by the garden with a hammer in his hand. The gray wooden boards from the barn lay on the grass near his knees mixed with other, newer boards whose golden color seemed somehow out of place.

Misty nodded back to him and headed for the woods behind her trailer. The garden hadn't tried to speak to her all day, and Misty wondered if it was waiting for her to offer an invitation. As she walked between the trees, Misty let her fingers glide over the trunks she passed, and she could feel them waking at her touch, their names unfurling like a cat stretching its long back into the sun. Trees had some of the longest names that Misty had ever heard. The only name longer was that of the mountains themselves, which she'd heard only a handful of times in her life, and even then only in fragments. There was no way that she could hold the mountain's full name in her memory. There wasn't enough room in her body or her mind for all that the mountain had been. She could manage a few old sounds that tasted like snow, a few grating, grinding plates that shook the bones of her feet and rattled her teeth. And the mountains would stir a little before her, a great beast lifting its head from a long sleep, slowly opening a single eye to look at her—this strange, small thing with not nearly enough hair or enough bones to make it through this world alone—before it dropped back into its slumber for another thousand years.

Trees were nearly that old and complicated. Their names were doubled and tripled and twined. Their names joined the names of other trees seemingly at will, and they talked to one another all the time, about the air and the passing of the clouds and the people who lived around them. They had deep, gentle voices, and they liked talking to Misty, or at least they liked trying. They would humor her all day, starting at the beginning of their memories, from the very first seed that had ever fallen into the first patch of waiting soil, and up and up and up. Their names wound and twisted through blight and beast and storms so great that Misty's shoulders quaked against the lash of the wind and water. The trees were old growth and new, their name the life of every tree that had ever withered before them so that they might have a chance to grow, and they boasted, often, of who was the oldest among them, though none of them ever agreed.

The trees filled Misty to the brim with wonder and a sense of unquestioned belonging. A rootedness so deep that she was surprised to find her legs could bend when she opened her eyes, surprised to know that she was a moving thing, a seed herself carried by strange winds.

If anything could help her figure out how to find the garden's name, it would be the trees.

When she was deep enough in the woods that she was sure she wouldn't be noticed, Misty sat down on a pile of dried leaves and closed her eyes. The shadows were deep around her and it would be dark soon, so she tried to hurry as she conjured her name one moment at a time. She noted the changes—the fawn's bloody hip appeared twice now, spliced with images of her dream of the green glass man, the trees knit dark above her, the sound of glass crunching close behind, Earl's shadow on the floor of the living room and her mother's throat contracting.

Misty was sweating by the time her name finished and her heart ached, too. This time her name didn't include a single memory of her father.

She waited for the trees to come find her and listened to the chorus of their names mingled with the names of the birds in their nests and the bugs wriggling through the earth beneath her, each of them filling her with light and dark in equal measure. And then the still water feeling, the shifting on its surface like ripples in a pond.

"Hello," the garden said. "I thought you might have forgotten me."

"It's just been a long day."

"Are you okay?"

"Yeah," Misty said, but images flickered between them. A dark window in an empty house, the little lines of light etched across her favorite quilt when she hid beneath it, a pale green light quivering on the wall.

"I've felt that way before," the garden said, and Misty felt grass growing all around her, but not on her, no trickle of water through her earth, nothing to shift, to change, nothing to keep her company. It was a dried and brittle feeling, like Misty would crumble between someone's hands the moment they touched her.

"It's lonely," Misty said.

The garden curled around her shoulders like a coat on a cold day. "We can be lonely together. Little you, little me."

Misty smiled. "I think I found somebody who could help us. The trees remember everything about the bottom. They have to remember you."

"Oh," the garden said. Its presence withdrew from Misty's shoulders and the air seemed suddenly colder. "That's a good idea."

"I think so. The trees know everything." Misty's chest swelled with a feeling of full earth after a deep, hard rain, and she knew the trees were listening and that they loved compliments.

"Do y'all know this place?" Misty asked. She shared images of the garden before the statue grew so the trees would know which piece of earth she was talking about. They didn't think of boundaries in the same way people did, and Misty had to be specific when she asked them questions or else she would get answers she never intended. "Can you tell me about it?"

A pause. A swell.

A tide growing closer, closer and then a burst of images as the trees exhaled their memories. Some of the trees started too far back, and Misty didn't recognize the bottom at all. There were fires and great elk and treacherous storms whose lightning flashed across the backs of Misty's eyes and filled her with the scent of ash. She waited as the trees' memories marched on until she saw the dogwoods that Dolly had talked about in church, the bottom before Misty's time, before the trailers. The memories slowed, as though the trees treasured this time, held it close. They showed her the dogwood trees in every season—withered by the snow and bright with blooming life and full of bone-white blooms that glowed in the moonlight and, when the blossoms fell, covered the bottom with a ghostly down. Misty felt a petal on her tongue, light and cool, tough and solid as leather, but delicate, too. The bloom dissolved before she could taste it and left her with a mouthful of cold rainwater.

The trees missed the dogwoods. They had known them, loved them.

Then a woman was there. Thin and brown-haired—the same woman the trailer had shown Misty, the same woman in the garden's memories. She wore a dress with little spiral designs stitched along the hem, and she hurried across a swinging bridge, the rope swaying under her hands. She walked through the dogwood grove and touched the trees gently, her hand caressing their trunks, following the ridged line of their bark. She spoke to them, though Misty couldn't make out the words.

Time sped up. The images mashed together too quickly, too many. Misty's chest contracted. A voice in her head pleading and then gone. Her arms stiffened. Her toes curled inside her shoes. She looked down at her hands and saw branches instead.

"Wait," Misty said, but the images rifled on.

Earl was there. Younger. He looked almost like Misty's father.

Then the trees were gone, ripped up by their trunks, their roots a tangled mess, the ground scored with deep runnels where the trees had been.

And then trailers, then people, then birds. The bottom took the shape Misty recognized until she appeared in the trees' memories, small and squinting up at the sun, holding her mother's hand on the day they moved into the trailer.

The memories ended and the woods grew quiet. The birds yielded their songs to silence. The bugs paused in their tracks. Everything listening, listening.

"Thank you," Misty said to the trees. She shared a memory from the summer before when Misty had crawled into Penny's bed and Penny had let her stay. It was a close feeling, a not-alone feeling. She turned her attention back to the garden. "Do you know who that woman was? The one with the trees?"

Misty walked back toward the trailer as she waited for the garden's answer. Her legs felt a little wobbly from the weight of the trees' memories and she walked slow, careful. The trees sent her passive images—deep greens and browns, the feeling of themselves stretched mile for mile, an expansiveness that made Misty's ribs feel like they were floating away from her, held only by the faintest memory of what it meant to be an *I* instead of a *we*.

"Are you there?" Misty asked the garden. Worry wormed into her stomach.

"I'm here," the garden whispered.

"Did you know that woman?"

Misty replayed an image between them but the garden cut it off, fragmented it so the image of the woman's face dissolved into a film of pale colors.

"She's part of the bad thing," the garden said. "She's part of the losing, the unnaming, the gone and hiding. She's not part of me."

"Oh. Do you remember her name?"

"Caroline."

The name had a weight that Misty could feel. The name like a hand on her shoulder holding her in place. Caroline was the woman her sister and William had talked about in the barn. The woman everyone thought Earl had killed.

"What happened to her?" Misty asked.

"I don't want to talk about that."

"But it might help us figure out—"

"No!"

The word smashed against Misty's sternum so hard that she actually took a step back. The birds above her lifted from their branches like they sensed the shock wave.

"I'm sorry," the garden said. "I don't want to hurt my little friend. But I can't think about Caroline. I only want to think about the trees. Little white blooms falling like snow. I remember those. They were good."

Misty rubbed her fingers across her ribs.

"I'm sorry," the garden said again, and the remorse spread through Misty like vines creeping. Her own heart ached with the grief the garden felt. "That was the wrong thing to do. I'll go now. It's okay."

Then it was gone.

Misty felt the garden's leaving like a shade drawn over a window, a shuttering, a closing. The silence in her head seemed greater than before now that she knew what it was like not to be alone all the time. She tried reaching out to the garden, but without a name there was no way to find it. There was only silence.

Misty leaned against a tree trunk. The roof of her trailer peeked through the trees, slim and dark. Their mother would be there, in the kitchen, and the television would be on, the volume turned down low, and there was a spot on the couch waiting for Misty.

Then leaves crunching.

Then twigs snapping.

Misty turned as William struggled through the undergrowth behind her. He came crashing over a tangle of brush and briar and stumbled in front of her. There was something held tight inside his hand.

"I been looking for you," he said.

"Are you okay?"

William shook his head. There were dark circles under his eyes and dirt on his chin and underneath his fingernails. His clothes looked rumpled, almost sleepy, like they hadn't quite woken up that morning.

He said, "I need help."

"What happened?"

"Mom is—" William shook his head. "She said Harold asked her to move in." William's lip curled and a stream of words tumbled from his mouth. "He said there's lots of room for us in his house on Beech Fork, and Mom said she was thinking about. She said it would be good for us but I don't want to leave. I want it to be just us again. Just me and her." William lifted his right hand and showed Misty a brown glass bottle. "I got this from Earl's garbage. It was just sitting there, and I thought if we could just do it again like we did before, then maybe something new will grow. She didn't like the last statue but she might like another one. I don't know what else to do." He handed Misty the bottle.

"What do I do?" she asked.

"Spin it." He pulled her wrist toward the ground until the bottle was lying on the leaves. "Like we did in the barn."

A screen door slammed in the distance and Shannon's voice floated through the air, calling William's name.

"I have to go," William said. "Harold's taking us to dinner. Please, Misty. It might be different this time. Please."

It was just her and William in the woods, and she didn't know what else to do so she wrapped her fingers around the bottle's neck and spun. The leaves underneath were too wet to let the bottle move much, so it stuttered and thumped against Misty's foot, ricocheting to the side, but William didn't pay it any mind. He leaned forward and kissed Misty on the lips, once, twice in a row. His mouth was hot against hers and his cheeks were damp. Their noses bumped together twice, and Misty flinched as William stooped to grab the bottle from the ground.

"This will work," he said. "I know it."

He turned and ran through the trees toward the sound of his mother's voice, leaving Misty in the woods alone.

Thirteen

That evening, Misty pressed her cheek against the window of her mother's car. She smushed her face as tight as possible, only leaning back when her nose began to hurt. No one noticed her contortions. Her mother was looking at the road, her sister toying with the small black purse in her lap. Penny seemed to be the same Penny that she had always been. Skinny Penny with her long limbs and earlobes that stuck out just a little too much. A gap between her front teeth and freckles from her nose to her chest. Dark-haired Penny with their father's blue eyes and their mother's wide feet. Nothing sprouted from her lips, nothing froze her into place, no part of her replaced, not yet, with glass. But Misty couldn't forget the way her sister had pressed her lips to the green glass man or the cloud of frost she had exhaled afterward.

And Misty seemed the same, too. Her reflection blurred in the car window. She only appeared in the shadows while the rest of her face was eaten up by the light, by other, stronger reflections. She'd kissed William again, or he had kissed her. She wasn't sure which it was or if it mattered, but just thinking about it made her stomach tight, so she slid away from the window and watched the road curve ahead.

The road to Aunt Jem's was two narrow blacktopped lanes whose edges were crumbling into the ditch lines. Their mother knew all the potholes, all the dips and divots, and she led their little car along the road like she was dancing with the pavement. There were dozens of hollers that branched away on either side of them. Some Misty knew, and many she didn't. Some were only a mile long, ending with a house or a creek or with the mountains. Some went for miles and miles, winding deep and deeper, crisscrossing with other hollers and with abandoned mining roads. It was hard to tell just by looking at the hills, but they were filled with people, with life.

Their mother's eyes moved from side to side as she drove. Careful, always. Watchful, always. She'd put on makeup before they left. The corners of her eyes were smudged with brown shadow, her eyelashes thick with mascara. There was a small tube of lipstick in her purse that she rarely used. Misty had seen her bring it out before, twisting the base until the deep-red stick appeared, but she usually just closed the lid again and dropped it back into her purse without ever putting it on.

"Will you be back to get us tonight?" Misty asked.

Their mother looked up at Misty through the rearview mirror. "No, Little Bit. I'll come get you in the morning. Like always."

Misty leaned her head against the back of the seat. They'd gone to Aunt Jem's a lot lately. At least once a week. They would spend the night, and their mother would be there in the morning. Sometimes she brought them sausage biscuits from the gas station where William's mother worked, and she didn't even scold them when they dropped crumbs onto the seat. Those were the good mornings.

Misty had asked if she could stay with their mother before, but their mother never said yes. These nights, she said, were for her and the girls' father. Private nights.

The car wobbled as they turned into Jem's driveway, which was really nothing more than a steep hill. The hill had been covered in gravel once, but the rains had washed most of the stone into the creek, leaving behind deep ruts and furrows.

"Hold on," their mother said.

The girls each grabbed hold of their door handles as the car lurched forward.

Misty couldn't help but smile when she saw Jem's double-wide. Jem had told Misty a story about her trailer and how it was cousin to another trailer that had turned feral years before. The trailer had kicked its owner out the back door and taken to the mountains. Its wallpaper peeled and its sinks filled with tadpoles and its walls skittered with mice. But the trailer had never felt more beautiful, more itself. No one had seen it for years, except on foggy nights when little girls could sometimes hear the creak of its underpinning as it ran through the trees. Jem said she knew that her trailer would do the same to her one day, but she had made her peace with it and only hoped it would toss her onto something soft when it kicked her out.

The grass in Jem's yard was knee-high because she refused to cut it. So instead of being blunt and green, her yard was filled with wildflowers and grasshoppers. She had a stick she carried when she went outside to warn away the snakes. There were colored Christmas lights strewn across the trees in the driveway that Jem kept lit every evening no matter the season, and wind chimes hung from the branches of almost every tree. When Misty opened the car door, the clamor of the bells brought goose bumps to her skin. Jem stood on the front porch, smiling. She held one side of her long golden skirt in her floured hand, revealing her bare feet and wide calves.

"Hello, sweet babies," Jem yelled. "Come give me some sugar."

Misty hurried up the steps and wrapped her arms around Jem and breathed in the smell of fry grease and the Fabuloso cleaner that Jem bought in bulk at the Dollar General. Penny followed and she didn't even wait for Misty's hug to end before she started her own so they all stood there, a tangle of limbs and sweat. Their mother followed with a garbage bag full of clothes clutched in her hands. She tossed it at Jem and smiled.

"That's for the clothing drive," she said. "It's all washed and dried. I'll help you sort everything next week."

Jem hugged their mother, too, and whispered something in her ear that made their mother laugh. It was a true laugh. Nothing forced or hidden about it, and it was one of Misty's favorite sounds in all the world.

"You got any of that ice cream with the cookies in it?" Misty asked.

Jem grinned. "I got us some this morning."

"It's a wonder I let them stay with you at all," their mother said. "Come in here with me. I need your ear a minute."

The girls followed Jem to the door, but their mother asked them to stay outside while she and Jem talked. "I won't be long," she said. "Y'all can pick me some of them pretty wildflowers of Jem's, okay?"

Penny didn't argue, but she rolled her eyes as she stepped off the porch, and she tugged the hem of Misty's shirt to keep her from lingering by the door.

"It ain't like you can hear what they're saying anyway," Penny said.

"What do you think they're talking about?"

Penny shrugged. Two of Jem's dogs ambled around the corner of the house, and the girls followed them back into the driveway. Plenty of hunting dogs got lost in the woods or were set loose to starve when their owners couldn't train them. Most of them seemed to find their way to Jem's hill, and she never turned them away. Gubby and Jake were two strays who had stayed for years, their hips stiff with arthritis, their muzzles slowly turning gray. They led Misty and Penny to the edge of the driveway where they lifted their heads and howled low, deep notes that joined with the ringing of the wind chimes.

Misty ran her fingers along Gubby's thick nose, and his name swelled in her knuckles. Dogs were easy to talk to, so willing to share every inch of themselves, so happy to be known.

"What do you hear?" she asked aloud and the rumble of an engine answered, then another. The sound was far off, but it grew louder, reverberating off the mountains until the headlights of her cousins' four-wheelers swept over the trees. Jem and Dolly's holler was one that went for miles, twisting and turning through oil and timber roads, intersecting other hollers, and Jerry and Jamie knew every inch. Misty led the dogs beneath a mulberry tree as Jerry and Jamie flew up the hill. Jamie popped a wheelie at the top, spewing a cloud of dust into the air, and Jerry followed him, slower, frowning.

"I have asthma, you fool," Jerry yelled as he cut his engine.

"Nothing the good Lord can't heal," Jamie said as he hopped off his four-wheeler. He paused long enough to give Misty a high five before he ran up the steps and into the house.

"Where's he going?" Penny asked.

Jerry shook his head. "Him and Sam have some kind of deal. He said he needed to get something. We're about to meet them up on the ridge—Sam and Charlene. Y'all wanna come?"

"Yes," Penny said before Misty could say anything about asking their mother for permission. She ran to Jamie's four-wheeler and climbed onto the back, leaving Misty to ride with Jerry. He eased off his seat so Misty could wiggle onto the worn cushion he'd tied to the racks. The plastic sides of the four-wheeler were warm against Misty's calves as she settled into place.

"You can hold on to the rack there, or you can hold on to me," Jerry said, turning until he could see Misty behind him. "It don't matter which as long as you don't fall off, all right?"

Misty wrapped one arm around Jerry's waist as Jamie came running outside. He had a plastic bag in his hand and a stick of beef jerky in his mouth as he hopped onto his four-wheeler and revved the engine.

"All right, children," Jamie said. "Let's ride."

Fourteen

The rumble of the four-wheeler's engine eclipsed every other sound as they flew along the road. They passed Dolly's house and the garden she and Jem worked and then Misty's grandparents' house, which had stood empty since her grandmother passed a few years before. The house technically belonged to Misty's mother, but they didn't live there. Misty wasn't entirely sure why, but she knew it had something to do with her father's family. Misty hadn't spent much time with her father's parents or with her uncle Danny, and she knew it might be unfair, but she wished they could move back here with Jem and Dolly and her cousins, away from the statue and the garden's voice in her head. It would be simpler here. Better.

The pavement ended not long after Dolly's house, and the four-wheeler dipped, wobbled, roared on over the dirt and gravel. There were oil wells further in the holler so a company maintained the roads. Beyond that, the roads had once belonged to a logging company, but had fallen out of use. The deeper they went, the more bumpy and rutted the ground became, the thicker and closer the trees grew, the greener Misty's view of the world until there were only leaves and branches and faint speckles of dark-blue sky.

Dolly's children, Sam and Charlene, sat on their own four-wheeler by the road ahead. Misty waved to them, and Charlene waved back as Sam revved the engine and pulled in front of Jamie and Penny. A cloud of dust swelled in front of them and Jerry pressed his nose into his shoulder to keep from breathing it in, but he still coughed and Misty patted his back gently.

The voices of everything around her were louder now. The trees and the bugs, the raccoons and ground squirrels and opossums, the flat tire that someone had left behind, its rusted rim glinting in the last rays of sunlight—all of them shared their names and spoke to one another. They were louder here than anywhere Misty had been, so far from the presence of humans, so comfortable with themselves. They regarded Misty and her cousins with curiosity and a lace of fear, and they delighted at the sound of Misty's voice as she shared a fragment of her name. It unfurled easily at first, but then came the memories of Caroline in the woods and then the brown glass bottle in William's hand and the press of his lips against hers. She pulled away. Her name ended and the sound of the world fell flat.

Misty didn't want to bring those thoughts here. She wasn't willing to wonder if the garden was still angry at her or if she would ever learn the sound of her family's names. It was better to close her eyes and let the wind whip through her hair, to shiver and rumble with the rev of the engine, to feel Jerry's shirt flapping against her chest and hear her cousins shout and holler as they drove through a narrow creek, the water splashing Misty's bare calves.

The air grew colder under the trees and the shadows thicker. The sun was just a faint red bleed above the highest ridge, and the light that fell on their path was yellowed and stormy. A few smaller roads branched here and there, but what they'd once led to had long disappeared—old logging sites, empty shacks, or paths that simply ended with no explanation. Some people dumped their trash here, and there were rusted truck shells and mattress springs that shot out of the tall grass like strange new flowers. Aunt Dolly always told them to be careful when they went riding. There was no way to be sure what they might find in the hills, or who, like they could go so deep that they might turn back time itself and ride themselves too far from the reach of their mothers.

It seemed almost possible as the road curved ahead and they started up a long hill. Jerry turned the headlights on and the new light only made the shadows darker, made the trees seem doubled, tripled, their branches trembling overhead.

Jerry was more cautious than his brother or their cousin Sam. Jamie drove on the side of the road, blasted through fields of wildflowers with Penny screeching behind him, her hands held out to catch the blooms between her fingers until she held a bouquet above her head triumphantly. Sam swerved as Penny let go of the flowers so Charlene might catch them. Charlene tied the Queen Anne's lace around the rack of Sam's four-wheeler, the thin white blooms shaking in the wind.

But Jerry held back. He was easy on the bumps in the road, choosing the smoothest path for him and Misty. Part of her wished that she'd beaten Penny onto Jamie's four-wheeler instead, especially when he did doughnuts in a wide spot in the road, kicking up clouds of dust that Jerry sped ahead to avoid.

"That looks fun," Misty yelled.

Jerry glanced back at her once, but she wasn't sure that he'd heard her until he cut sharply to the left, leading them along a road that ran parallel to the one they had been on. Sam and Jamie kept going below. Penny looked back at Misty through the trees, her hands held up in the air in question, but Jerry barreled ahead until Penny and the others were eaten up by the trees.

They drove so quick and so far that Misty began to wonder where they were going. Every minute they spent between the trees plunged them closer to nightfall. The air grew cold, and Misty wrapped her arms around her cousin's waist to shield herself from the worst of the wind.

Jerry stopped the four-wheeler in the middle of the road. He pointed the wheels toward the trees and left the headlights on so two dirty yellow beams cut through the darkness. He stepped off the four-wheeler and helped Misty do the same.

"Where are we?" she asked.

"I come here sometimes when I need to get away from Jamie and Mom. It's a good spot to think." He led her through the trees, holding up branches so she could sneak beneath them, warning her away from the briars, the gnarled roots of trees, the poison oak.

"I've never told anybody about this spot before," Jerry said. "Not even Jamie knows where it leads. You can get turned around pretty quick if you don't know exactly what to look for, but I found it by accident once." He stopped just ahead of Misty and held out his arm. "Just don't go past here, all right?"

Misty understood why when she stepped up to Jerry's arm. One more step and there would be no ground beneath her. The mountain suddenly dropped away, angled so steeply that not even grass grew on its side. Only the tangled, skinny roots of a few brave trees stuck out here and there, jutting beside sharp stones. Kudzu had begun to creep along its bottom, its vines like bony fingers digging into the earth. It would cover the whole mountain soon. Misty stared at the drop so long that she almost didn't notice what was below it.

Her trailer.

Her bottom.

She was looking at them from a new angle. This mountain ran along the side of the road that ran parallel to the creek she played in, and it took her a moment to reorient herself. Everything looked like doll furniture from above, like she could reach out and rearrange them any way that she wished. All it would take is the tip of her finger to nudge her trailer closer to the creek, one flick of her wrist to change the shape of the water, to make it wind around her yard like a moat that no one might cross.

William's trailer was there and Earl's and the garden, too. The green glass man glowed yellow-orange around his edges.

There were no lights on in her trailer and her mother's car was missing from the driveway. It looked so lonely. So small and empty.

"Pretty cool, huh?" Jerry said. "I almost fell the first time I came out here. Didn't expect it to end so sudden, but then I saw you down there." He pointed toward Misty's backyard. "Or at least I think it was you. Walking around after dark." He lifted an eyebrow at Misty and she smiled. "People think Jamie and Penny have all the fun, but that's because they don't watch us close enough. They don't always see us. Sometimes it's nice to be unnoticed. You can get away with a lot more if no one suspects you."

"Sometimes," Misty said.

"This is the closest I've come to that statue," Jerry said. "I tried drawing it from up here, but it never came out right. I always ended up drawing scribbles and swirls. It was weird. I can almost see why everybody is acting so strange about it."

"Mom is." Misty almost told Jerry about the green light on the wall and the way her mother's face looked as she hunted it, but it felt like a secret, like something she shouldn't tell.

"She's got a lot on her mind right now," Jerry said. "I know separating from your dad wasn't easy for her, but I think it was the best thing for now. Mom says they'll work everything out and be back together before long. The preacher has them going on dates and doing all kinds of exercises and stuff. They're trying."

Misty's hands grew cold. She looked up at Jerry, but he was looking beyond the trees, his eyes caught on the shimmer of the green glass man. She wanted to ask him questions, to ask where her father was, and what he meant by exercises from the preacher, but the only word she could think of was *separated*.

The word was like walking through a spider's web. It clung to her. It wrapped her up.

Separated.

"We should probably get back," Jerry said. "But you can come back here when you're bigger. If I share this spot with anybody, it ought to be you."

He squeezed Misty's shoulder before he turned back and walked through the trees. Misty followed him without really looking and climbed onto the back of his four-wheeler without really feeling the engine. She rested her cheek between his shoulder blades and held on tight as Jerry raced through the dark, but all she could think, all she could feel, was that word, over and over again like a song stuck inside her head.

Separated.

Fifteen

"Well, well," Sam said as Misty walked into Jamie's bedroom. "Look who finally decided to join us."

"We was about to start a search party," Penny said.

"She means a celebration party." Jamie walked into the room carrying a bag of chips. "Where'd y'all go anyway?"

"Around." Jerry winked at Misty. "Where's Charlene?"

Sam shrugged. "Jem walked her home. She doesn't like spending the night away yet."

Penny rolled her eyes but Misty nodded. She'd felt the same way as Charlene when she was eight, and still felt it now, sometimes.

Unlike Misty and Penny, Jerry and Jamie had bedrooms of their own. They were all crowded now into Jamie's room, which had a bed and a dresser and a recliner that he'd found by the side of the road. Jamie was the only one brave enough to sit in it since Jem swore up and down that the chair had a dark past and Jerry swore that it had mold growing underneath it. But Jamie loved the recliner where he sat sideways, his long legs draped over one arm.

Penny lay on the floor with a pillow propped under her arms and Sam sat beside her. Sam was the oldest of all of them. His life had always seemed far away from Misty's because of their age difference until last summer when Sam showed up at Misty's house in the middle of the night. He'd left Dolly's and refused to go back or to tell Misty's mother what happened. Sam slept in Misty's room that night, and it was only after everyone else was asleep that Sam told Misty and Penny the truth. Sam had gotten into a fight with Dolly over something, and he wasn't sure if he could ever go home again.

"Why not?" Penny had asked.

"I told her something about me that she didn't like." Sam had been sitting with his knees curled to his chest on Misty's bed. Misty went over and sat beside him, offered Sam one of her favorite stuffed animals to hug.

"What'd you tell her?" Misty asked.

"I told her to call me Sam instead of Samantha. I know everybody thinks I'm a girl, but I'm not. That's not me."

"Oh," Misty said.

Penny leaned on her arm and squinted across the dark. "Well, I reckon you ought to know who you are. I'm going to bed." Then she rolled over and pulled the covers over her head.

Sam laughed. "What do you think, Little Bit?"

"Well," Misty said, "I guess I agree with Penny."

"There's a first."

Misty smiled. She bounced her legs back and forth against the bed frame until Sam reached over and poked her on the arm.

"Is something wrong?" Sam asked.

"It's just...right now there's more girl cousins than boy cousins. And if you're not a girl cousin anymore, then that means we're even."

"What about Charlene?"

"Oh," Misty said, "I forgot about Charlene."

Sam laughed. "Anyway, I'm still on your side even if I'm a boy."

Misty smiled. "All right then. You mind if I sleep with you? Penny snores like an old man."

"Sure."

Sam rolled over onto his side and Misty fit herself behind him, slotting her knees behind Sam's knees and burrowing her forehead against Sam's back. Misty had worried, for a moment, if it was okay to hug a boy this way, but Sam still smelled like mint and cigarettes and still talked in his sleep so it seemed like nothing else ought to change, either. Ever since then, Misty had made a point to stop calling her cousin Samantha and called him Sam instead.

Misty sat on Sam's other side as he shuffled a deck of cards. His fingers were quick, but the cards were wider and shinier than Misty had ever seen. The backs were brightly colored—purple and gold and red—and they shone under the light. They must have been what Jamie had been carrying in the plastic bag.

"Can you go any slower?" Jamie said. "I didn't go all the way to Hell-for-Certain for a bunch of black magic for nothing. I swear that Lady Baker is a witch."

"I told you," Sam said.

"Yeah, but I figured you was full of shit, like usual."

Sam laughed. "Now you'll learn to take me serious. Do you have your question ready? You got to ask the cards a question before I cast them."

"I got it all right." Jamie slid from the recliner to the floor. "I want to know if Sherry's going to break up with me this weekend. I think she's cheating on me. She's been wearing this new eye shadow."

Sam rolled his eyes. "Not everything a girl does is about you. You know that, right?"

Jamie sighed. "I'm being serious here. I like Sherry. I thought about giving her one of Mom's old rings. You know, like a promise."

"You sure got Mommy's crooked nose," Jerry said, "but I forget you got her heart sometimes, too."

"Shut up," Jamie said, but there was no heat behind it.

"All right," Sam said. "We'll get to the bottom of this."

Sam shuffled the cards just like Misty's father did, except Sam looked at the deck while he did it. Misty's father had always looked at the person across from him, like he didn't even need to see the cards to manipulate them, and she'd always thought it was the most impressive thing a person could do. Her father had tried to teach Misty to play poker once, but she kept putting the cards in the wrong order, matching them by color instead of suit until he laughed and they'd made up a game of their own instead.

She hadn't thought of that in a long time, but now the memory pressed against her chest. It seemed like that would never happen again. Like she'd never see her father again, never know her family whole. Everything she wanted, she wanted because of them. Without her mom and dad together, there seemed to be no point in finding out where the statue came from or waiting for the garden to teach her how to talk to people. All the people she wanted to talk to would be gone and she'd be alone and none of it would matter.

Jem walked into the room just as Sam started laying down the cards. Everyone stopped. Jem carried a large plastic mixing bowl in her arms. She scraped off a spoonful of dark batter and popped it into her mouth as she stepped between Jerry and Penny until she stood over the cards.

Sam looked up at Jem and said quietly, "Don't tell Mom."

Jem hummed a little note. "And just what is this that I'm not seeing right now?"

"We're casting cards," Sam said. "Jamie has a question."

She looked down at the cards and then at her son. "Just don't go asking for what you ain't ready to receive." She handed the bowl to

Penny and walked back across the room. She said, "Brownies'll be done in ten minutes," as she shut the door.

Penny looked after Jem for a long moment before she turned back to everyone else. "Having Jem for a mom must be nice. If our mom came in and seen this, she would freak out."

Jerry snorted. "Yeah, Mom don't have much room to stand on when it comes to stuff like this. There ain't much she hasn't tried before."

"Or done a lot better than us," Sam added.

"But she ain't all roses," Jamie said. "Last week the water got cut off when I was in the middle of the shower because she used the bill money to buy some secondhand silk. She said it had a story that needed telling, and I told her I had a headful of suds to show DCFS for my negligence case."

Sam laughed. "She's always forgetting something."

"Like me," Jamie said, "at school when I was in third grade. She left me there for four hours once. I thought I was going to have to take to the woods and survive on moss and beetles."

"If only," Jerry said. "The point is, Pen, that everybody has problems."

"And none of them are bigger than my problem with Sherry," Jamie said, "so hurry up and lay them cards down, Sam. I ain't got all night."

Sam cast the three-card spread in quick succession, then flipped the first card up. The image was vibrant and violent. A church steeple stood in the center, its white brick ending in a point of light. A comet streaked toward it through the sky, and dark clouds roiled all around. An orange shadow flickered near the bottom like flames were slowly consuming it. But the worst part was the woman who tumbled from an open window, her hair concealing her features so she might have been anyone. Misty shifted a little further from the cards.

"Well, this ain't the best sign in the world," Sam said. "The Steeple is about upheaval. See, it's supposed to be something solid, right? The church. A foundation unmoving. But that's not the case. It's being consumed here. So you might have thought things were going well, but your relationship is about to undergo some sudden changes."

"I knew it." Jamie tossed his head back. "I *knew* it."

"Hang on, now, the cards ain't done." Sam rubbed his fingers across the back of the second card. "Contact is important. The cards have all kinds of things to say, and not everything is just in the image. It's in the feeling." Sam flipped the card over and sighed.

A mountain rose along one side, rocky and steep. A woman stood atop it, looking out at something that Misty couldn't see. She wore a long dress and held one hand out in front of her where a flame burned in the center as though she conjured it herself. She held a staff in her other hand, and the look on her face wasn't sad or afraid, but like she knew what was to come. It was like the story Penny and William had told in the barn about Caroline's sister, who took to the woods searching for her after her death.

But all Misty could see when she looked at the card was her mother searching for the green light in their house. Their mother, alone.

"The Wanderer," Sam said. "This can be a lonely card, but it's not always bad. I like to think that it means you're about to take a journey that will teach you a lot of things. But it's something you have to do on your own."

"On my own," Jamie repeated. "So it's happening. She's cheated.

If it's Conner Roark, I'll never survive. The shame will kill me right here on the spot. Jerry, hold my hand."

Jerry rolled his eyes and took his brother's hand.

Sam flipped over the final card. A man stood with a rifle in his hands. The ground at his feet was strewn with four other rifles as though there had been a battle there just before the card was made. Two other men walked away in the distance. The ground was bare dirt, but there was water in the direction that the men were walking. The sky was light and a few clouds drifted through it. Sam said that it was a card of endings, of separation. The battle was over and Jamie might never find closure but he had to learn how to let go.

Jamie fell back onto the carpet and covered his eyes with his hands. Penny crawled over to pat his shoulder. The longer Misty stared at the cards, the harder her heart beat. They all seemed so sad. So lonely. The woman falling from the tower and the woman searching through the dark and the man looking back on the people who were walking away from him. A card of endings. Of separation. Tears welled in her eyes and she brushed them away.

"What's a matter, Little Bit?" Sam said.

Everyone turned their heads toward her, and Misty looked away. She didn't want them to see her crying. She didn't want to ruin their evening.

Jamie leaned forward and touched Misty's ankle with a single finger. "You ain't got to cry for me. I know it's sad but I'll be all right."

"It's not that," Misty said. "It's…Mom and Dad. They're… *separated.*"

"Well, who the hell told you that?" Sam said.

Jerry winced. "I thought she knew. Penny knows! Why wouldn't Misty know?"

"Because she's *little*, you ignorant swine." Sam wrapped his arm around Misty's shoulder.

"Mom don't even know that I know," Penny said. "I heard Jem talking about it and made her tell me. They don't want either of us to know." She crawled over her cousins until she was sitting in front of Misty.

"Wait a minute," Jamie said, rising to his knees. "I just want to set the record straight. Somebody did something wrong, and…it wasn't me?"

Jerry punched his brother. "I'm sorry, Misty. I swear I thought you knew or I would've never said a thing."

"And it's not that bad," Sam said. "Mom and Dad have fought like this before. Mom went and spent a week at Jem's once. Left us at home with Dad. We ate spaghetti out of a can every night and had fudge rounds for breakfast every morning. Come to think of it, that might have been the best week of my life."

Misty smiled a little and Sam squeezed her shoulders.

"And Jem's divorced," Penny said. "So the worst thing that could happen is that Mom ends up like Jem."

"Lord help us," Jerry said. "One Jem is about all this world can handle."

"Don't cry," Penny whispered, and it was like they were alone for a minute, their faces just a few inches apart. Misty hadn't known the truth for two hours before she broke down in tears, but Penny had known for much longer and she'd never said a word. Penny wiped her hand across Misty's cheek and then frowned.

"I got your snot on me," she said, and Misty laughed.

"What can we do to make you feel better?" Jerry asked.

"You should take advantage of this," Jamie said. "We owe you now. Big time."

"Something sweet might help," Misty said, and the boys jumped to their feet.

They spent the next few hours finding things to cheer Misty up. Sam cast a spread for Penny, predicting great changes in her life and great battles to face. She got a faraway look on her face, the kind she'd gotten before she kissed the green glass man, so Misty asked if they could catch lightning bugs together like they did when they were small. Jem gave them old mason jars with holes cut in the lids. She sat on the porch and watched them as they ran back and forth, filling the jars with dozens of bugs. When they were done, they all retreated to the porch, setting the jars here and there, the bugs blinking out of rhythm. They passed the plate of brownies around until Misty's belly ached with sweetness and she lay flat on her back on the wooden boards of the porch, watching the stars shimmer in the sky.

When they released the lightning bugs at the end of the night, Jem told them to make a wish because the bugs would carry it away with them. Misty wished that it could always be like this. That her family could be together, be close, always. She didn't think of the statue or of the garden or of William. They never even crossed her mind.

Sixteen

Jem's bedroom walls were covered in framed photographs of Misty's family. New pictures of the cousins were mixed in with pictures of Misty's grandparents as she knew them—white-haired and wrinkled—but also pictures of them when they were younger. Misty's mother stared down at her from a tarnished frame. She must have been about Misty's age when it was taken. She sat on a fence, her body tilted back to look behind her as though someone had just called her name. Black-and-white photos mingled with colored photos, weddings and funerals, birthdays and candid moments— there was no discernible order. When Misty had asked why the photos were so mixed up, Jem told her it was because this was how she saw their family all the time. She saw her great-grandmother in Misty's smile and their great-uncle Story in Jamie's quick temper. So having the pictures this way felt more honest. More true.

Misty lay in the very center of Jem's bed with the covers pulled up to her chin. She and Penny had slept in the trundle bed beneath Jem's bed the night before. Misty had been awake for at least an hour, but she hadn't wanted to leave just yet, so she'd crawled into Jem's bed where the sheets were soft and the pillows piled just right. Outside, the voices of her cousins and her aunts drifted by. Inside, she heard the whispers of Jem's furniture, most of which were hand-me-downs from family or bought secondhand. The dresser's voice creaked like a rusty hinge, and the headboard sighed and scolded the curtains, which were eaten up by moth holes on one side. The side tables shared a story back and forth about the day they came to Jem's, but neither of them remembered it quite the same way.

Misty's stomach growled and she shuffled into the kitchen, leaving the warmth of Jem's bed behind. Jerry sat at the kitchen table with a ruler in one hand and a biscuit in the other. When Misty asked what he was drawing, he just shrugged and kept frowning at his paper. Jamie ran in from the living room, slung open the fridge door, and drank milk straight from the gallon, his throat working hard.

"Hey, Jamie, you want to go riding again?" Misty asked. "Mom usually don't come 'til after ten."

"No time today, Little Bit," Jamie said, wiping his mouth with the back of his hand. "I gotta get up with Charles Ray before he leaves."

"No time for a cup, either," Jerry said without looking up. "You know, nobody wants to drink your germs."

Jamie snatched the biscuit from Jerry's hand as he walked by. "You'd sure hate to know what I did to your toothbrush then."

"Jackass," Jerry muttered. And then, "Did you really do something to my toothbrush?"

The screen door slamming was his only answer.

"We could still go riding, Jerry," Misty said. "Like last night."

"Sorry." He got up from the table and shoved his papers under his arm. "I really have to finish this. Maybe next week, huh? When you come back?"

Misty stood in the kitchen alone. Everyone seemed to have forgotten what had happened the night before, how sad she had been and how sorry they'd all felt for her. Sometimes it seemed that if Misty never cried, no one would ever notice her at all. That the only way her family saw her was when she was wounded, bleeding, sobbing. Only the sound of her hurt was loud enough to cut through the noise of their lives and make them turn toward her instead. But the minute the wound was stayed, they all turned away again.

She missed the crawdads, suddenly, fiercely. She was closing her eyes to reach out for them when Penny shouted her name from the porch. Misty followed the sound outside where the wind chimes were clamoring and singing.

"What?" she said.

"Get your stuff together. Mom's on her way."

Misty gathered her things from Jem's room. She went back to the porch and sat in a rocking chair beside Penny. Gubby came up from the yard and leaned his big head against her bare feet until Misty scratched his ears.

"What's that?" Misty asked, pointing to a plastic bag by Penny's feet.

Penny pushed the bag out of sight. "Sam gave me his old casting cards. They're not like the ones he used last night, but they're good to practice on. He said he'd help me learn."

"Could you tell my future?"

"Maybe," Penny said. "I had a really nice time here. Didn't you?"

Misty nodded.

"It's so different here."

"Yeah."

"I like it better than at home."

"What do you mean?" Misty asked.

Penny shrugged. "I just mean that if something happens with Mom and Dad that we don't just have to be with them."

"But I want to be with them."

Penny rolled her eyes. "You want to be chasing that stupid green light all over the walls? Or waiting for Dad to lose his temper? You want to stay there with that creepy statue of Earl's and Earl lurking around?"

"There are other things."

"Not enough of them," Penny said. "I'm just tired of being stuck there all the time. It don't have to be like that."

Misty's heart pounded in her chest. Even though he'd been gone for a while, it felt like she'd just lost her father the night before, and now Penny was smiling and staring at Jem like she had a plan to fix everything. But there was nothing to fix their family except being together.

"What're you going to do?" Misty asked.

Penny sighed. "Nothing right now. But I was thinking of asking Jem if we could stay here with her for a while if things don't get better. Don't mess it up for me, all right? She won't take just me. It'll have to be both of us or nothing."

Penny grabbed her backpack from the porch as their mother's car lurched over the hill and rattled into the driveway. She threw her arms around Aunt Jem and then crawled into the back seat beside the only window that would roll up and down all the way. Misty waited until their mother honked the horn before she slid from her chair and followed.

Seventeen

It wasn't supposed to be this way.

The statue, the garden, William kissing her in the woods, Penny kissing the statue, their parents separated, Penny moving in with Jem.

Misty was supposed to learn how to speak her family's names. She was supposed to build a bridge between them all—a place where no one could lie, no one could hide. A place where they could be honest and safe. It would bring them all back together and they would be happy and no one would leave.

But everything was all mixed up now. Everything had changed.

Misty fought back tears as their mother pulled onto the highway. Penny had turned around in her seat to watch Jem's house until it faded. She was still turned that way, her head tilted against the back of the seat.

"Turn around, Penny Lee," their mother said, and even she seemed distracted. Her hand kept fluttering from the steering wheel to her throat to the dial of the radio. She touched the drooping fabric on the ceiling of the car, and her fingers left a faint imprint in the foam underneath that slowly sank as the fabric fell away again.

Penny flopped back into place and crossed her arms over her chest. "I miss it already," she said so low that only Misty could hear.

"You're not really going to go, are you?" Misty asked.

"Shh!" Penny hissed. She looked up at their mother but their mother wasn't paying attention to them. Her eyes were locked on the road. She traced the buttons on the radio with her fingernail, back and forth, up and down.

Misty swallowed. Her throat felt thick, like it was full of all the air she'd ever breathed, like she could suffocate on it. "Just tell me."

"You're going to get us in trouble," Penny said. She turned to the side so her back was facing Misty and pressed her face against the window.

Misty tried to reach out to the garden, but without a name, it was impossible to find. She could barely feel the bottom where they lived—it was a faint trembling in her chest but she couldn't hold on to it long enough. She couldn't even concentrate on the crawdads, couldn't remember all the pieces of their name. Everything felt so far away. Everything slipping between her fingers.

And if Penny left, there was no way Misty could put them back together.

There would be no coming back.

"Mama," Misty said.

Their mother pulled her eyes from the road as though it took a great effort. She looked at Misty through the rearview mirror. "What, honey?"

Misty felt the words sitting in her throat like briars. They stung her skin, they burrowed in, and she didn't want to rip them out. She didn't want to say them. But she didn't know what else to do. She couldn't let Penny leave so she said, "I saw Penny kiss the green glass man."

There was a long beat of silence as Penny lifted her head from the window and looked at Misty. Their mother's hand slipped, and the car veered onto the side of the road. Gravel pinged against the metal, and the car rumbled under Misty's feet as though it were laughing at her.

Their mother's eyes were wide as she looked at Misty again. "What did you say?"

"She snuck out of the house," Misty said, and the words tumbled out as though once they'd been freed there was no way to stop them, and she told their mother everything she saw the night she followed Penny outside. The chair Penny had stood on and the way the light swam on her skin and how she'd pressed her lips to the green glass man's face.

Beside her, Penny grew very still and very pale.

Misty expected her sister to scream or to lunge across the seat. She thought Penny would fight, would kick, would lie, would do anything to keep their mother from believing the truth.

But tears welled up in her eyes instead until one ran down her cheek.

Their mother turned around in her seat but she didn't stop driving. The car drifted over the double yellow lines this time as a curve loomed ahead. "Penny Lee, is this true?"

Penny refused to answer. She just kept staring at Misty.

Their mother glanced back and forth between Penny and the road. "Answer me," she said. She reached back and took hold of Penny's knee and shook her once, but Penny didn't move, didn't speak.

Misty fell against the door as their mother jerked the car into their holler. She'd never driven this fast, and plumes of golden dust rose behind them like storm clouds. Penny kept staring at Misty all the while, and Misty wished that she would do something, anything.

"I'm sorry," Misty whispered.

And there was something in the words that seemed to break Penny loose in a way that nothing else had. Her face tightened, contorted, and she lunged at Misty, smacking at her face and chest. Penny's fingers tangled in Misty's hair and Misty pushed back, trying to grab hold of her sister's hands. Penny shouted as she swung at Misty, but the words were garbled—*I hate you and I hate this place, I hate it, I hate it.* The car jerked to the side and slung Penny against the car door, breaking the girls apart.

"I hate you!" Penny shouted again, and her anger dissolved into tears.

Behind her, in the window, the garden flashed by in a blur of green. The car skidded to a halt on the grass and more dust flew into the air. Something gold glinted in the garden, something new.

A second statue had grown beside the green glass man.

Misty could only make out a long, slender shape before their mother unbuckled her seat belt and glared back at them. "Into the house. Now."

Misty opened her door but Penny kicked at her, sending her stumbling to the ground, and Misty whirled back at her. "You shouldn't have done it!"

"You shouldn't have told! You're just as bad as I am. She's been playing spin the bottle in the barn with William!"

"So have you!"

"She kissed him!" Penny shouted.

Their mother's door slammed, and then Penny's door was yanked from behind her. She almost fell backward onto the grass.

"You can't just whip me," Penny said. "It's not fair. She's done the same as I have!"

"That is enough." Their mother reached over Penny and unbuckled her belt and pulled her from the car.

The dust settled enough for Misty to finally see that they were not alone outside. Earl stood by the garden, and the preacher from their church stood beside him. Shannon was on her porch and she reached out her hand for William, who had been standing on the steps. He put his hand in hers, and she led him quickly back inside their trailer.

"It isn't fair!" Penny sobbed.

"Enough!" their mother yelled.

Everything stopped. There was no sound except Penny's labored breathing and the whine in Misty's throat that she couldn't stop no matter how hard she tried. Across the yard, Earl dropped his head and the pastor turned toward the green glass man. Its watery light danced across his shoulders.

"Into the house," their mother said. "Right now."

Eighteen

At first, Misty wasn't sure what she was seeing when she walked into the trailer. She stopped in the doorway until Penny pushed past her, slamming the door behind them. They were both still crying, though the tears had slowed, and by the time they looked around the living room, all their anger and hurt turned to confusion.

"What the Hell is this?" Penny said.

Long strands of green yarn zigzagged across the ceiling.

The first strand began in the center of the living room wall, the same spot that Misty's mother had first noticed the green light. The string was attached to the wall with a piece of tape and it ran from there to a point on the ceiling, from the ceiling to the far corner of the living room, from there to another spot on the opposite wall. Back and forth, up and down, the yarn intersected and crossed in sharp angles. None of the strands had been cut. They were still connected to the original ball of yarn, which slumped against the couch like their mother had just dropped it there before she left to pick up the girls.

"What did she do?" Penny asked. She stretched onto her tiptoes to touch the lowest hanging piece, but Misty reached out to stop her.

"Don't touch it," she said.

Penny jerked her arm away. "What's she going to do? Whip me twice?" Her finger grazed the green string before she settled back onto her feet. She followed the strands back and forth until she reached the most recent. The green light was still there, shivering on the wall beneath the string.

"She's tracking the light," Penny said.

"Why, though?" Misty wiped a tear from her cheek. She'd been so angry before, but now all she felt was fear. Fear of the whipping she was about to get, fear of the mother who would deliver it.

"I don't know." Penny sat down on the couch and put her head in her hands. "God, this is all so stupid."

"What do we do?" Misty asked.

"How am I supposed to know?"

The back door opened, drawing a gust of air through the house that swept through the green strings and sent them rocking slowly back and forth over Misty's head.

Their mother walked inside with a switch in her hand. The limb had been torn from one of the bushes in the backyard. It was thin and green and at least a foot long. The tip of the switch trembled as she stood with her eyes locked on the floor. Her mouth was a thin, tight line.

"Sit," she said, and Misty sat beside her sister on the couch.

"I know I didn't raise children like this. Children who would fight and scream at each other in front of strangers. In front of our *pastor*." She stopped. She took a deep breath. "And that's not the worst of it. The worst is what y'all did. Lying to me. Playing games. Putting your mouths God knows where for God knows what reason because I know"—she slapped the switch against the wall, and the girls flinched—"I know that I raised you with better sense than this."

Penny curled her knees to her chest.

Their mother took a step toward them. "Do either of you have any idea what people say about girls who go around kissing boys at your age? Do you have any idea how hard it is to come back from something like that in a place like this? To find somebody to love you and treat you right when they think you've been out there giving yourself away to anybody with their hands out? Twelve and ten. Neither one of you should have any idea what a kiss even is, and here you sit with your eyes down."

"You lied to us, too," Penny said.

Misty raised her head just to see the look on their mother's face as Penny's words sank in.

"What did you say?"

Penny lifted her chin. "I said you lied to us, too. Daddy ain't just working on the new excavator. He ain't just training no new miners. He's living with Uncle Danny down at them scummy little apartments. Y'all are separated. And we know it."

Penny's voice wavered, but only a little. Misty loved her in that moment and regretted ever doing anything that might cause Penny any harm. If she could have spoken her sister's true name then, Misty would have sent Penny every good feeling she knew, would wrap Penny in sunlight and dry grass and cool water on her ankles and Jem's buttermilk biscuits and the first day of summer vacation and their mother's laughter when she was really happy. She would have filled Penny so full of happiness that she would barely have felt the whipping that was to come.

And if she had her mother's true name, then Misty would have shown their mother what it felt like to be them, waiting to be hurt when they knew that they didn't deserve it—not this—but that it was coming anyway, and maybe her mother would have stopped. Maybe she would have snapped the switch in half and hugged them instead.

But all Misty had was her own small voice, and she was afraid that she might make it worse for both of them, so she sat there, quiet and alone, as their mother held out her hand and said, "Come here, Penny."

Their mother sat on the recliner. She still didn't look at them, but somewhere in the middle of the room. Penny stood sideways between their mother's knees so her back was to Misty.

"Pull up your shorts," their mother said. "You, too, Misty."

Penny rolled the hem of her shorts halfway up her thigh, making more skin for the switch to find. Their mother took hold of Penny's wrist to keep her from running when the pain started. She rested the thinnest end of the switch against Penny's shin and waited.

They hadn't been whipped often, but this was always the worst part. The moment before the impact came, the long, quiet seconds where the only sound was each other's breathing. The green light trembled on the wall, pinned beneath the yarn, trapped, at least for a moment.

Then their mother flicked her wrist back and forth so fast that her hand blurred.

Misty flinched at the same time her sister did, but Penny didn't lean to the side or bend her knees or pull away. She stood still and straight as the switch beat her calves, ankles, the backs of her thighs. It was the thinnest end that did the most damage, the slightest touch enough to burn as it tore away the top layer of skin. The switch made a mean sound, a quick little whistle of air, the dull smack of its body against Penny's body again and again and again.

When it was over, their mother opened her hand, and Penny walked to the kitchen to wait for Misty's turn. Tears welled in Penny's eyes and rolled down her cheeks, but she didn't lift her hand to wipe them away.

Misty took Penny's place.

She held out her arm, and her mother's grip was strong against Misty's wrist, was a kind of pain in itself. The garden knocked against Misty's mind like a small fist against a small door. The sound was persistent and loud, and Misty almost answered. She had missed the garden, and it was nice to know that it was still there.

But the garden sensed Misty's fear, and it wanted to know what was happening. Other things reached out, too—the trailer and the blackbirds sitting on the telephone line outside—all the little things that knew something was wrong, and they tried to help. They tried to send her images of comfort and safety, but Misty turned them away. She pushed them back so they couldn't sense her at all and she couldn't sense them, either. Misty didn't want them to see her like this. She didn't want anyone to know how much this would hurt.

And though she was ready, Misty still gasped when the switch hit her skin.

She leaned to the side, letting her weight fall into her mother's hand, but her mother didn't slip or slow or stop. She held Misty up as she whipped the switch against her calves, the backs of her knees, the tip of the branch bending as it flew, wrapping long red welts along Misty's thighs, its skinny tongue hungry for skin.

And though she'd only had two or three whippings like this, there was always a moment when the switch caught the same piece of skin that it had caught before and the pain doubled, tripled. There was always a feeling, just before it was over, that it might never end.

But it did.

Misty opened her eyes and let out a long breath.

"Go straight to bed. Don't come out until I call for you." Their mother didn't lift her eyes as they passed, but Penny stared at her the whole time, her hands balled into fists at her sides.

Misty propped her heels against the end of the bed frame so her calves and knees and thighs didn't touch her quilt. The wounds rose out of the pale skin of her legs as if they had been hiding there all along and all their mother did was bring them to the surface. Like some part of Misty, always, was bleeding, some part of her always waiting to be shown to the light. The welts were bright red and almost as thick as Misty's pinkie finger in some places. Each of them ended in a bright-red lash, a cut that welled slow, red blood.

Penny didn't check her wounds. She walked straight to their closet and pulled an old bedsheet from the back instead. She took the chair from under her desk and a handful of tacks from a jar. Penny hung the sheet from the ceiling. It wasn't quite long enough to reach the floor, but it was close. Only a few inches of space were left at the very bottom, just enough to watch Penny's bloody ankles walk back and forth as she checked the sheet for weak spots. The sheet stretched from one side of the wall all the way to the door, splitting their room in two.

She said, "I don't want you talking to me. Not never again."

Then she flicked the light off overhead and plunged Misty into darkness with not even the light from the corner of the window to shine through.

Nineteen

The strings on the ceiling had multiplied when the girls left their room to eat dinner that night. Before, the green light had been the size of a pencil eraser, but it was now the size of a dime and had moved from its place on the wall to a new point on the ceiling. The yarn followed. It traced a path through all the places the green light had touched, and the room was quickly filling with yarn. Misty had never thought about light that way—what it touched, how much, how often. But looking at the green strings made it seem like there was nothing that could hide from the light, no corner it couldn't find.

After dinner, the girls returned to their beds. William knocked on the door once, and his voice was small as he asked if Misty could come out and play, and their mother's voice was even smaller as she told him no. When he was gone, the house fell back to silence except for the occasional thump from the living room as their mother did laundry. Misty imagined her pausing with a pink sock in her hand to eye the green light as it swept from the ceiling to the floor. Misty imagined her mother's bare feet planted on the end table, her head tilted sharply to the side as the light zipped back and forth. Her mother prowling through the shadows with bruises under her eyes, her mother tangled in yarn, her mother made of yarn, so soft that the first time Misty tried to hug her, she would collapse in on herself, unspooling inch by inch until there was nothing left.

Cars came and went on their narrow road. The headlights flashed along Penny's window and the sheet hanging from the ceiling. Earl yelled at the cars from his backyard, threatening the people who lingered too long to steal glances of the statues from rear windows, until the sound of his voice blended together with the other night sounds—the crickets and bullfrogs and Penny's faint snores.

Misty opened her chest to the trailer, and then beyond. She found the crawdads beneath the front porch, the ones who had come to keep an eye on her, but they didn't answer her calls. There were at least a dozen crawdads now, and all of them were building burrows of their own. But they didn't stop when they reached the cool, dank water resting underground. They kept going, kept digging.

They burrowed toward Earl's trailer.

Misty roamed between them, sharing limited access to their eyes, their bodies, and each of them saw the same thing in the dirt: a faint green glow. Watching it was like watching a flame curl and writhe and catch. It was never quite the same, no matter how long Misty looked.

There was something else, too, in the dirt. Tree roots. Thick and white as bone, though there were no trees growing in that part of the yard. Old roots, then, remnants of the dogwood grove that used to grow there.

Misty tried to call the crawdads again, but they didn't answer. They kept following the green light toward Earl's trailer, digging deeper and deeper.

Twenty

Two days passed.

Misty and Penny woke early on Sunday morning, like always. Their mother was usually up by then, rousing them with the smell of eggs scrambling on the stove, but the house was silent. The last time they had missed church was nearly a year ago, last summer when all three of them had been sick with the stomach flu.

They still hadn't been given permission to leave their room so the girls stood side by side in their doorway, staring at their mother's closed bedroom door. There was no light beneath it and no sounds stirred on that side of the house.

"Should we go knock?" Misty asked.

Penny shook her head. She hadn't spoken to Misty for two days, but she still rolled her eyes, sighed, grunted, and, every now and then, nodded.

They both returned to their beds. They stayed there until almost noon when someone knocked on the front door.

"I bet it's Aunt Jem," Penny whispered from the other side of the sheet she'd tacked to the ceiling.

"Really?" Misty wanted to ask another question, anything to keep Penny talking, but she didn't want to try her luck.

The knock came again, a little louder.

Their mother's bedroom door creaked open. Her footsteps barely made a sound. Misty slipped from her bed and crawled toward Penny until they sat together by the bedroom door.

"Is Mom okay?" Misty whispered.

Penny pressed her finger to her lips and glared at Misty.

Their mother cleared her throat. The front door swung open. Misty couldn't make out what her mother was saying, but she could hear how her mother said it. The low, slow drawl of her voice. The occasional cough. Misty could almost see her mother's hand resting on her throat the way it did when she was nervous, like she wished she had something to clutch there, something to hold on to. The garden knocked at the back of Misty's mind, the same way it had been knocking for the last two days. Misty wanted to speak to it, but that would mean sharing her name, and Misty knew what was waiting for her there. The green glass man, the fawn's bloody hip, her whipping.

Misty ran her fingers along the cuts on her calves. Most of them had already scabbed over and some had covered with a thin, shiny layer of new skin, but the marks were still tender to the touch. She didn't want to face her new name yet. She didn't want to feel all that hurt.

"Who is it?" Misty asked.

"Earl." The disappointment in Penny's voice matched the slump of Misty's shoulders.

"What does he want?" Misty asked.

"He put a gate at the end of the road."

"Our road?"

"Do you know any other road?"

Misty frowned. "What would he do that for?"

"To keep all them people out. He says if they try coming out here again that he'll… Shoot, Mom laughed. I couldn't hear him."

Misty shivered at the sound of her mother's laughter. She didn't like her laughing with Earl, or near Earl. Just the thought was enough to make anger flare in her chest, but this time the anger was Misty's.

"He gave her a key to the gate," Penny said. "There's three of them. What kind of gate needs three... Shoot, shoot, go. She's coming!"

Penny shoved Misty out of the way, and they scrambled back to their beds. Misty had just enough time to sling her covers over her legs before their mother knocked once on the door and then swung it open. The light was so sudden and bright that Misty turned her head. When she looked back, her mother was standing in their room with the sheet that Penny had tacked to their ceiling caught between her hand.

"What's this?" she asked.

She looked at Misty, but Misty just stared at the sheet, imagining Penny on the other side doing the same thing. Their mother looked at Penny and raised an eyebrow.

"I wanted some privacy," Penny said.

"Dolly did the same thing to me once." Their mother ran her finger along the sheet. "It didn't last more than a few weeks, but it felt a lot longer than that. You girls can come out now. Earl put a gate at the end of the road so there won't be any more people driving up and down here. Just don't go any further than the front yard, all right?"

She dropped the sheet and walked out of the room, leaving the door open behind her. The television turned on in the living room and the refrigerator door opened. Misty crept across her room and looked out the bedroom door. The green strings swayed gently on the ceiling. The strings' path had grown in the last two days, creeping into the hallway, into the kitchen.

Misty waited.

She had been waiting for two days to leave her room, to go outside and be normal again, but now that she had permission, she felt almost stuck. Almost afraid to leave her bedroom. The world outside seemed suddenly larger. There was a second statue waiting in the garden. There was a gate at the end of the road. There was so much out there that for a moment she thought of staying in her bedroom forever. Curling the covers over her shoulders and falling into a deep and dreamless sleep. Misty went back to her bed and sat down again. She waited a little longer.

Twenty-One

The new statue didn't look like the green glass man.

It was gold instead of green. It wasn't shaped like a man, but a hand with the fingers curled gently at the knuckle. The wrist protruded from the earth like a tree trunk. The hand was six feet wide from one side of the palm to the other, and each finger about two feet long. Its golden skin was smooth and unmarred but for a single mark along the heel of its palm that was almost like a scar. The line was so thin that it only appeared in certain shades of light and seemed to blend into the hand the rest of the time. It was easy to imagine that the statue kept going, growing down the length of the arm to the crook of a wide golden elbow, spreading out to form a body hiding in the earth. There might be someone down there all the time, holding their breath while they held the garden up.

And when she looked at the hand, Misty couldn't help but think of William, too. How he'd held the brown bottle out to her when he found her in the woods. How he had put her hand on top of it and asked her to spin. And that day in the barn when they first played the game, he'd taken her last turn, his hand gripping the neck of the green bottle.

That was where all of this began, that day in the barn with his hand.

She wasn't sure how the statues were growing, but they seemed to be saying something about Misty and William and it made her stomach ache to look at either of the statues too long.

Misty turned away from the garden and slunk around the front of her trailer. She hadn't gone outside all day, but had waited until everyone was asleep. The moon hung in the sky with its body sliced in half, hiding between the trees like it was afraid to show itself, afraid that Misty might notice that part of it was missing. She followed its feeble light to the corner of her porch, crouched down, and looked underneath. The crawdad chimneys were still there, but the crawdads didn't emerge when Misty strummed her fingers against the ground. She waited and waited, but none of them answered her call.

Misty closed her eyes. She thought of her father brushing her bangs across her forehead, the rough calluses of his fingers, the little seams of coal dust that gathered in his knuckles, and the smell of him after work, like something long-buried in deep, cold earth, and a green bottle buried beneath the dirt, and William's mouth against her cheek in the barn, and his mouth against hers in the woods; the paper-thin feeling of her grandmother's skin inside Misty's palm; the rattle of her mother's breathing, rocking her, begging her to sleep; a fawn in the woods, blood on its hip and pain in Misty's leg, pain in her chest; a switch against the back of her knee, catching, catching her skin; a crawdad skittering over her thighs, resting on her belly; branches above her; birds screaming in the dark; the fawn struggling toward her; her mother sitting on the couch with her head in her hands; the bedsheet tacked to the ceiling in her bedroom and Penny's bloody ankles walking back and forth behind it; Earl's shadow on the living room carpet, growing, distorting; the green light quivering on the wall; the smell of Jem's bedsheets and the sound of wind chimes; cool water rushing over her ankles; blood rising to her skin, welling bright and red; white roots in dark soil; a feeling of sadness like many small stones stacked inside her stomach; the switch smacking the living room wall; a small cloud of cold breath hanging in the air; a burrow digging down deep into the earth.

Misty let out a gasp of air, her whole body shaking. Above her, bats circled. A half dozen of them, maybe more. It was hard to tell them apart from the darkness, their bodies so slim and black, their bodies sweeping around and around. She felt them like little drumbeats inside her head as they shared their names with her. The barn reached out and so did the trailer and the worms in the ground, and the sleeping redbirds woke and sang her a long and lonely note.

And then the garden said, "There you are, little little. What kept you so long?"

"I got in trouble," Misty said. Her stomach still churned with the sound of her name, but she was relieved, too. She'd been alone for two long days, and she hadn't realized how vast the silence was until something filled it. "I wasn't allowed to come outside."

She walked over to the garden and knelt in the grass. Earl had finished building the fence, so this was as close as she could get without climbing over. She reached under the lowest board instead and traced her fingers over the dry earth near the green glass man's base.

"That tickles," the garden said.

Misty smiled. "Really?"

"No, but it would be nice if it did, don't you think?"

"It would," Misty said. "So you're not mad at me anymore?"

"Mad?"

"The last time we talked. With the trees, remember? You went away."

The wind picked up and sent the tree limbs shaking, the tall grass bending. The garden said, "No. You got mad at me."

"When?"

"In the woods. You yelled about her. About Caroline. I was afraid."

Misty frowned. She didn't remember it that way. But she *had* been afraid of what she saw, of the memories the trees shared. So many things had happened since then that it was hard to be sure of herself. Maybe she had yelled.

"Are you sure?" Misty said.

"I thought you'd never speak to me again," the garden said. "And then you didn't answer when I called. For days and days I called. I was worried."

"I'm sorry," Misty said, though she still felt confused.

"It's forgiven and gone. Gone and away. Now tell me about this trouble you found."

Misty shared images of the car ride home and everything that followed. "It was awful. I didn't want to tattle on Penny, but I was just so, so—" Sadness bubbled in Misty's chest. It heated her cheeks and brought tears to her eyes, but she blinked them away.

"I know that feeling," the garden said. "When you're so full and there's nothing to do. There's no place for it to go. It has to come out somehow."

"I didn't mean to get Penny hurt."

"I believe you."

"Penny doesn't."

An image of the sheet that Penny had hung from their bedroom ceiling drifted through Misty's memory, though it seemed longer in her mind, blocking out all hints of light, and thicker, too, almost like another wall.

"She'll never forgive me," Misty said.

"She will."

"She won't." Misty didn't know how sad she was until someone asked, or how afraid she was until someone listened. It all surged inside her at once, but it felt good to say it, too. It felt good to talk. "And Mom won't, either. I was bad and now—"

"How were you bad?"

"I lied," Misty said. "I played a game I shouldn't have played. I yelled and told people our business."

"Those are things you did," the garden said, "not things you are."

Misty shook her head. "There's no difference."

"There is. I swear, I swear." Misty felt sunlight on her cheek like a warm touch. "Doing bad doesn't make bad when you're sorry. When you do better after."

"I guess. Maybe." She ran her thumb across the garden's dry earth, slowly, back and forth.

"I was whipped before," the garden said. "It isn't nice, but it isn't your fault."

"Whipped? Why would somebody whip a garden?"

"Oh." The garden's presence retracted, almost pulled away completely, and for a moment Misty thought that the garden had gone again. An image of Caroline jittered between them, her face breaking in and out of Misty's mind like static. Then the garden said, "I meant 'whipped' like hurt. Like when Earl dug me up."

"I know it sounds mean, but I don't like him. He's been acting so weird lately. And he put that gate at the end of the holler so nobody can get in."

"A gate?"

"Yeah. He doesn't want anyone seeing the statues."

Anger flared in Misty's cheeks, and the garden's voice was low and grating. "He's trying to hide them. That's all he does. Slither further and further away. But it won't work this time. I have help now. You and the crawdads and—"

"The ones from under my porch?" Misty asked. "I was worried about them. They wouldn't answer me when I called for them."

"They can't speak when they're working."

"Why not?"

"Because," the garden said, "they're going to help me until they're finished. That's what we agreed."

Misty drew her hand back to her lap. "I don't get it."

"It's something I learned a long time ago. I take a little of my name and a little of their name and I join us together. That way, they can help me make him stop." An image of Earl surfaced in Misty's mind, but it wasn't the Earl she knew. It was a much younger Earl, and Caroline was there, too, but her face blurred and disappeared almost instantly.

"But you don't have your name yet."

The garden's presence subsided for a moment, then returned like a wave lapping tentatively against the shore. "I have part of it. You helped me remember the dogwood trees. That's all I need, a little part."

Misty frowned. The garden's presence surged in her mind.

"This isn't a frowning thing. It's a good thing. The crawdads are helping me make Earl afraid," the garden said, and Misty felt the familiar simmer of hatred in her chest. "For what he did. What he does. I'm going to make people see him for what he is."

"How can the crawdads help with that?"

"They have little claws for digging, but I don't. I needed them."

Something about the way the garden said it made Misty feel nervous, but she tried to tamp the feeling down, to keep it hidden. The garden could sense everything that Misty felt and thought while they were connected, and she didn't want to upset the garden.

Misty looked back at the yard. More crawdad chimneys broke through the grass here and there. Most of them were clustered near Earl's trailer.

"Do they want to help?" she asked.

"It doesn't hurt them," the garden said, "and I'll let them go when they're finished."

"You can do that? Make other things do stuff?"

"That makes it sound mean," the garden said.

"I just worry about them. The crawdads are my friends."

"I won't hurt them. Promise."

Misty nodded. "All right. Well, maybe let them talk to me sometime, okay?"

"Soon," the garden said, "when their work is done. I'm feeling tired." Another image blinked through Misty's thoughts. Caroline standing by a dogwood tree, her fingers sunk into its bark. For a moment it seemed like Caroline was sinking into the tree, but then the image was gone. "I need to rest now."

"Okay," Misty said. "Well, sleep sweet then."

"You, too, little little. I'll see you soon."

And their connection was gone like a cold gust of wind slamming a door shut, so quick and sudden that Misty didn't hear the sound of a real door shutting nearby. She didn't notice William until he whispered her name, and by then he was right beside her. Misty jumped.

"Hey," he said, "were you talking to somebody?"

Misty shook her head. "No. Just sitting."

William looked up at the green glass man and smiled. "They're awful pretty, ain't they? Especially at night."

Pretty wasn't the word she would use but Misty nodded anyway.

William sat down beside her in the grass. "What happened to your legs?" He pointed to one of the cuts from her whipping. "Somebody got ahold of you good."

"My mom."

"Really?" William shook his head. "I didn't figure her for that. She seems so nice."

"Yeah, maybe. Until you give her a switch."

William smiled. "My mom used to be like that. She said she thought whipping was fine until my dad whipped me with a belt once. I don't remember it at all. She threw him out after that. I don't know which is worse, a belt or a switch."

"A belt sounds pretty bad."

"I guess so," William said.

Earl coughed from inside his trailer and William leaned back to get a look at his front door, but Earl didn't wake up. Not yet.

"Did you see the gate he put at the end of the road?" William asked.

"Not yet. He gave Mom keys to it this morning."

"Mine too. She about had words with him right there, but she was already late for work. She called me at lunch and said she thinks he's going crazy."

"Why?"

"He keeps talking about birds spying on him. And he thinks God's trying to send him some kind of message with the statues."

"About what?"

William shrugged. "I don't know. But he don't want nobody seeing them until he's figured it out. I don't care what he thinks as long as he don't hurt them."

Misty watched William watching the statues. His expression looked like a hand outstretched, waiting for another hand to meet it.

"What did your mom think of the new statue?" Misty asked.

William sighed. "She didn't seem to mind it as much as she did the green glass man. She still thinks he's creepy." He shook his head. "She's been acting funny, too. Sleepwalking. I found her in the kitchen the other night drawing on the cabinets with one of my markers."

"What was she drawing?"

"Trees, I think. It's all right, though. I ain't giving up on the statues. I still think they can get her to stay. I was actually thinking about that, and about you. There's something I wanted to show you."

"Okay," Misty said. "But I have to hurry. I don't want Mom catching me out this late."

"It won't take long. Promise."

Misty followed William to the barn, which looked cleaner than the last time she'd been there. The puddles of water and oil that had sunk into the earth had dried and fresh dirt had been added to the dips in the floor. William led Misty to the back wall, ducking beneath two sawhorses and a pile of unused lumber. He pointed out the bent nails jutting from the boards and told her to be careful. The back of the barn was even cleaner than the rest—the floor swept in long, even strokes, the cobwebs torn from the corners, like someone had been preparing the barn for something special. There were footprints like William's in the dirt and Misty overlapped them.

"Look through that crack there," William said, pointing to a gap between two boards.

"What am I going to see?"

"It's not scary," he said. "I promise."

There was a sinking feeling in Misty's stomach that made her want to turn back, but she couldn't think of a way to leave that wouldn't hurt William's feelings, so she pressed her nose to the crack in the wall. One half of her trailer glowed in the darkness. The trees behind it were honed to their black silhouettes. The wind rattled something in the hayloft overhead that sounded like paper.

"It all looks the same to me," Misty said.

William inched closer until he could see through the same crack that she was looking through. His breath was warm against the back of her ear. He smelled like milk.

"William?" Misty whispered.

He wrapped his arm around Misty's waist like a hug, but it didn't feel like a hug. It felt like a clutch, like a hook. She turned toward him but all she could see was the top of his head. His other hand slipped to the waistband of her shorts. His fingers pried beneath it until his skin was against her skin.

"Maybe we should go back to the garden," she said.

He took a step closer, his knees knocking against the back of Misty's knees until she had no choice but to press her hand against the barn to keep from falling. She held herself up as William's hand moved over her panties. His fingers kneaded her skin like he was searching for something in the dark. He leaned harder on her back until her muscles strained to support the weight of them both, their bodies clenched together. She pushed back, trying to dislodge him so she could stand, so she could breathe, but he was heavier than she was, and he rocked his hips against her, slowly, back and forth.

Misty pressed her eye to the crack in the barn's walls, groping for the yard, the woods, the dark. She willed herself outside, willed the barn into a window, her body into air. She willed herself small enough to slip away, but her body was there, her body bent awkwardly, her shoulders aching, and other feelings, too, that she couldn't understand. She tried to breathe slowly but her lungs wouldn't listen. She wasn't even sure what was happening, but she felt the same panic as when her mother closed her hand around Misty's wrist and held her in place, the lash of the whip hovering in the air, the same need to get away, and the same knowing that there was no getting away, not from her, not from this.

In her head a chorus played without an answer: *what did I do, what do I do, what did I do, what do I do.*

She dug her fingernails into the wooden board beneath her and the barn stirred. The barn whispered its name in her chest like a flame, guttering. Over and over again, it spoke, and Misty closed her eyes and listened. The harder she focused on the name, the more she felt the wood under her hand. The more she felt like the barn did—the more tired, the more sleeping, the older and grayer and softer. She felt sinking and crumbling. She felt less and less herself, less her body straining against William's, less her fingernails bent against the wood.

"It's okay," William said as he scraped the inside of her thigh.

Misty reached further, searching the trees. She found birds sleeping in their nests. One and then three and then ten. Dozens of them in the woods behind her trailer, all of them curled up safe and Misty clenched her fist.

"Wake up," she screamed to them, though her mouth remained cinched tight, her teeth biting into the soft skin of her cheek. "Wake up!"

The birds startled, their wings fluttering before they even felt the need to fly, their bodies responding to Misty's call. "Wake up. Please wake up."

William said, "I just wanted something nice to happen, and the garden seemed so lonely, and I was..."

The birds took to the air, the birds a lightness in her chest, a weight without a fall. They swept through the trees and flew toward the barn.

William said, "You touched the bottle and I kissed your cheek and now it'll be even better, what grows next. It'll be even better because of this."

The birds landed on the roof, a dozen, then two—their bodies red and brown and gold and blue. Their feet scratched the tin as they skittered for purchase, crowding together on the far side of the barn, the one where the sun took the longest to reach every morning. The garden sensed her fear and confusion and it called out to her, but Misty ignored its voice. She pushed the garden away and focused on the birds even as her connection with them began to falter and her body started to pull her back again. Her body, aching. Her body, afraid.

"Please," Misty said to the birds. Their heads turned back toward the woods, wondering why they had gone, yearning for the warmth of their nests. "Please don't go."

William said, "It'll be even better now."

A car pulled into the driveway.

William jumped away from Misty, and she sagged to her knees. She let out a long breath and the door in her chest slammed shut. The birds lifted from the barn, scraping and screeching, their wings buffeting the air. Misty pressed her back against the wall and turned so she could see William standing above her.

"Are you okay?" He stooped in front of her and squinted at her face in the dark. He stroked her hair with his hand, his fingers barely grazing her scalp like he was afraid to touch her now. "It's not bad, what we did. Okay? I have to go now. But it's okay, Misty. Everything's going to be okay."

William tore a splinter from the wall where Misty's hand had been, and then he was gone, ducking under the sawhorses and running through the door.

Twenty-Two

The sheet that Penny tacked onto the ceiling rippled when Misty opened the door and revealed, in a glimpse, her sister lying on her back with a flashlight in her hand, a book propped against her knees, three training bras slung around the end of the bedpost, and a backpack lying open on the floor. Misty walked to her side of the room and stood before the bedsheet.

She opened her mouth to call her sister's name, but something else came rushing up—heat in her cheeks, tears to her eyes. She could think of no name for what had just happened to her. If she made one up herself it would sound like the heavy suck of mud against bare toes, glass broken and glittering, glass cutting into skin, glass shattered and put back and shattered again.

There was a frantic feeling in her palms, as though they wanted to split at the wrist and sweep to the sky like bats circling. They wanted to never come back again, never to be part of a girl like Misty.

How could she tell Penny that?

How could she explain what happened in the barn without explaining why? If she told Penny about the barn, then she had to talk about the statues, too, the green bottle, and about how she spoke to the world, and how William thought that she was the thing that made the statues grow. That all of it, somehow, was her fault.

Penny's flashlight shifted. The beam landed on the middle of the sheet, its light concentrated in the center like a small, pale sun.

"I don't care where you went," Penny whispered. "I won't even tell if you just leave me alone, all right?"

The light clicked off and the springs in Penny's bed creaked as she turned to her side, her back pointed to Misty.

Misty sat down on the floor. She couldn't think of going to bed now. She didn't want to feel anything pressing against her back, no softness, no quilt, nothing. She drew her knees to her chest and touched the sheet that hung in the center of their room. The sheet shared its name with Misty—the feeling of fibers twining together, of many small things making one—and it waited for Misty to share her own but she couldn't. Not when she knew what would be waiting for her within it.

Tears spilled down her cheeks as she drew her hand away. She hiccuped and clenched her toes against the carpet to keep from sobbing, and she let the tears fall without really feeling them.

Eventually, the sun came up and pale-yellow light filtered through the room. Penny's snores softened and a cabinet door opened and closed in the kitchen as their mother started to make breakfast. Only then did Misty turn away from the sheet, when morning came and she knew that she wasn't alone. Only then did she roll onto her side there on the carpet and close her eyes.

That day, a spiral appeared behind the green glass man.

It was nearly as tall as Misty, its bronze back curved and curving. The spiral chased itself until there was nowhere left to go, until it ended in the center, its tip as sharp as a needle. When Misty looked at it she saw herself. She saw the way she felt—the tightness in her chest, the swirling of her stomach, around and around, unending, and she was more sure than ever that the statues grew from her and from William.

Earl touched the tip of the spiral once and jerked back his hand, gasping. He lifted his finger to the light where a bright-red dot of blood quivered on his skin.

Twenty-Three

It rained. A heavy, driving rain whose fists pounded against the trailer and overflowed the clogged gutters. A rain too much for the ground to hold so the water stripped the dirt from the driveway, carried it away to someplace new, someplace the dirt hadn't chosen. The rain pooled in the yard in shallow puddles, turned the crawdad chimneys into mud that weighed the grass down.

Misty wedged herself in the narrow space between the couch and her father's recliner. She pretended that it was a boat and the storm outside raged around her on a dark and choppy sea. She'd been traveling with a team of other boats but they'd gotten separated and now she was on her own. She'd taken a bag of chips from the kitchen cabinet and a handful of M&M's and those were her rations, all the food she had to last until she found land again. Her mother's green strings swayed on the walls and ceiling. Misty had taken a shed crawdad skin from the box under her bed—the last one the crawdads had given to her—and she ran her thumb gently over its translucent back. She tried to reach out to the crawdads in her yard, but they still didn't answer.

Or couldn't.

She wasn't sure exactly what the garden did to make the crawdads do what it wanted, but now it seemed as though the garden was the only thing the crawdads could hear. They were shut off from Misty in a way that made her uneasy. They hadn't even reached out to her when she'd been in the barn with William, even though they had to feel what was happening. They were the closest thing to her in all the world and now they were gone, too.

The front door flung open and Misty's mother hurried inside, little raindrops hanging like diamonds from the messy bun that drooped across her shoulders. The storm yanked the door from her hand, slammed it against the trailer, and held it there as the wind poured inside, bringing the scent of cold water and drenched earth. Misty tugged on the green string taped to the wall behind her, drawing her boat away from her mother. She huddled deeper into the shadows of the recliner.

Misty's mother watched the storm for a moment, silhouetted in the open doorway. The statues in Earl's garden glinted beyond her right hip. She seemed to be remembering something before she shook it off and pulled the door closed. She dropped a soggy envelope onto the coffee table and didn't notice Misty wedged in the corner.

Her mother carried a dish towel and a cold can of pop from the kitchen and knelt behind the end table. She shook the envelope until a stack of money slipped out, then dried each of the bills, even the ones that didn't look damp at all by pressing them gently between the folds of the dish towel before stacking them into narrow towers.

Misty felt a knocking at the back of her mind, like someone pounding on a door at the end of a long, dark hallway. It was the garden. It had been calling all morning just that way, a gentle, persistent push, and every time Misty had pushed it away. The trailer had called out to her, too, and the figurines on the television stand and the crows that lived down by the creek, and she'd pushed them all away. She didn't know how much the garden had seen last night in the barn or how much it felt through the connection it shared with Misty. But the garden had been there, briefly, and even that was too much. Even thinking of the barn made her feel frantic, like there was something small and clawed inside her chest that would tear her apart to get free. Her fingers felt sticky and warm so Misty wiped them on the carpet, but the feeling lingered, as though the damp was underneath her skin.

When her mother finished drying the money, she brought out a separate stack of envelopes from inside her purse. In her mind, Misty was still on the boat and her mother was an old witch woman who lived alone on an island. She was hunched inside her little cabin checking her spells, sorting her ingredients. The envelopes her mother pulled from her purse were weathered and worn. Some of them were coffee-stained, and others held together with pieces of tape. They were all labeled in her mother's neat handwriting: one for each of the bills their family had to pay.

The money disappeared from the table by inches, whisked into the envelopes. By the time the table was empty, most of the envelopes had been filled. Misty's mother looked down at each of them and frowned. Then she bowed her head. Her lips moved but no sounds came until she whispered, "Amen," and Misty mouthed the word like an echo.

Her mother reopened the envelopes like a magician reaching into his hat, hoping for a rabbit. She snatched a five-dollar bill here, a ten there, and eventually she took the only bill—a twenty—from an envelope marked SAVINGS and sat the money on the corner. She sighed, leaned back, closed her eyes. She seemed so still that Misty was tempted to reach out to her mother, to share her name and try to build a bridge between them. There was something about the softness to her mother's features and the quiet drumming of the rain that made it feel suddenly possible. Like maybe everything Misty wanted could come true after all.

But speaking to her mother would mean speaking her name, and that meant her mother would see the barn and William. She would see Misty pressed against the wall, and the thought of that alone made Misty's throat close up and her cheeks flush. Her mother had been so angry when she found out that Misty had played spin the bottle with William. She might think she was just playing another game, that she'd caused it somehow, and she'd never forgive Misty for what had happened. She'd never see her the same way again.

Her mother's eyes snapped open, and she caught sight of Misty's face peering between the couch and the recliner. She jumped. "Misty? Good Lord, I didn't even know you were there. What're you doing?"

Misty pressed the tape on the green string back into the wall and her boat pulled into the sand of her mother's island, creaking and leaking. She swallowed the sadness in her throat and whispered, "I'm on a boat."

Her mother lifted her eyebrows. She looked around Misty, and for a moment, the boat almost shimmered into existence, solid and whole, its great wooden sides creaking as Misty peered through a porthole. "Oh, I see. And what's the boat called?"

"The SS *Crawdad*."

Her mother laughed. "It's a very worthy vessel."

"You want to join me?" Misty asked. "There's plenty of room." She scooted back to make an empty space for her mother to crawl inside. If she came, they could go anywhere. They could sail the open sea and discover someplace no one had ever seen. They could do it together.

Her mother smiled. She leaned forward to inspect the narrow

space and Misty thought that, for a moment, she might really join her. Then she shook her head and said, "Why don't you come out here on land with me?"

Misty's heart sank a little, but she climbed out of her boat anyway, leaving the shed crawdad skin behind to guard her snacks. She poked one of the envelopes on the coffee table. "That's a lot of money."

"Mmm, it sure seems like it, don't it? It gets gone quicker than you might think. The electricity eats it up and the trailer eats it up and little girls eat it up." She pinched Misty's sides until Misty smiled.

"Where'd it all come from?"

"Your daddy left it for us."

"Is he here?"

"No, he dropped it off in the mailbox. He's working again."

"Oh." Misty leaned her head against the couch, and her mother smoothed her bangs away from her face. "Is he going to come back?"

"He'll be by for a visit soon."

"What about for good, though?"

"I think so. Sometimes grown-ups just need time apart for a while. To get things right."

Misty nodded as though she understood, but she wasn't sure what her parents had gotten wrong in the first place. Being apart seemed like the wrong thing to do, not staying together. She said, "I wouldn't mind some time away from Penny."

Her mother smiled. "I thought that way about Jem and Dolly when I was your age, but now I don't know what I'd do without them."

Misty snorted. "I know just what I'd do without her."

"Oh yeah?"

Misty nodded. "What's that money over there for?"

"Well," her mother said, "you know it's the Fourth of July soon.

There's going to be fireworks in town tonight, and I thought we could all go together. Take some blankets to put on the hood of the car and stop at Dairy Queen for some chicken tenders."

"And a Blizzard?" Misty said.

"And a Blizzard."

"I'm going to get Oreo." Misty smiled and for a moment she forgot all about the barn and the garden and her father and the statues. "Is Penny coming?"

"Yes, your sister is coming."

"Is she getting a Blizzard?"

"Yes."

Misty sighed.

Their mother smiled. "We just have to hope the rain lets off, or they might have to cancel it all together."

The rain did let off, and they all piled into their mother's car that evening and drove into town. Town was the place where Misty and Penny would go to high school one day, the place with four restaurants and two stoplights, the Save A Lot, a long bridge decorated with little American flags on sticks, and a crowd of people. The fireworks always took place over the football field near the high school. People parked all along the road, and some walked to the field with blankets and folding chairs while others sat in the beds of their trucks. They bought food from the restaurants in town or brought food of their own, and everyone milled around talking and laughing.

Their mother found a parking spot behind Dolly's truck. She spread a blanket on the hood of the car and helped Misty and Penny on top. She tucked napkins into the collars of their shirts and spread the food they'd bought between them.

"Don't let it get cold now," she said, stealing one of Misty's fries.

Dolly and her daughter Charlene came pouring out of the trunk, and Jem followed in her favorite pair of coveralls, one buckle undone to show a bright-yellow shirt beneath.

"I swear you just about glow in the dark in that thing," Misty's mother said.

Jem grinned. "That way you'll never lose me."

"There's no chance of that," Dolly said. She hugged Misty and Penny both, but she hugged their mother the longest.

"You been on my mind a sight lately," she said. "Every morning I wake up and see your face when you tried to cut your own bangs. You remember that?"

"It's hard to forget," their mother said. "Where are the big kids at?"

"Sam said they were all going to LeeCo for a fireworks show with their friends," Dolly said. "They're supposed to be back before ten."

Jem snorted. "I swear Jamie told me they were going to Caney Fork. It's untelling what's going on between the three of them. They're as bad as we were."

Dolly straightened the hem of their mother's shirt. "Did you talk to Mrs. Gray yet? She was asking about you."

"If you're wondering if she's still alive, the answer is yes." Jem shook her head. "That old woman's going to outlive everything but the cockroaches."

Dolly smacked Jem's arm. "She's three cars down. In the blue van. Go on and say hello. We'll keep an eye on the girls."

Dolly waited until their mother was out of sight before she twisted Misty's calf to the side to reveal the pale ghost of the cuts from her whipping. "Them's some awful mean-looking marks on those legs."

Misty pulled her leg away. She didn't like anyone seeing the marks, especially Jem and Dolly. She didn't want them to think worse of her for what she had done to deserve the whipping.

"I've had worse," Charlene said.

"Please," Dolly said. "The worst you ever got was a pat on your behind."

"Which explains some things," Jem said. Charlene stuck out her tongue, and Jem nodded to the child as though her tongue were evidence. "The good Lord said it Himself: 'Spare the rod.'"

"It must be nice to pick and choose the things you and the Lord agree on," Dolly said. "I don't reckon I'd have turned out worse if Daddy had spared me the belt a few times."

"I swear that man could catch a bare piece of skin thirty feet away in a dense fog." Jem rubbed her arm as she talked, but there was a hint of pride in her voice. "Daddy couldn't walk a straight line if his life depended on it, but he sure could whip an ass."

"Nearly broke Beth's jaw once with that buckle," Dolly muttered. "I don't see you bragging about that."

Penny sat up straighter. "Do what now?"

"You heard me," Dolly said. "She was about a year older than you."

"And came sneaking in the house after midnight," Jem said. "Come on now, Dolly. You know Beth'd never do something like that to these girls."

"And I told myself I'd never whip mine a'tall, and I intend to stick to that," Dolly said. "Just because they did it to us don't mean we got to do it to our own. You girls don't deserve to be hurt, you hear me? You're good children. Of course you are—you're related to me." She kissed first Misty and then Penny on the cheek.

Misty uncurled her legs and stretched them across the top of the hood. She'd been so afraid that Jem or Dolly or the garden would think less of her because of the marks, but when they found out, all they wanted to know was if she was all right. They didn't treat her poorly—they still loved her, whipping and all.

"Hush now," Jem said as Misty's mother walked back over. "We sure missed you at church, Beth. You ain't getting sick on us, are you?"

"I'm not sick," their mother said. "Just tired. And I didn't know they'd started taking attendance."

Dolly sighed. "Well, you missed a real humdinger."

Jem shook her head. "Sister Cheryl got filled with the Holy Ghost about ten minutes into the service. Took off down the aisles like a bat out of Hell."

"After the preacher gave that announcement about Revival, everybody was beside themselves and it turned into a worship service," Dolly said. "They sang your favorite song, too. I swear that Ida Day has got the prettiest voice in the whole congregation."

"That old bullfrog?" Jem said. "I'd rather listen to Sister Trish and her niece, that little dark-haired thing—what's her name?"

"What announcement?" their mother asked.

"You ain't heard then?" Jem asked.

Misty's mother shook her head.

Jem glanced at Dolly. "He said we was going to have Revival on location this year." Jem added air quotes to the word *location*.

Their mother frowned. "What does that mean?"

"He wouldn't say." Dolly shrugged. "But the rumors are already flying that it's going to be at that garden of Earl's. An unveiling of sorts for them strange things that's been growing in your yard. You never did let us come and get a look."

"Yeah," Jem said, "we need the backstage tour."

"I thought Earl didn't want nobody to see them," Misty said.

Their mother looked back at her. "Where'd you hear that?"

Misty shrugged and Penny said, "He put that gate at the end of the road."

"Do what?" Dolly said.

"That man ain't right," Jem said. "I think it's what he did that's eating him alive. Killing Caroline, covering it up. You can't lie about something like that without paying the cost."

Misty's mother crossed her arms over her chest. Her face looked dim and pale, like someone had turned off the light inside her. "He has been acting awful strange. I saw him in his yard just this morning stomping at the ground, telling something to stop watching him. I don't know what's going on with him, but it ain't right. And it sure don't need an audience."

"Beth!"

Everyone turned toward the voice and found Shannon walking along the rows of cars, one hand waving wildly in the air. A man walked behind her wearing a button-up shirt and dark jeans. Misty searched the road for any sign of William but couldn't see him anywhere. She sat the rest of her food down and drew her knees to her chest.

Dolly shook her head. "Is that Shannon? I swear half that woman's clothes come from the newborn section at Kmart."

"Hush," Jem said. Then, smiling at Shannon, she called, "Hello, stranger! Been a while since I saw the likes of you."

"If you'd ever get out of the truck and come say hello when you get gas down at the store, you might see me more often," Shannon said.

"But then I'd have to see everybody else," Jem said, and they laughed.

"I can't argue with you there. I wouldn't mind a few days off from that bunch myself, but little boys need food for some reason. Lots of it." She turned to the man with her and squeezed his arm. "Y'all know Harold Whitehead. He's a boss at Blue Diamond. Goes to church up on Big Creek. His mom's the secretary of the elementary school up that way."

"Oh, yes," Dolly said, "I reckon you worked with my husband. Wayne Phelps."

"Yeah, yeah. Me and Wayne go way back. He's a fine man," Harold said. "Tell him I was asking about him."

Dolly smiled. "He'll be glad to know you're doing well."

"Is William with you?" Penny asked.

Shannon's smile faltered. She glanced at Harold and then away again. "No, honey, he's at home."

"We wanted to bring him," Harold said.

"Of course," Shannon said.

"But he's getting to the age where they start to act out. Talk back. Sometimes he don't treat his mother with the respect she's earned." Harold squeezed Shannon's shoulder, and she smiled at him.

"You know how it is, Beth," she said. "Kids don't have a clue what it's like to be a parent and be working. They don't understand what all it takes and sometimes they just… Well, they start taking you for granted, and you get used to the way things are—"

Misty's mother nodded. "I understand."

Shannon smiled, relieved, but Harold kept talking. "The way I was raised, a belt could straighten out about any problem a child had. A few good slaps never did anything but good for me. Especially for boys. If you don't teach them consequences, they'll cause nothing but trouble."

Shannon looked at Harold. "Hon, would you mind getting my jacket out of the truck? I thought I could tough it out, but it's a lot colder than I thought."

He nodded, gave a little wave to Misty and her family, then walked away. Shannon waited until he was a few cars down before she turned back to Misty's mother and sighed. "I swear I don't know if I'm doing the right thing half the time."

"That's motherhood for you," Dolly said.

"I reckon that's the truth. Harold is a good man, though. Strict, but good. And he means well. He wants William to do good in life, you know? He wants him to have something when he grows up. He wants us to have something now. It's so hard getting by on your own all the time." Shannon looked overhead as a firework exploded in the air, sending a shower of dim red sparks streaking through the sky. "Oh! It's starting. I better get back to Harold before I lose him in the dark. It was good to see you girls. Have fun!"

Shannon ran back along the edge of the road, her hair lit by the lights of a passing car. Jem and Dolly and Charlene all crawled into the back of her truck and Penny went with them, claiming she could see the sky better from there. Misty watched her sister to see if she whispered anything to Jem about moving in with her, but Penny seemed occupied with the fireworks. Misty's mother climbed onto the hood of the car beside Misty and stretched out on her back. They lay side by side with their arms touching, both of them watching the sky so that it seemed the sky was all that existed, that they floated together on the back of a dark and calm sea with no thought of where they would land or when.

More fireworks exploded. Children screeched with joy all along the road, and some of the younger ones started to cry. People oohed and aahed at the colors and the designs, which were almost identical to the year before, but they seemed different every time somehow. The hood of the car was still warm from the engine, and the warmth seeped into Misty's shoulders. Bullfrogs croaked in the ditch lines by the side of the road, and the sound was like an echo of the greater boom of the fireworks. The explosions resounded in Misty's chest until she felt like she was part of them, like she was bursting in the sky, like she was filled with light.

There was so much around her that she wouldn't mind being a part of. The lights, the noise, the crowd. The grass swaying slowly back and forth. A creek that trickled sluggish and cold beside the road. All the cars lined up together, their engines ticking as they cooled. She wanted to hold on to all of it for a little while longer.

She closed her eyes and thought of her mother counting money at the coffee table, the little speckles of rainwater that darkened her shoulders; the crawdad's empty shell in her hands, the light pouring straight through it; a green light underground, writhing like a flame; her father brushing her bangs across her forehead, the rough calluses of his fingers; the green bottle spinning on the floor of the barn; the birds on the roof, crowding together, the scrape of their claws; the rattle of her mother's breathing, rocking her, begging her to sleep; William's hand on her hip; a fawn in the woods, blood on its hip and pain in Misty's leg, pain in her chest; a crawdad tangled in her hair; William's hand creeping lower; Earl's shadow on the living room carpet, growing, distorting; a weight on her back, pressing and pressing; William's breath against her ear, the smell of soured milk and hard-packed earth and—

Misty opened her eyes.

The door inside her chest slammed shut and her mother jumped.

"Did you say something?" she asked.

Misty shook her head.

Her mother smiled. "I swear I thought you said something. It must be these fireworks. Ain't they pretty?"

Tears welled in Misty's eyes, multiplying the fireworks above her, turning them blurry and dim. Names changed. Names were honest. The whipping hadn't been in her name this time, but William had. She didn't know how to make something disappear from her name, how to control it all on her own because it wasn't just her choice. And if talking to the world, to the garden, or even to her family meant that she had to relive what happened in the barn, then she would rather be quiet. She'd rather be alone.

Shed

Once the crawdad's old shell has
withered, it's time to let it go.
The old body fights to keep hold of itself as
the crawdad struggles to cast it off.
Eventually, the old shell yields and is discarded.
What's left beneath is different—newer,
but weaker. Vulnerable to attack.

Twenty-Four

A name was like a map. Even with just one part of it, Misty's friends could still find her. But if Misty chose not to answer their calls, then all they could do was stand at the door and knock. Eventually, she thought, when enough time passed and her name changed drastically, her friends might not be able to find her anymore. Even if they looked, even if they wanted, Misty would be lost to them.

But still, she ignored them.

She turned away the barn and the trailer, the crows who lived in the dead trees down by the creek, the redbirds and bluebirds, the starlings and blackbirds, the killdeer with their thin, delicate legs. She turned away the rabbits burrowed under her trailer and the groundhog who lived under Earl's barn. She turned away the mice and the owls, the worms and centipedes.

Days passed, but eventually everything stopped trying.

Their voices fell away one by one until only one remained.

The garden came to Misty every morning and every night. She knew just by the knocking who it was. Three little raps that reminded Misty of a stone skipping across a pond—three jumps until it sank below the water and was gone.

And for nearly a week, Misty turned the garden away, too.

Misty tried on three outfits in a row, but none of them felt comfortable enough to play in. Every shirt felt too itchy or too tight. The waistband of her shorts dug into her belly, or the elastic was too loose and slipped over her hips. The fabric was wrong—too soft, too hot, too clingy. Static crackled her hair as she ripped off another T-shirt and flung it behind her, where it hit the bedsheet Penny had tacked to their ceiling.

"What're you doing?" Penny said. Her foot appeared under the sheet and kicked the shirt back to Misty's side of the room.

"Getting dressed."

"It sounds like you're fighting the clothes, not wearing them."

"Why do you care?" Misty asked.

"I don't."

Penny's feet disappeared back onto her bed and the room returned to silence. Misty grunted as she tore off a pair of pants that had been her favorite just a few weeks ago, but now made her skin feel sticky and hot.

But even without the clothes, her skin felt strange.

There was too much of her that touched the world, too much of her to find. Everything reminded her of her body, and her body reminded her of the barn. What she wanted was a new body—something smaller or lighter. A bird body or a snake body, any body, really, that was not her own.

She picked up the clothes that she'd worn the day before and put them on. The clothes didn't feel *good*, and they smelled like sweat and dust, but they still felt better than anything else, so she gave up and went outside.

Misty walked down to the creek. She didn't bother to roll up the hem of her shorts, but sank herself knee-deep in cold water. She searched for crawdads under the heavy stones, tipping them up, muddying the water. But every stone that she turned was empty. The crawdads had all been called from the creek by the garden. They were buried deep in the earth, digging.

Bells tinkled nearby. They were so faint and faraway that at first Misty forgot what the sound meant. Then she looked up and saw William standing on the hill. He held on to the old swinging bridge chain as he stumbled onto the sand. His shoes squelched as he walked toward her. Misty's mouth felt dry, her cheeks warm. She thought briefly of running, but her legs didn't seem to be hers anymore, her hands numb and faraway.

"What're you doing?" William asked.

"Playing."

"Can I help?"

Misty didn't say anything, so William walked past her. Water splashed onto his shirt, leaving dark stains behind. "You know, my cousins built a dam in their creek once. With rocks and stuff. They turned it into a swimming hole. I bet we could do the same thing here."

He bent down and cleared a spot beneath the water, then started stacking stones in place. Misty watched him for a while, then started to help. They worked together for an hour. William never mentioned what had happened in the barn. He acted as though nothing had changed, and Misty began to wonder if it had happened at all. If maybe she had imagined that evening, the press of William against her back, the weight in her chest. Maybe it had been someone else, some other boy in William's skin, someone meaner and heavier.

It would have been so much easier to believe that, so she tried. And she went on working as though they had only ever been like this, only ever friends.

Penny came by once to see what they were doing. She stood on the hill overlooking the creek with a little bag in her hand. Misty was sure the cards that Sam gave her would be inside. Penny had taken to playing in the woods by herself, casting cards, not coming home until almost dinner, looking tired and lost. "What're you doing?"

William dropped a stone in the water. "What's it look like we're doing? Long division?"

"Praising the Lord?" Misty said.

"Bass fishing?"

"Cooking your dinner?"

Penny peeled herself away. "Y'all are just a bunch of smart-mouth fools, you know that?"

William waited until Penny disappeared into the trees before he said, "Has she been extra sour to you lately or just to me?"

"She's been that way to everybody lately. Mom says it's part of growing up."

"I guess everybody turns into a jerk like Earl eventually."

Misty laughed.

"Hey, you want to play something else for a while? My hands is getting tired."

"Like what?"

"We could play Wolf," William said. He smiled.

Misty's stomach did a funny twist. She'd played the game with William before. Sometimes they pretended that they were being chased by a pack of wolves, and they had to come up with traps to keep themselves safe. Sometimes they took turns being the wolf, and the other one had to run, to hide, to stay alive.

"We'll play Wolf for a while and then we'll play something else. Whatever you want," William said. "I'll be the wolf first."

Misty opened her mouth to suggest something else, but William had already turned his back to her and closed his eyes. He started to count out loud, slowly, and then faster. He would chase her whether she ran or not, so Misty turned and ran through the creek, the water splashing against her thighs. She ran into the trees, searching for a place to hide, until William's voice cut through the air, calling her name.

Misty ran toward her trailer instead. If she was near her family, then she might be safe. Misty paused in her backyard, bending to inspect a cut on the bottom of her foot when she heard William crashing behind her. She ran through the front yard and around Earl's trailer, where more crawdad chimneys had appeared. The ground was damp with water and uneven around the chimneys, dipping and shifting as Misty ran around them. William was right behind her, his face bright red.

Without thinking, Misty ran into the barn. It was the only place left, and her legs were tired, and her foot was throbbing from the cut. William followed her inside.

"Wait," Misty said, a second before his hand touched her face. He hovered beside her for a moment before he kissed her, his mouth missing hers by an inch, so he tried again. He backed her toward the corner, their knees knocking together until Misty tripped and landed hard against the ground. William knelt in front of her. He didn't even try to close the barn doors.

He was quicker this time. Less afraid. Misty didn't have a chance to scramble to her feet before he was on top of her. His chest pressed against her stomach, and all the air rushed out of her lungs and refused to come back. Not even her breath wanted to be a part of this, every inch of her trying to escape as William shoved his hand

under the waistband of her shorts, the only pair she found that she
didn't mind wearing anymore. He yanked them to her knees.

"My cousin showed me this," he said.

He pressed one hand against Misty's arm to hold her still as she
tried to scoot closer to the wall. He held her in place as a rock dug
into the soft skin of her shoulder. William moved above her, talking
all the time, and when she didn't move, he moved her. Misty stared
to her side, looking for something to hold on to, something to speak
to. A couple of loose nails lay on the ground near her head so she
grabbed them and held them in her palm. Misty shouted for them
and the nails responded with their name. They had deep voices, grating and gray. They spoke pressure, spoke the hum of the earth a
hundred miles beneath. They swallowed darkness like air and Misty
swallowed, too. She followed the nails back until her bones felt like
long veins of oil buried deep beneath the mountains, felt herself not
bigger but wider, and she would be something else one day, something that the pressure of the earth made, forced into a new shape
that people would love to tear open and rip out, and the mountain
knew, and the mountain trembled.

When it was over, William took the nails from Misty's hand and
left her behind. She stayed in the barn long after he was gone.

She knew what she needed to do to leave, but she couldn't seem
to do it. She thought of the steps in her mind—stand up, pull up her
shorts, brush the leaves and dirt from her hair, make sure no one was
looking, walk through the door—but her body didn't listen. It felt
both empty and heavy at once. Both hers and not at once.

She sat up and scooted to the side until her back was against the
wall so she could see anyone who came through the door long before
they saw her. Loose bolts and screws littered the barn's floor, a rusted

tool bucket, the handle of a broom, a pile of deflated tires in one corner and a few busted rims in another. Any of these things—any one of them at all—would be nice to talk to. Any one of them could fill her with a story that wasn't her own.

Misty closed her eyes and tried to reach out to them.

She thought of the sheet hanging down the center of her bedroom, Penny's bare foot beneath it kicking her shirt, Penny's ankle, bloodied; the green bottle spinning on the floor of the barn; William's hand fumbling with her waistband—

Misty opened her eyes. Her heart pounded in her chest. She could feel the things around her now, could hear their still, small voices reaching out to her so she tried again.

Penny's bloodied ankles beneath the sheet; a crawdad's empty shell in her hand, the thin translucent skin, so light, so empty; her mother's shoulders speckled with rainwater; the fawn in the woods with blood on its hip; William's mouth on hers—

Misty dug the heels of her palms into her eyes.

More voices gathered near her. The barn tried to send her sunlight. The rims tried to send her warmth. The birds flew down from their trees and landed on the roof and they sent her wings, sent her sweeping and feathered and flying.

But it was just fragments. Misty needed a connection whole and bright, something strong enough to swallow all these feelings in her chest. She closed her eyes.

Green strings crisscrossing the ceiling in the trailer, swaying gently in the breeze; the smell of rainwater and fresh-cut grass; her mother rocking her as a child, begging her to sleep; William's hand on her hip; her father brushing her bangs over her eyes; the wind whipping her hair as she rode behind Jerry; Sam turning over the cards to read

Jamie's fortune; Penny's bloodied ankles beneath the sheet; William's chest against her chest, the weight of him pressing her down, down, down—

A sob broke from Misty's throat. She smacked her hands against her face, trying to chase the feeling away, to stop the tears.

The barn tried to help. So did the birds. They wanted to help make things better, but she had to let them in, and she couldn't. Misty didn't want to relive what had just happened. She didn't want any of them to see her that way, either. If they did, they might blame her, hate her, never speak to her again.

Misty couldn't stop the images from coming and she couldn't stand them, either, and she was caught in the middle with nowhere to go.

"It's okay."

The garden's voice was slick and soft, a deep, dark water rippling in Misty's mind.

"Don't hurt yourself," the garden said. "Please."

Misty pressed her hands against her face. She cried and cried until she didn't anymore. Until she couldn't anymore.

"There now," the garden said. "It's all right."

"No," Misty said. "It's—"

"I know," the garden said. "But you don't have to think about any bad things anymore. I don't need your whole name to talk to you. Just a part. Any part at all."

"But—"

"Hush, hush," the garden said. "You don't ever have to say your name again if you don't want to. Not never ever again. We can make our own names, me and you. I'll show you how. Dry your face now."

Misty wiped her face with the hem of her shirt and dried her damp hands on her shorts. She tucked her hair behind her ears.

"See," the garden said. "We're getting better already. We can choose our own names if we want. We don't have to have any part that we don't like. Doesn't that sound better?"

Misty hesitated. Not using her name would mean cutting herself off from her other friends—the barn, the crawdads, the trees. But if they knew what happened, they might leave her anyway. It seemed easier, somehow, to abandon them than to be abandoned by them.

"Yeah," Misty said. "Okay."

"Your mom is in her bedroom and Penny is napping. If you go to your room now, nobody will even notice. But you have to be quick, quick, all right?"

Misty pushed to her feet. The barn tilted a little in front of her, and her legs felt woozy and unsure. She stumbled forward until her body caught up and she slipped through the barn doors.

"There you are," the garden said. "See, we're just fine, you and me, you and me."

Misty crept through the front door and hurried into her room. She shoved all of her stuffed animals into the crack between her bed and the wall because she couldn't stand them looking at her. She curled on top of her quilt with her back to Penny. All of the other voices fell away— the barn and the birds and the trailer—until it was just Misty and the garden, and the garden stayed with her until she fell asleep.

Twenty-Five

Misty's mother propped the front door open with a chip of broken concrete. She tore the quilts from the windows until the whole house was filled with light. Rain dinged against their roof and the air that drifted through the door smelled fresh and cool. Her mother ignored the new statue in the garden, though Misty found it harder not to look. A bridge had grown there in the few hours between night and day, grew heavy and bronze, but it only grew partway. The bridge ended in the middle, right where it curved the highest. It stopped where it should have bent back toward the earth, like it didn't want to be a bridge at all, so it made itself impossible to walk. No one could ever cross it. There was nowhere to go except back to the garden.

The bridge was just like her. She'd tried to talk to the world after what happened, but it didn't work. Misty couldn't face her name so she'd never speak to the trailer again, to the birds or the barn. She'd never learn her family's names. She'd never know the sound of their voices inside her head. She was alone now, except for the garden, who curled like a shadow in the back of Misty's mind.

Above her, the green strings crisscrossed the ceiling, swaying gently. They caught hold of one another, snagged, loosed themselves again. Misty sat on the couch with a blanket wrapped around her shoulders while her mother stood in the kitchen, her arms sunk wrist deep in a bowl of ground beef and cracker crumbs and ketchup. The meat made a soft, slick sound as she kneaded it between her fingers.

The phone rang and her mother jumped. She rinsed her hands in the sink, picked up the phone, and said:

"Hello.

"No, no, I'm fine. Just making supper.

"They're all right. Stir-crazy from being cooped up from the rain.

"It's untelling.

"Oh. I thought Peanut was doing that. Idn't that his job?

"Well.

"I ain't mad. I just thought it'd be nice if the girls got to see you once in a while.

"Well.

"Be safe."

She let the phone clatter to the countertop. Misty pulled the quilt around her face like a shawl and waited for her mother to smile and call her Mary Magdalene, but her mother never looked up. Instead, she put the meat into a pan and poured more ketchup on top, then washed her hands with water so hot that it turned to steam on her skin. Her mother turned to walk toward the back door but stopped, her hands caught inside a dish towel. Her mouth had gone slack, her hands stilled, so it seemed for a moment that she had frozen in place.

"Mama?" Misty said.

"It's back." She stared at the space just above Misty's head. "I thought that if I opened everything up... With all this light, how could we even see it? I thought I could drown it in light."

She dropped the towel on the counter and slipped a roll of tape around her wrist. She clutched the waning roll of green yarn in her fist.

"Move, baby," she said.

Misty moved to the end of the hallway, her blanket trailing behind her like a long cape. Her mother's knee sank into the couch as she crawled across it to the green light, which darted out of sight as soon as she touched it.

"Did you see?" she said, almost laughing. "That's what it does. Just as I'm about to catch it, it moves away again. It's smart, Misty. It knows."

She taped the yarn down and turned, her eyes roving over the trailer, searching for the faintest hint of green. She found it above the kitchen window. She held the yarn in her hand, unspooling it as she walked, careful not to pull hard enough to loosen the tape from the wall. She connected the last point where she'd seen the light to the newest point, and just like before, the light wavered and wobbled and was gone.

Her mother laughed outright this time. "I'm so tired of this."

She chased the light from the window to the ceiling to the television stand. It landed on the carpet and on the recliner where Misty's father used to sit and on the handle of the front door. Their mother taped everything that it touched. She hunkered and shuffled as the web of green strings grew tighter and tighter. She crawled on her hands and knees through the kitchen to tape the light down as it hovered in the center of the floor. The yarn was quickly vanishing until she could hold it all in the center of her left hand, the right hand poised in front of her with a piece of tape, ready.

Their mother's skin was sheened with a bright layer of sweat, and all the muscles in her face were constricted, her shoulders pulled tight, her hands contorted, the knuckles bent like she was holding on to something that Misty couldn't see, something that she couldn't let go of, not now, not ever.

"Do you see it?" she asked.

Misty let the quilt fall from her shoulders. She leaned past a piece of green yarn to look into the living room. The wind picked up and sent the strings twisting and turning, pulling at the tape that bound them to the room.

"No," Misty said.

"It can't have just… I was getting closer." Their mother's shoulders slumped. "I don't understand. I thought…"

She looked at Misty and stopped. Her eyes widened until they seemed round as moons. They ate up too much space, those eyes, took in too much light. Misty could see the whole room reflected in them, hovering, like when her mother blinked, the whole world might disappear and take Misty with it. She took a step back.

"Mama?" Misty said.

"Don't move, baby."

The last of the yarn unfurled in her mother's hand as she bent over a low-hanging string and crawled to Misty. On her knees, they were almost the same height, and it was one of the few times Misty had looked at her mother this way. Her mother pressed the last bit of string to the center of Misty's chest. The green light hovered there, now as big as a silver dollar, the edges of it jittering and shaking like it was about to pull itself apart. The light shivered and then it went still. For a moment, it was a perfect green circle right in the middle of her, and then it was gone.

Misty's mother blinked. She grabbed Misty's shoulders and turned her around. Her hands roved over Misty's back, lifting the hem of her shirt and prodding her skin, her mother's fingers hot and clammy. She turned Misty back and pressed her palm to Misty's forehead, searching for a fever that wasn't there. Her eyes darted over Misty's face, her body, her hands, and when she found what she was looking for, she pulled Misty against her chest and hugged her for the longest time. Penny came out of their bedroom to ask about dinner, but she stopped when she saw them, and she stood by the door and watched them until the meatloaf started to burn.

Twenty-Six

Misty didn't recognize the sound of her father's truck pulling into their driveway that night until his door slammed shut, but by then his feet were already pounding up the steps and his fist was pounding on the door. She'd never heard her father knock before.

Penny stood in their bedroom doorway with a hand on either side of the frame. When Misty tried to step past her, Penny grabbed the hem of her shirt.

"Don't," she said.

"Why not?"

"Something's wrong," Penny said. "I saw it in the cards."

Misty looked at her sister. It had been more than a week since Penny tacked the sheet between them, but it felt much longer than that. It felt like Misty hadn't looked at her sister's face in months and that Penny had aged years in that time. There were dark circles under her eyes, and the beds of her fingernails were stained with dark-blue ink. Late at night, Misty had heard the sound of scribbling coming from Penny's side of the room.

"Are you okay?" Misty asked.

"I'm just tired," Penny said as their mother opened the door.

"Where are the—" Their father's voice cut through the silence like a thunderclap, but the question he'd meant to ask died as he saw the green strings taped to the walls. "Beth. What—what's going on?"

"We have to talk. Say hello to the girls and then come to the bedroom."

"Say hello? I'm not going to say anything until you tell me what this is. This is all about those statues?"

"There's been a light." Her arms had been crossed over her chest until then, but she let them go, splayed them at her sides like she was trying to convince their father that she wasn't something small anymore. "You haven't been here. You don't know what we've been dealing with."

"We agreed on that," he said. "Don't try to make me feel bad for something you said you wanted from the beginning. I want to see the girls."

Their mother stepped back. She collided with a half-dozen strings and her weight pulled them taut. The sound of the tape straining against the wall was faint, but it seemed louder in the quiet. It wouldn't be long before one of the pieces broke, but their mother didn't move, her back pressed against the strings like she needed the support.

Misty's father seemed bigger as he shut the door, bigger in front of their mother, bigger than the strings. He'd grown a beard since the last time Misty saw him and his face looked younger somehow than it had before.

"Hi, Daddy," Penny said.

"Hi, baby," he said. "I've missed you both."

Misty nodded but she didn't speak. Their father held out his hand like he was presenting them to their mother.

"Look at their faces, Beth. They're terrified," he said. "What's going on?"

"You haven't been here," she said.

"I'm here now. And this is going to end now, all right? You called me over. You said I had to come, and now I'm here and I'm fixing this. You hear me? All this, this bullshit with the strings. With them statues. It's over right now."

Then he seized a handful of strings above their mother's head and ripped them down. Their mother flinched as though he'd torn the strings from inside her chest. She stood perfectly still as their father stalked around the living room tearing down the rest of the strings. His legs tangled in what fell to the floor, and he kicked the strings off as he moved into the kitchen, rattling cabinets and knocking over the salt and pepper. The only sound in the room was the tape being torn away.

When he was satisfied that the strings had been removed, he walked into their mother's bedroom and came back with a metal baseball bat.

"What're you doing?" their mother said.

"I told you. I'm ending this."

"Girls, go back in your room, all right? Shut the door."

Their father slung the front door open and strode outside into the dark. Their mother followed.

"He's going to hit the statues," Penny said. There was laughter in her voice. "It won't work."

Misty and Penny walked from one doorway to the next, standing shoulder to shoulder. The air outside had cooled, but it was still humid and sticky. It clung to the backs of Misty's knees and her palm and the hollow behind her ear, all the little places that no one else seemed to notice but the heat. The garden knocked against Misty's mind, and she answered with a scrap of her name, but a scrap was enough for the garden.

"What's happening?" the garden asked.

"I don't know," Misty said. "Something bad."

So the garden stayed with Misty in her mind, like someone standing just beside her in the dark of an empty room. Penny grabbed Misty's hand as their father walked up to the green glass man, cocked back his arm, and swung.

Their mother's hands flew to her mouth, and she stopped in the middle of the yard. The only light in the bottom came from the sodium lamp over the barn, and it outlined everyone in orange— their mother narrowed to a thin line of fire at her shoulder, their father's face full of sunlight as he swung, and the green glass man glowing and shivering and not moving an inch.

The sound of the bat hitting the glass was almost like a church bell. High and bright, a single piercing note over and over and over again. After a few swings, Misty could almost feel the reverberation in the soles of her feet.

"He can't hurt them," the garden whispered. "Why do men think the only way to fix something is to hit it?"

Misty shook her head. Even if she could talk to her father now, if she could build a bridge between them, she wouldn't. His face was set in hard lines, his arms moving like pistons, pulling back the bat and swinging and swinging and swinging. Even if he heard Misty's voice in his head, it didn't feel like he would listen. She'd wanted so badly to speak to him for so long, but that feeling was changing. She had hurts of her own now, and the longer she looked at him, the less he seemed like the kind of person she could share them with.

Earl walked onto his front porch and stood with a beer in his hand. William came out behind him and the two looked like different versions of the same thing, like a timeline of growth and all William had to do was shoot up and out a few inches and he would be the one standing there instead of Earl. And even though William wasn't looking in her direction, Misty still took a step back, tried to hide. Her stomach ached and the garden swirled like a summer breeze along her throat and into her chest, warming her from the inside.

William tugged on Earl's shirt and said something. Earl rested his beer on the rail of the porch and walked back inside his trailer. The beer wobbled, tipped, fell onto the grass below. The porch rail was uneven. The more Misty looked, the more she noticed how Earl's trailer seemed to dip forward, like it was leaning toward the garden. There were dozens of crawdad chimneys strewn across his yard now, and the ground was beginning to sink as the crawdads dug the earth's insides out.

When her father's bat produced not so much as a dent on the green man's chest, he turned his attention to the golden hand. He swung for the wrist and then for each of the fingers one by one, but the hand never closed, never flinched, never wrenched itself from the earth to flee. It sang its own, deeper tone as the metal bat struck its palm over and over.

Earl came back with a gun in his hand. He checked the chamber, held it up, and fired a single shot into the air.

Penny closed the front door.

She led Misty back to their room and sat with her on the edge of her bed until the sound of their father's truck peeling out of the driveway and onto the road faded to a distant hum, then lost itself beneath the screech of the crickets. Until the front door of their trailer opened and closed again. Until their mother's sobs wrung themselves dry.

Twenty-Seven

If Misty could speak Penny's name, she thought it would sound like the pop of bubble gum blown too wide and thin and pink. The sticky, soft way it peeled from her cheeks after the bubble burst, how it tried to hold on to everything it touched. Penny would be a wind chime in a high wind, the desperate clinking of the metal, the bells jarred and humming, giving out not a song, but a cry, a warning that something was about to change. Cinnamon candy held in the well of a jaw, dissolving, cracking, gone. She'd be the squish of fingers through damp hair, the froth of shampoo, the scratch of fingernails against the soft tangle at the very nape of the neck, a knot of dark hair like reeds twisting at the bottom of a deep, green lake.

Penny sat beside her in the back seat of their mother's car. She had a notebook in her lap, and they passed the ink pen back and forth playing tic-tac-toe. When Penny won too many games in a row, she would suddenly start playing worse, her O's becoming too wide for their boxes, and Misty would win knowing that Penny had let her win, but was happy all the same.

When they pulled into Dolly's driveway, Penny pushed the notebook into her overnight bag. "I still don't see why I can't come."

"Because," their mother said. "I need some time with your sister."

Misty shrugged when Penny looked at her. She couldn't say anything with their mother there, but Misty had noticed a difference in their mother since the day the green light landed on her chest. A kind of desperate searching in her eyes every time she looked at Misty. She had come to their bedroom door three times a night since then and stood, silent as a shadow, just watching. Just making sure.

Penny sighed. "Well, I'm coming back when Dolly gets up tomorrow morning. First thing. I ain't sticking around to watch Charlene slather mayonnaise all over her fried bologna."

Penny skulked into Dolly's house without bothering to wave goodbye, but Dolly waved from the window, her hands dusted white with flour. Misty rarely went on trips with her mother alone because Penny was always there, Penny asking questions, Penny angling for ice cream or a toy at the store, and without her noise, the space between Misty and her mother felt wider, emptier.

Her mother gripped the wheel as Dolly shut the front door behind them. She said, "I think we need help."

"Okay," Misty said.

"I know this has been a hard summer for both you girls, but I wanted us to have a chance to talk. Just me and you. And then we're going to the prayer meeting. It's the best place I can think of for heavy hearts."

They were both silent during the rest of the drive down the long, twisting roads. They passed the old gas station with its windows boarded shut, and they passed Elder Mason standing at the mouth of his holler, staring up into the sky. Every day he woke and dressed and walked the three miles down to that same spot. He never accepted a ride, even when it was raining or snowing. He waited there until dusk, then turned and walked home again. No one knew exactly what he waited for, but Misty always felt sad when she saw him standing there with his wispy, graying hair and thin plaid shirt. She wanted to hand him something warm to drink and stand beside him so at least he wouldn't have to wait alone for one day.

Her mother's car rumbled as they drove, and sometimes the engine went quiet in the steepest curves and her mother whispered, "Come on, Betty," under her breath as the wheels evened out and they kept chugging along. The car was box-shaped and gray, and both rims were missing from the wheels on the right side. The fabric on the inside of the roof was starting to come loose. It billowed like a circus tent, caught the breeze from the open windows, and ruffled until their mother couldn't stand the sound. She'd brought thumbtacks from the kitchen and tacked the fabric in place, but the billows didn't go away—they just became smaller, stretching between the tacks. The car had a topography of its own, a special, hilly landscape that mirrored the one outside as though the two had spent so much time together that they were beginning to look alike.

The car had belonged to Misty's father once, and it still smelled like coal dust, and there was a bright-yellow sticker on the dashboard that read *CAUTION: HOT WORK AREA*. The engine had a particular whine to it after it had been driven for a while, a kind of high-pitched grind that was so fine and thin a sound that Misty could barely hear it some days, but she heard it on the drive and was comforted by it until Misty's mother pulled into the church parking lot and shut off the engine.

There were only a couple cars in the parking lot and almost twenty minutes before the prayer meeting started so they waited. The windshield fogged at the corners and then everywhere, completely, so the world outside disappeared. The engine ticked as it cooled, and for a while it was the only sound between them.

"I don't think I've ever brought you to a prayer meeting before, but it's a lot like church, except there's no preaching or singing. They'll have a prayer line. Brother Baker is here and Brother Daniels. He's from up Stinnett. Brother Cleveland is usually here. He's from Harlan."

Misty toyed with the handle of her umbrella.

"Do you—" Her mother faltered. "Is there anything you want to tell me before we go in? Anything you need me to know?"

Her mother's hands moved from her lap to the steering wheel and back again. She stared straight ahead through the foggy window, and before Misty could think of an answer, she was talking again.

"I know that you ain't been sleeping good lately. I check on you girls at night. I think one of the best things about being a mother is when you put your kids in bed. Not because they're not awake or because you want them gone, but because I can stand there in the doorway and say they are right there, and I know exactly where they will be, and I know the sound of them sleeping, and they will be okay until morning. Everything will be okay until morning."

Her mother's hand fluttered along the wheel. "I know that you ain't been eating much, either. I haven't said anything because girls change. It's hot and sometimes you lose your appetite. Your granny said that Aunt Jem made it by a whole summer just sucking the juice from honeysuckle blooms. Now, I don't know if I believe it or not—I sure don't remember Jem ever refusing a meal—but I guess what I'm saying is that I know sometimes you just don't want to eat. It's funny to be growing up, and it's fine, sometimes, to act different. Until it ain't fine anymore."

Her hands squeezed the wheel once, white-knuckled until they released and fell to her lap. "You know, I don't think my mama knew a thing about me when I was your age. She loved me. And she tried to raise us right, keep us fed and clothed, but it was hard and Daddy, well, your grandpa was a good grandpa but he wasn't much of a husband or a father to any of us. He drank a lot and he was gone a lot and Mom had enough on her hands. So as long as we weren't bleeding or screaming, she didn't ask many questions. And I didn't know anything about her until I was fully grown. I was pregnant with Penny before she told me that she had a tattoo."

"Granny had a tattoo?"

"Yep. A friend of hers did it. Right here." She touched Misty's shoulder with her finger. "They used an ink pen and a screwdriver or something else like that. I can't remember all the details. It was awful, though. Got infected and everything, said she thought she'd die from the pain, but she didn't. It was her initials before she got married. Peggy Ann Combs. Said she didn't ever want to forget. I wish I had known her better before she passed, and I wish she'd known me better, too. Did I ever tell you that me and your daddy are going to counseling down at the church?"

Misty shook her head, even though Penny had told her the truth days ago. She'd never heard her mother talk so much at once, and she was afraid that if she spoke up, the gates would shutter closed and her mother wouldn't speak again for a day at least, maybe never again.

"We've been going for months now. We decided that he would stay with your uncle Danny for the summer. Try to give us some space to think things through. Not forever. Just for a little while. It was my job to tell you girls about counseling and about how your dad wouldn't be staying with us. I wanted to right from the start but every time I looked at you and Penny…" She shook her head.

"And I don't know why they left it to me, neither. The preacher tells me that I'm your daddy's helpmate. He had me write it down one week and write out all the things I thought a good helpmate should be. He never asked your daddy to do that. He never asked your daddy what he could do to help me. And I called him last night so he could help me. I told him I was scared and I didn't know what to do about the statues and you girls, and I wanted him to come and help me figure it out. But he came and tore things down and that wasn't help. Not the kind I wanted."

Misty almost reached out to her mother, almost put her hand on her knee, but there was a kind of frantic energy around her, like all the green strings she'd hung on the walls of their trailer had connected something inside her and she had to let it out before she burst.

"And the thing is that most days I think everything will be okay. That everything *is* okay because one day all this suffering, all this pain will be over and I'll be given the first true rest of my life in Heaven. I'll be at peace. We all will. And my mom will be there, and she won't be angry anymore because all her burdens will be lifted. And my granny and Dolly and Jem and all of them will be as happy as they deserve. So it's easier to go along and to pray and believe that it's all worth something and that what I'm doing is right, even if it hurts, and the hurt proves it somehow. The hurt shows what I'm willing to do for God. But if you don't believe for sure in Heaven—if you're not completely sure all the time that it's worth it, then it's so much harder to keep going. It's so much harder."

Misty's mother stared out the window. Her breath fogged in front of her mouth, and a tear slipped down her cheek. She wiped it away absently.

"You know them clothes I brought to Jem's house? In the big bag? We gather things up for families that need them. Whatever we can do to help. This time it was a woman who left her husband. He wasn't a good husband and she needed to go, but she had to leave the state to be safe. We got her set up and sent her off in the dark of night. She's called already and we know she's okay. But she'll be wearing some of my old shirts wherever she goes. They'll be living this life I'll never see and sometimes…sometimes I just wonder…"

When her mother looked at Misty again, she jumped a little, like she'd forgotten that Misty was there or forgotten how small she was, how round her face, how dark her eyes.

Her mother said, "I shouldn't have told you all of that. See, there's a way to say too much when you're a mama, but I can't figure out exactly what's enough or what's too much, so I say too much and then feel bad and go back to saying nothing at all. Lord, Misty. I'm sorry, okay? I'm sorry for all of this, for me and your daddy both, but we're trying, and whatever it is that's been weighing on your heart this summer, I think tonight will help. This is what your granny would have done for me. 'Go to God,' she said, so we're going."

She took Misty's hand and gave it a tight squeeze.

"Come on," she said, wiping her eyes. "Let's get inside."

Most of the people attending the prayer meeting were older and sick. There was a whole row of people near the windows who were in wheelchairs or walkers. There were women with oxygen tubes wrapped behind their ears and one man with a blue hospital mask over his mouth whose cough sounded wet and rattling, like his lungs were filled with water and stone. One older man came over to Misty's pew and offered her a stick of gum. He offered her gum at every Wednesday night service, and Misty smiled as she took the silver foil from his hand. He smiled back and nodded, his face lined with wrinkles, his glasses smudged in the corners. His cane trembled as he walked a few rows down, stopping now and then to offer gum to the other children. Misty was unfolding the foil when her mother cleared her throat and held out her hand.

"I don't trust that man," her mother said. "He never got married. Always acted right quare. He lives alone at the top of that big, old hill, and he only ever gives gum to little girls."

Misty opened her mouth to tell her mother that she'd just seen him give a piece to a boy in another pew, but her mother narrowed her eyes and Misty sighed. She put the gum in her mother's hand, and her mother crumpled it up and dropped it in her purse. Men were supposed to be nice, but they couldn't be too nice or people would stop trusting them. They became quare, and quare didn't seem like a good thing to be. Misty wasn't sure at what place in the middle men were supposed to be, but it seemed a very narrow spot. She kept her eyes on the little old man as the preacher walked onto the pulpit and spread out his arms.

He said, "Thank you all for being here tonight. I know many of you have come from far away to get a touch from the Lord, and we're so glad that you could come. The Lord tells us in James that if any among us is sick to call on the elders of the church and ask them to anoint you in His name. We've got oil here that we've sent to churches all over the states, down as fur as Georgia and it's been prayed over by some of the best men I know, and they all believe that there is a healing in store for you. I say there is a *healing* in store for all of you who are weak and weary, burdened and ill, and whatever it is that you carry. We're going to help you carry it tonight."

He stomped his foot hard enough to make his glasses almost slip from his nose. He tipped back his chin just an inch, and when he spoke this time, he spoke in tongues.

Chills broke over Misty's arms, though it was not the first time she'd heard the preacher speak this way. The sound was unlike any other language, as though for God to speak through one of his faithful, he had to bend them first, to reshape their mouths to hold His name. The preacher's tongue became a round thing rolling across his teeth, and the words rolled with it. There seemed to be no space between the words at all, just one long sound connected. And the only reason the word ended at all is because it was in such a small body, such a worldly vessel.

In the mouth of God, the sound might never end, might go on and on and on, might tell and untell and retell the universe from beginning to end, unravel it and start again. Such force couldn't be contained in a preacher's body or in any body for long, lest their teeth be ground to dust inside their mouth and their body collapse under the weight of all they'd known. The preacher stomped again and the words stopped.

The preacher's nephew stood near the front. He was a tall boy, thin with curly, blond hair. He interpreted what the preacher had said as, "The Lord our God, our Father, He protects us."

"Bless him, Jesus," Misty's mother said.

"He is the Father," the preacher repeated, smiling. "What a wonderful message from our Lord tonight. Isn't it something the way He gives His gifts? One may speak with God while another is made to listen and understand. I can say the words, but I need young Joshua's help to hear them. I think there's a lesson to be learned in that, don't you?"

He walked from one end of the pulpit to the next, bouncing a little as he went. "The Lord knows how important community is. So he spreads his gifts across all His children to remind us that none of us can make it on our own. None of us can do it all alone. We need each other. And we're going to help each other tonight. Praise Jesus."

"Amen," Misty's mother said, and the church murmured back.

"Amen, amen," Brother Baker said. "We've got three Brothers here who will be glad to pray with you and anoint you in His loving name. If you can't come to the front, we'll come to you, don't worry. But we'll get started now. Come on up," he said. "Don't be afraid to take what the Lord has promised to His children."

A line formed, and then another, and then a third—one for each of the preachers standing by the altar. The preachers anointed their fingers with oil and rubbed the oil against the forehead of the person in front of them. The preachers held on to the ill, the grieving, the tired—sometimes grabbing their arm, sometimes their shoulder, sometimes pressing three fingers to the slick stain of oil on their skin and pushing back to emphasize their words and press the healing into them.

When the prayer was over, the healed sat by the altar or returned to their pews. Some cried. Some whispered different prayers beneath their breath and looked up at the ceiling with their eyes closed. Others stayed up front and lay their hands on new people with the preacher, multiplying the voices and the healing.

Misty stood in the first line beside her mother. Across the church, Penny's homeroom teacher, Miss Gail, was being prayed for in the third line. Her hands were clenched into tight little fists by her side. Her head tipped back and her eyes closed and the oil shone against her forehead. The overhead light glinted across the oil, and even though the light wasn't green or etched on glass, there was still something about it that made Misty feel uneasy. There were people standing all around Gail, praying, crowding her. The preacher held Gail's shoulder in his hand and another hand pressed against the small of her back and another rested along the nape of her neck.

Misty took a long, slow breath. She tugged her mother's hand. "Mom, I don't feel so good."

"What?"

"I don't feel good."

Her mother put her palm against Misty's forehead. "We're almost there, baby. Just hang on a few more minutes. We'll leave as soon as it's done."

Misty was still watching Miss Gail when Brother Baker pressed the tips of his fingers to her forehead. Misty's eyelashes fluttered. The oil on his fingers was cold and slick and heavy. She waited for it to drip into her eyes, but it didn't. The oil dried quickly, solidifying, changing against her skin, changing her skin.

"Lord bless this child," Brother Baker said.

Misty's mother wrapped her hands around Misty's shoulders, rooting her in place. Another woman moved to the right of Brother Baker, and Misty lost sight of Miss Gail. There was someone else on Misty's left side, and Misty was somewhere in the middle of all those bodies who were taller than her and bigger than her and they were all touching her. The weight of their hands pressed against Misty's forehead, her shoulders, her arms, the small of her back.

The people who weren't touching Misty held their hands up to God as they prayed for her. They prayed her peace and wellness; they prayed her out of temptation and suffering, for it was the smallest among them who would inherit the Kingdom of God. Her mother's hands trembled against Misty's shoulders, and Misty trembled with them. She tried to step back, but there was nowhere to go where someone else wasn't already holding her in place.

Misty closed her eyes, hoping it might be better if she couldn't see the people. But it was worse in the dark. Those hands could have been anyone's hands. They could have been William's hands and they were, all of them. William now and William a year from now and William grown into the shape of Earl and the shape of her father and William green and glinting and they wouldn't let go. They would never let go.

Someone shouted in tongues. Someone said "Amen" over and over and over again.

Misty started to cry.

She was still crying when the prayer ended and the people backed away, but their touch followed her. They rubbed small circles against her back and shoulders as her mother turned toward the door. Misty's breath hitched in her chest. She kept her eyes closed as her mother walked her through the church, as the car started and the floorboards shook. Outside, the trees were dark and slick with rain, and the headlights quivered through their branches.

"It's okay," her mother said. "I cried the first time, too. Everybody does. Just let it all out, baby. Ain't nothing to be ashamed of."

Misty cried harder, and harder still because maybe she couldn't stop. Now that she'd started, there would be no end. She would go on and on until her body emptied and wilted and shriveled and a strong wind would blow through the bottom and carry her across the mountains. She'd never come back down again, would become a cloud one day, would lose herself one drop of rain at a time until she was gone forever.

"Come on," her mother said when they pulled into the driveway.

Misty held her mother's hand as they walked inside. The lights were off, and they fumbled through the dark together. The strings still hung limp and green from the walls, and her mother yanked a few out of her way. She came back from the kitchen with a snack cake in her hand, the kind she used to pack in Misty's father's work lunch.

Misty clutched the plastic wrapper as they walked back to her bedroom. Her breath whistled through her nose as she breathed and she concentrated on that, on getting enough air to keep her moving. Penny's side of the room was empty since she was spending the night with Dolly. Misty's mother stroked her hair as she sniffled and trembled.

"Did it help?" she asked. "I swear, I thought it would help."

Misty didn't answer and her mother stayed with her until Misty closed her eyes and pretended to fall asleep. Her mother left the door cracked so a narrow beam of pale-yellow light fell from the kitchen onto the bedroom floor.

When her mother was gone and the house was quiet, Misty kicked the covers from her legs. She tried to blow her nose on an old T-shirt she found under her bed, but nothing moved. She couldn't breathe right, and she could still feel everybody's hands on her body. There was a weight, small and precise, on her shoulder, and another on her back, and another on her neck.

She rubbed her hand across her skin to chase the feeling away, but it persisted.

She was hot, almost fevered, but cold, too. She was tired, but wide awake, and being torn between these extremes meant that she was nothing at all, and that would be nice. It would be nice to be nothing. It would be nice not to have all this skin around her bones, its heaviness, its sweat, its dampness behind the knees and dryness between her fingers, its invitation to other people to be near it, to touch it. William was there, too, among all those strange hands. William was the brightest, hottest touch in the places that she wanted to feel the least.

It was all too much.

Misty wanted to scream, but she didn't. She couldn't without waking her mother, and she would bring her own hands and her own worried face and Misty didn't want to see her mother again right then.

So she called out to the garden instead, and the garden was there immediately, like it had been waiting for Misty to call.

"What's wrong?" it asked.

"I—I…" Misty didn't know how to finish the sentence.

"It's okay," the garden said. "I can help. I can. You just have to tell me what you want. What is it?"

A sob broke loose from her throat, and Misty bit down on her fist to keep the noise from growing. She stood up and her ankle caught on the box beneath her bed. The crawdad skins shuffled inside, the sound of them like sand falling between fingers. Misty bent down and opened the box. The skins were the pale color of early morning fog as it gathered at the tips of the trees. She ran her fingers over their ghostly skins.

"I want to be like this," Misty said. "Like the crawdads."

An image of a molting crawdad hovered between them.

"You can do that," the garden said. "It's your skin for the making and unmaking. Are you sure you want it gone?"

"I'm sure," Misty said. "I'm sure, I'm sure."

"Okay," the garden said. "There's just one way I know to make things listen. You have to rename them, like I did with the crawdads.

I learned that a long, long time ago." An image of Caroline flashed between them and was gone. "So you take a little of your name and you mix it with your skin's name. You put them together, so you can control it. Can you do that?"

"I guess," Misty said.

"Go on and try. I'll be right here."

Misty closed her eyes. If she could speak to her skin, she could tell it to leave. She could tell it the truth: that it was the problem here, it was what was wrong. If she could be free of it, just for a while, then she might be able to breathe again.

And if her skin had a name, it would be a skillet pressed to a bare hand. It would be a knee on a throat, a hand on a mouth, the last strained breath escaping. It would be a boulder, her skin, would be the mountain and everything beneath it.

Misty called out to her skin as she knew it—a knot tied in fraying rope, a skillet pressed to bare skin. Knee on throat, hand on mouth, a hiss of air between hot fingers. Boulder old and heavy, mountain old and heavier. Press and pressing.

Knee on throat, the fawn's bloody hip, fraying rope, a green light trembling on the wall.

Knotted hip, bloody rope, a green light trembling on her throat.

She spliced herself together until she could feel something beginning to change, a separation. She told her skin what she wanted. All the soft parts sifted from all the hard, because she didn't want anything on her that could be kneaded or molded or changed. She wanted a slick body, rigid and edged. She wanted a clean body, light and simple.

Her body resisted, at first. It knew what it was. It knew it belonged together and that together was all that it knew, but Misty insisted.

"You're doing it," the garden said excitedly.

She thought of her skin like a dress that didn't fit anymore and all she needed to do was reach the zipper in the back and release herself from this, her body.

"Almost there now," the garden said.

There was a looseness behind her ears every time she ran her fingers over her cheeks, so Misty pulled harder. She tugged at her skin. She kneaded her forehead. She pinched her earlobe between her fingers and yanked hard and thought of her skin's name, the one she had given it. And there, among her touches, something happened.

Misty pushed her fingers against her forehead, and her skin slid back and slipped away. She pressed her hand against her cheek, but this time she didn't feel skin.

She felt something hard and clean and cool.

She felt bone.

Misty walked to Penny's desk. She dug through her sister's black purse until she found a compact mirror. She flipped it open.

Her skin hung around her neck like a hood.

Her face wasn't where it used to be, her face a folded pile of flesh behind her, and there, looking back at her in the mirror was her skull—her white-boned skull glowing, faintly, in the darkness. Her jaw was there, and the two dark divots where her nose should be. Her eye sockets were round and empty and darker than the dark.

Misty pulled at her shoulder. Her skin slid down her neck, revealing more bone, more glistening whiteness.

She kept tugging and pulling, bending her elbows, shimmying her hips, until her skin fell to her feet with a sound like her mother's hands slicking through the meatloaf.

Her clothes came away with her skin, and Misty stepped out of herself.

The mirror revealed the joint of her shoulder and, when she turned, her spine.

She could still see, though it was not the sight she knew before. The colors had been replaced with black and white, everything a duller version of the skinned world. She could still smell, too, but only faintly, and every sound was muffled and distant, like she was hearing the world through a heavy fog. Everything felt further away from her than it ever had been before.

There was no pressure, either, not even when she put her thin-boned hand against the curve of her hip. She sat on the edge of her bed, but she couldn't feel the familiar softness of the quilt beneath her. She bounced up and down once, and her heels clacked against the floor.

She tried to laugh, but no sound came out. There was no tongue, no lungs to make the noise, so she was silent except for her bones clinking together. There was no garden in her head, either, no other voice, no voice at all.

Misty was alone, truly.

She bent and collected herself from the floor. Her skin was heavier than she ever expected it could be, but she lifted the weight easily. These bones had been holding it up for years, after all. They knew just how to hold her.

Misty laid her skin on her bed. She pulled the covers back and arranged herself carefully. Without her bones to hold her up, her limbs folded over themselves. They bunched and pinched and crooked, but she didn't deflate. She looked almost the same as she did before, full and round. What held her together now, she wasn't sure, and she didn't care, either, as long as she was outside herself. Still, she spent the longest time smoothing her body out until she was lying on her back with one arm slung over her head and one foot dangling off the edge of the bed.

She was a small, freckled thing. She was bruised and she was breathing, still, boneless as she was. Her chest rose and fell with the beat of her heart. She pressed her skull to her belly and heard the faint rumble of her insides, the music of her body, still moving. Her eyes were open, staring blank and brown at the ceiling until Misty closed them one by one.

She didn't feel sad looking at herself. She didn't feel lonely or angry. For the first time in a long time, she didn't feel afraid, either. She didn't feel anything at all.

Twenty-Eight

Misty slept until noon the next day, and when she woke her body felt sore and strange, as though when she'd pulled her skin back onto her bones she'd missed something. Her skin sat a little crooked on her frame and everything hurt—her knuckles puffy and tight, her heels pinching every time she took a step, and her eyes dry and gritty. She hadn't gone anywhere in her bone body the night before. She'd only wandered around her bedroom, picking things up, sliding them between her ribs, testing her new body's limitations. She'd thought about going outside, but Earl had taken to sleeping by the garden at night and Shannon usually came home after dark and there would be no way to explain herself if someone saw her. The worrying had been enough to keep her inside for one night, but the worry was wearing off in the light of day, and all she could think about was where she would go that night.

Misty shuffled into the kitchen to scavenge some cold biscuits, but there was no plate on the stove. The dishes from yesterday's dinner were still in the sink, their rims growing crusty. The clothes her mother had worn to the prayer meeting the night before lay in a pile by her bedroom door, which was shut, and no light peeked through from underneath.

"She didn't make breakfast," Penny said from the couch. "And we're out of cereal, too." She crunched loudly on her next bite of cereal to let Misty know that at least someone was eating that morning.

"When'd you get home?"

"Few minutes ago. Dolly dropped me off."

Misty squinted against the midday light pouring through the windows. The strings still hadn't been cleared from the walls so they hung limp and green. Something about them looked sad now that they weren't chasing the green light, like streamers the day after a birthday party.

"Do you think Mom's okay?" Misty asked.

Penny shrugged. "Where'd you all go last night?"

"Church."

"Why?"

"She thought I needed praying for."

"Did they lay hands on you?"

"Yeah."

"About time, honestly."

Misty rolled her eyes. "I'm going back to bed."

"Fine. You know, I think I'm finally going to ask Jem about staying with her. So I might be gone by the time you get up."

"About time, honestly," Misty said.

Later, in the bathroom, Misty peeled back her face and let it hang along her neck just to be sure that she could. It was her mouth that freed her, the lips stretched to a thin pink O around her skull, her mouth a dark cave from which she emerged, clean and white. From the side, it looked like she was trying to swallow herself whole.

The skinned parts of her were still capable of sensation. Her fingers rubbed the cotton of her shirt and knew its threads, but her skull couldn't hear the whispered rasp of her touch. When she skimmed her palm along the plate of her skull, her skin felt the cool smooth-ness of her bone and the little ridge where something joined her together, but the skull felt only pressure, only the weight of Misty's hand. Her teeth were still set firmly in her jaw, and their clack echoed across the bathroom as she opened and closed her mouth, like she had twenty jaws, all of them clicking, all of them hungry.

Misty snaked her hand, still plump with skin, through the hollows beneath her jaw until she reached her eye sockets. She wiggled her fingers back and forth like worms wriggling from the earth. She hung her mother's favorite pair of gold earrings along the shelf of her jaw, there where her ear should have been. She was tempted to slip her skin off entirely until Penny banged on the bathroom door and demanded to be let in.

The garden spoke to Misty that afternoon. It had overhead Earl talking about Revival and wanted to know if the church was really coming to see the statues. The garden seemed excited by the idea. It filled Misty's body with a buzzing, jolting energy that made Misty's head ache.

"I'm sorry," the garden said. "How are you feeling?"

"Tired," Misty said.

"It takes a lot to do what you did. To separate yourself. I know."

"Will anything bad happen now?" Misty asked.

The garden hesitated. "There are always consequences." An image of Caroline staggered through Misty's mind. She wore a dark dress that flashed in the moonlight, the hem covered in spiral stitches. Caroline ran between the trees and out of sight. "But I think the consequences are better than what you escape from. Don't you?"

All those hands on her skin. The feeling of never being alone, never being untouched. The weight of William on her chest, his face above hers. The images rifled one after the other and Misty couldn't stop them from coming, couldn't stop the garden from seeing what she saw. Misty shook her head and chased the images away.

"I can't go back," she said.

"I know." The garden's voice was sad. "Neither can I."

After dinner, Misty and Penny sat on the floor on either side of the sheet. Misty took out a small blue knapsack that she'd gotten during her first week in Brownie Scouts. The Scouts had disbanded a month later when the only mother willing to hold meetings at her house filed for divorce and the school didn't think she would be in the right frame of mind to lead a troop of young girls. Misty packed everything that she might need the next time she left the house, but everything she could think of would be useless without skin. She wouldn't get hungry or thirsty in her bone body; she wouldn't get cold no matter how cold the night became. She emptied the bag and hung it at the end of her bed.

Penny asked, "Are you sick?"

Misty leaned down and looked under the space beneath the sheet. Penny's legs dangled over her bed, the heels bouncing back and forth against the bedspring. She bent forward, probably about to check the same gap, so Misty leaned back before their eyes could meet.

"You've been acting funny," Penny said. "You were making noises in your sleep."

"No, I wasn't. When?"

"Earlier. When you took a nap."

"No, I wasn't."

"I heard you."

"Fine."

"Fine." A book closed on the other side of the sheet and landed on the floor. "I saw William today."

"So?"

"He was asking about you."

"What'd you tell him?"

"Nothing. Are you mad at him?"

"No," Misty said.

"Are you sure?"

"Why're you talking to me anyway? Ain't you still mad at me?"

"Yeah."

"Fine."

"Fine," Penny said.

Misty shoved to her feet and sat on the edge of her bed. The hem of her nightgown was frayed. It had been Penny's once, and somewhere along the way a hole was worn into the hem, then patched, then worn away again, and Misty rubbed her finger along it, wearing it bigger so her mother would have no choice but to buy Misty some clothes of her own instead of forcing her to shuffle through life in Penny's hand-me-downs.

"Are you sure you're not sick?" Penny asked.

"No," Misty said. "I'm just tired."

She waited until Penny was snoring before she slipped out of her skin and arranged her body on her bed. She pushed herself onto her right side so her back faced Penny. She slumped her body over a pillow and let her mouth dangle open a little. Not enough for anyone to notice that the teeth were missing, but enough to leave a small stain of drool on her pillow. She leaned back and looked at herself, still breathing. She pressed one bone finger to her own throat and felt her heart fluttering under her skin. Misty didn't look deflated or emptied without her bones, and unless her mother tried to pick her up and saw how her body sagged and draped, nobody would ever notice that she was gone.

She crept down the hallway and clicked through the kitchen to the back door. The green strings on the walls didn't make her feel sad as she passed them. Nothing made her feel sad anymore, not in her bones, not her mother or father or Penny or Caroline or William or the barn. All of it, everything, was so far away.

There were just her and her bones and all the places they could go. Everything would be different in this body—the creek, the yard, the road, her school. She wanted to take her bones to all her favorite places. They'd been concealed by her skin for so long, hidden away from light or air or water. It seemed only fair that they got a chance to see things now.

Misty's feet bones sank into the heavy sand at the bank of the creek as she walked toward the water. She left deep impressions behind, not of whole feet, not of girl feet, but of something else. Something strange and sharp, something that might have been bigger than Misty, with a dark beak and claws, and she walked back and forth leaving as many prints as she could.

She clinked her way across the stones on the bottom of the creek to the very center, the deepest dip where the water ran the fastest. She sunk herself into this darkest water. She wedged her hip bones into the silt and stirred a wave of mud that settled and cleared until she could see the white shining bones of her body beneath the surface.

The water made Misty a moving body filled with moving bodies—the sand sifted between all the small bones of her feet and the minnows congregated in her ribs, kissing their small, slick mouths to Misty's bones. They never knew that she was there, that she wasn't one of them. There were no crawdads that night. All of them had abandoned the creek for new water, deep water down under the earth of Misty's yard. Misty tried to call out to them, to call them home again, but nothing happened.

She tried for the minnows instead, but there was silence in her head, a kind of emptiness she'd never felt before. Her mind didn't crowd with the memory of the minnows, all their sights and sounds, their strong, insistent weight. She pressed her hand bones to the silt beneath her and felt only pressure, the vague sense of an ending that she could not pass, but no memories, no heat, no long and winding history. She ran her finger bones through the water and picked up a heavy stone and tugged at a clump of submerged grass bleached almost white by the water, but nothing reached back to her.

Had she been wearing her skin, she might have felt something like sadness. She might have wondered a little longer what it meant to be without her voice in this body, whether it was better or worse, but her bones didn't mind the change. They barely noticed at all.

A cottonmouth slithered out of the grassy hill behind her and onto the far bank of dark-gray shale. The snake didn't slow when it reached the water's edge. It didn't recognize that anything had changed because it belonged to both the land and the creek. The snake swam with its head peering out of the water. It flicked its skinny tongue at Misty, tasting the air. The snake watched her with small, black eyes, but Misty wasn't afraid.

There was nothing that a snake could do to a girl's bones.

There was nothing left on her that anyone could harm.

Misty pinched the snake's head between her fingers when it swam too close. She didn't let go even as it writhed and switched, not until she had seen as much of its small snake face as she wanted. Its scales were all dark gray to Misty's missing eyes, but when it opened its mouth, the snake's throat was a bright, shining white. If she could leave her own body, maybe she could slip her way inside another. The snake's mouth was not nearly big enough to fit her bones, but it might have been nice to slip into the snake's skin and feel the long, taut length of scales, to think of nothing but the next small thing darting in front of her, jaw hinging wide, belly full and tight. Misty opened her finger bones and the snake splashed into the water. It jerked fast toward the shore, rustling the tall grass as it escaped onto the land.

She didn't feel cold when she left the creek, but she dripped clear water that left dark stains on the ground behind her. Her bones bobbed up and down as she walked past her trailer. The yard was becoming more and more uneven. There were dozens of crawdad chimneys and more were appearing every day. The crawdads carried the earth away and the yard sank lower, too heavy now to support itself, like a chest without its ribs. Water pooled in little dips and hollows and splashed against Misty's anklebones, and she didn't know whether it was warm or cold, whether it smelled fresh or stale, and she didn't care, either.

The green glass man glinted as she passed the garden, and Misty stopped.

She noticed, for the first time, a thin crack running along the green glass man's chest. It was so thin and spidery that she almost lost sight of it even as she stood right in front of it. The crack snaked up and around his shoulder and disappeared.

Misty stepped back and looked up at the green glass man. His body reflected her body back to her like a strange mirror, and if she stood just so, their bodies almost matched—the white bones of her arms aligned with the green sweep of his arms, the curve of her hips slotted into the narrow green space above his legs, as if she completed him somehow, made him whole. Maybe he'd been waiting just for this, for Misty to step inside his body so he could take the bones she'd grown and use them as his own. All she had to do was slip through his glass like light through a window, and she'd never have to think or feel again. Everything would be gone. The green man would take care of it all.

Misty shook her little bone head.

She didn't want to see the world from inside the statue's chest, didn't want green and murky. She wanted her own body, hard and smooth, so she turned and left the green man standing in the garden alone.

Misty walked up the driveway and onto the single-lane road that ran the length of her holler. Already she was beginning to forget what was behind her, the glint of light off her bedroom window, the shape of the creek, the statues looming in the garden. Everything she might want lay ahead of her, not behind her, after all.

Misty's feet bones skittered across the pavement as she walked. The feeling reverberated through her shinbones and her hip bones until her jaw clattered up and down, shaking like a new tongue with a new song.

Her holler was not very big. The road ran in a straight line past Misty's trailer before it met a fork in the road. To the right, the road became a bridge that crossed the creek and joined the main road, which could take her almost anywhere if she walked it long enough. To the left, the road was unpaved, the dirt rutted with worn tire tracks. There was an oil well at the end of the road, and another further on, along a path that was so guttered and worn that it had to be reached by four-wheelers if at all.

She took the right path out of habit more than anything else. She sat on the edge of the bridge and let her feet dangle over the side. The moonlight sifted through her ribs and cast a small, dark shadow on the creek below. Cars passed by on the road, their headlights illuminating Misty's bones, making them glow temporarily. She wasn't sure how long she sat there, watching the water trickle in the creek, but the sky was beginning to lighten when she stood and walked to the edge of the road.

She'd never gone beyond this spot on her own. If she turned right, she would be walking toward her school. Left would take her to her aunts' houses and toward town. She paused there, waiting for fear to find her and drive her back home. She was always afraid—of the dark, of being alone, of saying something wrong.

Bone Misty wasn't afraid of the road or the cars that might pass or who might see, but there was still enough of her old self there to keep her from taking that one last step.

At least for now.

Back in her room, Misty unfolded her body. It had slipped while she was gone, the neck bent at an unnatural angle, like she was trying to crawl into her own chest. She grasped either side of her mouth in her bone hands and let the rest of her body dangle between her knees. She was heavy and hard to hold. She kept sliding, wanting to puddle on the floor. Her eyelids fell open and stared, blank and brown, at the sheet hanging down the middle of her room.

Misty stretched her mouth open and wiggled her feet inside.

She let her skin swallow her bones a little at a time.

The sensation was faintly warm and her bones slicked as they met her skin, things rearranged, brushing past each other, accommodating.

She made it to the hips before she noticed something different.

The skin was tighter than it was before. It didn't slide the right way, swift and easy like pulling on a sock. Misty let the skin fall a couple of inches and tried again, pulling gently, and then pulling harder, but both ways gave the same result—no movement, no whole body, just her skin bunched and heavy in her hands.

Somehow, in the few hours she'd been separated, her bones had grown but her skin had stayed the same.

She didn't match anymore.

Misty leaned back on her bed and levered her hips toward the ceiling. Her mother had done this before when she tried to squeeze into a pair of old jeans from high school. The jeans looked almost as small as some of Penny's, and it was hard to believe that their mother had ever had a shape different from the one she had now. Misty wiggled her hip bones back and forth as she pulled her skin, urging them together, begging them to remember each other.

There was a faint pop as something gave. Her skin slid over hips.

She finished the rest as quick as she could before her body decided that it liked itself better alone. It didn't need bones after all. It liked the deep dark nothing that Misty left behind, and it didn't care if she ever came back. Misty pushed her face over her skull and the pain came with it, throbbing in her hips, burning in her shoulders, all her joints filled with needles and knives, the fiery, persistent ache of being born.

Twenty-Nine

Misty could feel every inch of skin on her body the next morning, and every inch hurt. Every inch ached or burned or bruised every time that she moved so she lay very, very still on her bed.

But it still didn't help.

The pain crept into her forehead. It settled between her eyes and spread behind her ears. Her knuckles hurt and the soles of her feet and the little place where her jaw connected beneath her ear. Acid bubbled in her stomach and soured her throat. She ran her tongue over her teeth, which were fuzzy and soft feeling, and her whole mouth tasted brittle and brown as dry leaves. The sheets on her bed smelled like earth and skin and sweat and fabric softener. Her pillow had a harder scent, an older, unwashed smell, like the nape of Misty's neck after she'd spent the day outside. Her feet scratched against the sheets as she kicked the covers down so she could feel the air on her skin, something light and empty.

But at least this pain was certain. At least this pain was clear. Gone, momentarily, was the dense fog of what had happened in the barn and the long days that followed. Gone the stomachache of what it all meant. At least for a little while.

"You have to get up," Penny said for the third time. "We're leaving for Dolly's in a few minutes."

Her shadow darted back and forth along her side of the room, picking things up and slamming them down again, and every sound throbbed behind Misty's eyes.

Penny said, "If you don't get up soon, Mom's going to come in here herself. I told her you was playing, but I don't think she believed me. I don't know why I was lying for you anyway, except I think you might be sick or something. But if you're sick, then I should tell Mom."

"I'm not sick," Misty said.

"Then what are you?"

"Tired."

"You're always tired."

"Well, leave me alone then and I won't be so tired."

"Something ain't right with you," Penny said. "It ain't been for a while now. You think I don't notice things but I do."

"I'm fine."

"Fine," Penny said. "Be like that. But I'm not going to cover for you again, you hear me? I won't do it. Now you can either get up and get dressed or lay there and rot for all I care but I'm going to Dolly's."

The door clicked behind Penny, and the air rippled across the sheet.

Misty rolled onto her side and covered her face with her pillow. She felt a tentative knock on the back of her mind, and she reached out to the garden.

"I saw you last night," it said, "in your little white bones."

Misty smiled. "I went out for a while."

"You should be careful. You might scare someone if they see you out." An image of Earl drifted from the garden's direction. "Some people might not be so understanding."

"I tried to be careful."

"How are you feeling today?"

"Sore," Misty said. She explained how her skin hadn't fit when she tried to get back in, how she'd had to struggle to return to her body. "Why do you think that happened?"

"I don't know," the garden said. "What we do isn't... It isn't normal. It's not the way names usually work. So strange things can happen."

Caroline appeared in the garden's thoughts. She stood in front of a tree and whispered something to it, her lips pressed tight to its bark until her skin scraped and bled. She dug her fingers into the tree's trunk until it looked like the tree started to give, like her fingers were sinking underneath. The image fractured and disappeared.

"That was Caroline," Misty said. "Wasn't it?"

"Yes."

"Can I ask you something about her?"

The garden didn't answer.

"It's just... I thought that maybe you'd seen what happened to her. Back when Earl hurt her. And maybe that's why you forgot your name."

"Something like that."

"Is that why you don't like to talk about her?"

"I don't like to talk about her because it's her fault," the garden said, its voice rising in Misty's head until she had to squint just to bear the noise. "She was a foolish woman. She got herself hurt and me hurt, and it's her fault that things are this way. Nobody ever liked her. Did you know that? Nobody at all."

"But what did she do?"

More images surged through the garden. The branches of a dogwood tree heavy with bloom, a man's voice in the distance, a feeling in her arms like she was being ripped apart, pain bursting through her chest until Misty almost screamed.

The garden's leaving was like a door slamming shut in Misty's chest. Her head throbbed with every beat of her heart, and it hurt to breathe too deeply. From the next room, her mother called her name and told her it was time to go.

Dolly's house was a fifteen-minute drive from Misty's trailer. It wasn't a long trip, but there was something about the mountains that made it seem much longer. There was so much more than just distance between them. There were thousands of trees and brambles and vines, endless pounds of kudzu, countless dips and hollows and bumps. There were a dozen hollers between Misty's and her aunts, and each of them had families and creeks and pets and people of their own. And every one between them added to the weight and the distance so that going to Dolly's house felt like a great journey.

It didn't help that their mother never drove above thirty miles per hour.

"We need out of the house. It'll be good for us." Their mother smiled through the rearview mirror at Misty and Penny as she talked, but her hands couldn't be still. It was always her hands that gave her away, like all her nerves and worries retreated there when the world became too much. They buzzed in their mother's palms until the fingers had to move. So she cleaned or straightened or weeded or shoveled or mended. She found places where the house was falling apart or not even falling, but just leaning a little too far to one side, and she fixed it. Every time, she fixed it.

Dolly and Jem were already in the garden when they arrived. They wore loose T-shirts and ankle-length denim skirts, just like

Misty's mother, with their hair pulled into high ponytails that swung as they turned to wave.

Their garden was much bigger than Earl's. It covered a whole hill that had been tilled many years before by Misty's great-grandfather. The garden wasn't flat, exactly, but it was flatter than any other ground nearby. The soil had been worked for decades and was darker and richer for it. There were a dozen rows of corn and three long rows of potatoes, half-runner beans and tomatoes and one lonely eggplant at the end, which had been Jem's idea.

"Eggplant," Dolly said, toeing the green leaves with her tennis shoe. "Have you ever heard of such a thing?"

"Everybody's heard of it except you, you old Philistine." Jem adjusted the leaf that Dolly had touched as though she might transfer some of her ill will into the plant and tomorrow they would wake up to find it shriveled and dark.

Dolly frowned. "I don't know how it growed this fast. You only planted it a week ago, and now look at it."

"Some of us just have that special touch." Jem winked at Misty.

"Well, I still think it looks obscene," Dolly said. "Reminds me of Ned Hacker's nose. You remember him?"

"The woodworking teacher?" Misty's mother asked.

"That's the one," Dolly said. "I hated that man. He was always squinting at me in the lunch line."

"He knew you was stealing milk," Jem said. "And say what you want about the man's nose, but he always smelled right. Like Old Spice. That's how a man's supposed to smell. Like a cold morning. Something to smack you in the face and wake you up."

"What do you know about the right kind of man," Dolly said, laughing. "You couldn't even hold on to the one that you had."

Jem's expression tightened. "You know, that'd bother me more if he'd been worth holding on to."

Misty's mother cupped Jem's elbow and Jem turned so no one could see the look on her face and Dolly rolled her eyes and the moment was over as quickly as it had begun. Still, Misty could feel that something had happened, the air sparking and humming around her aunts, but she couldn't be sure exactly what it meant. She could only watch the space widen between Dolly and Jem as Jem walked down the row of beans, tearing off stray leaves that had yellowed and dried and some that were still fresh and green.

Dolly squeezed Misty's shoulder so tight that Misty almost cried, her body still sore from the long night it had lain empty on her bed, but she closed her eyes and bore the touch because Dolly's hand was also warm and worn in all the best ways. Dolly leaned down and pressed a kiss to the top of Misty's head.

"I've sure missed you girls. You can go and dig some new potatoes if you want. Whatever you get, we'll cook up tonight. We'll ask Jem to fry us some of that chicken, too. Lord knows it's one of the only things the old girl does right."

"I'll show you how right my aim is in a minute." Jem pointed the sharp end of her hoe in Dolly's direction.

Misty walked toward the lower half of the garden, which was closer to the creek and to the shade of a long line of maple trees. The dirt was stiff and dry. It crumbled under Misty's feet, the earth shifting so she couldn't walk straight or easily. Her stomach ached as she tensed to steady herself. She stumbled past a mound of earth seething with little red ants and plopped onto a patch of shade at the edge of the garden.

She had missed her family. She didn't know how much until she saw them again, standing all three together—Jem and Dolly and her mother. The shape of them was so near the same as they bent their backs toward the earth or squatted in front of the beans. Their hands were deft and quick. They carried five-gallon buckets everywhere they went, squatting on the white rims or leaning their stomachs against them for balance as they worked. The beans fell with a hollow thump into the bottom and then with no sound at all as the buckets grew fuller and fuller. When they were finished with one task, they would carry the buckets to the bed of Jem's truck, turn back, and start again.

They talked as they worked, almost without ceasing, but there was quiet, too, long stretches of nothing but the slide of the dirt beneath their feet and the rustle of leaves. Misty felt a deep content-edness sweep over her just looking at the garden, but it was hard to be happy when her body hurt so much, and when the world was still so loud. The birds were calling overhead and there was a cicada somewhere, whirring and whining, its voice a high-pitched keen that worked against Misty's head like a saw.

Penny dropped the head of a hoe beside Misty. The metal piece had been pried from its handle so only the flat spade was left with a little piece of metal where Misty could wrap her hand. Penny had another of her own, taken from the back of Jem's truck. The women gave these to the children when they wanted to help because even now their limbs were too short to hold a hoe properly. It was easier this way, to give them less to control.

"They're talking about the statues," Penny said.

"What are they saying?"

"Not much. Just a bunch of 'good Lord' and 'I'll be.' Mom's tell-ing them that she thinks something's wrong with them. That you and me ain't been acting right lately. Especially you."

"Did she really say that?"

Penny shrugged. She dug carefully into the small trench where the potatoes were hidden underground. She had always been the best at this, the most patient. She coaxed a small potato out of the dirt and into her palm. She rolled it back and forth, blowing the dust from its mottled skin.

"Do you hear that bug?" Misty looked around.

"Which one?" Penny asked. "And you know what else there is? There's all the crawdads in the yard. And Mom said that the statues are starting to change. There's cracks in all of them now. I asked her if it was because of Dad hitting them with the bat, but she said she saw the cracks before that."

"I saw them, too," Misty said. "In the green glass man."

"You know what I think?"

"Not much," Misty said.

Penny stuck out her tongue. "I'm trying to be serious."

"Fine. What do you think?" She covered one ear with her hand to block out the drilling whine of the cicada. It seemed to help for a moment, but then the sound amplified and changed directions, coming from overhead.

"I think the statues is poison," Penny said. "I think they must have done something to the air. They're probably doing something to the water, too, since they grow right there in the ground. I think that's why you been acting so sick lately. Because they got to you, too."

"If they're poison, then why ain't you sick?" Misty asked.

"I don't know. Maybe I'm stronger than you. I never get colds as much as you, and I never had one ear infection when we was little. All you did was cry. Mom says it herself."

"So it's just me that's dying then?"

"I never said you was dying." Penny dropped three more potatoes into the bucket and turned to Misty. "Do you think you're dying?"

Misty sighed. "No."

Penny went back to working, the quiet *chh-chh-chh* of her hoe parting the earth, and the pop of the beans from their vine as their mother and aunts walked down a long row of half-runners. Misty kept looking for the cicada overhead, squinting against the sunlight filtering through the leaves, but she saw nothing but green and gold. She closed her eyes and tried to reach out for it. Some of them spent years underground, sleeping, and their names were filled with dream language, strange and twisting, like a whole other world that the cicadas knew, a whole separate life they lived before they lived. She'd spoken to them before in clips and whispers, little conversations about the taste of the earth and the way it felt to disappear, but she didn't know any of them very well, and they didn't trust her now. They shied away from her calling because she wasn't sharing her name. The cicadas didn't want to speak to her without it.

So Misty tried what the garden had taught her. She took part of her name and she took the name she knew for bugs in general—not just cicadas but anything like them—and she joined them together in her mind. It felt different this time, but she kept trying. She asked them to stop their noisemaking, to stop, just for a little while, so her head might ease its aching, so she might be able to close her eyes and rest beneath the trees. She just wanted some quiet.

For a moment, nothing happened.

Then Penny screamed.

Misty startled, falling back onto her elbows. Penny jumped to her feet. She stared down at the ground with her face contorted.

"What is it?" Jem yelled.

"A bug!" Penny said. "I think it's dead."

Something landed on Misty's shoulder, and she turned her head slowly. A great black-shelled beetle was tangled in her hair. Its body was stiff and unmoving, but Misty couldn't help but smack it away.

There was another soft smack, and another as bugs poured from the trees.

Beetles of all shapes and colors, cockroaches with their wings rustling in flight, dog ticks, centipedes, ladybugs and assassins, spiders by the dozens—yellow spiders and black, spiders with long, thin legs and with squat heavy bodies, their bellies thick with eggs. All of them fell from the trees around the garden and from the cornstalks and the vines. They landed on Penny's shoulders and at Misty's feet, and Penny screamed for their mother as Misty turned and vomited. Her stomach was like a fist punching through her, and what came out was hot and yellow and thin. What came out of her felt exactly like she did.

"Oh Lord, Misty. Beth, it's Misty," Dolly said.

All three of the women came high-stepping in her direction, but it was Jem that reached her first. Jem scooped Misty's hair away from her neck and held it. One damp strand stuck to her chest, and she smelled what the inside of her smelled like. Her stomach rolled again, but Misty could only cough this time.

"Was it the heat, you think?" Jem asked. "Or the bugs. Good Lord, what has happened to these bugs?"

Misty started to cry. Her mother lifted her onto her shoulder, and Misty wrapped her legs around her mother's waist without thinking, some old instinct from the days she had reached for her mother most often, the days when her mother had always been there. She carried Misty across the garden with one hand held tight to Misty's head.

"It's okay," her mother whispered. "Everything's okay."

Penny followed, close enough that Misty could see the faint speckles of dirt on her sister's cheeks like freckles. She jumped and whipped her hand through the air occasionally as she felt the ghost of a bug land on her, but she held on to Misty's hand, too, even as their mother dumped Misty into the back seat of their car. Outside, the sound of the whining had stopped, every sound had stopped until the car engine rumbled to life and carried Misty away.

Thirty

Dolly lived in a shotgun house that had been built by Misty's great-grandfather. Rooms had been added onto the house over the years, and the porch had been boarded up to make a nursery when Charlene was born. For the longest time, weeds still sprouted between the floorboards. Dolly would stomp them down, shove them into the cracks, until finally they sealed all the holes and insulated the floor. A bathroom was added onto the living room and a sewing room onto Dolly's bedroom, though it had become more of storage closet, packed with boxes and old toys, musty church clothes slung across Sam's discarded twin bed.

The floor was dark-brown linoleum and, in the winter, covered with rugs to keep their toes warm, although the rugs had been shed for summer and all the old scuff marks and scars were visible on the floor. The furniture was a mix of hand-me-downs from Dolly's mother and her husband's family. There were three couches in the living room, none of which matched, a large television in the corner, and shelves for Dolly's porcelain figurines.

Misty's mother carried her inside and put her in a cool shower while her aunts cooked. Her mother sat on the toilet while Penny lingered in the doorway, fetching towels, clean socks, a glass of apple juice—whatever Misty asked for.

Before long, Misty was dried and dressed in her favorite purple pajamas, sitting on a pile of blankets in the living room. Her cousin Charlene stared at her from the other end of the couch.

"What happened to you?" Charlene asked.

"I got sick," Misty said.

"What kind of sick?"

"Puking sick."

"Is it catching?"

"I don't reckon."

"Are you sure?"

Misty shrugged.

Dolly's older child, Sam, walked in from the kitchen and leaned his hip against the couch. His long hair was tucked into a baseball cap. "Just be glad whatever you got ain't catching, Char. The rest of us sure are thankful."

Charlene stuck her tongue out and chose a seat on a different couch. Sam took her spot, sitting with his legs folded beneath him.

"What's a matter with you, Little Bit?" Sam asked.

"Not feeling good."

"Mom's got some ice cream sandwiches hid in the back of the freezer. You want me to steal you one before I go?"

"That might help," Misty said. "Or you could take me with you."

"You don't want to be where I'm going, especially with a belly-ache. Some friends of mine are going night riding up on Four Seam. Jerry and Jamie are coming with me. Danny Turner said he'd let me drive his four-wheeler."

"Just be careful."

"I will."

Jamie and Jerry came through the door a minute later. They all stopped to check on Misty, teasing her, ruffling her hair before they left with a plate of food each.

Penny hovered around Misty most of the evening. She even packed Misty's plate to overflowing with fried chicken, boiled new potatoes so tender they fell apart on her plate, half-runner beans slick with oil, and a chunk of corn bread dripping with butter. Everyone watched Misty take small, deliberate bites. Even when they were tending to their own plates, they still looked to her from the corner of their eyes, offering to get her refills or a fresh paper towel or asking if she needed another pillow.

It was just like the way everyone had gathered near her when she cried at Jem's house. Again Misty found herself hurt, and again everyone was kinder than they had ever been. She didn't understand why it had to be this way. Maybe she could tell her father about William and the barn, about the hardest, strangest hurt she'd ever known, and it might be the thing that would bring him back, would bind them, forever, as a family. A hurt so great that he couldn't ever leave her again.

But she couldn't bring herself to talk about it.

She wasn't even sure her family could help her anymore. And even if they could, she was tired of being the one who was hurt and in need of help.

When the plates were cleared, her mother and aunts went to the front porch to tend to the day's harvest. They moved Misty's blankets and pillows onto the porch swing so she could sit with them while they worked. Penny and Charlene played with Charlene's pet turtle, a squat little thing with a crack in its shell and a heart painted over it with pink nail polish. They tried to force lettuce into its retreating mouth until they lost interest and played in the yard instead, chasing lightning bugs back and forth through the tall grass.

Misty's mother broke beans while her aunts shucked corn. Her mother held the beans four at a time in one hand, pulling their strings from top to bottom and back again, then breaking them into four pieces that fell into the bucket at her feet. Misty could time the sound of the beans hitting each other with her own heartbeat, until the two were entwined.

Dolly said, "Did I tell y'all Billy Ray Sizemore came by here the other evening? Right about suppertime and I hear that old Thunderbird of his come wheezing up the road. Handing out campaign flyers."

Jem snorted. "The man can't do his job but he sure likes to keep it."

"He brought a load of gravel to us last summer," Misty's mother said.

"Well, it's good to know he did something for somebody." Jem pointed at her with a cob of corn, half-stripped, the yellow kernels glowing in the dim light of evening. "He's been promising us he'd get somebody to mow the sides of the road since March. I about hit Dolly coming around the curve there at the mouth of the holler. I couldn't see her coming."

"Oh, come on, now," Misty's mother said. "Dolly drives this road like it's a roller coaster. Always has."

"She did wreck Daddy's truck that one winter," Jem said.

"And his hatchback the summer before," Misty's mother said.

"You know, now that I think about it, Dolly, you was probably the reason we was so poor." Jem bopped Dolly's knee with her ear of corn. "If you didn't drive as sloppy as you put on lipstick, then we might have been able to afford a few things."

"Like a harness for that mouth of yours," Dolly said. "Y'all just making this mess up. It was Mom that wrecked the hatchback, and I didn't so much as wreck that truck as be the one unfortunate enough to be driving it when the poor thing finally fell apart. The steering wheel was held together with rubber bands, for God's sake."

"We had to start it with a screwdriver. And it never did have a heater that worked," Jem said.

"You didn't need a heater when the suspension was broke. That thing bounced us up and down so hard driving to church that the friction kept us warm," Misty's mother said.

They all tipped their heads back and laughed. When they quieted, Dolly shook her head and said, "I still don't remember wrecking that car."

"Well, that's too bad," Jem said. "None of us belongs only to ourselves. We don't always get to decide who we are, and you, sweet sister, are a menace."

The chairs creaked as the women rocked back and forth. Misty pressed her foot against the porch railing to set herself swinging, crooked, side to side. She tucked her blanket under her chin and winked at her mother when her mother winked at her. The air was cool and the crickets were singing, the bullfrogs croaking down by the creek. There was no garden in sight except for the one growing corn and beans, not glittering, gleaming statues. There was no barn except Dolly's, which was full of old tractor parts and a run-down Ford her husband kept promising to bring back to life. All the bugs were where they were supposed to be, all of them still living. Misty hadn't meant to hurt them earlier. She'd only wanted some quiet. A little rest. But the garden said that joining names wasn't normal. There would be consequences, like Misty's skin growing too tight. Misty wondered what might happen to the crawdads if the garden didn't release them soon. Somewhere, in the distance, a whippoorwill called three times in a row, paused, called again.

"Do y'all remember Caroline Lewis?" Misty's mother asked.

Dolly laid her hands in her lap and frowned. "Earl's wife?"

"Yeah, but before that. Do you remember anything else about her?"

"What's got you thinking about her?" Dolly asked.

Misty's mother shook her head. "I don't know. I've just had her on my mind lately. I keep trying to remember what she was like before."

"Well, she was a little older than us," Jem said. "I only saw her every now and then. She used to spend a lot of time down by the creek near y'all's trailer, Beth. Long before Earl ever bought that land."

"She always walked to school, too," Dolly added. "Never would take a ride from anybody even when they offered, not that anybody offered that often."

"And she used to sew those patterns on her clothes, remember?" Misty's mother held her finger to the air and traced a circle round and round. "Little swirls. She'd sew them right there in class on the skirt she was wearing. Purple and red and green. I always thought she was brave for picking colors like that. They only made her stand out more."

Misty thought of the dress she'd seen in the garden's memories, the one with swirls sewn along the hem.

"And she sang a lot," Dolly said. "Under her breath, all the time, singing. I had to stay after school once when I got caught skipping class and Caroline was there for something else. Singing to herself the whole time and never a whole song. She'd start with some Lynyrd Skynyrd and switch to 'Prayer Bells of Heaven' partway through and then finish with something else. It about drove me crazy so I finally asked her why she did that. She said, and I'll never forget this part because I got chills all up and down my arms when she answered. She said, 'It helps keep the noises out.'"

Jem nodded as though she understood. Misty's mother ran her

fingers back and forth over the thin strings she'd stripped from the beans, gathering them in the center of her lap and then casting them apart again.

"I had forgotten all about that until now." Dolly shivered. "I guess I try not to think about her. I always end up feeling guilty."

"Why?" Misty's mother asked.

"I don't know. I always think maybe I could have done something to help her. Befriend her. She seemed so lonely all the time. Always by herself. And then she ended up with Earl, and then she ended up gone."

"He did it," Jem said. "I don't care what the sheriff could or couldn't prove. No body don't mean no crime. Especially in this county."

The three women fell silent and Misty closed her eyes. The garden had told her that everyone hated Caroline, but that didn't seem true. Her mother didn't hate her, and neither did her aunts. They'd felt sorry for her and what happened.

Then why did the garden hate Caroline so much?

Misty had thought that the garden had seen what happened to Caroline, that maybe it had been there on the night she disappeared, but maybe Misty was wrong. Maybe there was something she was missing.

Dolly sighed. "Well, now I'm depressed."

Jem leaned over and smacked Dolly's knee. "I'll cheer you up then. I got some good news this week. Jerry won his art contest at school. Got fifty dollars for it. I think he's done spent the money on some kind of charcoals, but it was his own to spend. I told him: do what you want."

Misty's mother smiled. "That's wonderful. He could light them crayons up in church, now. Made the prettiest little flowers."

"What'd he draw?" Dolly asked.

"Y'all will laugh," Jem said. "But he drew a picture of Great-Great-Granny Cora Beth. Your namesake, if you recall, Beth, even though you never did believe the stories."

Misty's mother rolled her eyes.

"Lord, Jem. Don't tell me he drew her as a tree," Dolly said.

"What else could he draw? He did a whole series. Illustrated the story we were told. He called it part of our cultural tradition or something, compared it to farming during the Depression, how we've always managed to find a way to survive."

Dolly leaned back and sighed. "He got that much right. You know, if we had a team, that'd be our name. The Findaways."

Misty's mother smiled. "What would our mascot be?"

"Something pitiful," Jem said. "A little rat or something. Starving, of course. Or a hammer."

They laughed.

"What about Granny Cora Beth?" Misty asked.

Misty's mother bent forward until her head was level with Misty's. "Well, Little Bit. I thought you was finally sleeping."

"On and off," Misty said. "I'm on now."

Dolly smiled. "Go on and tell her then, Jem. Give her a bedtime story."

"Lord, y'all. There's a reason I ain't told her this myself," Misty's mother said. "I don't like filling their heads all full of nonsense."

Jem rubbed her palms across her skirt to clean them. "You'll take them to church every week to learn about men walking on water and taming lions, but one woman becomes a tree and suddenly there's a line to draw."

"That's different," Misty's mother said.

The sun was nearly gone by then and one half of Jem's face glowed with sunset fire, the other side cast to shadow as she leaned forward. "How's it different?"

"Because," Misty's mother said, "those are Bible stories. They've got morals. They teach them something."

Jem scoffed. "They're all stories, Beth. Every one of them. Except this one is part of us. Cora Beth is a part of us. Besides, you've got some awful funny-looking glass people growing in your yard to be telling somebody where to draw the line. You telling me this world ain't strange? That strange things don't happen every day of the week?"

"Those stories scare me more than the Bible ever did." Misty's mother worried the bean husks between her thumbs.

"Why?" Dolly asked.

"Because," Misty's mother said. "Sometimes it's worse to think there's another way when you're stuck in an old one."

Everyone fell quiet. A weight grew in the air between Misty's mother and her sisters, a weight that Misty couldn't quite understand. So much of growing up was that way. A feeling in a room that she'd just walked into. A feeling hanging between two people that she loved. A sense of something gone slightly wrong, but when she asked, no one would tell her the truth. And that was where childhood lay, in the shadow of knowing that something was wrong but not knowing what it was or why it was or how to fix it, so she was left standing in front of her mother, her mother tired and bleeding, her mother with a ragged hole chewed through her chest, her mother saying, "It's fine. Everything is fine."

"That's why we tell the stories," Jem said at last. "To remind us there's another way. A better way. We tell stories so we can find it."

Misty's mother sniffed. "Tell your story then."

Jem leaned back. "Will you stay and listen?"

Misty's mother said, "If I had anywhere better to be on an evening as pretty as this, don't you think I'd already be there?"

"And keep it short, Jem, will you? Some of us are about ready for bed," Dolly said.

"Y'all are the sourest bunch of grapes I ever knew," Jem said. "You listening, Misty, baby? All right. Well, the short version is that a long, long time ago, back before even Aunt Dolly roamed the earth, Cora Beth Combs come to this very same holler with her husband and their seven babies. They were trying to make a go of it farming, and he was working in the mines. Well, it wouldn't long before he was killed. A tunnel collapsed on fourteen men and that was that. Cora Beth was on her own. She tried for a while to figure things out, but there was hail and then a drought. The crops was thin and the babies was thinner. She had to think of a way to keep them all from starving.

"So Cora Beth did what any mother would do, what any Combs woman has ever done: she found a way. Some of my aunts said she did it by eating apple seeds and drinking cold earth, but it started slow. Her growing little green apples right out of her hair. Her skin got tougher and her bones got stiffer, and before long she was rooted in place, right there in the front yard. But she bore apples like you wouldn't believe. The biggest, fattest apples in the county, and she kept her babies fed. Mind you, just about every one of their teeth fell right out of their heads, but they survived.

"Now, this next part is my favorite part. See, a lot of people in the world have decided who gets to be special and who don't. They act like special is in their blood, their birthright, but most magic don't work that way. Some people have to make their own. Out of love or spite or need. It's not always good. It's not always safe. But it doesn't belong to just one person. Cora Beth knew that, so when other women came to see her, she helped them. She taught them everything she knew, and the women took it away and made their own magic. All kinds of ways for all kinds of people. And Cora Beth wasn't the first, neither. This kind of thing has been going on long before we came here. We ain't the type to wait for someone else to save us. We take care of each other. Half the food on this porch is getting donated to people here in the community. That's the only way we get by. Together."

Jem leaned back and took a deep breath, then went on with her story.

"Now, Cora's oldest daughter married a decent man in town, and he come and took over the farm and helped her raise her little brothers and sisters. They made it out of that year, and they kept that apple tree standing until a storm took it out in '87. Split the trunk right in half. But we keep her alive by remembering her, don't we, ladies?"

"Who could forget that story?" Misty's mother asked.

"Now you can tell it to your babies one long, long day away," Jem said. "Let them know they're special. Just like you."

In the morning after they packed to leave, the five of them stood on the same porch for an hour saying goodbye.

Their mother said, "Earl called this morning to give us notice about Revival. The whole church'll be in my front yard this Sunday night. Are y'all coming?"

Dolly shook her head. "Char's got some play she and her friends wrote together. They're putting it on in the backyard, and we promised to take her to Applebee's after."

"And I feel a sickness coming on." Jem rubbed her fingers across her throat. "You're welcome to bring the girls by and eat dinner with us. We'll find us a movie and forget all about them statues."

"Maybe," their mother said. "I'll let you know."

Aunt Jem pressed a covered plate of food into Misty's hands. She knelt down before Misty and looked at her hard in the early morning light.

"Don't you forget," she said. "There's magic in this little body of your'n. Don't you never doubt it."

She kissed Misty twice on the cheek and stood on the front porch to watch them leave. Misty waved at her aunts through the rear window of the car until the road curved away and the mountain swallowed them up.

Thirty-One

William took Misty to the barn three times the next week.

Every time she opened the door or looked out her window, every time she crept onto the back steps, he was there. She asked him to go down by the creek or to pick wild strawberries with her in the woods, but he didn't want anything else. He didn't seem to hear her at all as he shut the barn door behind them. And every time he closed the door, Misty felt cold all over and her bones tried to slip free from her body but she held on to them for a little while and promised that it wouldn't be long.

Each time William gave Misty something to hold—an old toy car that he'd taken from his room, one of his mother's gold earrings, a plastic Christmas ornament with a manger scene painted on it—and each time he took it from her afterward.

William talked to her in the barn. He said:

"Revival is soon.

"Mom said she would come to the service. She promised.

"She's been packing up some of our things. I think she means to move in with Harold at the end of summer. I keep unpacking the boxes at night, but she won't talk to me about it.

"You don't have to scrunch your face up like that. This don't hurt.

"I keep thinking, maybe the garden could change other things. Maybe it could make other things better, too."

Three new statues grew that week, and William said, "These are for you," as he pointed to a silver ax with its blade stuck in the ground like it meant to cleave the whole world in two. He pointed to a bird with its wings spread wide, its clawed feet barely dug into the earth below so it was hard to imagine how the statue supported its own weight, how it stood there when it should be tipping, falling, flying. He pointed to the last statue and the largest of them all—a tree that grew in the very center of the garden. Its trunk was wider than Misty, and its branches spread over everything below and cast faint shadows on her upturned face.

The statues didn't make as much sense this time. The bird had to have been from her memory of the first time William had taken her to the barn. She had called out to all the birds asleep in their nests and they'd come for her. They'd tried to help. She'd asked the trees for help before, too, so maybe that was why this one grew, but she wasn't sure. And the ax must have come from William, something he thought or remembered or wanted.

It seemed like the statues had been saying something about her and William, but she couldn't read them now. She couldn't understand.

"Do you like them?" William asked.

The tree was made of bright, clear glass so Misty could see straight through it to the other side of the bottom, but the view was distorted. Twisted, turned, so the trees on the other side of the garden seemed to be growing upside down with the sky pooled at their feet. Misty was a thin slip of gray cloud inside the glass, her features blurred until they disappeared, and she couldn't even see herself as she nodded and William smiled.

Thirty-Two

This time, when Misty shed her skin, she didn't stop at the bridge.

She didn't even pause as she crossed the highway into a nearby yard, past a fence and a dog tied to a post with a heavy chain, who lifted its ears and tipped back its head and let go a single, mournful bellow as Misty crept past its owner's window where the owner slept inside. She turned right, toward her school, and kept going.

It was after eleven and everything was shut down tight, everyone sleeping. Every now and then a car passed by. The glare from Misty's bones was so sudden and bright that most people thought her a road sign and kept driving.

The trees were denser along the road, the kudzu thicker, and Misty plucked little leaves and boughs as she walked beside the main road. She stuck the green things in the gaps between her bones. She replaced the tendons with maple leaves and two long strands of supplejack that she wound around each knee, filled her ribs with wisteria and spread mud around the sockets of her eyes to catch the pollen and dust floating by. Lightning bugs drifted around her, blinking their sleepy lights. She caught them and brought them to rest in her body, let them climb over her bones and her blooms, giving off faint yellow light that pulsed like a heartbeat until she was almost whole again.

The road widened, forked, and turned. It opened into a hundred small hollers like her own that switchbacked through the mountains like veins. She passed her elementary school with the lights blacked out and the fence shut with a heavy padlock. She waved to an old woman sitting on her front porch in a rocking chair, smoking a cigar. The woman lifted her hand and waved back, the bright-red point burning in her other hand, smoke drifting lazy from her mouth. Misty passed a man hauling hay into the back of his truck, singing a church hymn that she remembered vaguely from somewhere before.

She didn't think about where she was going. Her thoughts floated around her like a dandelion puff that had been blown to pieces, each individual idea drifting in a different direction. She followed whatever looked prettiest or the path that seemed easiest. She only wanted to get further from home, from the barn, from whatever it was that bothered her so much about that place. The further she walked, the harder it was to remember what had troubled her so, and the less trouble she felt at all. And she thought, *This must be what it felt like to be William.* To be skinless: bold and unafraid. To not worry all the time about what might hurt you or what your hurting might do to other people. This must be what it felt like to be a boy.

Fireworks lit up the sky over an old strip job and Misty followed the light to a ring of four-wheelers arranged around a wide-open space. Teenagers filled the middle, some dancing in the blare of the headlights, others drinking or laughing, their long-limbed bodies covered with skin and sweat and one another. Music came from somewhere, pared down to only the deepest sound to Misty's missing ears, the bass line and the drums. Misty didn't recognize the song, but her bones recognized the rhythm. They responded to anything that reminded them of a heartbeat. Even the pounding of her feet bones on the pavement was enough to please them, and whatever beating thing that they could feel, they yearned toward, wanting more.

Misty strummed her toe bones over the gravel, and the sound reverberated through her body until it came to rest in her jaw, buzzing. She bent her knees, first one way and then the other, letting her hips rotate in their dried sockets, and that was a vibration, too, a gentle grinding that shook the leaves from her ribs. Dried mud flaked from her eyes and fell like snow between her finger bones as she began to dance.

What her body did was something in between what the girls were doing in the light of the four-wheelers and what she'd seen her aunts do in church. Her bones bounced a two-step over the thinning grass, her arms loose at her sides. She lifted them to the air and let her fingers clink together until that vibrated down her arms. She let her bones drop toward the ground, catching them at the last moment and slowing them, bringing them back to stillness before they jerked, clacked, danced again. She made her own music as she moved toward the trees, a shaking, humming grind of bone on bone. It almost made sense why the women danced in church, why bodies moved at all—because they needed to. She needed to.

Just as she began to twirl in a slow circle, a voice called out, "What the hell is that?"

A boy walked to the edge of the four-wheelers. He crossed their line of light and entered the shadows, squinted in Misty's direction. "There's something over there," he said. "I ain't shitting you, Cody. Turn the damn Kodiak around so I can see. Point them lights over here." He lifted his voice toward Misty, shouting, "Jesse Graves, if that's you, I'm gonna stomp a mudhole in your ass, you hear me, little boy?"

The boy stalked across the field. Whatever part of Misty was left that understood the set of a boy's shoulders when he meant to hurt someone told her to run, so she ran.

She jumped over a fallen tree and into the darkness of the woods, which made it even harder to distinguish between what was solid and what was not. Her vision had darkened even more since she left her body that night, and now everything was creeping toward black. A light flashed over the trees—the light of a four-wheeler arcing in her direction. A distant rumble followed her, and she felt the wheels crunching over the gravel more than she heard them.

An old mining service road ran along the woods, and two of the four-wheelers broke away from the pack to follow it. A girl clung to the back of the boy who'd spoken to Misty. She held a flashlight in her hands, but the beam was too weak to break through the trees. It only muddied the woods, making it even more impossible to tell one tree from another. The service road was almost as overgrown as the woods themselves, sinking with deep potholes and runnels as big as ditch lines from the summer rains. The four-wheelers bounced and squeaked, the boy shouting every now and then that he could still see her running, so Misty ran faster.

If they cut through the woods, they might catch her, and if they caught her, then there was no way to know what they might do. Her bones might remind them of their own bones, their own bodies bare and quaking, their own self split, and seeing themselves that way might make them do strange or terrible things. She might be divided between them, a bone for every hand, a bone for every tooth in their heads. She might be broken apart and carried away until her body forgot it was a body and not just a rib or a finger or a spine.

Misty ran as fast as she could before she thought she might shake herself apart and do the boy's work for him.

She ran past a ramshackle guard shack on the hill of a strip mine. The bare light bulb that hung from its ceiling flickered to life as she passed, illuminating a single metal chair tipped on its side, the wooden walls papered with blueprints of the mine, the inside of the mountain made real and whole and tacked to the walls outside itself. She ran along a hill covered with mining equipment. The backhoes and dozers and one dump truck as wide as the mountain itself thundered to life, their engines revving as Misty's feet bones dug into the damp earth. She wound her way between them and down the other side of the hill. She ran straight through the middle of a trailer park, the lights flaring in each of the windows, flickering and stuttering. Televisions blinked off and on in rapid succession and blenders whirred in their cabinets and the wind chimes on all the porches rang with sound, like there was some great force surging along with Misty, something riding in the wake of her bone body. And everything near her felt it. Everything near her answered the call of whatever was left of Misty still clinging to her bones shouting *help me help me help me*.

She didn't stop until she stumbled into the parking lot of a small convenience store. The lights blared so bright that even Misty's failing eyes could see the reds and the golds of the tobacco signs hanging from the windows. Her bones jarred over the asphalt, shaking her back to herself, and she turned to look through the woods she'd left behind. Somewhere along the way, she'd lost the four-wheelers, and already, she was forgetting what it was that sent her running. There seemed to be nothing there that would ever harm her—just a few dark trees, their leaves shifting gently under the moonlight.

A door opened, and a beam of light fell on the asphalt in front of her. Misty walked toward it, only stopping when a woman came out, lugging four bags of garbage behind her, a cigarette clutched between her teeth. The woman mumbled something under her breath that Misty couldn't make out, but she could see the cigarette bobbing in her mouth, forming words that shook the ashes onto the collar of her shirt.

The woman hauled the garbage to a dumpster near the trees, then stood shaking and smoking. Misty crouched behind a tall stack of pallets. From this close, she could barely smell the kerosene imbedded in the wood.

The woman by the dumpster looked familiar. She was lean and tall and felt the way a baby bird looked—fragile and flailing, like something just learning to fly, something that could be incredible, soon, if it caught the right wind. She finished two more cigarettes before she stubbed out their flames with the heel of her white Keds and walked back to the door. She leaned inside and shouted, "I'm going home, Sandy. I did my share of the work. Well. Come right on and try to stop me then. I'll do to you what I did to your cousin in fifth grade. That's what I thought. Goodnight, hon."

She grabbed something from inside and came back with a purse slung over her shoulder. The bag punched her hip with every step and something inside it sounded like church bells ringing over and over.

Misty followed the woman to her truck. She crept into the bed as the woman coaxed the engine to life and forced the truck into gear, the whole frame jerking forward and back. Misty curled one hand around a bag of something that felt like oranges and held on as the truck rocked out of the parking lot and onto the road. The wind whistled by overhead. A few minutes passed before the woman wedged the sliding rear window open so a thin trail of gray smoke could emerge. The smoke held itself together long enough to reach the roof of the truck before the wind ripped it apart.

Sound blared through the open window—static and bits of gospel music, static and something upbeat, static and Dolly Parton. The woman inside sang along to "Jolene" with all her heart. The sound of her voice overpowered the thrumming and jarring of the truck until Misty could feel *her* vibration in her spine. Not the road and not the busted suspension and not the growl of the engine, but the woman's voice pleading with Jolene.

Overhead, the stars whirred past between the thin, dark arms of trees. It was like God was pulling a curtain fast across the sky, and the world was going with it. What waited at the end, Misty wasn't sure. She stretched her leg bones a little further apart, planting them on the metal sides of the truck so she might feel more of the road humming through her, pooling in her joints and ricocheting through her skull.

The woman turned and turned again and every road she chose was curvier than the last, and every song she sang was sadder. The sky lightened. The world became easier to recognize as the stars became harder to find until they were almost indistinguishable from the sky.

The truck stopped. Misty's skull bumped against the back of the bed and a faint cloud of dust lifted from the back tires. The truck shuddered as the woman shouldered the door open and slammed it again. The top of her head was visible from Misty's angle. She tapped a cigarette from its pack and stuck it between her lips. She stared in the direction of the garden for a moment before shaking her head and shoving the cigarette back into place. She walked away without a word.

Misty sat up. For a moment, she didn't recognize the sight of her own trailer. She had rarely seen it from this direction. She was always looking at it from her own yard or from the woods behind her house, but rarely from here in William's driveway. It looked different from this new angle—the roof was flat and gray, the front porch leaned a little where her mother had shored up a broken post with a stack of cement blocks.

On her other side the statues glinted in the pale morning light. The crack in the green glass man was clearer from this angle, and thicker than she remembered. There were other cracks, too—in the golden hand, in the spiral with its pointed tip, in the tree. All of them looked like they had been damaged somehow. Like they were falling apart.

Earl sat in a plastic folding chair in front of the fence he'd built, his body slumped to the side. The sunlight filtering through the green glass man's chest turned to the color of seaweed as it rippled across Earl's face. There were dark circles under his eyes and his skin was loose around his throat like he was slowly shrinking away from himself.

Misty descended the back of Shannon's truck carefully. Her bones clanked and thudded on the metal until she jumped onto the grass. Earl's trailer was even more sunken than before. It canted dangerously forward and two of the posts that held his front porch up had splintered from the pressure. White crawdad shells littered the ground— the kind the crawdads shed when they molted. Misty picked one up. It crumbled between her finger bones and drifted through the air. She followed another and another until she found a crawdad lying in the grass behind Earl. She nudged it gently with her finger but the crawdad didn't move.

It was dead.

Misty cupped it between her hands. She could see no reason for the crawdad's death—nothing injured, nothing missing. It was just gone, surrounded by the ghost of its former selves. She looked across the yard and spotted three more crawdads lying motionless in the grass.

Had she been in her skin body, Misty would have cried. She would have buried the crawdads under her porch and prayed for them to make it safely into the Ever, which is where crawdads went when they died.

But her bones didn't feel anything at all except the faint tug of a memory, something about the garden, about names and consequences.

It was not desire that drove Misty inside. It was something much older than that, older even than need. It was something Misty didn't know how to name, but if she could, it would have sounded like grease popping on the stove and the rumble of her mother's voice through the wall of her bedroom when Misty wasn't supposed to be listening and the roar of her father's truck and Penny, too, the way she drummed her fingers against the walls when she was tired of waiting for dinner. It was the heartbeat of her family, the steady, familiar drum of them that called to Misty's bones, and she answered.

Back in her room, Misty sat on the edge of her bed with her body gathered around her waist. She forced her skin over her hips until her dark mouth gaped toothless up at her, still hungry for the body that remained. The parts of her that were already joined throbbed a dull and distant pain that she didn't have time to consider. Her body felt even smaller than last time, fighting every inch that she tried to rejoin. She knew that if she kept leaving, there would come a night when she couldn't force the two back together. And on that night, she would have no choice but to leave her body behind.

Misty hadn't thought much about what that meant. Where she would go, what her mother would do, what would become of her bed and her toys and her clothes. Her brain just kind of blinked off when she thought that far ahead, gave way to a gauzy kind of static until she turned away from it again and thought of other things.

Still, it was a risk she took every time she shed her skin now, and every time it got harder to return.

On the other side of the sheet, Penny stirred, coughed twice, and was silent again. Misty pushed her right arm bone through the right arm skin, but her hand slowed through her forearm. Her hand stopped before it reached the end, the skin tightening until she could push no further.

Misty craned her neck and braced her foot against the bed. She pulled hard with her left bone hand, the little knuckles clenched tight together, tugging the right arm into place until something stretched, almost broke. Her shoulder burned once the skin slotted into place and her hand tingled. Misty opened and closed her fist trying to chase the feeling away, but the pain lingered.

She forced the other arm inside the same way, struggling, pushing, before she finally fit inside herself. She peeled her skin over her face like a mask. Her eyes were sore inside her head and when she opened her mouth to yawn, her jaw cracked. Misty sat on the edge of her bed with her bare feet on the floor, panting and shivering and aching, when a voice came from the other side of the room.

"Where'd you go?" Penny asked.

Thirty-Three

Misty froze. She hadn't noticed the shadow standing on the other side of the room or the two small feet poking beneath the sheet. She couldn't remember if she'd noticed Penny on her way back into their room, if she'd stopped to make sure she was sleeping. There was no way to know if Penny had seen her bones, and no way to ask without giving herself away.

"I can hear you breathing," Penny said.

"How long have you been awake?" Misty asked.

"I heard your big feet clomping around over there. You sound like a herd of cattle, you know that?"

Misty exhaled slowly. Penny hadn't seen her then, only heard her.

"Well," Misty said, "go back to sleep."

"I can't. I'm awake now."

"I'm not. I'm sleep-talking."

Penny snorted. "You want me to read your future? I've been practicing. I'm not as good as Sam, but I've cast some cards. I did some for me. For Mom and Dad."

"What did you see?"

Penny was quiet, and Misty took that as an answer. Whatever she saw must not have been different from what they saw—the distance, the separation. Misty clenched her fist into a hand, and her skin slid across her bones like it was ready to leave again.

Penny's shadow slipped across the sheet like clouds across water as she retrieved something from her desk. She sat on her side of the room, her bony knees poking from her nightgown. "Come sit on your side."

Misty slid from her bed. She tried hard not to groan as pain erupted in her knees and ankles, all her joints angry at the new weight they had to bear. They had been just bones before and they begrudged the heft of her body, all that flesh, the heart, the lungs. It was all too much.

"Sit with your knees like mine," Penny said. "Yeah, just scoot back a little. Fine, then, sit right there if you want to be like that. Lord. I'll make it work."

She dealt the cards in a half circle that joined Misty's left knee to her right like the arc of the sun across the sky.

"Okay," Penny said. "This here is like your life, see. I'll start over here at your birth and then we'll finish on the other side with your death. So this first card is what you started with in life. Oh. A queen. And of spades, too, wow. I guess that means you, well, you was born with a lot. Or at least something. You're not like a five of hearts, you know? You're not just any old card. You never was, right from the start."

Penny's cards didn't look like Sam's. They were just an ordinary deck of cards that had been shaded and colored. It was a practice set.

"This next one is where you are right now. Three of spades. The spades is the most powerful suit, so that means you've got a powerful imbalance going on in your life somewhere. Something went wrong, I think. Something you probably didn't expect. That's not good, is it?"

"I don't know," Misty said. "You're the one reading the cards."

"Well, it's not good. It means you've got some problem you're holding on to. You should probably talk to somebody about that, you know. The cards can also help give you advice when you need it."

"I'm tired, Penny. Can't you—"

"*You're always tired.*"

"And you're always bothering me. Just turn the next card, or I'm going to bed and you can read the sheet's fortune."

"Fine. God, you're raw. The next card is…another spade, really? Did you do something to these cards?"

"How could I do anything to your stupid cards?" Misty asked.

"I don't know. It's just strange is all. Well, this one is you in a couple years, you know, so in middle school. It's a face card so that's good. You're out of the imbalance. You're stronger than you are right now. You've got direction. You've got places to go."

"Like bed," Misty said.

"Like the orphanage if you keep it up with that attitude."

Misty smiled.

"High school you is going to go through a dark phase. You'll probably get into a lot of trouble. People will see that you ain't as sweet as you pretend to be, which is about time, really."

"I'm still sweeter than your old vinegar butt," Misty said.

Penny flipped the next four cards all at once. "Let's just get this over with if you're going to be so rude to your… Wait. Are you sure you didn't mess with my cards? I won't be mad if you did. I just want to know."

The three of spades appeared again at the end of the deck— the same card that represented Misty's present also represented her death. Misty picked up the card and flipped it over. The images had not been colored or shaded like the rest of the deck. It looked like it came from a separate set of cards altogether.

"It must just be an extra," Penny said, reaching beneath the sheet and taking the card from Misty's hand. "I don't know how that got in there. I've done this a hundred times and never drawn this one. Well, now the whole thing is ruined."

"Why?"

"Because you can't have the same card twice."

"Why not?"

"You just… You can't. It don't make any sense. How would you even read it?" Penny laid the card back in place. "I mean, I guess I'd call it a bad omen. Like unless something changed you might never get the rest of your life, since these two match. Your now card and your end card is the same, see. So you might… Well…you might die soon."

Misty stood up.

"Where are you going?" Penny asked.

"To bed."

"You can't just go to bed on that."

"Watch me."

"What happened in the garden?" Penny asked. "I saw you right before them bugs fell. I watched your face, and it looked like… It looked like you was talking to something. Your lips was moving."

"No they wasn't."

"They were! And you've been acting weird all summer. I know something's going on." Penny moved toward the door. She wrapped her hand around the sheet and pulled it back an inch. "I'm coming over."

"No," Misty said. She grabbed the sheet just above Penny's hand. "You wanted this here and we're keeping it here. You don't just get to change the rules."

"Then tell me what happened."

"Nothing is happening."

"That's a lie, Misty. Mom knows something's wrong. Everybody does."

"I ain't the only one. You kissed the green glass man. You want to tell me why you did that, huh? You want to talk about that?"

Misty could hear her own voice yelling, the sound rising in her throat every time she spoke. Their mother would hear before long. She would come check on them and make everything worse. The thought of Penny knowing what was happening terrified her. Because then they would all know—her mom and dad and Shannon and Earl. They would know what William did in the barn. What Misty did. They would see her there on her back. They would see her that way forever, and none of them could look at her the same for as long as she lived.

Misty yanked the sheet out of Penny's hand. "Just go to bed, Penny Lee. Just leave me alone."

Penny's hand dropped but she didn't let go of the sheet. Her fingers toyed with a loose string. "I don't know why I kissed him. I mean, I do, and I don't. I just got so mad at Mom and at Dad and everybody. Nobody ever wants to listen to you when you're twelve. They act like nothing that happens counts, but it does, and I just wanted to spite all of them. I wanted to prove them all wrong. And…"

"And what?"

"I don't know. I thought the green man was kind of neat at first. Everybody was acting all dumb about it but he was different. Special. So I thought if I kissed him, then maybe I could be, too."

"What?"

"Special, I guess. I wanted to feel special."

Penny's hand crept back across the sheet, her four fingers clutching the fabric against her palm. It was hard to imagine Penny as something small or soft, something vulnerable. She seemed so much herself that there was no room for anyone else, no room for doubt.

"I wish I hadn't kissed him, though," Penny said. "Now my lips will probably fall off. It's probably killing me, too."

Misty almost laughed. She almost eased her hand back and let Penny pull the sheet to the side. Almost told her what she'd been wanting to tell someone since William first took her to the barn.

But the telling.

The saying.

Just the thought made her throat close up and her bones slip away from her skin, her hand pulling back, her arm trying to escape her body until Misty had to clench her fist to keep her skin from slinking away.

Penny pulled the sheet in one direction while Misty pulled in another.

"I told you the truth," Penny said. "Misty."

One of the tacks popped loose from the ceiling and skittered across the carpet. Penny's face appeared in flashes—the corner of her head, her hair frizzed with sleep, one eye squinted almost shut. Misty pulled her arms back and pushed Penny away, aiming for the dark square of her chest. Penny fumbled back. The desk thumped as it scooted against the carpet. Everything atop it shifted. A cup of pencils upturned and rolled across the top, and then nothing. Silence.

"I wanted to help." There were tears in Penny's voice. The words lifted and fell on little huffs of breath that she caught to keep from crying. "You don't got to be like this. You don't get to treat somebody that way."

"I'm fine," Misty said. "Just leave me alone." But her voice cracked, too.

"Fine," Penny said.

Two small hands shot beneath the sheet and collected the cards. The mattress creaked as she climbed onto it, the quilt rustling hard as Penny kicked it into shape. Misty climbed into bed, too. She lay on top of her quilt, her hands straight by her sides. She stared at the ceiling and listened to the sound of her sister's breathing. She tried to match them, tried to breathe as calm as Penny did, but her lungs wouldn't listen, so she wheezed and she trembled until she cried.

Thirty-Four

By noon that Sunday, cars started to appear on the side of Misty's road. Men from her church cut the tall grass on William's side of the yard. They crushed the crawdad chimneys beneath their work boots and poured sawdust into the deepest pits until the ground was almost even again. The men stopped their work occasionally to stare at the statues in the garden, their faces lit with green and golden light, their hands hanging limp at their sides.

Misty watched the men through a crack in her front door while nursing a glass of corn bread and milk. She pushed the corn bread to the bottom of the glass before spooning some into her mouth. The milk was sweet to the corn bread's earthiness, the oil and the cream mixing together to make something that was the better half of both. There was still enough crunch to the crust, and little pieces of hard bread broke between her teeth and mixed with the milk to make something softer, something that slid smooth and effortless down her throat. Misty's movements were gentle. Every time she so much as turned her head, she was punished for the long night she'd spent outside of her skin. Even the spaces between her toes and fingers felt like the skin had been flayed, her throat raw every time she swallowed.

Yet, there were no bruises on her body. She'd checked that morning in the shower, searching for even the smallest discoloration to prove that something had happened to her, that something was happening to her. But there was nothing to show for any of the pain she felt, not now, not in the barn. Nothing that she could hold in her hands and say, *Look, this is what I mean.*

Penny poked her head from their bedroom and looked down the narrow hallway at Misty. "Is Mom out yet?"

"No," Misty said.

Penny shut the door without another word. After last night, Misty thought they might spend the rest of their lives that way, speaking a handful of words, only talking to ask each other directions or to pass the buttermilk, nothing more ever passing between them until Misty couldn't even recognize Penny, their faces losing all their similarities until they didn't share the same broad nose or freckled skin, until they weren't sisters at all.

Misty closed her eyes and leaned her head against the wall. The garden hadn't spoken to her since the day she'd gone to Aunt Dolly's house, the day she'd asked about Caroline. She still didn't understand why the garden seemed to hate Caroline almost as much as it hated Earl. As far as Misty could see, Caroline hadn't done anything wrong, nothing, at least, that deserved that kind of anger.

And even though the garden scared her sometimes, she still missed the sound of its voice, its constant presence. Misty missed having someone around. Her sister ignored her. Her father hadn't been home in days. Her mother seemed to be more lost inside herself than ever before. It was hard to be alone.

Misty inched the door in her chest open. She thought of the crawdads clinging to her clothes, following her onto the bank of the creek; their slick backs and thick claws; their empty skins scattered across the front yard; her mother's finger brushing her bangs over her face; the slick feeling of her skin sliding from her bones; Penny's hand on the sheet, trying to pull it away, trying to find Misty on the other side; William's hand against her hip—and then a familiar presence bubbled up in her head before she even finished her name. Its name was like silt running between her fingers, the hushed crinkle of a morning glory closing its petals for the day, the pop of a bone from its socket.

She hadn't spoken to the crawdads for so long that she almost broke the connection in her excitement. Instead she shared as many images and feelings as she could, all of them trying to express three little words: "I missed you."

The crawdad filled her with the feeling of shallow water, the creek after it had gone without rain for days and days, the dry tops of the stones peeking through, a sense that there was nowhere to go, nowhere to run. The pain of molting, the deep, suffocating tightness of a shell before it was shed like a hand around her throat, closing tighter and tighter. Their bodies scattered across the grass, lifeless, the same ones that Misty had held in her bone body.

The garden said that using the crawdads wouldn't hurt them, but that wasn't true. They were in trouble. They were hurt, dying, and they asked for Misty's help.

"What can I do?" she said.

The crawdad shared a fragmented image of the garden, but the focus was on the soil below the statues. It shared an image of the ground beneath—pale white tree roots breaking through the dirt, grasping for purchase, a green light shimmering faintly underground, and a brief flash of Caroline's face.

Then the image was gone and the crawdad was gone with it.

Misty reached out for the crawdad again, but another voice answered instead.

"Misty?" the garden said. "I want to apologize. I shouldn't have yelled at you before. I'm sorry. I've been working very hard for tonight and I took my worry out on you."

"What do you mean?" Misty asked.

"All the people," the garden said. "They'll finally come. They'll finally see the statues. They'll see what Earl did, how he isn't what they think he is."

"You mean about what he did to Caroline?"

"Yes."

"I thought you didn't like her."

The garden hesitated. "It's not about liking. It's about right and wrong. I need them to understand. Will you be there tonight? Will you come?"

"Yeah," Misty said, "I'll be there. But I wanted to ask you about the crawdads. Did you let them go yet?"

"Almost. We're almost done. I have to go now. There's still so much to do."

The garden's voice disappeared before Misty could say another word, leaving her alone on her living room floor. She reached out for the crawdads but they didn't answer. They had to be under the garden's influence again, trapped under the earth where the green light shimmered and shone.

By five thirty, the little one-lane road that ran beside the bottom was already crowded with cars. People started to park along the main road, squeezing onto the grass sides of the hills with the thinnest of inches between their tires and the crumbling mountainside. One good gust of wind would be enough to tumble them down into the creek below. People walked across the highway, over the bridge and into the holler. They followed the light of the sodium lamp over the garden, which burned bright orange and buzzed like a hornet's nest. The women's heeled shoes clacked against the pavement and then grated over the gravel driveway before sinking into the worn grass of the yard.

By six, the sun had started to set, and Earl stepped back and watched the crowd. He wore a collared shirt and a pair of dark slacks, his hair combed to the side and stiffened with gel.

"He shined them shoes within an inch of their life," Penny said. She pressed her forehead against the banister of their porch. From up high, she and Misty could see everything that happened. People waved or asked after their father at first, but after a while no one seemed to notice them. This was as close to the service as their mother would allow them—the porch and no further.

There was only a handful of chairs near the garden where the elderly could sit with their oxygen tanks propped against their knees. Everyone else stood in the grass or by the driveway, some leaning against the mailboxes by the road. There were a hundred people there at least, though it was hard to count them when they were packed so close together. The crowd swelled like a lung, inhaling and exhaling, shuffling then still.

Sunset changed the bottom. Had Misty ever been able to believe that the statues were something good, holy even, she would have believed it at sunset as the light bounced between the metal and glass, the dying rays of red-orange burnishing the edges of the green glass man, tracing the arc of the bridge, coloring the hand and the spiral, the ax, the bird, the tree. It set them all ablaze, like they were burning with a sun-forged light hidden somewhere deep inside. For a moment, right before the sun sank behind the trees, the statues became a light of their own and the whole bottom glowed with fire-light warmth.

The men and women from the church noticed the change. Their voices slowed. Some people cut off midsentence and turned away from their friends or family, leaving them gape-mouthed and staring. The children quieted. Some pointed, some clung to their mothers' skirts. One man fumbled with the side of his oxygen tank until he turned the dial up, forcing a blast of fresh air into his trembling lungs.

William appeared beside Earl. He was dressed in an outfit almost identical except smaller in every way, and he had no dress shoes to wear so he wore his darkest tennis shoes instead. His eyes roamed over each of the faces in the crowd, his eyes shining with their own reflected light until they seemed like two fire-heated coins glowing.

Misty gripped the porch banister and her skin slid over the small bones in her hand, tried to sink and fall away. The skin of her shoulders loosened, too, and her jaw sagged, peeling away from her teeth. She hadn't meant to call her skin away. She didn't want to leave her body, at least not right then, but it seemed like her body was deciding without her now. She shivered twice and her skin shuddered back into place.

Their mother opened the screen door and stepped onto the porch at almost the exact time that William's mother walked out of her trailer. Shannon wore a long, black dress with sleeves down to her elbows and the silver chain of a small bag slung across one shoulder. Her dirty-blond hair was pulled back from her face. She was dressed for a funeral more than for church, but she still looked pretty, and

younger, somehow, without so much volume in her hair. She waved
and started across the yard toward them.

"You girls be good," their mother said. "If you go back in the
house, I want you to walk around to the back door so you don't
distract nobody. This is just like church, remember?"

"We know," Penny said.

"I'm glad you're here," Shannon said, leaning against the porch.
She squeezed Misty's knee and winked at her. "You mind if we stand
together? Safety in numbers and all that?"

Misty's mother smiled and joined Shannon on the grass. They
walked across the driveway and merged with the back of the crowd.
They were about the same size and shape, though Shannon was a
little shorter, a little thinner. They talked with their heads bent close
and their arms crossed over their chests. They'd lived within feet of
each other for the last three years, but Misty had never seen them so
close for so long. There was something about Shannon that made
their mother afraid. What scared her, Misty wasn't sure, but she
knew what fear looked like, and she saw it in the slant of her mother's shoulders and the tightness of her eyes on the rare occasion when
Shannon came over.

Maybe she was afraid that if someone saw them standing side
by side for too long that they would notice how similar they were.
Misty's mother may have worn longer skirts and scrubbed the kitchen
harder and never cussed in front of company, but she could be loud
and stubborn and brittle, too, just like William's mother. The only
difference was that Shannon didn't hide it from anyone. She didn't
even try, maybe because she had too many other things to worry
about, like keeping her truck running and food on the table. She was
doing it all alone so she didn't have time to conceal herself as neatly

as Misty's mother did, but the more Misty looked, the more she saw their sameness. They could have been friends, once.

The crowd grew as dark settled over the bottom. There was a comfort in the hushed murmur of all those familiar people and the faint crunching of shoes over gravel. Misty drew a blanket over her arms and closed her eyes. It was hard to tell which parts of her hurt, if it was her eye or the eyelid, the skin or the bone that ached, but the pain diffused throughout her body, settling into her like a familiar ghost as she listened to the crowd.

It seemed like all the worst things she feared were far away from her there. William wouldn't hurt her now, not with so many people near. And the statues looked almost pretty in the dying light of evening, softened and melting into shadow. The garden was still silent, refusing any attempt that Misty had made to speak to it or the crawdads that afternoon. It was easy to imagine that the garden had never spoken to her at all. She'd only caught the edge of some other whispering, sneaking thing that fluttered too close and there was no danger, not to her or her family, not that night.

Misty didn't realize she'd fallen asleep until the garden knocked against the back of her mind, but this time the knock was loud, like a fist pounding inside her skull. Misty answered just to make the feeling stop.

"They're clapping for him," the garden said. "Why are they clapping for him?"

Misty looked at the garden. Earl stood in front of the fence with his arms spread out. The statues rose behind him and the crowd was clapping. Earl smiled.

"I don't know," Misty said.

"I thought they would notice."

"Notice what?"

"The statues," the garden said. "I thought they could see what he did to her." Images of Caroline fluttered through Misty's mind. "But they don't. They don't even care."

"What happened to her?" Misty sat up on the porch. Penny was slumped beside her, one bare leg poking free from her blanket, one foot dangling off the edge of the porch. It was full night, and the crowd had nearly doubled in size since Misty closed her eyes. People filled not only the yard all the way to the creek, but they stood along the road, too. They craned their heads and smiled as Earl continued to speak, turning now and then to point at the statues like he'd made them himself.

"She was like you," the garden said. "She could talk to things. She could make things happen. She never told anybody about it except for Earl. She thought she could trust him."

The crowd clapped again. Someone shouted "Hallelujah" and anger flooded Misty's body, heating her cheeks and the palms of her hands. The garden's voice grew louder.

"But he was mean to her. He always was, right from the start. He hurt her until she didn't want to be hurt anymore and she thought she'd found a way out. She'd heard stories before. About women who could change themselves. Turn into other things, like trees."

Earl lifted his hands and shouted something, but his voice sounded dim and far away. Misty could only hear the garden whispering in her head, could only think of Aunt Jem and the story of Misty's great-great-grandmother.

"She tried to convince the tree to bond with her," the garden said, "but it told her she was too young. Too healthy. It said she should find another way to keep living, and come back to it when she was old and gray. It promised it would bond with her someday, but she was so tired of living. Of fighting. So she used our little trick. She bound her name with the tree's and she joined it anyway. She felt bad at first, but she was free, finally, from Earl and from everybody who treated her bad and called her names, free from everybody who ever hurt her."

A woman joined Earl in front of the fence. She smiled at him and said something to the crowd. Then she started to sing.

"But then Earl found her," the garden said, "and he cut her down."

Images flashed in Misty's mind: Caroline's hands sinking into the trunk of the dogwood tree, a light blinding and green inside her head, her vision shifting, changing, her body stretched and emptied, her roots spreading beneath her, digging deeper and deeper into the earth.

"He thought he killed her," the garden said, "but he forgot the roots."

White roots in dark soil, the green light flickering over the backs of the crawdads.

"Does that—does that mean she's still there?" Misty asked. "In the ground?"

"She never left."

Misty shook her head. "Is she okay? Can I talk to her?"

"You already have."

Misty looked across the crowd of people at the statues. A tree, a spiral, an ax. She thought the statues had been about her and William and what happened in the barn, but maybe she was wrong. Maybe...

"Are you Caroline?" Misty asked.

"I was," the garden said. "Once." And then she slipped away from Misty like she had so many times, gone before Misty could ask her to stay.

The woman in front of the garden continued to sing. The sound of her, so pure and clean and bright, carried across the bottom like an unexpected rain, and Misty's mother turned up her face so she might hear it better. Goose bumps broke across Misty's arms as the woman's voice reverberated between the trailers, caught in the dim space between all those bodies and trees that echoed the song back to her, that seemed to be singing along, like there were a hundred versions of that woman hidden all throughout the bottom and all of them, all of them were singing.

A woman near the back of the crowd began to stomp her feet. Her head was bowed almost to her chest, and little clouds of yellowed dust rose from her ankles. Shannon stepped back to give the woman more room, but the woman latched her hand around Shannon's wrist, and Shannon began to dance, too. Her head fell back, exposing the long, pale line of her throat, then she whipped back just as fast. Her body jerked in four different directions, each part of her wanting to be somewhere else. She was pulled toward the earth, the sky, the barn, the pulpit, and so turned in spinning circles with her arms clenched tight at her sides.

The crowd shifted to allow the women room, and the more women who danced, the more who followed. One woman stood with her arms spread at her sides, bending forward and back, slow and even. Another shouted, another wailed, and the sound of them reverberated against the trees and returned, doubled, even stronger, until the women cast it out again.

Misty's mother lifted her eyes to the stars. Her whole body shook from top to bottom and she began to dance. Her feet stuttered over the grass, the blades worn to softness by so many feet. She clenched her hands into fists and pressed them to her chest like she was holding on to something there, some invisible line that kept her from floating off into the dark.

The air seemed to shimmer with some new feeling that the women shared, like the first crack in an egg, but not the breaking. A thin and perfect line racing through something that had been whole once, bound up tight, but the women were gates, opening; they were a lock, snapped. Burst, they spread, up and out, out of themselves, a firework crackle that sparked and sped back toward earth. A sheet pulled back to reveal the true shape of the thing beneath, a sheet that snapped their spines straight and sent them tumbling, tumbling.

It was a shed-and-gone feeling, like the slough of Misty's skin from her bones, the heavy weight of all she carried pooled around her feet; it was an emptying, an outing, a fall and pouring.

"All these women know how it feels," Caroline said, her voice surfacing suddenly. "To be hurt. To have nobody care. Do you see the one in the red dress? With her hands in the air?"

Misty watched Miss Gail dancing by the pulpit, Penny's homeroom teacher who'd been at the prayer meeting the night everyone laid hands on Misty.

"She has nightmares every night," Caroline said. "Something happened to her like it happened to you and she dreams about it. And the one spinning around and around?"

Misty looked at Shannon.

"She's been hurt like you and me. Again and again. She doesn't think that anyone will ever love her like she is."

"That's not true," Misty said.

"And the one beside her. Do you know what happened to her?"

Misty's mother stomped her feet in quick little bursts, her face held up to the sky, her hands gripped into tight fists at her sides.

"I don't want to know," Misty said.

"No," Caroline said, "no you don't. But I know. And it has to stop somehow. All this hurting. Do you know the easiest way to find a person's name?"

"How?" Misty had wanted to know the answer to that question for so long, but she didn't want to hear it like this.

"All you have to know is what's hurt them most," Caroline said. "You just need that one sharp piece of them that they never could let go of. The thing they never could say. And you can make them do almost anything."

"What're you going to do?" Misty asked, but the garden, Caroline, was already gone.

There was no music, because there were no voices left to sing. All the women were raptured, their bodies taken and shaking to a song that only they could hear. The bottom was dark except for the glow of the sodium lamp, and beneath it, the women's bodies writhed.

William walked through the crowd of twisting women. They danced around him, and even with their eyes cinched tight, not a single woman came close to touching him. He stopped in front of his mother. Shannon spun on the tips of her toes, her heel falling and rising, but never resting for long. A shallow divot formed in the dirt beneath her.

William said something, but Shannon kept spinning. He said it again, louder, and again until Misty heard his voice over the stomping of the women's feet: "Mama?"

But the women kept dancing.

They danced as the men gathered near the pulpit and talked in quiet whispers, glancing now and then at the women's bodies.

They danced as Misty's father came walking down the road

toward the trailer. Penny was slouched at Misty's feet, drifting in and out of sleep, and their father looked between them and the women and the pastor. He found Misty's mother in the crowd, dancing with her chin dropped to her chest. His hands hovered by her shoulders like he was afraid to touch her, like she was sleepwalking and it might hurt to wake her. He tilted his head and looked down at her face, but she didn't look back. She was looking at something else, something far away and inside herself that no one else could see. Sweat pooled along her forehead, running in thin streams along the back of her neck. Dark stains appeared on the back of her gray blouse until it clung to her like a second skin. Misty's father said something, whispered close to her mother's ear, and then he grabbed her shoulders. The muscles strained beneath his shirt as he tried to hold her still.

"Beth?" he said.

Next time, he shouted.

But still, she danced.

Thirty-Five

Someone called 911. The only ambulance in town came and picked up the oldest woman who was caught in the spirit, strapped her to a gurney, and hauled her away. The rest of the women had to be taken in cars, forced through narrow doors, their arms pinned to their sides but straining all the while, fighting until they shook loose, pale hands jittering at the ends of their wrists like birds struggling to fly.

William cried. He clung to his mother's dress as someone forced a seat belt over her waist and shuffled William into the back seat. The other men remained blank-faced, their mouths set in rigid lines.

Misty's father tried to send her and Penny inside the trailer, and they went, for a moment, but they both ran onto the porch and caught one last glimpse of their mother's bare foot twitching through the open door of their father's truck before he shut it and ran to the other side. Gravel pinged off the sides of the trailer as he peeled away.

For twenty minutes the girls had been home entirely alone, and all they could do was sit on the couch side by side. A few green strings still clung to the walls, held on by thin scrapes of tape. They shifted in the breeze from the open door.

"Are you hungry?" Penny asked after a while.

Misty shook her head.

"Me neither."

"What's going to happen to Mom?" Misty asked.

Penny shook her head. "I don't know. I never seen anything like that."

"Me neither."

"I'm going to take the sheet down," Penny said.

"What?"

"In our room. I'm going to take it down."

"Okay."

"I don't think I've been very nice to you. I mean, you ain't been nice, either, but two wrongs don't make a right. And I don't know what's wrong with you, but I know that something is, and me acting wrong ain't going to help anything."

"What?"

"I'm saying sorry."

"Oh."

"Do you forgive me?" Penny asked.

Misty nodded.

"All right. Can I ask you a favor?"

"Is that the only reason you said sorry? So you could ask me a favor?"

"No. Geez. Give me a minute to ask, all right?"

"Fine."

"I keep thinking about those two threes. And how your now is the same as your...as your death, and I just don't want you to do anything to make that happen, okay? Do you promise?"

Tears welled in Misty's eyes as she nodded.

"A nod is a promise, okay?"

"Okay."

Dolly's car spun across the driveway a few minutes later, kicking gravel and dust into the air. She and Jem were arguing when they got out of the car and their voices echoed through the empty yard, the grass trampled flat, the statues glinting with waning moonlight. The minute they came through the door, they tried to feed the girls, but neither of them had an appetite. Penny asked if they could sleep in the living room, and Dolly dragged the mattresses from their beds and piled them full of pillows. She let them sleep with the television on, and Misty listened as Dolly and Jem whispered in the kitchen.

"What did he say?" Dolly asked.

"No change. They've got the women knocked out now. I reckon they had to about break out the horse tranquilizers to get them under, but they're all sleeping. It ain't a coma, he said, but it's close."

"A coma?" Dolly's voice rose an octave.

"Will you keep it down, big mouth? I don't want them girls to worry."

"I know, I know. I just… A coma? Ain't that worse?"

"Not in the state they were in. I guess this buys the doctors some time to figure out what's going on. If that head doctor don't have some answers soon, I'm going to go down there and show him the real meaning of 'emergency room.'"

They whispered some more about blankets and breakfast and what they would do with their children tomorrow before they walked into Misty's mother's bedroom and shut the door. Misty looked over at Penny, who lay beside her on her back, her eyes wide open and staring at the ceiling.

All night Misty tossed and turned in bed. Her skin felt too sweaty, too close, too much. It was all too much. She didn't know what to think about the garden now that she knew it had been Caroline all along. And that she had been trying to tell the world what happened to her all this time, praying that someone would listen. That someone would hear.

But no one did. Not even Misty. All this time she thought that the statues had been her fault somehow. That she had been making them happen with William and they reflected her own pain back to her, but it hadn't been her. It had been Caroline.

And now, because of this, her mother was sick, her mother trapped in some faraway place for real this time, maybe for good. And Misty didn't know how to help her, how to make Caroline set her mother and the other women free.

Misty clenched her hands into fists and her skin slid over her bones, the tips of her fingers gone numb as they tried to slip free of their skin.

But she couldn't shed her body now.

Not when there were so many things happening.

Not when she wasn't sure if she'd be able to get back into her skin this time.

All night Misty reached out to the garden, to Caroline, searching through the dark for any hint of her voice, but there was nothing, nothing to be found.

Thirty-Six

By the next nightfall, Misty's trailer was packed with family.

Two cookers boiled on the stove, filled with Misty's mother's favorite vegetable beef soup. Dolly's husband, Wayne, sat on the end of the couch with his hands spread apart while Charlene threaded different colors of yarn through his fingers. Every now and then he looked up from the baseball game on television to tell her how nice the braid would look on his key chain. Watching them made Misty's chest feel tight so she looked away.

Jem's sons, Jerry and Jamie, sat by the back door with loose-leaf paper and markers scattered between them. Sam sat outside on the concrete steps, flicking a lighter on and off. Misty climbed behind Jerry and stretched out across the washing machine and dryer. She pulled the hem of her T-shirt up so her back could rest against the cool metal. Even with both doors propped open, the house was muggy with the damp heat of too many bodies held too close together. The heat made Misty feel small, like there wasn't enough room in her body to hold her. Her skin weighed on her with such dogged insistence, demanding every moment that she be aware of this weight, these bends, these empty palms. She stretched herself as far as she could so that no part of her might be touching any other part of her. She tried again to reach out to Caroline, but there was nothing but silence in her head.

"Did you hear about Jerry's art award?" Jamie asked.

"Jem told us," Misty said. "I'm real glad you won."

"Yeah, thanks," Jerry said. "I was surprised."

"No he wouldn't." Sam leaned his head back. "Don't let him pretend to be modest."

"He beat the rest of them by a mile," Jamie said. "You should have seen the girl who got second place. Drew a bunch of lopsided cats with people teeth. Teeth just like mine and your'n."

Sam laughed.

"Them poor cats," Misty said.

"Them poor cats is right. And my poor eyes. I dreamed about them cats for a week straight afterwards. Probably won't ever be the same." Jamie shook his head. "They put Jerry's pictures in the hallway down at the courthouse for a whole month. Mom about pitched a fit, thinking they was going to keep them."

"She wants to hang them in the living room," Jerry said.

"Where?" Jamie asked. "There ain't a spare inch of wall that woman ain't hung something from. It's hard to think something is precious when she puts every damn thing she owns on display."

Sam leaned back and looked up at Jerry. "Well, one good thing came out of it. Tyler Bowling told Jerry that he thought he was the most talented person in the school."

"Nay," Jamie said, "the whole county."

"Country!" Sam yelled.

Jerry's cheeks pinked. "Come on now. Wayne might hear."

Jamie rolled his eyes. "Who cares what Wayne thinks. I'm almost broad enough to take him now."

"Take him where?" Sam asked. "Out for a nice steak dinner? He'd wipe the floor with you and your toothpick arms."

"I just don't want anybody giving me another speech," Jerry said, "about how hard it is to be quare and why can't I just meet a nice girl. I keep thinking one day they'll wake up and see that it's not bad."

Sam snorted. "Don't hold your breath, bub."

"Well, something has to give, because I ain't leaving just because of a bunch of ignorance." Jerry scribbled out an errant line, then grabbing a fresh piece of paper, started over. "Even if I have to show them myself."

"I ain't showing them nothing but the back of my head when I finally move out of here," Sam said. "I'm taking my quare ass up north."

"We shouldn't have to, though," Jerry said. "I don't want to leave."

They all fell quiet. Sam leaned back and cupped Jerry's elbow with his hand, held it gently in place as Jerry drew mountains across the page.

"You know," Misty said. "I don't understand why it has to be bad. 'Quare' sounds like a nice thing, don't it? Like...like..."

"Some kind of diamond or something," Sam said.

Misty smiled. "Yeah."

"Or one of them far-off places nobody can find on a map," Jamie said.

Jerry smiled. "I like it better the way y'all say it."

Jamie scooted closer to his brother, stopping only when their bare ankles touched, their shoulders resting against each other. Sam rested his head on a stack of fresh paper, and Misty rolled onto her side so she could watch Jerry drawing. His hand swept across the page and a dark line followed, smooth and even. He paused now and again, the ink bleeding a dark spot where his hand had stayed too long. The line curled back and around until he'd drawn the trailer where they sat, right down to the glob of tar that had dripped above Misty's window years before and dried there, big as a hornet's nest. He handed the drawing to Jamie, who rested it against the linoleum and began to color it in. Jamie's hand scrawled, scratched, and jerked. The marker squeaked under the pressure as he mixed yellow with red and brown. The colors he chose seemed to make no sense—the blue streaks in the grass and gray in the windows—but when he was finished, he pushed the drawing across the floor toward another pile of paper, and it looked right somehow. It looked like the way Misty imagined the trailer when she'd spent the whole day at school, some combination of solid lines and shifting colors, part memory and part truth.

"Can I have that one?" she asked.

"Huh?" Jerry said. "The trailer one? Sure, but I could do a whole lot better. Here, let me have your hand." Jerry reached for the nearest blue pen and Misty held out her hand. The tip of the pen felt cold against her skin, a little scratchy. Jerry switched pens a few times before he finally leaned back and squinted at her palm. "It smeared a little, but it looks all right. What do you think?"

"Not bad," Jamie said, "but you forgot something." He added his own marks, his tongue stuck between his teeth. "See now, that's just about perfect."

"My ass," Sam said. "Give me that purple one there. No, the darker one."

Misty tried to imagine what her cousins were drawing, but it was impossible to tell. The lines blurred together, overlapped, until Sam leaned back and smiled.

"There," he said.

"What're you all doing?" Penny asked. She had a biscuit in one hand and the television remote in the other.

"We're making art," Jamie said.

Penny walked over and inspected Misty's hand. A smile tugged at the corner of her mouth. "Can I add something?"

"Why not?" Jerry said. "Everybody else has."

Penny took a pen from the floor and added her own careful lines, though they trailed past Misty's palm and onto her wrist. "There now. Come on. William's at the door. I told him to get lost, but he says he needs to talk to you."

Misty turned her hand toward herself but Jerry grabbed her wrist. "You have to wait 'til we leave to look at it, all right? Until all this is over and your mom is back home. Then you can look at it."

"But—"

"It'll be better that way," Jamie said. "Like a surprise."

"You promise?" Jerry asked.

Misty slid from the dryer and onto the floor. She gripped her hand into a fist. "I promise."

"Hey," Jerry said. "I think your mom's going to be okay. From what my mom's told me, she's real tough, like the rest of them."

"Yeah," Sam said. "It'll take more than the Holy Ghost to take a Combs woman down."

Misty smiled and followed Penny through the warm air of the kitchen and living room to the front door. William stood on the porch. His eyes were rimmed red from crying.

"Hi," he said.

"Hi," Misty said.

"Well." Penny frowned. "He said he needed to talk to you."

"Just for a minute." William glanced inside at all the people glancing out at him. "On the steps, maybe."

Penny crossed her arms over her chest. "I can come, too."

"Why for?" William said. "I just want to talk to my friend. You know, my mom's in the hospital, too, the same as yours."

"Go on," Misty said. William wouldn't try to hurt her with so much family around. And there were some things Misty wanted to say to him, too. She pushed Penny toward the couch. "I won't be long."

Jem called that supper was ready as Misty followed William outside. Everyone piled into the kitchen except for her. William walked past the steps and across the yard and didn't stop until he reached the garden fence. He sat on the grass, leaving enough space for Misty to sit beside him, but she kept standing.

The statues had just finished their firelight burn, but they still held a faint glow of light at their very centers. The ax's blade glowed at the edges like it had just been pulled from the forge, and the tree's branches shimmered golden.

William said, "Have you talked to your mom?"

Misty shook her head. "No. Jem and Dolly talked to Dad. They said nothing's changed."

"That's what the doctor told Earl. Somebody called my aunt Rose and she's supposed to come and get me in the morning. She's going to take me to her house with her two rotten boys."

"I'm sorry," Misty said.

"I wish they'd just let me stay here by myself. I can't fix nothing if I ain't here with the statues. We have to do something to make this right."

"How?"

"I don't know. I figure it's got to be you."

"What's got to be me?" Misty asked.

"Everything. All this started with that bottle I planted, and you touched it. You're what made the difference."

Misty's eyes prickled with tears. "Did you ever once think that the statues wasn't a good thing? Or what you did in the barn?"

"We did that stuff in the barn. Both of us."

"No."

William scowled. "It was the only thing to keep the statues growing. We had to do that. It can't be bad if something good came from it."

"Nothing good did! Nothing good ever did!"

Misty backed toward her trailer. Her feet sank into a hollow that the crawdads had made and cold water splashed across her calves, her toes sinking between blades of grass to the soggy earth beneath, something like mud, but thicker, congealed. Her bones shifted inside her foot, her skin sagging, because even when she didn't mean it to, her body was begging to be gone.

Caroline knocked at the back of Misty's mind and she answered, frantic.

"You should be careful," Caroline said.

William stood and took a step toward Misty. "What'll we do then? We could try going back to the barn. That might help." He reached for her hand, but the skin slipped right through his grip.

"No," Misty said.

"We got to try something. We could… We could bury something else in the garden. Something bigger. Something I ain't tried before. I thought about… Well, I thought about—" He took a step closer. "What do you think would happen if we went under there? What do you think the garden could do for us if we planted ourselves instead of some stupid bottle. It took everything I gave it, and it gave me something back most every time. It made them better, too. What do you think it could do for us if we gave it a chance?"

"Tell him to try," Caroline whispered. "I'll take care of him."

"No," Misty said aloud.

"But we have to. We have to fix my mom." William caught the hem of Misty's shirt between his fingers and pulled. He wrapped his hand around her shoulder, his fingers sliding under the collar of her shirt. He was crying again, his chest heaving up and down like there was something inside him that was fighting its way out. "Misty, you have to fix this. You got to."

"Run," Caroline said. "Now, Misty. Run!"

Misty pried William's hand from her shirt. She pushed him away, turned, and ran. She curved right at the bank of the creek, her feet sliding in the grass, and darted for the trees at the back of her trailer. William followed. He called her name softly, not loud enough that her aunts might hear through the open door. The light from the trailer poured into the backyard, and Misty caught a glimpse of everything as she turned her head—William running behind her, her aunts silhouetted in the light from the small kitchen window, the empty back room with the drawings scattered across the floor.

Then the trees blocked her vision. Branches whipped against her face. Twigs pulled at her hair, and she ran, ripping them loose, not watching where she went. She stumbled over a dip in the ground, scratched her palms on an upturned rock, kept running. William was faster than her, and all he had to do was follow. He didn't have to clear the path or know the woods. He only had to know her, the pale cloth of her shirt floating in the darkness.

"Don't let him catch you," Caroline said.

And Caroline's memories burned through Misty's vision. They flashed in front of her eyes, blotting out the trees, eating away her path. In one blink there were the woods she was running through, and in the next blink were the woods that Caroline knew, the woods that Earl would buy and cut and change. Ahead of her, a dogwood tree stood in a little clearing, its blooms glowing under the moonlight, and Misty knew that it must have been Caroline's tree, Caroline's memory. And even though the image was years gone, she could recognize the place where the garden would be, the place that would become her home, and she ran toward it through the dark.

Something inside the tree moved like water. The bark rippled and shifted until a face emerged from the trunk, its cheeks whittled with dark wood and light, its eyes sunken. There was no long brown hair, no bruises on her arms, but Misty still recognized Caroline as she rose from the trunk like a dark wave. Above her, in the branches, were dozens of birds of all shapes and colors. They crowded together, their wings rustling and shifting.

William called Misty's name just behind her, but she didn't turn her head. She kept running toward Caroline's memory.

But Earl was there, too.

A younger Earl, taller and broader than Misty remembered.

Earl with an ax in his hand.

"Please," Misty said.

She pried the door in her chest open and called out to everything in the woods. Everything she'd ever spoken to. The poplar and maple and elm, the little rocks grown smooth at the bottom of the creek, the kudzu stealing along the bank, the wildflowers bobbing in the shadows with their dim faces turned toward the sky. She called the earth, the dirt, the underneath. Called the worms and all the skittering bugs, called every bird in every nest.

"Please," Misty said. "Help me."

And Earl said something to Caroline as Misty ran closer. Sweat beaded on his skin. His mouth twisted in a snarl as he drew the ax over his head. The birds screeched in the branches, their beaks opening and shutting, their feathers splayed. They swarmed at him, trying to chase him away. One of the birds scratched the palm of his raised hand, drawing blood, but it didn't stop him. Nothing could stop him.

Misty closed her eyes and jumped over a fallen log just as Caroline sank down the tree, down, down to the roots, where she could hide.

Where she could wait.

The ground swelled beneath Misty. The ground sank and spread, made a space just big enough for her. Above her, Earl swung the ax in the memory as Misty landed with a jolt hard enough to knock the breath from her lungs. The ground rushed in around her. It sealed her up inside itself until only a small circle of light remained a few feet ahead, like the entrance to a crawdad burrow. A few specks of earth fell onto her cheeks and Misty brushed them away. William's footsteps pounded the earth above her, but he sounded hollow from underneath.

"Misty!" he called. "Misty!"

A crawdad wriggled through the soft earth beside her and plopped onto the tunnel where she lay. It paused in front of her mouth for a moment, just long enough for the water in its burrow to seep through into Misty's. The water was cold and dark and sweet-smelling. It trickled inside, wetting Misty's knees and elbows, splashing against her cheek. The crawdad started digging a new hole into the earth, a new place for the water to follow, and she wondered, for the first time, how much of the bottom was left. All those long days of digging and tearing, all those burrows, all those chimneys. The potholes and the hollows in the yard, the trailer sinking like everything beneath them had been replaced by darkness, by cold, sweet water.

Above her, William's footsteps receded, then vanished. His voice was replaced by the whirring of the crickets. Misty crawled along her tunnel until she reached the round circle of light at the end.

She climbed out over the damp leaves piled high from last year's fall. She looked behind her. A little mound was there that hadn't been there before, the ground rising up to meet Misty's fall, forming a hill the exact shape of her body as she curled on her side in the dark.

As she watched, the hill collapsed.

The earth crumbled and fell and the mound deflated again. The earth returned to the shape it had been before.

"Are you okay?" Caroline asked.

Misty shook her head. She didn't have a name for the feelings twisting through her. If she did, she might have called them away.

"Misty!" A woman's voice called from somewhere between the trees, though it was hard to tell if it was Jem or Dolly. Misty wiped the dirt from her cheeks.

If she turned back home, William would still be there, just across the yard. He wouldn't leave until his aunt came in the morning. Until then, Misty's house was filled with people. Her house was too loud, too bright, too warm. Penny would ask what had happened. She'd want to know why Misty had been crying. Her aunts would want to know, too, with their warm hands and their concerned faces. Her cousins would crowd around her, taking up all her space, breathing up all the air. There'd be nowhere to turn without touching some-body and nowhere to go where she might find quiet. It would be like the church all over again, all those hands weighing her down. And she didn't know how to answer them. She didn't know how to make any of it stop. Her father was gone and her mother was lying in the hospital alone. She might never wake up again, and there was no way that Misty knew to fix it. There was nothing she could think to make things right again.

Misty closed her hand into a fist and felt the bones slide together beneath her skin. Her hand went numb slowly, and then altogether, until she couldn't feel the place where her arm ended. Her hand was empty, blank, and endless.

"Misty?" Caroline said just as Aunt Jem called her name again.

Misty turned and walked further into the woods.

Thirty-Seven

Misty hid her skin in the hollow belly of a maple tree.

She rested her chin on her chest, tucked her arms around her knees, curled her toes so they might fit inside the tree instead of sprouting like mushrooms from its bark. Her eyes refused to stay closed so they stared, bewildered, at her own palms as if wondering what had happened to bring them to such a place.

Already, Misty felt lighter.

Already, the heavy weight of her mother's dancing and of her family crowded tight into her house and of William's hand at the collar of her shirt and William's hand on her neck and William's hand—already the weight was lifted. Even as she ripped some brush from the ground and arranged it around the trunk to hide her body, she had forgotten half of what had sent her running out of her skin. It didn't seem like such a terrible thing anymore. Nothing did.

Misty turned to walk further into the woods, thinking of the way her bones would rattle if she walked upstream through the creek, of the silver flash of minnows between her toes, and the kudzu she might wrap around her shoulders like a cape, the kudzu peeling from the mountain to trail behind her feet, the mountain sliding away, the whole world unraveling in her wake.

Penny stood a few trees away, her hands cupped around her mouth. She was calling Misty's name.

Misty froze. She'd been so focused on hiding herself that she hadn't heard Penny coming through the woods. Now all Penny had to do was turn around and she would see Misty there, standing alone in her soft glowing bones. Misty waited.

Penny turned. She looked to the other side instead where Jem and Dolly struggled through the dark. They carried heavy flashlights, and their denim skirts were hiked to their knees so they could fight against the underbrush. Misty cowered behind the tree where her skin waited, her name echoing faintly around her.

William crashed through the woods with his own pocket flashlight sputtering a narrow beam onto his feet. He stopped just shy of Dolly, his narrow chest heaving as he looked up at her the way an ant might look at a mountain.

"What did you do?" Penny yelled.

She whipped around and stormed toward William. When she reached him, she planted both hands on his shoulders and shoved. His foot caught something in the grass, and he hit the ground hard.

"Penny!" Dolly yelled.

"What did you do to her? What did you do?" Penny punched at William's chest and belly. He tried to scoot away, but he was caught, helpless until Dolly wrenched Penny to the side, her fists still swinging. "He did something! He came to talk to her and now she's gone!"

"Have you seen her?" Jem asked. She shone her flashlight in William's eyes until he squinted, then lowered the beam to his chin.

"No," William said. "She—she said she was going back home. And I went back home. And that was it. I thought she was with you."

"He's lying!"

"Penny," Dolly hissed. She wrapped her arms around Penny's elbows as Penny squirmed and kicked the ground.

Jem loomed above William. Her dark hair had come loose from her bun, and little hairs were plastered to her cheeks and forehead. Her skin looked pale blue beneath the faint moonlight, the dips, the peaks, the wrinkles of her face lost to Misty's eyes and she seemed to swim in space above William, an extension of the trees themselves. She seemed, for a moment, much bigger than herself as she leaned down and took William's hand in her own and helped him up.

"Son," she said. "This is very serious, what's happening. I need to know you're telling us the truth."

"I ain't lying," William said.

Jem looked back at Dolly. Dolly shook her head.

"He's lying, Jem." Penny dropped her chin to her chest and slumped in Dolly's arms.

"Go on home." Jem pointed the flashlight through the woods. "If you hear or see her at all, you tell one of us, all right? Go." When William was far enough away, Jem turned back to Penny and Dolly. "I don't trust that little thing as far as I could throw him, but what can we do? Take Penny back to the house. Get her something to drink and calm her down. We're going to find your sister, Penny. I promise you that. And I'm awful proud of that right hook of yours, but we can't do a thing if we lose our heads. So go on."

"Should I call the hospital?" Dolly asked.

"Not yet. Give us some time before we scare everybody half to death. I'm going to walk through the woods and meet you back in the yard. Get everybody lined up and ready to search."

When her family turned away, Misty climbed the maple tree as quick and quiet as she could. She'd never been able to climb trees in her skinned body. She'd always been too afraid of falling. There'd always been so much of her to hurt, so much skin to cut, so much softness to lose, but her bones didn't mind at all. It never occurred to them that they could break, so they didn't hesitate as she swung her legs onto a heavy bough. She rested her ankles in an empty bird's nest, the bottom littered with bright white shards of egg.

Below her on the ground, Jem walked slowly between the trees. She swung her flashlight back and forth, calling Misty's name.

By morning, everyone in the family had searched the woods, the bottom, the road, the creek. Jamie and Jerry walked side by side, shouting. Sam stood in the middle of the woods and closed his eyes like he was searching inside himself for Misty. Charlene carried a plate of biscuits that she refused to put down, thinking Misty hungry, thinking food enough to bring her back when nothing else could.

Even Earl came. He never once opened his mouth to call her name, but he stood not far from her tree and tipped back his head and closed his eyes. He stood there in the deepest black of night, and Misty knew that he was praying for her. She could almost feel the words lift up between the trees like fog rising from the mountains.

Every hour that passed, her family's voices grew fainter until Misty couldn't hear them at all even as she watched Penny standing in the distance, the muscles of her throat straining as she yelled until Jem wrapped an arm around Penny's waist, picked her up, and carried her home. There was a moment near dawn that Misty saw something shimmering in the distance—the dark shape of a woman with her hand outstretched and a bright flame flickering at the end. Whether the flame came from a lantern or from her hand, it was impossible to tell. But Misty could have sworn that the woman looked right at her before she turned and walked away.

Eventually, the woods emptied and the sun returned. Misty's bones didn't ache from sitting so long in the same position, unmoved.

Her bones didn't feel, didn't need, didn't care. The longer she sat on the branches, the harder it was to remember why she'd come there in the first place. It was better this way. This body better than her own had ever been, kinder than her skin, gentler than her own heart.

She shimmied down the trunk once she was sure that no one was coming back. The sun was already creeping toward afternoon, and almost a day had passed since she ran from William and took shelter in the woods. She scooped her skin from the hollow of the tree, meaning to find a final place for it to rest, somewhere that it would never be found. Just to be sure, she slipped her arm inside her mouth and tried to fit herself back into place. Her hand barely made it past her shoulder before the skin tightened, slowed, stopped. She wiggled her fingers in her upper arm, trying to press forward, but there was no use.

Even if she wanted to go back, she couldn't.

Too much time had passed. Too many things had happened. She'd outgrown herself at last, and her body wasn't hers anymore. Her body hadn't been hers for a long, long time.

Thirty-Eight

Misty's head lolled back and her eyes stared at the grass as she carried her body through the woods. She stopped by a hickory tree whose branches yawned toward the sky. There were holes in the ground from the squirrels digging up the nuts as they fell. The earth was soft, a little damp. She couldn't smell it anymore—the rich, dark dankness of the ground—but she had loved that smell. She'd scooped a handful of dirt into her mouth once because of that smell, because she wanted to know if it would melt in her mouth or turn to silt between her teeth, because just the smell hadn't been close enough. She'd needed to know it better, to feel it as part of herself.

Misty laid her body beside the hickory tree. She was a tangle of limbs, her knees stacked atop each other like firewood, her fingers splayed, her jaw slack. She wore one of her father's shirts, OSHA written in bold, white letters across black fabric that had faded near gray after years in the wash. The sleeves reached Misty's elbows and the hem swung almost to her knees, past the frayed end of her favorite blue-jean shorts with a plaid patch sewn into one of the back pockets. She'd taken the shirt from her mother's dresser after their father took her away to the hospital. Misty thought Penny would say something cruel to her, but when she saw the shirt, Penny had walked into her parents' bedroom and came back wearing one just like it.

Misty slotted her finger bones into the holes that the squirrels dug into the soft earth. Her arms didn't grow tired the way they did when they were skinned. She didn't sweat or lose her breath. She dug slow and even, pulling back the dark earth growing darker the deeper she went. She wrenched stones loose and tossed them over her shoulder. She broke roots as thin and creeping as spider's legs. Her body piled in a heap beside her, her feet bare and her forehead resting on the fallen leaves.

As she dug her grave, Misty considered that it might be easier if she left her body somewhere it might be found instead of hiding it. If she tossed herself from the bank of the creek so she was half-submerged, one shoe kicked off, her dark hair floating in the slow current. Like she'd tripped and fallen, like she'd hit her head just a little too hard. She might coax the copperhead from its hiding place and hold it up to her skin, let it have its pick of which tender places it would bite. It wasn't like she would feel the venom anyway. Nothing could burn a skin that wasn't hers; nothing could pierce her or cut her, not anymore. She could prop herself against a sycamore, her body curled tight around the wounds that killed her, like she'd been walking home when she was overcome and her life ended beneath the watchful trees.

Then her family would know, at least, that she was gone.

But even her bones felt wrong about that. Even then, unskinned, she didn't want anyone to find one part of her without the rest. If she left, then her skin left, too, her skin as gone as her bones would be. It made sense to her.

Of course, her family would miss her. Their faces blurred in her mind, overlapping, joining, until they seemed to be a single person who looked a lot like her. They might never stop searching for her, but they would never find her, and eventually, they would move on. They would build the house their mother dreamed of, and Penny would never have to share her room again. She'd carry Misty's backpack all through high school, and anytime someone mentioned how childish it looked—bright purple with little stickers fading along the front pocket—Penny would whip her eyes at them and say something so cruel and quick that eventually people stopped asking. Penny would learn how to cast cards not for herself, but for Misty, and every year she would draw the same spread—the three at the beginning and the end. Penny would keep the sheet she tacked across their room tucked under her bed as a reminder. She'd take it out every now and then and stare at the stitches, half-expecting to see Misty's shadow dart across it just like it had on all those nights that summer.

Her father would come home. No one would say that it should happen. There wouldn't be a discussion or an agreement, but he would be there again one morning, at the table drinking a cup of black coffee, and they would go on as if it had always been that way. He would kiss Penny on the forehead every night and read her stories before bed the way he'd always meant to when she was small. Penny would indulge him for a while, though she could never fall asleep to the sound of his voice, always waiting for him to get up and leave so she could relax into the familiar space of his absence.

One summer night a few years after Misty left, her father would drink too much at his brother's house and demand to be driven into town. He would wake up the only tattoo artist he knew and beg to have Misty's name inked on his chest, right across the rib he had broken when he was ten years old, falling from the back of his father's truck. The man would oblige, but the minute the needle hit his skin, her father would say he wanted a crawdad instead. He wouldn't know why, but it would feel right, and he would carry it with him for the rest of his life, catching sight of it from the corner of his eye some mornings as he got ready for work, his skin working the crawdad into motion like it was burrowing into his chest.

Her mother and all the other women would wake up. It might take a while, but Misty was sure that Caroline would give up once she knew that Misty was gone, when she realized that she was alone again, alone for good. The statues would stay or they would crumble. The crawdads would be released back to themselves and find their way home to the creek. They would remember Misty in their stories, an image of her passed between them through generations. Caroline would recede deeper and deeper into the earth until she forgot herself completely. Any sadness or doubts Misty had about her plan were left buzzing in her skin, and Misty's bones were sure that the world would return to normal in her absence.

When her mother got back home, it would break her heart to know Misty was gone, but after some time, she would recover. She might even go back to school. Get her GED and take some poetry classes at the community college, writing long elegies in a little leather journal that she bought just for herself. Every summer she would come back to the woods and read them to the trees. From sunup to sundown, she'd stand beneath their shade, the hot air heavy on her neck, her voice cracking to barely a whisper as she recited all the things she thought Misty might have been that year.

"You would be taller than me by now," her mother would say and she would look up, her chin tilted just a fraction of an inch, and she would see Misty in front of her, Misty made of light and sundust, Misty's eyes dark and smiling, and she would cry the way she did every year, every month, every week.

Her mother and father and sister would draw closer, the three of them closing up like a pine cone before a storm, shielding the soft core that had been exposed by Misty's leaving. All she'd wanted for so long was for her family to be together, and now she realized that all they needed to make that happen was for her to disappear. She would be the wound they couldn't recover from, the one thing that would bind them together forever.

As for herself, she wasn't sure.

Her bones were quickly losing their ability to hear or see, so she would take to the woods. There were miles and miles of forest within the mountains. She would follow the nearest trail for as long as she could, and then she'd lie down somewhere soft and wait until she forgot every moment of her life, every happiness and every hurt. The grass would sprout through her ribs. Wildflowers would bloom in her eye sockets. Chipmunks and ground squirrels would gnaw on her finger bones, their little teeth etching runnels into the bone until they plucked them away and carried them off to their nests, to their children, to the far ends of the woods that Misty had never seen before.

Snow would fill all her empty spaces. It would melt and freeze and thaw again, cracking her skull and splitting her vertebrae, sinking her deeper into the ground.

It would peaceful, at least.

It would be over, at least.

By the time Misty had dug a hole deep enough for her body, night had come and the stars blinked sleepy eyes at her between the trees. It was almost impossible to see in the dark, her senses lost so that only her own brightest bones were visible, and the smooth, pale circle of her face as she rolled herself into her grave.

Her skin made a soft, thumping sound as it hit the earth.

Misty climbed down and arranged her limbs. She tilted her chin back and pulled her hair onto her shoulders. She ran her finger bones through the dark strands, her knuckles snagging on tangles and knots, and she did her best to break them free. She was careful of her tender scalp even when she wasn't in it. She could still feel the thin skin pulling from the time they had been running late for church and their mother told Penny to brush Misty's hair. It had felt like Penny took out every wrong that Misty had ever done, every pinch, every ounce of trouble she'd ever caused on Misty's scalp that day.

Misty pulled the hem of her T-shirt over her belly. A scar etched its way along the bottom of her rib cage, glinting like water beneath moonlight. She'd seen a little gray kitten walking along the mouth of her granny's well and climbed up to catch it before it fell, but fell herself. Her leg got tangled in the rope and she tumbled to the side. A nail tore a small wound on her side that bled through three handfuls of paper towels before it slowed. Her granny called it her spear wound and said she bled more than Jesus on the cross.

Misty straightened her feet, but they kept sinking to the side, the toes curled slightly inward. She ran her finger bone along the thin scar on the sole of her foot from when she'd stepped on an old soup can in the creek. The tetanus shot had ached for a week afterward.

She straightened her shorts over a dark patch of skin on the back of her thigh, discolored by an old burn her father promised would heal with time. She had taken to sleeping on the couch the first summer they lived in Earl's trailer. There was something about their room that made her throat tight. Her father had kissed her on the cheek before he left for work one morning, and as he bent down, the lid on his thermos slipped off, and the hot coffee spilled all over the back of Misty's leg.

And just below the burn, a little hook of a scar on the side of her right knee from her last whipping. All the other marks from that evening had faded.

There were so many hurts that hadn't killed her. So much pain she had forgotten.

And there were other things, too.

A little mole on her ankle that was the exact size and shape and place of the mole on her mother's ankle. It was proof, her mother said, that Misty was hers. Even if the Lord put a hundred Mistys on this earth, she would find her.

The little dimple on her shoulder that her mother said came from her uncle, who died before Misty ever met him, but he was there, tied to her through their bodies. He had been a good man, her mother said, and Misty always wished she could have met him.

Her legs were long for her age, and her father said she had baseball calves—strong and muscled—hill-climbing legs that let her scurry up mountains and across the creek, that ran her through the woods until she didn't have to run anymore.

But every place Misty touched had been touched before.

William's hands were needing, seeking things that dimpled her skin and gripped too hard and lingered long after he was gone. She'd had that tight-throat feeling every morning since he took her to the barn, struggling out of sleep to a body that was not her own, a body warped beneath his hands, reshaped until it was what he needed it to be for as long as he needed it, until she couldn't bear the feeling of herself and she had to escape.

Misty took one of her hands inside her own so that she was reversed—the bone cradling the skin. There was something smudged against her palm so she held it up to the light where her fading eyes could make out the shape.

It was the drawing that Jerry and Jamie and Sam and Penny had made.

It was Misty.

She stood on the center of her palm. The ink was a little blurred from her sweat, but she could still see herself there, standing on what might have been a mountain. Jerry had drawn her smiling. He'd drawn her in the light of a pale-yellow sun that bled across her fingers. There were little dots of freckles on her face and Jamie must have added those, his pen tapping against her hand like Morse code. There was grass at her feet and flowers everywhere, and Sam had added those. And just off to the side was a crawdad. Its body was almost as big as Misty's, its claws dark and lopsided, but it had a crooked smile drawn onto its face, too. Penny had left out most of its legs, but it was a crawdad all the same.

That was what they saw when they looked at Misty.

Not marks, not bruises, not pain. Just her, standing in the warm sunlight in a field of flowers. Just her, happy.

Misty placed her hand gently on the ground. She brushed a line of dirt from her cheek and smoothed the hair away from her eyes. She lifted up her arm and fit herself into the crook of her own shoulder. She wrapped her bone arm around her own waist and rested her skull against her chest. Her body was cool and solid beneath her, her body a small, persistent weight, a pressure that hummed inside her bones.

Misty lay beside herself for a long time.

This was the kind of touch she'd wanted—a gentle, easy touch, a resting touch that didn't ask for anything too much, and never asked without giving back. If she'd had her tongue, she would have told herself how sorry she was, not for what William had done to her, but for what she had done to herself.

All the blame she'd taken into her skin.

All the guilt and the hurt and the shame that she'd held inside her body until it couldn't bear the weight of it anymore and she had to shed herself just to breathe.

She'd been so afraid that her friends and family would abandon her if they found out what happened in the barn that she ended up abandoning herself. She hadn't escaped their leaving at all. She'd done it for them.

Misty thought back to the day when William had come down to the creek. Before spin the bottle, before the garden, before the green glass man grew and everything changed. She remembered herself lying by the creek with the crawdads crawling over her, and all she had wanted was for her family to be okay, for someone to talk to, to listen.

It had never occurred to her that they might already be okay or that, after all she'd been through, she might still be okay, too.

If she left now, she would never know. And she wouldn't just be leaving herself. She'd be leaving her family, too.

Misty pressed her jawbone to her cheek in a kiss.

She sat up and pulled her mouth open gently. She apologized even though she couldn't speak inside her bone body. She thought over and over again how she had been wrong to blame herself. Wrong to send her body away when she needed it so much.

Misty pushed her leg bones over her tongue first, her toes curled as she slid them down her throat, her belly, her thigh. Her body adjusted, allowing the bones back into their old place. She expected the pain to be worse than before. She expected to break into her body like someone stealing, someone claiming, but her body remembered these bones.

Her body recognized Misty and welcomed her back.

And as she slipped into her skin, Misty had an idea. She wasn't sure that she could fix everything that had gone wrong, but she knew a place to start.

She pulled her body over her knee bones and slotted her hips back into place; she covered her spine with tissue and cloaked her arms with skin. She paused before she pulled her face over her skull again. She took one last dim look around the woods, gone almost to black now just before the sun rose. She could pick up only the faintest line of light above the trees before she slipped her skin over her head and joined herself again.

Grow

There is a brief window of time
that exists between the
shedding of the old shell and the
hardening of the new shell.
It's the only chance for the crawdad to grow
before its new body hardens once more.
The only chance to become truly
different from what it was before.

Thirty-Nine

It was still dark when Misty rounded the corner of the trailer, though the edges of the sky were beginning to lighten. She threaded between dozens of crawdad chimneys until she sunk her leg almost to the knee in a pit of water so cold that it took her breath away. She pulled herself free and stood shaking beside it. The yard was littered with holes and hollows. Most of the grass was submerged in clear water. Earl's trailer had slipped from the blocks that held it aloft and sunk to one side of the yard. The windows on that side had shattered. Glass glittered in the grass, and a pale curtain drifted out to float in the wind.

Penny watched the curtain flutter from the front porch. A can of warm Pepsi lay beside her feet along with a bag of Misty's favorite half-and-half cookies.

There were four cars parked in the driveway, but her father's truck wasn't one of them, and there were no noises coming from the trailer. Misty hesitated, not wanting to wake anyone just yet, not wanting the noise and questions that would follow. Then Penny turned her head.

Her face didn't change at first. She stared at Misty as if she didn't quite recognize her. Then her eyebrows lifted a fraction of an inch. Her face crumpled. Penny heaved three great breaths before she pushed herself from the porch. She wobbled, stiff, down the steps and across the grass. She didn't seem to notice the water that splashed onto the hem of her nightgown or the way she teetered back and forth. She wrapped her arms around Misty's shoulders and Misty hooked her arms underneath. There was still a flicker of terror in Misty's throat at being touched. Even though this wasn't the same as what had happened in the barn, the panic was the same, the need to push away, to run.

Misty said, "Lord, you stink."

Penny hiccuped a laugh and pushed Misty away gently. "That's because we've been rooting around all over the place looking for you."

"Sorry."

"Where did you go?"

"I hid."

"Where?"

"The woods."

Penny crossed her arms over her chest. "Didn't you hear us yelling for you?"

"I need your help," Misty said.

Penny frowned. "What kind of help?"

"I just need you to come with me."

"Where?"

"To the garden."

"Oh. Well. Okay. There's something I need to tell you first."

"What?"

"William went missing, too. Right after you did."

Misty tried to swallow around the tightness in her throat, but the feeling wouldn't budge. It lodged there, pressing and pressing, so her words had to fight their way free. "Has anybody found him yet?"

"No. Earl's still out looking. We have to call the police today. We was going to call them about you, but you're here now. Have you seen William?"

Misty shook her head. "What about Mom?"

"I heard Aunt Jem and Dolly talking, and they said something about comas. Nobody'll tell me what's going on."

"But everyone's still here?"

"Yeah. Nobody wanted to leave in case you came back. We was up real late looking for you. We went to the school and to Jem and Dolly's houses and their garden, all the way into town. Jem was convinced you was up at the pond, the one we went to last summer. She said you liked the water. You should have seen her face when you wasn't there." Penny shivered. "You're lucky you didn't have to. We should go tell them you're back."

"Wait," Misty said. "Can we do this first?"

"I've been nice, Misty, but they need to know you're all right. Jem cried. I ain't never seen her cry. She punched a hole in the living room wall after, but still. She was crying there for a minute."

"I know." Misty rubbed her hand across her face and the bones shifted beneath, trying to escape. Now that her bones knew they could slip free, they tried to leave of their own accord, chased away by her sadness, fear, or pain. "But we need to do this first. Please, Penny. I have to do this, and I don't think I can do it by myself."

"Will you tell me what's been going on then?"

Misty nodded.

"Okay," Penny said. "Okay, but we have to hurry."

A faint mist clung to the barest tips of the trees, and it grew thinner with every step they took toward the garden. Any minute now, the sun would lift above the mountains and tear the mist apart, scatter it back to whatever it had been before. Earl's trailer was empty and so was William's. The creek trickled and cars passed by on the main road and birds chirped in the distance—the holler just as alive as it had ever been.

Caroline knocked at the back of her mind and Misty answered.

"I thought you were leaving," Caroline said. "You ran off and shed your little skin again. I saw you bone-walking through the trees. I saw the home you dug for yourself by the creek."

"I changed my mind," Misty said.

"He didn't."

"Who?"

Caroline's voice faded and Misty heard another sound beneath. Something small and humming, something full of static.

It was William.

She wasn't sure how she knew, but she did. He had planted himself in the garden just like he'd planted everything else, just like he'd told her the night before. He planted himself so he might come back bigger and stronger, so all his cracks might be glossed over, so he might shine.

"It won't work," Caroline said. "He's almost gone."

Misty stopped when she reached the fence and turned to her sister. "He's gone."

"Who?" Penny asked.

"William. I think he planted himself here."

Misty hoisted herself over the fence and landed in the garden. The statues had always been cooler than everything else, and the air between them was like an early November morning. The garden soil had partially frozen so that every time Misty took a step, the dirt crunched beneath her bare feet, broke apart, and crumbled.

"Wait. He planted himself? Like in the garden?"

Misty nodded.

Penny climbed onto the fence and sat on the top rail. "What's going to happen to him? If he comes sprouting back out of this field, then I am done with this place. Honestly. I'm moving in with Aunt Jem."

Misty shook her head. "I don't think he's coming back. He thought he could. That it'd be just like the statues. He thought he'd come back and he wouldn't feel bad anymore and his mom would be okay."

"What'd he feel bad for?"

Misty toyed with the hem of her shirt. She'd gotten back into her body for this, to come here and help. But for a moment it seemed like a terrible idea. A small part of her wished that she'd stayed inside her bones instead so she wouldn't have to answer Penny's question. Then she wouldn't have to tell the truth. The skin around her mouth loosened, wanting to leave her, but Misty grit her teeth. She took a deep breath and said, "Do you remember when we played spin the bottle?"

"Yeah," Penny said. "That feels like forever ago."

"Well—" Misty began, but a voice cut through her thoughts, stopping her.

"What're you doing?" Caroline asked. "You're not going to tell her, are you?" Her voice filled Misty's hands with shards of gravel, slicking her throat with the oil that leaked from Earl's truck and onto the dry dirt.

Misty ignored Caroline. "It didn't start there. In the barn. Not for a while. I guess it started a long time ago, though, with me. With what I can do."

"You ain't making any sense," Penny said.

"I don't know how to tell you what I have to tell you." Misty's throat contracted and the sadness crested, pushing up and up until there was no place left to go. "I'm afraid."

"Of what?"

"I don't know."

"Why would you tell her?" Caroline whispered. "She doesn't know about those hurts. She's not like us."

"Will it help if I look away?" Penny asked. "I can turn around, like when the girls is changing in the locker room. I don't have to see you to hear you."

Misty nodded and Penny swung her legs around until she was facing the trailer instead of the garden, and it did help somehow. It eased some of the pressure in Misty's chest not to be seen. All this time she had hoped to find a way to talk to her family without words. It felt like the only chance she had of being heard. But she'd been wrong. No matter which way she did it, the truth was hard. It hurt.

Caroline said, "If you tell her, then she'll leave. That's what they do. And then you'll be like me."

Misty covered her eyes with her hands. "That's not true."

"What isn't?" Penny asked.

"Nothing," Misty said. "Just…the first thing I have to tell you is about me and the second thing is about William, but I'm going to start with him." She slotted her fingers together and the bones wiggled beneath, begging to leave. She clenched her hands tight to hold herself in place. "It was after we played spin the bottle. I saw him outside that night, and we planted the bottle together. In the garden. It just looked so lonely, and we was both sad because of Mom and Dad and his mom and Harold. And then the green glass man grew. So William wanted to keep planting things. And then…" Misty pressed her fingers against her cheeks. "I don't know which parts to tell you."

"None of them," Caroline said. "You can stop now and she doesn't have to know. You can come down under here, right here, with me and you won't ever have to tell anyone again. You'll be safe."

Misty's mouth filled with the taste of dust, of green. Her arms laced with bone-white roots that pulled her down. Tears poured over her cheeks, and her breath hitched in her chest.

"Hey," Penny said. "It's okay. You're doing okay. William planted the bottle and the statue grew and..."

"And he wanted them to keep growing," Misty said. "So he got another bottle and he asked me to spin it and he planted that one, too. And another statue grew. And then we went back to the barn, but we didn't... It wasn't me and him. It was him. And he did things." Misty's chest heaved. The skin on her shoulder drooped and she held it back up with her hand, forced herself back into place. She wrapped her arms around her chest and squeezed and squeezed. "I didn't like what he did, but I didn't know what to do. And I didn't want to tell nobody."

"He—" Penny paused. "Did he...hurt you?"

Misty nodded and Penny knew it somehow without ever turning around. Penny's shoulders slumped like her body wanted to leave, too.

Caroline was silent, listening.

"And it went on," Misty said. "For a while, it went on. And things kept growing, and I thought it had something to do with what I am. What I can do."

"Wait, what can you do?"

"I don't know," Misty sobbed. "I don't know what it's called. I ain't never met nobody who could do it but me. I talk to things sometimes. Birds or crawdads. The barn. And sometimes they talk back to me. In my head. They use pictures. Sometimes they use words. I want you to look now, Penny."

Forty

Misty walked through the garden to the place where the statue of the bird stood on its clawed feet, its wings outstretched, always on the edge of flying, but never really leaving. A thin crack etched its way over the bird's eye and splintered across its beak. If she wanted, Misty could use her name to make the statue turn back into what it had been before. She could split herself into even more pieces and undo what Caroline had done. Everything would seem normal again.

But then she wouldn't be any different from Earl or William or Caroline.

It didn't have to be that way, though. She could give them a choice, like the one she had made to come back to her body.

"You don't have to do this," Caroline whispered.

"If I don't, then everything's going to get worse. There's already cracks in the statues. Some of the crawdads died."

"I didn't know that at first," Caroline said. "I swear. I didn't know that calling something out of its name hurts it. But if you do it long enough, it can kill it. I think—I think when you rename something like your skin, it stops changing. Stops growing. And names have to change to be names. They have to grow. I should have known. That's how I felt my whole life. Stuck."

"It don't have to be that way," Misty said.

She cupped her hand around the birds' feathers. They were hard and cold beneath her palm, and Misty shivered. She aimed her words at Caroline. "I thought these statues were about what William did to me in the barn. That maybe I was making them, somehow." And just the thought was enough to make Misty's shoulder slump again, her body eager to fall to her feet, to abandon her to her bones, but Misty held on. "But then I figured it out. You made the statues. You said you didn't when I asked, but you mixed your name in with theirs and made them change. Didn't you?"

Caroline didn't answer.

Misty said, "There were birds in your tree that night. When Earl found you. They were scared for you. They didn't want you to get hurt."

"They were the only friends I ever had," Caroline said. "Nobody else cared what happened to me."

"That's not true. My aunt Dolly wishes she had helped you when she could. She remembers you singing 'Prayer Bells of Heaven.' Do you remember that?" Misty hummed a few notes from the chorus, and the ground shuddered beneath her feet. "Dolly feels bad all the time for what she didn't do."

"She should!"

"I know," Misty said. "It wasn't fair. But it's not fair what you did to these things, either. What if this doesn't want to be a bird? Are you going to keep it like this forever?"

"No," Caroline said.

"Then let it go. Let it choose for itself."

Misty opened her chest and called out to the thing that William had buried, the thing it had been before Caroline turned it into a bird—a Christmas ornament with a manger scene painted on one side. Misty reached back to the day she had held the ornament in her hand, the cool weight of it in her palm, the glitter of its stars scratching her fingers as William backed her against the barn wall, and all the while she had been worried about breaking the ornament, worried about squeezing too hard, afraid that it would shatter. And the ornament had spoken to her. It had shown her every tree it had ever hung on, filled her head with the bright reflection of green and red lights, the smell of pine needles and plastic, the rip of wrapping paper, a dozen faces reflected in its glass. It had been there for her when she needed it most, and she thanked it over and over again. She shared the memory with Caroline and she smelled the barn again— musty and dry—and she felt the heat of the day collect on her skin and the sticky touch of William's palm on her wrist, and her whole heart ached.

She said, "You don't have to be a bird anymore. Not if you don't want to."

The sound that came next was like ice cracking on a frozen pond, something deep and shifting, giving way. There was a jolt in the air, like something had fallen from a great height, and Misty felt it reso- nate through her.

When she opened her eyes, the bird splintered.

A crack raced along its middle and then spread into another crack and another until there were dozens racing across the bird's wings, its throat, until the bird collapsed—a thousand little pieces falling. The pieces stirred a cloud of dust as they landed, and when the dust settled, the ornament was lying on the ground just as Misty remem- bered it.

Penny didn't move an inch. She gripped the fence beneath her, her mouth hanging open slightly. All she saw was Misty touching the statues. She didn't hear what she said to Caroline or to the bird, and Misty couldn't imagine how it must look to her as Misty turned to the ax.

"This is what he used," Misty said to Caroline. "And it was terrible, and I'm sorry that he did that to you. I'm sorry that you didn't get to be what you wanted."

"He killed me," Caroline said.

"I know."

"And nobody even cares. Nothing even happened to him. He gets to live. Still. How can that be fair?"

"It's not." Misty's whole chest heaved. She felt so full of sadness and hurt—her own and everyone else's. She wasn't sure that she could bear it much longer. Misty's trailer reached out to her. It offered her a different feeling—a dozen different hands reaching for its front door. A lighter touch. A so-glad-to-be-here, can't-wait-to-rest touch. Misty let the feeling settle over her as long as she could.

"Earl's alive," Caroline said. "And I'm not anything anymore."

"You're Caroline," Misty said.

She wrapped her hand around the blade of the ax. She closed her eyes and thought of the toy car that the ax had been before, the slick of its wheels on her palm, the dent on its roof, the scratched paint that she'd stared at as she lay on her back. The car had spoken to her. It had shown her the pinch of fingers on its sides, the steady, guiding weight of a hand as its wheels grated over pavement and carpet and tile and dirt. The way it felt to be lifted in the air, to do impossible things, the sunlight glinting off its windshield, and further still, back to its making, back to heat and compression, back to the earth, back to where Misty lay with her eyes cinched closed counting off the seconds in her head. There had been a rock grinding against her shoulder then as William's weight doubled on her chest, and she'd been so thirsty. That was all she could think of, her whole body narrowed down to the heat in her mouth, the frantic desire to get up and get a drink of water.

"You were a toy car once," Misty said. "You can be that again. Or be something else. Or stay the same. I don't know what you want, but you get to decide."

As she touched it, the ax seemed to melt, its blade liquefying and pouring down, taking the handle with it, until the whole thing dissolved onto the ground and the dust lifted and settled, leaving the toy car behind.

Misty stepped back and traced her finger along the spiral. Her reflection stared back at her, her eyes puffy from crying, and the dark shadow of Penny sitting on the fence behind her.

"Caroline?" Misty said.

Her voice was small when she answered. "I'm here."

"You used to sew these onto your clothes. My mom remembers that. She said she thought you was brave."

"No," Caroline said. "She didn't like me. None of them liked me."

"My mom did. She remembers you sewing these onto your clothes in class. In bright colors. She said she always liked them, but she never told you."

"Why not?" Caroline asked, and the *why* echoed through Misty, reverberating between her ears, her ribs, until her whole body buzzed.

Misty pressed her hand to the spiral.

"Wait," Caroline said. "If you take them all, then I won't have anything left. I won't have anything at all."

"They're not yours," Misty said.

She closed her eyes and thought of the first night in the barn, how afraid she had been, how unsure of anything other than that something wrong was happening to her and that there was no way to stop its happening. The day replayed in front of her and in front of Caroline, all those moments Misty had run from, all those seconds she would have done anything to avoid.

The spiral snapped in half and then in quarters and then in countless little pieces that fell to the dirt. The piece of wood that William had ripped from the barn was all that remained when it was over.

Misty wiped her cheek against her shoulder and kept going, kept crying. She pressed her palm to the golden hand scarred by the birds' claws and it crumbled into the brown glass bottle that William had brought to her in the woods. She traced her finger along the arc of the swinging bridge and it fell, piece by piece, to the ground, returning to the nails she'd clutched in her hand. She pressed her forehead to the dogwood tree that Caroline had been, briefly, the thing she'd wanted most in the world, but it fell, too, and became Shannon's gold earring.

The sun was higher by the time Misty turned to the green glass man. It was the first statue that had grown and the last left standing. Its body was webbed with a series of thin cracks, Caroline's hold on it stretching, almost breaking already.

Misty put her hand on the statue's chest. "This was Earl, wasn't it?"

"Yes," Caroline said.

"You didn't deserve to be hurt," Misty said.

"It was my fault. I should have left. I should have hurt him first, and worse than he ever hurt me. I shouldn't have done what I did to that tree, but I was so afraid. I was so afraid that he'd kill me before I had the chance to leave."

"You did bad things," Misty said. "That don't make you bad. Not if you try to do better afterward. Remember?"

"I don't want to be her," Caroline said. "I don't want to be gone."

"I know." Misty knelt on the ground, her fingers trailing down the green glass man's body. She rested her head against the place where his knee should have been and shivered as his cold seeped into her. "You know what I hate?"

"What?"

"That I don't get to pick my name," Misty said. "I get to pick some of it, you know. But not all of it. I don't want William to be part of my name."

"I don't want Earl to be part of mine, either."

"But I can't change it." Misty wiped her hand across her face. "But that don't mean I ain't other things, too."

"You are," Caroline said. "You're a sweet girl. And brave and funny and smart."

"So were you," Misty said. "I think we would've been friends, don't you?"

"Yeah. Yeah, I think we would have."

Another crack appeared in the green glass man. It raced from the bottom of his feet to the top of his head. It raised up a little, just enough to cut Misty's hand if she wasn't careful. Then the crack spread out, multiplying until the statue was more broken than whole. Misty turned her head as the statue crumbled in front of her and the dust rose around her face. When she looked back, the green glass bottle was lying on the dirt.

"Misty—" Penny said.

"I'm not done yet."

Penny nodded.

If Misty picked up a shovel and tore the garden apart, she might find William there, somewhere. Or at least parts of him that she might recognize. But whatever William had been was gone, and there would be no bringing him back. He'd made his choice, and now Misty made hers.

She pressed her palm against the dry, cold earth. Her whole body ached for Caroline, and she poured every ounce of that into her hands, cast it around the garden like a gentle touch.

"I liked myself," Caroline said, "a long time ago."

"I like you now," Misty said.

Caroline curled in Misty's palms like two heavy stones. "I did all this so Earl might have to answer for what he did to me. I thought it would make it better if he did, if I could see it. Isn't it better now that William's gone?"

Misty ran her fingers through the dirt. William would never come back, and that meant he would never take her to the barn again. Never hurt her again. But just the thought made her fingers loosen and numb, the skin slipping from her knuckles until she clenched her hand into a fist and held on.

"He's gone," Misty said. "But it's not."

"I just wanted both. To see him punished and to let go of what happened so I could move on. But it looks like some people only get one of those things."

Misty didn't know what to say so she sent the feeling of her family through her fingers—the excitement she felt when she heard her father coming home from work and the way her mother would brush her bangs off her forehead so she could kiss the skin between Misty's eyes and the feeling of Penny and their cousins gathered close together, trying to do all they could to make Misty feel better.

In return, Caroline filled Misty's palms with tree branches, her chest with bark as hard as bone, her fingertips with bright, new leaves just blooming. "Will you remember me when I'm gone?"

"I will," Misty said. "I promise."

An image flickered in Misty's mind, weak at first, then stronger, as Caroline shared her name with Misty. A woman stood in front of Caroline, and when she smiled, Misty's chest filled with warmth; an old house sat on top of a hill with its front door open, the smell of warm bread wafting through the door; the taste of cherries, bright and sour; a bird landed on the curve of her knee and sang her a bright, pretty note; a red feather tucked under her pillow for good luck, one in her pocket to keep her safe; someone pounding on her door, yelling, as she hid in her closet; a grove of dogwood trees, their branches heavy with white blooms; the feeling of a branch puncturing her arm, her body changing, morphing; the taste of cold water and earth on her tongue; the smell of honeysuckle and hot coffee; the whisper of a cotton dress against her skin as she walked barefoot down a long, empty road; Earl holding out his hand to help her up; the tip of an ax glinting in the moonlight; and Misty was there, too, her fingers brushing through the dirt; birdsong, all around her, endless.

Then it was over.

Caroline was gone. So was William.

For a while, neither Misty nor Penny said anything. The sun rose a little higher and its light warmed their shoulders. There was a slight breeze that rocked the door of the barn back and forth, its hinges creaking. Misty dug her fingers into the garden's soil. It wasn't as cold as it had been before. It would be a long time before it was warm again, but it might be, one day. Something might even grow there again.

Penny slid from the fence and toed the green glass bottle, frowning as she touched it. Misty's skin felt loose around her throat, and it would have been so easy to tilt back her head and let her skin slide away. Then she wouldn't have to hear what Penny had to say. Then she wouldn't have to know what her sister thought of her now, or if she blamed Misty, if she thought she should have run from William or fought harder.

Penny said, "I'm sorry."

Misty squinted up at her. "Why?"

"For you being hurt," Penny said. "And for not knowing it. Not helping. I'm sorry."

Penny brushed Misty's bangs out of her face like their mother did. She tucked the longest hairs behind her ear. It was a gentle touch. Soft and light. Misty cried. Penny knelt down and wrapped her arms around her and Misty buried her face in Penny's shoulder. They held on to each other and Penny rocked gently from side to side, the way their mother did, and they both cried until Jem opened the front door and squalled.

"Is that Misty? *Misty*. Dolly, get out here!"

Jem stumbled down the front steps and across the yard. She wore a long, purple nightgown hemmed with lace. Her hair was braided but falling fast apart, and her thick calves were covered with pale-blue veins. She ran to the fence, reached over the top board, and pulled Misty up and over. She pressed Misty to her chest, and Jem smelled just like baby powder and cheap laundry detergent.

"Oh, honey," Jem said.

"Misty?" Dolly yelled from the porch. "Lord, Jem, if you're strangling her, save a piece for me. Oh, I could just skin you alive, little girl. Move now, Jem, let me lay hands on her."

Jem replaced Misty with Penny and the aunts traded the girls back and forth, laughing and crying and asking questions without giving anyone enough time to answer.

"Good Lord, look at the garden," Jem said. She looked between Misty and Penny, their eyes swollen and puffy from lack of sleep. "You girls have a story to tell," Jem said. "I can see it. Now ain't the time for it, but I know it's coming. Tell them, Dolly."

"The doctor just called. Your mama woke up. She was asking for you girls first thing. Come get your clothes on and we'll go see her. We'll get breakfast on the way." She kissed them both on the forehead. "We ain't done with you, Misty, not by no long shot, but we'll be happy for a while. Are there any biscuits left? Beth always loved my biscuits."

Jem rolled her eyes and followed Dolly back across the yard. "Come on, babies. We can't keep your mama waiting."

"We'll be there," Penny said. "Just a minute."

Jem looked between them again, nodded once, and hurried Dolly back inside.

"You fixed it," Penny said.

Misty shook her head. "I just helped a little."

"And Mom. She's better."

"I hope so."

"We should tell her," Penny said. "About what you told me. She'll want to know. You can decide when, but I'll be there when you do, all right? If you want me to."

Misty nodded. Penny walked across the yard without asking her to follow. When she opened the front door, noise rushed out—a dozen voices chattering, a pan rattling on the stove, the roar of the television. It fell quiet again as the door clicked shut.

A crawdad chimney swayed by Misty's foot. A little piece of the base had been kicked away so the top wobbled in the breeze. She knelt beside it. She'd spoken to the crawdads for as long as she could remember, had felt the weight of their shells on her back, the rush of the water inside her skin. She'd known them digging and climbing, buried and lost, known them gone. Now she needed them to know her again.

Misty closed her eyes. She thought of her mother handing her a cookie that was half-light and half-dark, her mother dancing in the bottom, her feet pounding against the grass, her eyes cinched tight; a sea of green strings taped to the ceiling and the walls, swaying in the breeze; Penny's hand gripping the sheet in their bedroom, about to pull it away; birds screaming in the dark; a crawdad skittering over her thighs, resting on her belly; Jem's face bent down toward the garden, a hoe in her hands; corn bread crumbling in her mouth, soaked in sweet milk; a ring of coal dust around her father's neck after work; William's face running behind her through the trees, chasing her into the open; a burrow leading deep, deep underground; white roots in dark soil; casting cards laid out from knee to knee, her future spread before her; the itchy feeling of her clothes too tight against her skin; the clink of her bones against the pavement; the barn doors looming ahead of her; Jerry's face knit tight in concentration as he drew a picture of Misty on her palm, and Jamie dotting her freckles, and Sam giving her a field of flowers, and Penny adding the crawdad, all of them adding the things that she loved best, that they loved best about her; the whisper of skin sliding free of bone; the whisper of skin sliding back into place.

The air grew warmer around her and the sky filled with the sound of birds calling. When Misty opened her eyes, the bottom was full.

Redbirds and bluebirds and starlings and crows perched along the roofs of the trailers and the barn, crowded the branches of the trees, their feathers ruffling and settling, all of them drawn close to her.

She'd been so afraid that what happened in the barn would be there in her name and she'd have to watch it over and over for the rest of her days. That maybe honesty meant keeping nothing for yourself and she'd have to give all her secrets away in order to speak her name.

And it was there, in its way. The barn. William's face.

But the world didn't need to know what happened to Misty in order for her to be honest. She just had to know for herself, to be okay with herself. It was still her choice who she told and who she didn't.

Beneath her, the crawdads called back.

The ones who were closest to the surface pushed through the earth and into the yard, and the ones furthest away turned their weary claws toward the surface and began their long walk back. Some of them had miles to crawl, and for days crawdads would appear in the yard, surfacing from small holes and trudging, slowly, toward the creek.

Misty flexed her fingers and her skin stayed in place, her body attached to her at least for the moment. She led the crawdads back to the creek, taking careful steps as a long line formed behind her, dozens and dozens of crawdads with their dark shells glinting in the sun. Their voices like leaves skittering in her head, all of them happy, so happy, to hear her again. The crawdads crawled over her bare feet as she walked, the tap of their claws tickling her skin as she led them back to the water.

Shift / Shed / Grow / Shift / Shed / Grow

Misty will forget.

Already she is forgetting as she leads the crawdads back to the creek, her chest humming with their names.

Two weeks after her mother wakes up, Misty's mother will file for divorce, and she and Penny and their mother will move into their grandmother's old house beside Jem and Dolly. Their cousins will come over for breakfast on Saturday mornings. Jem will plant wildflowers in their yard that bloom so full and so fast that there'll be no place to step without touching them, and Misty will lie on her back and roll through them with Penny at her side.

Earl will move. No one will know where or why, and no one will ask many questions. The trailers remain where they always were, their roofs slowly falling in, the windows cracking. They will be home to birds and mice instead of people.

With Jem's help, Misty will buy a memorial for Caroline—a slick gray stone with her name in bold letters and a dogwood tree etched beneath. They will set it there in the garden, which will grow a little more green, a little more full every year. Jem will talk about Caroline more often, and so will Dolly, and so will Misty's mother, and Caroline's stone will become a place for women to lay their burdens down. They will visit her in the dark of night before they move or start a new job or end a marriage. They will press their hands against the leaves of her tree and they will know, somehow, that things will be okay.

William's face will fade.

Misty will forget the exact color of his hair and the gap between his teeth. By some other kind of magic, some kindness of chemicals in her brain, she will forget the way that Shannon screamed when she came home to an empty trailer. She will forget the look on her face, like an old house that had sunk into itself, and the way Shannon clawed at the garden like she had known that what was left of William was there, somewhere, beneath the earth. She'll forget the way Shannon's body slumped to the side when she found her golden earring buried in the dirt.

She'll forget the barn and the weight of William's hand on her hip and the shape of the toy car in her hand.

She'll dream about the crawdads now and then and spend most of her summers down by the creek at Jem's house with a vague feeling in the back of her mind like she knew the taste of that water, knew every crook and bend to follow, like she could never get lost as long as she was near it.

Every year she'll speak less and less to the world around her, finding it harder and harder to remember the names she'd learned. She'll tell herself it was all a dream, a fairy tale she'd told herself to make up for how lonely she had been as a kid.

Then, when she's seventeen, the boy she likes will lean over the armrest of his car just a little too fast and kiss her just a little too hard. Misty's panic will be fierce and immediate.

Her body will remember a barn.

Her body will remember a boy.

Her body will remember, this time, to run.

She'll push the boy away until the back of his head thumps against the window. Her throat will feel like the size of a straw, and she won't recognize the sound of her own breathing. She'll stumble outside to get some air, just a little more air, and when her palm touches the passenger door, the car will stutter to a start, the engine revving once before it dies. The boy will leave her there, alone in the parking lot of a movie theater. She'll watch the back of his blond head until he disappears around a curve.

Misty will sit there for an hour with the soft glow of neon lights flickering over her shoulders and the taste of cold earth in her mouth. She'll wait for Penny to pick her up, and while she waits, she'll slide a ring on and off her finger and feel the bone slide beneath it, feel a cold bloom in her skin, a numbness. She'll think of the barn and of William, of cold creek water and green strings and the particular music of her bones. She'll wonder, for the first time in years, whatever happened to Earl.

The truth will come back to her that night and never fully leave again, but it will be a muddied truth, a blurred and bending truth that she more feels than remembers every time she shuts her eyes.

The summer and William and the barn and the names.

She'll wish for those years of forgetting, wish for a time when she didn't remember her body like this. But the memories will keep surfacing in dreams and in shudders. Every touch will be his touch again, her body remembering over and over, stuck in a loop that she'll have to find a way out of again; even after all of the work she did as a girl.

She will return to the bottom, to the creek. She will sit by Caroline's stone, rooting out the weeds, clearing off the space so the inscription of Caroline's name shines beneath the sunlight. The trailers are still there, but they are rusted, sunken, empty. The barn is falling to pieces, its roof half-gone, its door unhinged. Rats nest in its corners, snakes lurk in its shadows.

Sometimes Penny will come, too.

And when Misty asks her what she remembers about that summer, Penny will shake her head, her hair cut short now, her hips wide like their mother's. She'll say, "I remember being angry all the time. And you cried all the time."

"I did not."

"Did so. You were always getting me in trouble."

"Until you hung that sheet up in our room."

"What? Oh yeah. I forgot all about that. God, I was terrible. That whole summer was terrible. And then I felt even worse when you told me, you know. What happened in the barn."

And Penny will wait until Misty stops crying before she holds out her arms and Misty will crawl into her sister's lap and they will sit that way until nightfall, until Penny whispers, "You were so strong. I never saw it when we were kids, but you were, the whole time. You are."

And Misty will remember the sheet, her sister's bloody ankles, the casting cards laid out in a half circle in front of her, telling her future.

Sometimes her mother will come.

She will hold Misty's hand in her own hand, which is older and wrinkled and soft. She will take a long breath and say, "I thought it was a sign from God. That green light. I thought if I could just keep it out, if I could just find it, then nothing bad would happen to you girls."

"But it did," Misty will say.

And her mother will hang her head. "You were so quiet after. Even when we moved. I thought maybe you'd never be able to forgive me for not being there. You even stopped playing with the crawdads."

"The crawdads?"

"Don't you remember? They used to crawl all over you like you was their mama or something. You loved them. They loved you."

And Misty will remember the feeling of the crawdad's feet across her own as she led them back to the water, and the burrows in the yard, the way Earl's trailer canted to the side, the green light deep underground.

Sometimes Jem and Dolly will come.

They will sit on either side of Misty like two great bookends there to hold her together. They will straighten out their long denim skirts and sigh when Misty asks what they remember.

"I remember that eggplant," Jem will say. "Thirty-five pounds the day that my former sister over there cut it from the vine."

"It was sucking the life out of my tomatoes. Something had to be done."

"There'll come a day when I get to cut a cord on you, and we'll see how kind I am."

Misty will laugh, and then laugh harder. Laugh until something shakes loose inside her and tears well in her eyes. Dolly will get a frantic look on her face, but Jem will grow calmer.

"I remember how little you was," Jem will say. "I remember how hurt you looked all the time, and me wishing I could do something about it."

"And looking for you in the woods. I was so scared. I never knew how much room you took up in my heart until I couldn't find you. Do you remember? She was gone, and then she was just back, and everything was different. You looked different."

Jem will start to cry and so will Dolly and so will they all until it passes and they load into Jem's truck and then into her house. They will eat fried chicken until their stomachs hurt and sit on the porch listening to Jem's stories until her voice grows hoarse.

And Misty will remember William standing in the woods, Penny pushing him to the ground, the white glow of her bones in the dark, her body lying in a shallow grave that she dug for herself, and the feeling of her skin slipping over her bones.

She will call Sam, whose voice is deeper now, but his laugh will have the same staccato rhythm. He'll promise that he'll visit soon, and he'll tell Misty that he remembers the night they caught lightning bugs in the yard, how it was the last time he could remember playing together. He has one tattooed on his arm, always glowing. "It reminds me that there are good parts of home, too. Things to come back for."

When Misty visits Jerry and Jamie's apartment, Jamie will answer the door with a textbook in his hand and coal dust around his neck. He'll lead Misty to the kitchen table where Jerry is threatening his life if he doesn't sit down and study for his finals like he'd promised. Jerry's art sits in frames all around the walls, pictures of Cora Beth as a tree, of his mother surrounded by the flowers she grows, of Jamie leaning out an open window, laughing, and of Misty, too, standing side by side with Penny. They will all be there in Jerry's careful lines.

"I remember drawing on your hand that night," Jerry will say when Misty asks about that summer. "Remember? We was all crowded in the back room there. The next morning my legs was covered with bug bites."

"Oh yeah," Jamie says. "You looked like a plague victim. That's the night Misty went missing. I thought Mom was going to tear the world apart to find you."

"The drawing helped," Misty will say, and she will smile when she says goodbye to them and they each kiss the same spot on her forehead.

And she will remember the image of herself inked on her palm. She will remember Caroline, an ax raised in the air, the way the ground swallowed her whole. Lying on the dark ground with her arms wrapped around herself.

But even with all that she will remember, there will be other things, so many things, that she forgets. Misty will struggle with knowing that something terrible happened to her, to feel the phantom weight of a hand on her hip, but not to know for sure what it was. She will hate piecing herself together through other people's memories, but she will keep trying, keep asking, keep telling the truth again and again until it's there.

Her name.

Longer now, and more twisting now, and heavier than it has ever been.

But the world will be there, too, crowding at her feet, the birds circling above her, the bugs wrestling free of the ground, the trees stretching their roots, the crawdads hurrying from the water, because they missed her, this girl. Because they remember her, too.

Reading Group Guide

1. Misty's idea of inner names includes memories and sounds, things remembered and lost. What does that mean to you? Can you think of anything that would be a part of your name?

2. Compare Misty's and William's home lives. How are they each coping with the challenges of their families? Do they understand each other?

3. Misty thinks her family only notices her when she's sad or hurt. Have you ever felt like that? What did you do?

4. Why do you think Misty decides to tell her mother about Penny kissing the green glass man? Was there another choice she could have made?

5. Do you think that corporal punishment is ever justified for children? Besides the physical pain, what does Misty notice and remember about being whipped with the switch?

6. How does the environment interact with Misty's emotions? Would that relationship still exist without her empathy? How might it be different?

7. Throughout the book, Misty and Penny reach out to each other but always seem to miss. What prevents them from supporting or helping one another?

8. Misty encounters several dangers when she takes off her skin. What are they, and how does she eventually overcome them?

9. Caroline explains that she thought she could punish Earl *and* move on, but she might only get one of those things. What kind of justice do you think she gets in the end? Is it what she deserved?

A Conversation with the Author

How did your experiences as a Kentuckian shape the setting of the book? What do you think people overlook when they think about Appalachia?

I think Appalachia has often been a useful tool and talking point for those in power, which is something Elizabeth Catte talks about far more eloquently than I can in her book *What You're Getting Wrong about Appalachia*. It's a book I recommend every time someone asks me a question like this. And I think Appalachia still exists as a monolith to many people, which often means they overlook things like the sheer existence of and therefore the contributions of black people and other people of color in Appalachia (take the Affrilachian poets, for example), or the long history of social, economic, and labor activism, or rural queerness, or the fact that Appalachia is an incredibly large place that includes cities and various religions and far more complexity and nuance than it's often depicted with (check out Roger May's photography series *Looking at Appalachia* to get an idea of the scope of the region). I know all these things to be true about my home. And when I write about it, I try to hold as much as I can in my work, and to write with honesty and conviction and with magic, too.

What draws you to fantastical storytelling? How do you think

elements like Misty's empathic abilities and the statues in the garden contribute to the story you're telling overall?

Part of this answer is simple: I've always been drawn toward the fantastical and frightening. Even from the early stages of writing this book, I knew that *Every Bone a Prayer* would have a kind of magic system and that this system would be fundamental to the way the world worked. That's just part of who I am as a writer. But the other part of this answer is more complicated. Like a lot of my work, this book deals with trauma and its impact on people and families and its impact on how our identity gets made and remade. I'm influenced by my own experiences as a survivor, as someone who grew up in a violent home, as someone with PTSD. Trauma, and our responses to it, can be incredibly surreal. Flashbacks can thrust you back in time. Dissociation can numb your body, fog your thinking, make it feel as though you're watching your life like a movie on a screen. Memory loss is common, which means whole parts of your life can be lost. So when I try to capture or re-create the experience of trauma on the page, the tools of the fantastical, the strange, the surreal, become some of my best options. Those tools help me get closer to the lived, embodied experience of trauma, the way that it *feels* to be going through such big, frightening, often sudden disruptions. So there's this strange way that creating a realistic portrayal means using the most unrealistic elements.

One of Misty's biggest obstacles is the sense of being alone around other people, unable to connect with them. Why did you choose to focus on this?

Misty's loneliness emerged fairly quickly when I started writing. A lot of the conditions of her life naturally led there—she lives in a

very rural, very mountainous, very small town without access to a
lot of distractions; she's growing up in a place and within a religion
that often encourage silence when it comes to violence or abuse; she
has an ability that she fears sharing with others because she's not
sure how they'll react. There are a lot of things that Misty is holding
back. And in regards to her ability, there's also a whole part of her life
that is so much bigger and brighter that she wants to share but feels
unable to. She wants, like most of us, to be known, understood, and
loved for who she is. But when the abuse begins, all of these circum-
stances become even heavier. Misty's confusion and shame and fear
grow and she feels even more alone. If she's going to find healing,
she has to reach out and find that connection, but with every event,
every page in the book, reaching out feels further and further away.
The cure and the poison are tied, as they so often are.

**You deal extensively with the power of names throughout the
book. Tell us how you feel about names, and your own name.**

When I started publishing, I decided that I wanted to write under a pen name. Not in an attempt to obscure my true identity, but
actually to get closer to it. When I married, I didn't take my part-
ner's last name, and I knew I didn't want to publish under my birth
name, either. They were both just different men's names. Neither
really felt representative of me or my work. *Blooms* was an easy choice
because it was a nickname given to me by my grandmother. The
story goes that I, like many children, hated wearing clothing and
would strip naked as soon as we got home from anywhere. Granny
teased my mother about it one day, asking, "Why don't you ever
buy that youngin' any bloomers?" *Bloomers* got shortened to *Blooms*
and it stuck. So not only did using *Blooms* as a pen name link me to

a kind of matriarchal lineage, but it also linked me to a time in my life where I was unafraid of my body. Where I could happily move through the world in the most vulnerable way. For me, one of the most difficult parts of recovering from sexual violence was trying to heal my relationship with my body. Taking the name *Blooms* is part of that healing. It links me not only to the women in my family who helped make me who I am, but also to myself—a name that is proof that I didn't always fear or distrust my body. That I embraced it once, wholeheartedly. *Blooms* is proof that I can do that again. Every day that I choose compassion over shame, love over judgment, I am actually returning to myself, to that little girl I was. *Blooms* gives me hope. That's the power of names.

Beth and her sisters are an interesting team, as are Misty and Penny. How did you go about exploring the sibling relationship? Do you have siblings?

The relationships in this book were definitely one of the most joyous parts of writing for me. Beth, Jem, and Dolly were especially fun to work with. When I started a scene with them, the dialogue felt like it was springing onto the page—I could hear them all so clearly in my mind. I drew on my own experiences with my siblings (an older brother and sister) and from watching my parents' relationships with their siblings. I spent a lot of time with my extended family as a child, so I was often surrounded by aunts, uncles, and cousins. And there was always banter and teasing and joking with care and tenderness sandwiched somewhere between. And as a book, *Every Bone a Prayer* is really concerned with relationships, identity, and connection. Misty's ability (or inability) to feel close to the people she loves is one of the driving forces, so capturing these sibling relationships felt like a vital part of the narrative. And I am always striving toward nuance and complexity. Sibling relationships are wonderful, but they're also really annoying. Sharing such proximity, vying for the same attention and resources, reaching different stages of life and development at different times. Growing up together can be tense, full of falling out and hating each other, then being best friends ten minutes later. I wanted all of those things to be present here.

The moment when Misty examines her body and recalls the ways she has lived in it has an aching sort of tenderness. Do you think our bodies are always our homes, or is that a choice we have to make?

I want the answer to this question to be yes. I want to believe that our bodies are always our homes even if we don't always feel that way. But I also know that our bodies are not separate from the world and our relationship to them is not defined solely by us or our feelings. That was one of the driving questions of the book: How do you reconcile with the parts of yourself, your body, your experience that you did not actively choose? What do you do with those pieces? Can you love them? Can you accept them? Can you erase them? I don't have an easy answer, especially not for everyone. I can only answer for me in saying that every day I am trying to come home to myself, every day I am trying to give myself the love and care that others often denied me. I am trying to be better to myself and my body than the world has been. And through that, hopefully, find a kind of peace and understanding, a new relationship with my body.

Where do you start a story? Do you know the ending when you begin?

I often have *an* ending in mind when I begin work, even if that ending changes. Knowing where I'm going puts guardrails around the story and keeps me focused, helps me sort through the imagery, symbols, relationships, etc. Novels, especially, have a tendency to sprawl. There's just so much that you *could* do that I find it helps to put at least a few limitations on myself. And the initial inspiration for my work often comes in many forms—a snippet of dialogue between two people in a moment of tension, an image of a character when their guard drops and they are alone and their face tells me something they've never said before, a flash of setting that invites me inside. It's often something small. A bright, fleeting spark without context, usually without even a hint of plot, but there's always promise. And the promise is enough to get started.

How do you strike a balance between the topics that are heavy and the ones that are beautiful?

This is something I think about a lot because I want my work to feel authentic, and in order for that to happen, I believe there has to be a mix of good and bad. No matter how dark or dire things seem, there's also hope, laughter, community, family, love. The fact that these things happen alongside one another doesn't negate them, but it does complicate things. So I try to be mindful about including those moments of reprieve, like in Misty's relationship with her cousins or when she gets to go see the fireworks in town. Even something as seemingly small as the moment when Misty eats cornbread and milk near the end of the book. I don't think the comfort and kindness of those small moments should be neglected. Especially when it can feel like we (as Americans) favor narratives of pain and suffering, especially the pain and suffering of certain people. The only value in a story doesn't come from how harrowing or raw it is, just like the value in a life doesn't come only from what a person has survived. I think there can be something unfair and maybe even dangerous about focusing too much attention on pain. It flattens life in a way that doesn't seem real. It's messier than just moments of hurt. Messier because those moments often exist in tandem with great hope and fear and courage. I try my best to value each part of a life, of a story, and to give my attention to the whole complicated mess.

Acknowledgments

Here, at the end of all the work to bring this book into the world, I am struck by the number of times that I almost set Misty's story aside. There were days when I felt I might suffocate on my own doubt and worry, days when it felt easier to give up rather than press on. And I am struck by the number of people—*so many people*—who were there to set me on my course again.

In the midst of some of my darkest, smallest days, I found a friend in you, Scott Lucero. And how many lives have we lived together since then? How many strange and fantastic adventures? I have cherished every one.

Then, as an undergrad, I walked into your office, Derek Nikitas, and received such encouragement, such generous feedback. You put books in my hand that helped me understand my own work better, and I can't thank you enough. And in that same year, R. Dean Johnson, your compassion and excitement made me want to write again, to write always.

Yet I still wasn't sure I could ever make it as a writer when I joined the MFA program at the University of Mississippi. Elsa, Sarah, Matt, and others helped change my mind. So did my instructors—Kiese Laymon, Tom Franklin, Beth Ann Fennelly. And Molly McCully Brown especially and forever: you plucked me out of my shell and showed me gentleness when I least expected it. I am grateful every day for your friendship.

To Billy Meyers: Without your counsel, I don't think I ever could have finished this book. You helped set me on a path of healing and joy that I hope will never end.

My 2017 Clarion cohort: Amanda, Amman, Amy, Emily, Ghis, Jane, Karen, Lucy, Luke, Macky, Nina, Patrick, Peggy, Rachel, Ren, Sanjena, and Ted. On week six, I shared the first chapter of this book with you. Your feedback and encouragement helped me see that this was a story worth holding on to. C. C. Finlay and Rae Carson, my week five and six instructors, your clear-eyed and warmhearted counsel helped me find the right place to begin this story.

But even after all these people, all their love, months later, I still doubted this book. In that doubt, I shared it with Dorothy Allison at the Tin House Winter Workshop in 2018. Your feedback and stories and encouragement gave me the strength to keep going once again.

And when it was ready, I sent the manuscript to you, Harper, because I knew that no one else would be able to see it quite the way you could. You are a light that I look for in the dimmest and loneliest moments of my life, and I know that you will always be there.

And, Ames, you were there for every panicked text, every ounce of angst that I could offer (and I offered much). You are one of the steadiest friends in my life, and I am so glad you are here beside me.

To Alexandra Levick, who read the culmination of all this work and saw something worth investing in. Thank you for being my agent, for every frantic, nervous email you answered, for every kind word. To Shana Drehs and the team at Sourcebooks, who believed in Misty and in me, who gave so much love and energy and care to every single word. You all made my dream come true, and I will always be thankful for that.

To my family who exist beyond timeline, beyond doubt, beyond memory. To my mother for believing in me first and most fiercely. To Brian and Niki—my brother and sister—I want to apologize now, because I will surely spend the rest of my life writing you both into different characters and faces and strange, far-flung places. But it's only because I wouldn't have made it this far without you, and I wouldn't be nearly as strong as I am now had I not survived the two of you throughout childhood. I love you all.

And finally, finally: to Sam. Thank you for spending hours teasing out the materiality of magic with me, for all the late-night trips to Sonic, for running me hot baths, for all the silly voices and silly songs, and for making everything, even the dreams that scared me most, seem possible. The greatest story I will ever tell is the one I am making with you.

About the Author

Photo by Karen Osborne

Ashley Blooms has published short fiction in *The Year's Best Dark Fantasy & Horror*, *Fantasy & Science Fiction*, *Strange Horizons*, and *Shimmer*, among others, and her essay "Fire in My Bones" appeared in *The Oxford American*. Ashley is a graduate of the Clarion Writers Workshop and the Tin House Winter Workshop and received her MFA as a John and Renée Grisham Fellow from the University of Mississippi. She was raised in Cutshin, Kentucky, and now lives in Berea, Kentucky. Visit her online at ashleyblooms.com.